LAST DANCE ON THE STARLIGHT PIER

LAST DANCE ON THE STARLIGHT PIER

SARAH BIRD

THORNDIKE PRESS
A part of Gale, a Cengage Company

Copyright © 2022 by Sarah Bird.
Photographs are used with permission from the collection of Carol Martin.
Thorndike Press, a part of Gale, a Cengage Company.

Thorndike Press® Large Print Core.
The text of this Large Print edition is unabridged.
Other aspects of the book may vary from the original edition.
Set in 16 pt. Plantin.

**LIBRARY OF CONGRESS CIP DATA ON FILE.
CATALOGUING IN PUBLICATION FOR THIS BOOK
IS AVAILABLE FROM THE LIBRARY OF CONGRESS.**

ISBN-13: 978-1-4328-9773-4 (hardcover alk. paper)

Published in 2022 by arrangement with St. Martin's Publishing Group.

Printed in Mexico
Print Number: 01   Print Year: 2022

*To Colista McCabe Bird, RN, 1920–2001,
who sang and danced her way through
the Great Depression and World War II.
Thank you, Collie Mac, for telling me
about all the fun you had
watching a dance marathon.*

You should have seen the things they were giving babies instead of milk. I remember seeing them put salt-pork gravy in milk bottles and putting a nipple on, and the baby sucking this salt-pork gravy. A real blue baby, dying of starvation. In house after house, I saw that sort of thing.

— John Beecher, activist poet and journalist who wrote about the Southern United States during the Great Depression, from *Hard Times: An Oral History of the Great Depression* by Studs Terkel

That was a time when people's emotions were raw to begin with. Everyone knew the Depression would be endless. So laughter was hard to find. We all fought in our own way. Mine was the marathons.

They helped me survive. Helped a lot of people survive. I was part of the little army that won the war of the Depression.

— June Havoc, vaudevillian, marathon dancer, and sister of Gypsy Rose Lee, in her memoir *Early Havoc*

GALVESTON

Dance Marathon. Galveston, Texas
Sunday, July 3, 1932
4:25 a.m.

Zave? Where is Zave?

With that question, consciousness thunders back. How long have I been out? Long enough that the wet sand of the narrow beach abutting the Starlight Pier has chilled me despite the muggy night.

I search for him in the crowd. He is not there.

I try to stand and I fail.

No one notices. Not the other dancers. Not the sloppers who'd fed us or the trainers who'd beaten the knots from our muscles or the floor judges who'd determined who stayed and who was eliminated.

They gape, wide-eyed and stricken, mesmerized by the terrible volcano beauty of the Starlight Palace as it burns in the night.

11

A tongue of flame leaps so high into the night sky that it licks at the pale sliver of moon. The fire burns twice. Once in the inferno the dance hall at the far end of the pier has become, and again in the rippled waves lapping at the shore.

Low blue flames escape and snake along the pier, nosing their way toward us. The flames search for the ones who got away. They search for me.

I shake my head, trying to rattle the vision loose. I've gone squirrelly. That's what barely sleeping for five days will do to you. The fire roars. I sit up and its heat warms me.

The few remaining windows ringing the top of the Palace explode. Firemen, leashed to the shore by their hoses, yell orders. Police shout at the crowd and shove them back. In dim, faraway voices, my marathon friends — Minnie, DeWitt, Lily, Ace, Patsy, and Lynette — yell questions at each other.

Spectators are perched along the top of the Seawall seventeen feet above the beach. They watch just as they'd watched us dancers during the show. It is the Fourth of July holiday weekend and the Starlight Palace had been packed beyond its two-thousand-person capacity, all the way up to the rafters. That's where the "cheap seat people" perched. People who pulled mustard-and-sugar sandwiches on day-old bread out of paper bags because they couldn't spring for a hot dog on top of the dime early-bird admission that let them stay all day. People who knew what it was to go to bed hungry and wake up hungrier.

People like me.

Just a few hours ago, we'd all been jubilant, drunk on bootleg hooch and hope, because Franklin Delano Roosevelt — our guy, the one who was going to pull us out of the goddamn Depression and give us back our jobs and our dignity — had just clinched the Democratic nomination in Chicago.

The oil execs, bootleggers, and movie stars in the high-dollar box seats up front didn't really care who the president was. For them, the Crash of '29 had never happened and the Depression was someone else's bad news. As long as people were putting gas from their refineries in cars, buying hooch from their illegal stills, and going to pictures made in their studios, they would be fine.

But, whether they were worried about where their next dividend check or their next meal was coming from, they had all come for two things.

They'd come to forget.

And they'd come because they'd read the stories.

About Galveston.

About me.

About Zave.

A few seconds later, the fire defeats even the sea, and what remains of the Starlight Palace surrenders. The skeleton of the dance hall wobbles against the lava-bright flames. Its blackened bones dance their last dance.

"Zave," I beg, though there is no longer any hope that a dark-haired man — hands in his pockets, light on his feet, favoring his right leg because of the injury that had brought us together — would emerge from the inferno. What materialized instead was the question I knew I would have to live with for the rest of my life.

How had I become a person who would cause the man I love to kill himself?

■ ■ ■ ■

THREE YEARS AGO

■ ■ ■ ■

CHAPTER 1

Galveston
June 1, 1929

The humidity that day was extreme. Shoes turned velvety green with mildew. Towels hung out to dry came in so damp they had to be cranked through the clothes wringer again. Saltines drooped limp as slices of bologna.

But nothing and no one was going to wilt me. Not today. I had already been a lot of things in my young life — vaudeville performer, dance instructor, waitress, dishwasher, pants presser, babysitter. And other things I won't mention. Mostly, I was always what Mamie, my mother, needed me to be to earn money.

Today, though, today was the first day of the life that I chose.

By some miracle, I had won a scholarship to study at St. Mary's Hospital School of Nursing located on Galveston. I sat up even straighter on my dusty maroon velvet seat aboard the Houston-Galveston Interurban Railway. Even though the island was barely more than an hour away, this was my first visit.

The cabin — sleek and modern as a rocket ship out of a *Buck Rogers in the 25th Century* comic strip — was the perfect vehicle to launch me into my future. I was so terrified of what lay ahead and so thrilled about what lay ahead that, had I been a dog, I would have stuck my head out the window and panted and drooled from sheer excitement.

But, being a seventeen-year-old girl from Houston's notorious Vinegar Hill neighborhood determined to hide who she really was, I sat up primly and folded my hands in my lap instead. My palms were sodden with sweat and butterflies churned through my gut. This was worse than any case of stage fright I'd ever endured back on the vaudeville circuit.

School had just let out and jolly vacationers packed the car. No one else onboard appeared to have a care in the world. Not the women in crisp white linen dresses and open-toed sandals. Or the men in straw boater hats. Or the boys in sailor suits. Or the little girls with long curls and short dresses with bloomers.

A party atmosphere pervaded the car. The men talked too loudly. Mothers let their children stand on the seats. A couple of the women, giggling behind their hands at their daring, lit up cigarettes and carefully blew the smoke out the window.

Everyone acted like naughty children playing hooky. And why not? Back on Vinegar Hill, we all knew that Galveston was a wide-open town where Prohibition was a suggestion instead of the law of the land. Where gambling wasn't considered any worse than chewing tobacco. And the prostitutes who worked openly along Galveston's infamous Line outnumbered spotted dogs. The island was drenched in a dark and irresistible glamour so potent that the biggest-name entertainers in the country performed in the nightclubs, casinos, and supper clubs there. Duke Ellington. Glenn Miller. Sophie Tucker. Harry James. Phil Harris. They all came.

What impressed us most, though, was that the whole operation had been created and was still run by a pair of brothers who'd emigrated from Sicily. They'd started out as poor as any of us, working as barbers, cutting hair for a quarter a head. When the island's biggest bootlegger, looking for an inconspicuous spot to stash his hooch, offered the brothers a dollar a case to hide his haul, they snatched up the deal. But, though they didn't know much English, they knew business. Instead of taking the payoff, they bought their way into the bootleg business. In an astonishingly short time, the brothers, and their network of family members, had created a glorious empire of vice and were running the island.

I tried to recall the family's name but could only remember how all the small-time Vinegar Hill chiselers always spoke of the island's ruling family with a combination of admiration and fear.

"Don't ever cross that family," they'd warned us kids who stood around, soaking up their street-corner wisdom and lies and not caring which was which. "Unless you want to end up in the Gulf of Mexico. Halfway to Havana. With your throat slit. And nobody in the entire state's gonna do a goddamn thing about it. Because that family's got every deputy and every sheriff in the county in their pocket. Shitfire. That bunch even owns the goddamn Texas Rangers."

An empire of vice, even if it was run by a family, seemed an odd place to start a new, a decent life, but my one and only chance to leave Vinegar Hill and Mamie behind waited for me on Galveston Island. If only I could impersonate a normal girl well enough to seize it.

Gripping my hands so tightly the knuckles whitened, I forced myself to concentrate on the view. We were hurtling across the Galveston Causeway. A vast flatness of sea and sky extended as far as I could see. A flock of gulls circled in a vortex outside my window. They hovered so close and so nearly motionless that I could almost touch them.

When a chubby boy in short pants tossed the crust of his sandwich out the window, the birds responded as one. In perfect synchronization, they all angled their bodies toward the crust and pivoted as if they were one creature. The sunlight momentarily transformed the flock into solid white paper sculptures. The origami seabirds floating in the sunlight were the purest, most beautiful sight I had ever seen.

I relaxed. What was I so nervous about? A place was waiting for me at St. Mary's. My scholarship application had already been accepted.

Under false pretenses.

My mother's hissing reminders became the voice of all the doubts slithering through my head.

We passed under the high arc of a sign

that read "Welcome to Galveston. Play-ground of the Southwest."

Three porpoises, their sleek bodies arcs of silver, leaped from the water at that moment. They dove back under and a fizz of hope bubbled through me.

CHAPTER 2

The street approaching the school was lined
with palms and hedges of oleander that
dripped gaudy pink blossoms. Not the tiniest hint of a breeze blew. Ahead lay St.
Mary's Hospital School of Nursing. A ten-
foot-high fence of black wrought iron surrounded the austere collection of two- and
three-story brick buildings. It seemed like
something out of Charles Dickens, too
severe to belong to this free and easy city.

Young women in white uniforms crowned
with white caps glided serenely about the
grounds. My stomach tightened into a hard
knot at the prospect of trying to pass as a
normal girl among them. I would have to
keep my trap shut and try to blend in as
much as possible until I got the lay of the
land.

A giant statue of Jesus' mother stood atop
the portico at the hospital entrance. Daddy,
who'd been a Catholic, had always called

23

her "the BVM," short for Blessed Virgin
Mary, just like she was his pal. I passed
beneath Mary's sorrowful gaze. Her head
was tilted down and her expression was sad,
as though she already knew that I was going
to disappoint her.

Inside, the hospital was a serene world of
silent corridors with ceiling fans quietly
circulating air that smelled of floor wax,
carbolic acid antiseptic, and Flit mosquito
spray. It smelled like the hospital where
Daddy had died. Where the nurses had been
so kind and did so much to relieve his suffering.

I followed a sign marked "School of Nursing" and headed down a broad hallway.
Almost immediately two nuns approached.
They glided forward in their long black
gowns and brimmed veils. Their faces
floated between starched white headbands
and high bibs. They seemed like sentries,
guards posted to repel intruders like me. I
quickly glanced away and pretended to be
fascinated by a painting of a saint in a
loincloth, porcupined with arrows.

"Hey." A peppy voice startled me. "You
must be Evie Grace Devlin."

The voice belonged to a girl my age
dressed in a uniform of blue chambray with
puff sleeves and a Peter Pan collar covered

24

by a crisp white Mother Hubbard apron.

How did she know my name?

"Sorry to spook you. I assigned myself to meet the new probie and since you're the only one around here who's not either in a uniform, a habit, or a bed, I figured that had to be you."

With her masses of dark curls, thick, unplucked eyebrows, and the slightest hint of a mustache, she had the innocent but determined aspect of a curious woodland creature. A friendly chipmunk, maybe.

"Probie?" I asked.

"Probationer," she clarified brightly. "Beginning nursing student?" she added when I didn't respond.

I nodded and she gave me a once-over so obvious that the Vinegar Hill girl I was suppressing wanted to tell her to take a picture, that it'd last longer.

"You'll do," she announced.

I'll do?

Though I winced at her comment, like all the smart players who kept their cards close to the vest, I said nothing.

"First thing, you need to check in with the director of nurses. Let's go."

Without another word, she throttled off down the hall, leaving me to stumble behind. Slowing down, she reached back, ordered, "Here, give me that," and snatched my suitcase away. "You pack light," the chipmunk observed, hefting the case up and resting it on top of her head like a safari bearer.

What an oddball. I figured her for some lonely do-gooder whose only hope at making friends was picking off newcomers like me. Fair enough, I thought. I'd take any acceptance that came my way.

I followed her through a swinging door and the world of silent serenity fell away. We entered a hive thrumming with purposeful activity. A student nurse pushing a cart clattering with dirty lunch dishes hurried past. A white-coated doctor with round glasses and a goatee dictated notes to a nun holding a clipboard. A young nurse hurried up a flight of stairs carrying a metal tray loaded with metal hypodermics that clattered with every step.

Chipmunk raced on. A cluster of girls dressed in chambray uniforms like the one my guide wore approached us. Expecting them to ignore my oddball escort, I was surprised when they all lit up like the Fourth of July, shouted excited greetings, and converged on her like they were autograph hounds and she was some kind of starlet.

"Make way, probies," she said, shoving through the giddy throng. "I've got the new probationer here and we're late to meet the Director."

Apparently, I thought, as we pushed on, this girl wasn't the lonely do-gooder I'd had her pegged as. In fact, she seemed distinctly popular. Then I glanced back at the girls who'd been so eager to talk to her and saw that some of them were whispering madly to each other and casting odd looks her way. Looks that I couldn't quite interpret.

On either side of the wide hallway, doors opened to large wards. Men's Surgical. Labor and Delivery. Bone Deformities. Women's Surgical. Children's.

I paused outside the children's ward and peered in at a large room swept by radiant light beaming in from high windows that reflected off polished floors. Two long rows of beds made up with snowy white sheets were occupied by sick children.

At one bed a nurse took a child's temperature. At another, a nurse helped a little girl sip from a straw. Several rocking chairs were in use by nurses holding limp or sleeping children. It exuded the calm efficiency of the ward my father was in near the end.

"Amazing, isn't it?" my guide asked, staring at the magical assembly line of care.

"Everyone knows exactly what to do," I marveled.

"After three years, we will too," my new acquaintance assured me.

"Maybe."

She heard the hesitant yearning in my voice and, as if I'd passed a test I hadn't known I was taking, she stuck her hand out. "Sofia. But if you call me that, I'll clock you. It's Sofie."

"Evie Grace, but you already know that."

A white-jacketed orderly, gliding up silently behind in his rubber-soled shoes, his vision obscured by the tall, metal cart he was pushing, nearly crashed into us.

"Jeezo, probies," he hissed, the steel instruments laying atop his metal cart and rattling wildly as he veered past.

"Aw, go soak your head," Sofie called after him, sounding exactly like one of my tough-girl friends on Vinegar Hill. "Can't let anyone run over you, right?" she asked me.

"You can say that again. Sofia."

Sofie balled up her fist, pretending she was going to punch me.

I smiled, figuring that, as long as I could joke with a person, anything was possible.

CHAPTER 3

At the Director's office, a diminutive nun who had one of those ageless, merry faces that could have belonged to either a happy old woman or a wrinkled toddler slapped both her hands on her desk, rose to her full height of maybe four ten, and burst out, "There you are."

"Meet Sister Theonella," Sofie said. "Officially she's the assistant director, but don't believe it. Sister T runs the place."

"Hardly," Sister T answered, taking both my hands in hers. "And you must be Evelyn Grace. Oh, how we have been waiting for you." Her openhearted warmth made me suspicious. Openhearted warmth on Vinegar Hill meant that someone was going to run a con on you.

At the Director's door, Sister Theonella stopped to gather up the long, draping sleeves that covered her hands before rapping three times.

An exceptionally peevish voice echoed out from behind the closed door demanding, "Sister T, did I not *explicitly* instruct you not to disturb me for any reason?"

Sister T gave Sofie a conspiratorial wink and opened the door.

Since I towered over the elfin nun, I had a clear view of the Director's office. Everything in it was shadowed except the boss nun's face. Or rather, the rectangle of face that pressed out between a stiff white headband and a tight, starched bib like bread dough that had risen too much. When she lifted her head to glare at me, the intruder, her rimless spectacles caught the light and hid her eyes behind two circles of silver.

Unbidden, the memories descended. Of Detroit. Of the men in the audience.

I jerked my thoughts away from a past I was determined to bury.

"Shut the door, Sister," the Director commanded. "And if you disturb me again, all privileges will be revoked."

Her threat was so chilling that I feared food and air might be regarded as "privileges" in this alien world I'd landed in. The only thing that was familiar was the Director's imperious manner. Just like Mamie, she exuded the same cast-iron belief that the world revolved around her.

Undaunted, Sister T asked impishly, "Are you sure? Because look who I have here."

The instant Sister T pushed Sofie forward, the Director's bullying manner vanished. "Sofia," she said, rising slightly from her seat. "Come in, please."

The three of us entered.

"Sister," Sofie said, "I just stopped in to bring you the new girl so that you can sign off on her admission."

"New girl?" the Director asked, her tone sharpening. "But the probationer class has already assembled."

Sister T gestured at the Director's desk. "I put the application that we approved right there alongside her admission form. If you'll simply sign, we'll get her settled in."

My pulse thudded as the Director scrutinized my application. Surely I would be found out now.

Clearly displeased, the Director asked, "Is this the charity position that was confirmed during the time I was away in St. Louis at the Motherhouse?"

"That's right," Sofie answered. "All you have to do is add your signature and we'll get out of your hair."

With a thin smile that appeared to cause her pain, the Director said, "Sofia, if you

31

wouldn't mind, perhaps I could have a moment alone with . . ." She searched the form.

"Evie Grace," Sofie supplied.

The Director dropped her imitation of a smile the instant the door closed. Tapping my answers with the point of a needle-sharp pencil, she asked, "Your father and mother are both dead?"

"Yes," I replied, only half lying. My father had died when I was young and Mamie, besides never wanting to be a mother to begin with, had told me I was dead to her if I stopped paying her bills and went to nursing school. So, if I was dead to her, how alive could she be to me?

"You graduated from Sam Houston High School?"

"Yes," I answered brightly, since that was one hundred percent true.

"With a grade point average of B minus?" she added, more disapproving than curious.

"I had to work two jobs to support myself and my mother. When she was alive, that is."

"I see that you worked in the school lunchroom and taught at a dance school. What sort of dance school?" she said, as if she were asking "What sort of prostitution ring?"

"The Bennett Academy of Dance. My

32

uncle Jake owns it. Mostly I helped him teach cotillion and debutante classes."

Another half-truth. It had been years since I'd taught with Uncle Jake. Not since all the Houston swells had fled downtown for the new suburbs, like River Oaks, leaving Jake with barely enough customers to keep the school open. But dance instructor looked better than my other part-time job, babysitting for the women who turned tricks at the nearby train depot.

"And I see that the rest of your schooling was out of state."

"Yes, Sister."

That was completely true if you considered "schooling" to be learning math from watching the all-night poker games played on the vaudeville circuit and being taught to read backstage by Marvin the Man of Marvels.

Marvin had enthralled audiences by tying his shoelaces, brushing his teeth, and buttoning his shirt. All by himself. And they were all marvels because Marvin had been born without any arms. Marvin could have read without my help, but after four or five shows a day, he was tired of being marvelous, so I held his books and turned the pages, and he helped me sound out words.

"Evie Grace Devlin," Marvin used to tell

me when I was sad or tired or in pain. "A person can do anything they put their mind to. Why, look at you? Two arms! Kid, the world is your oyster."

The Director stopped reading, speared a question, peered at me above her glasses, and asked with sharp alarm, "You are *not* a Catholic?"

If there was one question I wished I could have lied about, it was that one. But if you marked that you were Catholic, you had to get a form signed by your parish priest swearing that you were a "regular communicant" at his parish. And I wasn't a regular anything. Anywhere.

"Not technically," I hedged.

"Not technically," she repeated, staring at me coldly.

I hadn't fooled her. She saw who I really was. She saw the half-moons of sweat beneath the arms of my too-short dress. She smelled the stink of a girl who bathed using a pot of tepid water warmed on a hot plate and shared an outhouse in the alley with four other families. A girl whose last meal had been a cup of coffee and a doughnut eaten too long ago to keep her stomach from growling during the most important interview of her life.

The Director wrinkled her nose at the

growling that marked me as the pitiable, half-starved beggar I was.

"No, no, no," she said, putting the pencil down. "This will not do at all. We have never had a girl who was not Catholic at St. Mary's. And we have certainly never had a girl who frequents *dance* halls."

Just as I had never corrected Mamie, I didn't correct the Director. Because there had never been any point.

"Sister T and Sofia," she continued, "have gotten caught up in some dangerous ideas of 'reaching out.' Of seeking out a 'broader' range of students."

She folded her hands. "I'm sorry that they decided to use you as the poster child in their little campaign to change this school, but I am the guardian of St. Mary's and I take my responsibility to uphold spotless moral standards very seriously. Galveston's finest families entrust their daughters to me and I shall never betray that trust by allowing unsuitable girls in. I cannot approve an admission that was made behind my back. You are not suitable."

Already absorbed in another document, she held out the application I had poured all my dreams into without so much as a glance in my direction. Gutted, unable to move or even speak, I simply stood there frozen until she rustled the application impatiently.

I took it from her and left.

CHAPTER 4

"What's wrong?" Sofie asked when I stumbled out of the Director's office. "You look like you just swallowed a bug."

"I am unsuitable."

"What? Is that what she said? What a pill."

"Problems?" Sister T asked, joining us.

"She told Evie she's 'unsuitable.' "

The little sister rushed to reassure me. "Don't pay any attention whatsoever. You have been selected. Sofie and I want you."

"Apparently she doesn't."

Sister T exchanged eye rolls with Sofie and told her, "I told you she hates Protestants."

"Yeah, I know," Sofie said, shaking her head in amazement. "It's like something out of the Middle Ages. What she hates even more than Protestants, though, is poor people. No offense," she said to me.

"None taken."

"This simply isn't right," Sister T said with a fierceness I wouldn't have suspected

37

of the little nun. "Thirty years ago, I stood beside that woman at the Motherhouse in St. Louis when our class took the pledge to care for *all* our patients without regard to race, creed, color, politics, or social standing. How can we do that if we only train girls who are white, Catholic, and well-off?"

"We can't," Sofie said with an almost offhanded determination. "Stay here," she told me before marching back into the Director's office and shutting the door.

I didn't realize how desolate I looked until Sister T said, "Don't fret, little one, all will be well."

Any other time, I would have hooted at being called "little one" by a pixie runt a foot shorter than me, but all I could manage was a sad nod.

Peering up, she observed, "I don't like your color. You've gone quite pale. Why don't you have a seat and I'll go and find a snack for you from the ward kitchen."

Embarrassed, I answered quickly, "Don't bother. I'm fine."

I couldn't think about eating. If I did, the light-headed wobblies that came with hunger, real hunger, would overtake me, and I refused to wobble. Not in front of all these do-gooders. Not in front of anyone. Not when I already knew how this story was going to end. How it always ended when the one in charge made up her mind.

"Thanks a bunch for trying to get me in," I told Sister T as I gathered my things.

"You're not leaving, are you? You should at least wait for Sofie to come out."

Why? I wanted to ask. So she could keep pretending that she had the pull to get me in? I didn't know what the Chipmunk's game was, but I was done playing. Plus, if I stayed another second, I might have started crying. And I didn't cry in front of anyone. Ever.

"I have to get back to Houston," I lied. Not only didn't I have anyone or anything to get back to Houston for, I didn't even have the fifty-five cents fare for the train. I'd have to hitch.

I was already out the door when a voice called after me, "Hang on. Where are you going?"

It was Sofie. "What's it to you?" I asked, mad that I'd let myself be used.

"A lot," she shot back. "Since you're going to be my roommate."

I squinted at her. Hard.

"You're in."

"Oh, I am, am I?" I asked, letting my acid tone communicate that I was not the chump she'd played me for.

39

"Yep," she responded cheerfully. "You're a full-fledged probationer. Signed, sealed, and delivered."

I didn't believe her until she handed me my application. Which now had the Director's signature on it.

Too baffled to be either jubilant or relieved, my only thought was, *How the hell did she pull that off? And is it a con?*

With a thumbs-up and a wave to Sister T, Sofie grabbed my arm. "Come on, we're getting out of here. I need to show you Galveston."

The light-headedness returned as she rushed me through the polished corridors, dodging orderlies pushing gurneys and white-coated doctors leading coveys of students. Though the familiar headache and exhaustion that came when it had been too long between meals clouded my thinking, I tried desperately to figure out if all this was for real, because I couldn't see any way that this ditzy girl had managed to change the steely director's mind.

Had she forged the signature she'd shown me?

I was bracing myself for the next ugly surprise when we reached the street and Sofie flagged down a trolley. Oddly, it ground to a halt even though we weren't at

said, "Sure, Connie. Will do," her smile had tightened.

Expensive motorcars — a Duesenberg convertible, a Jaguar roadster — purred along the boulevard as sleek and exotic as the jungle cats the last was named for. I imagined their drivers and glamorous passengers to be playboys, debutantes, heirs and heiresses to vast oil or cotton fortunes.

This was my first real-life glimpse of the gilded princes and princesses of the Roaring Twenties that I'd read so much about. Far from roaring, though, the '20s had reached the shotgun shacks and abandoned factories of Vinegar Hill only as the most distant of echoes. A party that none of us had been invited to. But here in Galveston, thanks apparently to Sofie's family, that party was in full swing.

On the other side of the street a gaggle of pretty girls in billowy summer dresses strolled arm in arm, their Cuban-heeled sandals dangling from straps hooked over a finger.

"Oh, jeez," Sofie said, quickly turning away.

But the girls had already spotted her. Waving and calling, "Hey, Sofie. Sofie!" they dodged traffic, trying to cross the boulevard to reach her.

"Let's go," Sofie ordered, storming away. We double-timed it down the promenade, slowing down only when we'd left the girls far behind. Sofie stopped in front of a plaque embedded in the seawall dedicated to "Those Lost in the Galveston Storm of 1900."

Silently, I read about the hurricane that had killed twelve thousand people and totally flattened the island. "It's still the worst disaster in American history," Sofie said. "Can you believe that the survivors decided to rebuild? On a sandbar island. They had to raise the city seventeen feet."

"That is kind of crazy."

"Yeah, I guess we're all nuts," Sofie agreed, obviously proud to be the inheritor of such audaciously stubborn insanity.

The next stop was a sprawling two-story structure that floated above the beach like an enormous luxury liner on tall piers. A flag fluttering in the gentle breeze identified it as Murdoch's Bath House. Every inch of the structure was covered with advertise-ments for everything from Hires Root Beer to Kelly's Tires. But the biggest one read "Bathing Costumes. Men and Women. Girls and Boys. 10 Cents a Day. *Wash the Salt Off!! Private Shower 25 Cents.*"

"You can't be a real islander," Sofie said,

"until you're officially christened."

We joined the line of customers in street clothes on the walkway. On the beach seventeen feet below us men wearing ties and women in fluttery dresses and cloche hats strolled leisurely. Beach umbrellas scattered along the shore were an Easter egg hunt of bright color.

The bathhouse was a vast warren of rooms and noisy activity. Sofie led me to a counter where, for the twenty cents that she produced before I could object, the attendant gave us two wire baskets, with a towel and a bathing suit in each one.

Glancing at my pale skin, she pointed to the beach umbrellas for rent. "You'd better give us one of those as well."

The locker room was crowded with women shedding their city clothes and wriggling into the black suits they'd just rented. Their excited chatter echoed off the tile.

Completely at ease among the happy tourists who didn't recognize her, Sofie shed her clothes. I pivoted away and quickly hoisted the straps of my suit up over my shoulders. Thankfully it was baggy enough to hide my washboard chest and protruding pelvic bones. When I turned back around, we faced each other in our identical swimsuits, and Sofie exclaimed, "Look. We're twins."

I couldn't help laughing at both the enthusiasm and the utter ridiculousness of her statement. Her voluptuous figure, olive skin, and black curls were the polar opposite of my own tall, bony silhouette, pale, freckled skin, and flyaway blond hair. "Right," I joked. "No one will ever be able to tell us apart."

"Well, maybe not *identical* twins." She laughed along with me.

It felt so wonderful to laugh that I caught a second wind and my hunger seemed to vanish, along with some of my doubts. I thought again how hard it was for me not to like, or even trust, someone I could kid around with.

CHAPTER 6

We rushed down the stairs that funneled visitors from the bathhouse onto the sand. For an instant the blazing, late-afternoon sun blinded me and the world became an overexposed mirage. When my eyes adjusted I was staring at a silver-blue vastness that went on forever.

The delighted screams of skinny kids bobbing in the warm, docile waves echoed along the shore. The screams were met by warnings from mothers stretched out on towels not to go out even one inch farther. The warnings and happy shrieks blended with the laughter of fathers joking about how hung over they were from all the bootleg hooch the night before.

But it was the waves that mesmerized me. The ocean foamed white and tan at the shoreline then opened onto a shimmering avenue just waiting to carry me out farther than I could see. Maybe even into the future

I'd dreamed of.

"Is this the first time you've been to the ocean?" Sofie asked gently.

Though I'd "been" to the ocean several times back in the vaudeville days when we'd played Atlantic City, all I'd seen then were the footlights and the backstage of the Globe Theatre. First as my father's tiny, comic dance partner and then, when his lungs got too bad, as the toe-dancing Pint-Sized Pavlova whom Mamie claimed was only three years old long after I'd turned six.

"My first *real* time," I answered.

"Oh, probie," Sofie responded, oddly delighted by my answer, "you are the best. Come on, I'm taking you to my special place far away from the crowd."

Shouldering the beach umbrella like a rifle and still gripping the bag of burgers, Sofie set off at a brisk pace. Grateful for my second wind, I followed.

The soft sand gobbled up my long strides and I moved to the strip of beach packed hard by the waves. Sofie glanced back. The humidity had transformed her curls into a dark nimbus floating around her face. Laughing, she broke into a run.

Loping after her, I passed ladies with toenails painted red stretched out on towels, sunning their legs. A mustachioed man in high-waisted trunks building a sandcastle with turrets that flew pieces of sea grass for flags. Skinny boys chasing after one another, flinging wads of seaweed that marked sunburned backs like dribbles of black ink on pink paper.

I wondered what all the happy vacationers must think of me, a ridiculous, tall, bony, eternally hungry scarecrow of a girl galumphing past like a crazy person.

I ran until there were no people and the neatly tended tourist beach disappeared beneath random piles of timber tumbled by the waves into smooth driftwood and hillocks of seaweed baking in the sun that smelled of sulfur.

I stopped. Sofie was nowhere in sight. Was she hiding, spying on me? Was I the butt of some perverse joke?

The only structure this far down the beach was the ramshackle hulk of a once-grand edifice sitting at the end of a pier jutting far out into the Gulf. I visored my eyes against a sun that had suddenly gone from radiant to blinding to read the peeling paint on its side.

As I was making out the words "Starlight Palace," patches of dazzling brilliance began to flash through my vision. A film of sweat, clammy and cold even in the heat, suddenly coated my body. The hope-filled horizon I'd discerned earlier disappeared in the seething glare. The cries of the gulls grew piercingly, painfully loud.

And then the screeching and the glare, the hunger and the doubts stopped. All was blessedly quiet and dark and I was back in the only place where everything could ever be made right and whole again.

"There she is. There's my darling girl. There's my little nurse."

It was my father's voice, but all I could see of him were his hands reaching out atop the clean, crisply ironed sheets. And then my hand, small and warm and pink, appeared beside his. His was large and cold and tinged a bluish color that I hated. I tried to warm his hands with mine. To make that chilly blue go away.

But a crimson flower blossomed across my vision. The terrible flower filled me with panicked terror as it turned into my father's handkerchief spotted with red. I had to do something. I had to make the red flower and that awful bluish color go away. I wanted the hands that held me and protected me and guided me through the dance steps that mirrored his to come back. I had to save my father.

The nurse returned. The kind one in the winged cap with the gold pin gleaming on her chest. The one who adjusted his pillows so he could sit up and eat the soup she brought him on a tray with extra crackers and a glass of milk for me. The one who set up a cot beside his bed for me to sleep on when Mamie didn't show up to take me home at night.

She would save my father.

The nurse held a straw to his bluish lips and crooned in a voice that was comfort itself, "Take a sip, sweetie. Come on now. Just one little sip."

But the straw never reached my father's lips; it touched mine instead. I tried to explain that I was not the one who needed to be saved, my father was. That I would have no one without him.

"Just one sip," the voice urged. "It'll make you feel better."

I sipped. A sweet, cool bubbliness filled my mouth. I was so thirsty and it tasted so good that I couldn't stop myself. I drank and when I opened my eyes, he was gone and I was alone again.

"Good girl," Sofie said.

CHAPTER 7

We were huddled in the patch of shade cast by the rented beach umbrella. With each sip, the memory of my father faded farther away, and I was left with the familiar sadness of all the mornings I'd woken to realize that he was gone and wasn't coming back.

"Here," Sofie said, handing me one of the burgers. I wanted, badly, to merely pick at it, to act as though I could take it or leave it. I tried to save a shred of dignity by eating slowly, casually. And I failed. That hamburger, still warm from the grill, with the exact right touches of mustard, pickle, slice of tomato, melded into impossible deliciousness by a layer of melted cheddar, was the most delicious thing that had ever passed my lips.

Sofie watched me devour the sandwich with the same rapt pleasure I'd felt when I was able to coax my father into swallowing a few spoonfuls of porridge.

"You're looking better. Not exactly rosy, but not scary. Great nurse I'd make," she said with a snort. "Letting my first patient die of starvation. Jeez, kid, why didn't you tell me you were hungry?"

That was a question only a person who'd never been hungry, really hungry, would ask.

We sat on the empty shore and stretched our legs out into the water. The tickle of sand being sucked away beneath me was exquisite. The water rippled with wobbling bands of sunset color.

A whistling chirp caught my attention. The calls trilled in a way that could only be described as "piping." Without having ever seen one except in books, I knew that the covey of small birds darting past were sandpipers. They wound in and out of the water in flawless unison, their tiny legs blurring into a ridiculous churn of motion that made us both smile.

Since evening was coming, I had to know if I could trust Sofie. If I couldn't, I needed to start hitching before it was full dark. So, wiping mustard from my fingers, I asked her straight out, "Why did you go to bat for me?"

Instead of answering, Sofie picked up a shell that had tumbled to rest between us and started drawing random squiggles on the sand. After a while, she said, "First, tell me why you want to be a nurse."

I knew I should just play the grateful charity girl. But I couldn't. I'd lived too long under the control of one spoiled, willful narcissist. Before it got any darker, I had to know for certain that my future wouldn't be dictated by another. So I shot back, "Why don't we start with you?"

My tone caught her attention. The island princess was not used to being challenged. Her eyes went dark and complicated.

When she didn't answer, I probed further. "Why do you care so much about me getting in?"

"Sister T and I —"

I stopped her. "Don't give me that hooey about wanting to expose the other girls to some random non-Catholic poor person. That might be the reason why Sister T is pulling for me, but you? What's in it for you?"

Sofie backed away and said haughtily, "I'm not sure I like the tone of your question." The next second, a startled look came over her face. The snooty front dropped and she said, "Actually, that, *that* tone is exactly why I went to bat for you."

"What are you talking about?"

I sensed the silent debate raging in her head. She glanced around as if, on this completely deserted stretch of beach, someone might be listening. After staring hard into my face for several long moments, she seemed to decide something and said, "Evie, I've had a lifetime of people being nice to me. Kissing my butt. Telling me what they think I want to hear. Because of my family. I pulled for you because you're not BOI. You don't even know or care that BOI means Born on the Island. You didn't grow up on Galveston Island. You don't know my family and you don't owe them a thing. You're not awed by them. Or scared of them.

"Look, I'm not an idiot. I know what my family is. I know where the money comes from, and I am sick of existing in this strange limbo where everyone acts like my family's business is importing olive oil and I'm just this dumb, innocent Catholic girl and the business has nothing to do with me."

Barely pausing for breath, she continued urgently, "But it always has. And it always will unless . . . Unless I carve out a place for myself separate from them. Otherwise, I am going to end up marrying some guy who'll immediately become part of the business and then what? I'll have five kids and join the Altar Guild? Spend my life making flower arrangements and living for the 'highball at nightfall' like the other wives? All while pretending I don't know about the mistress my husband's got tucked away in the penthouse suite at the Buccaneer."

I didn't know what to say and Sofie, reacting to my silence and embarrassed then by her confession, tried to dismiss it with a weak laugh. "Hey, forget I said anything. I just thought that, with your background, where you came from and all, you might understand. That, if I had even one friend I didn't have to put on an act for, the next three years wouldn't be so, you know, lonely or something."

Without giving me a chance to speak, Sofie hurtled on. "Stupid, right? I don't know what I was thinking. Forget the whole thing." Waving her hand around as if fanning away a bad odor, she said, "Listen, don't worry, you've got a place at St. Mary's, no matter what. We don't really have to have anything else to do with each other."

She started to fold up the umbrella. I put my hand on hers and stopped her. After a pause, still searching for my thoughts, I said, "You know, Sofie, people talk a lot about how important it is to 'be yourself,' right? And to find someone who accepts you for who you are. And I'm sure that's wonderful and all. But that's not what either one of us needs right now, is it? I know it's not what I need. I need someone who will accept me for who I *want* to be." I paused, and, feeling like one of the poker players I used to watch backstage as he pushed all his chips in on a bet, I said, "Sofie, I can be that for you. Maybe you'll be that for me."

My skepticism had brought out hers and she reminded me, "You still haven't told me why you *really* want to be a nurse."

Uncertain how to start, I answered, "Okay, you leveled with me, I'll do the same. First, I'll tell you the smart reason. I want to be a nurse because if I don't carve out a place for myself separate from my mother, I'll end up back in Vinegar Hill. I'll get a job. Get knocked up. Get married. Get beat up when the world beats him up. Or worse."

I almost told her the "or worse" path. The one Mamie had laid out for me in Detroit. But that was one secret I had to keep.

Sofie no longer sounded rich or entitled or naïve or anything but human when she asked, "And the other reason?"

"The stupid reason?" I asked, stalling for time.

"Tell me," she prompted.

"Because I lost the only person in the world who loved me, the only person I loved, because I didn't know enough to save him. I didn't make him go to the hospital soon enough. I didn't force him to stop working. I didn't make him leave my mother."

"How old were you when he died?"

"Almost five. I told you it was stupid," I said defensively. "I know that I was too young to really do anything. That I'm crazy for feeling this way. That he's gone and nothing I ever do will bring him back, but —"

"Stop. Nothing your heart tells you is true is crazy. It may not be entirely logical, but it's never crazy. I'm glad you told me. I can't have any more lies. I just can't."

"Me neither," I said, thinking of the one lie I still had to hide and swearing that, with Sofie at least, it would be the only one.

"We're really going to do this, aren't we?"

I nodded.

"Promise?" She held up her little finger. The gesture puzzled me until I recalled the normal girls back at Sam Houston High doing this and I quickly held up my pinkie.

She twined hers around it and I answered, "Promise," as she shook it.

As if to celebrate our vow, thousands of bulbs blinked on at the end of the pier, transforming the heap of graying timber that they outlined into a castle of light.

"What's that?"

"A giant albatross around my family's neck?"

I darted a *What?* glance her way.

"The Starlight Palace."

"The electric bill must be staggering."

"The price of pride," she said.

"So it's completely abandoned?"

"Except for him." She pointed and I noticed that one of the lights was moving. A watchman.

"He's out there a lot. Comes at all sorts of odd hours," Sofie continued. "Probably just some guard that my father hired as part of the pretense that, any day now, the famous — the *historic* — Starlight Pier is going to be reopened in all its former glory."

Though I nodded, I knew immediately that the man was not a watchman or a guard. Back on Vinegar Hill, an arsonist everyone called Jimmy the Torch used to keep us kids spellbound by showing off his inside info.

"The worse the economy," he'd tell us like we were a class of junior firebugs, "the better my business. We call it Jewish lightning

61

when a business is about to go under and it mysteriously burns. Don't know why. Most of my customers is just regular panicked Christians."

Jimmy had warned us about the arsonist's worst enemy: fire insurance investigators. "Look out for guys in bad suits nosing around your target property. Regular watchmen never wear suits. And if they got clipboards and are taking notes, poking around where they got no business poking around, you are in big trouble 'cause the insurance company is wise to you."

The guy poking around the Palace wore a bad suit and he was making notes on a clipboard. I said nothing.

Sofie gave a fond chuckle as she gazed at the Palace. "There's such a long story behind that old place. It was the first structure rebuilt after the hurricane. Galveston loves the Palace. I'll tell you the whole story about how my family's been trying to bring it back to life, because we have time for stories now, don't we? Time for all the stories."

"We do."

I spent more than a thousand days at St. Mary's, but that first one, the day that Sofie and I became friends, allies, was the most important one of all.

Chapter 8

When the rising bell clanged at five on my first morning of nursing school, it was like pushing off at the start of a three-year bobsled race. Though the days seemed to last forever, the months roared past, borne on an endless stream of classes and work and constant learning. And, true to our promise, I backed Sofie up and she backed me up every step of the way.

Like all the other probationers, for the first three months we worked our fingers to the bone, rarely being given anything more important to do than take dirty sheets to the basement laundry, a place even hotter and more humid than the rest of the hospital. Though I griped along with the other girls about how we were being worked to death, with three meals a day, hot baths, and work that felt important, it was a vacation compared to dancing five shows a day or working two jobs while going to school.

I was a model nursing student, having learned early from Mamie to keep my trap shut and do what I was told. Only once, toward the end of that trial period, did I grow lax.

Sofie and I were in the courtyard after class with some other probies, a bunch of game kids with more pepper on them than the average Galveston Catholic girl. I'd taught them to play stickball the way I had back on Vinegar Hill. Bases were loaded and I was up to bat. Roswitha, a beefy Polish girl with a wicked fastball, was pitching. Before she wound up she taunted me, "Better duck, you Holy Roller beanpole! I'm gonna knock your block off!"

"In a pig's ass, yuh big Polack!" I yelled back. Too late I noticed the Director peering down from a second-story window. The instant she caught my eye, she beckoned me to her.

The Director had clearly hated me from the get-go. She probably hated Sofie and Sister T just as much, maybe even more, since they'd boxed her in. But it wasn't safe to hate them. Me? I was fair game. For three months, hoping I'd quit, she'd bullied me. I got the longest hours, the worst work assignments, and the most canceled free

64

hours. But that afternoon, she tore my hide off.

"If at any time, anywhere," she warned, "you ever bring another speck of your guttersnipe filth into my training program, you shall be back on the train to Houston so fast it will make your head spin. And, no matter how much misguided charity might have been expended upon you, you will be out. I shall never allow a Vinegar Hill degenerate to wear the pin of a St. Mary's registered nurse. That is all."

"You scare her," Sofie told me later, trying to explain why the Director persecuted me and would continue to do so until the day I got my pin.

"Scare her? What on earth does she have to fear from me?"

"Change. Sister T told me that the reason the Director was called back to the Motherhouse was to be counseled. Sister doesn't know why exactly, just that it's very unusual and very bad and means that change is in the air. So she's scared and taking it out on you. Also she hates Protestants."

"You Catholics are weird," I joked.

"No argument there."

From then on, unless I was alone with Sofie, I buried the street tough from Vinegar Hill. I gave the Director nothing to find fault with, and, over the next three years, I learned how to be a nurse.

I learned how to change sheets beneath a patient without disturbing her. I learned how to make a passable, lump-free junket for those on a bland diet. How to apply a hot, wet dressing on an infected wound and wrap it in a rubber sheet. How to seal a rubber collar around the neck of a polio patient confined in an iron lung.

I learned how to prep a maternity patient for delivery with a shave and an enema. How to prepare a sterile field for surgery and snap a pair of latex gloves onto a surgeon's scrubbed hands. How to become a silent sentinel on night duty, beaming my flashlight into dark rooms without disturbing the patient.

I was always chosen to assist when the prostitutes who'd contracted syphilis from working the Line came in for fever therapy. I tried to distract the women and keep them hydrated while they sweated in the heat cabinet. When the treatments didn't work, I learned how to ease the suffering of end-stage syphilis. How to bathe them when they passed on, lay them out, and wrap them in shrouds for the morgue.

I had another special duty and, though their name was never mentioned, it involved the Amadeos. With no explanation, I would simply be called into a private exam room. There I'd help splint the mangled fingers of card cheats, put casts on the broken legs of deadbeat debtors, and stitch up the pulverized faces of embezzling club managers. The injured were whisked in and out of private entrances. No notes were ever taken. No reports were ever filed. Even, or more accurately, *especially,* Sofie didn't know about these cases.

Painkillers made a few of the injured chatty. From them I heard about the ones who didn't make it to the ER. The mob guys from out of town who'd tried to encroach on Amadeo territory. The bootleggers who attempted to undercut the family. Anyone in the organization suspected of ratting. There were never stories in the papers. Just whispers about an oil barrel dumped fifty miles off the coast. Or the Texas Rangers "taking care" of things. No one pried too deeply. Least of all me. The family funded my scholarship and, I figured, this was how I paid them back.

True to the pact we'd made that first day, I never mentioned these visits to Sofie. I had too much at stake, because every lecture I attended, every fracture I helped set, every feverish child I soothed, every incision I cleaned and bandaged made me even more certain that I was put on Earth to be a nurse.

Just as Sister T had intended, I became the school's token poor Protestant. Most of the girls didn't know what to make of me, but because I was Sofie's friend, they put up with me. Dancing was my ticket to full acceptance in St. Mary's resident hall. Many an evening, after the books were shut and we'd clocked our hours at whatever ward we were rotating through, the girls would sneak into the room I shared with Sofie.

We'd crank up Sofie's Victrola and I'd teach the girls just as I'd once taught classes of debutantes and kids in cotillion. When we started having mixers with the med students and interns at Sealy Hospital, my classmates clamored to learn the newest dances. I taught them the Charleston and the Texas Two-Step. Then they insisted upon learning the naughty dances, and I showed them the Shimmy, the Grizzly Bear, and the Bunny Hug.

I also did what Sister T had hoped I would: I taught the sheltered girls about poverty. I taught them never to expect a person who couldn't afford food to tell you that they were hungry. Remembering our first day together, Sofie nodded with thoughtful reflection when I said, "A person with any pride will starve to death before they'll admit they're too poor to buy food."

In short, I was supremely happy. For the first time in my life I loved what I was doing, I had friends, hunger was just a memory for me to share, and after tomorrow no one could ever take any of it from me.

Tomorrow, I would get the pin that told the world that I was somebody. That I was a registered nurse.

CHAPTER 9

May 8, 1932

"Can you believe it?" Sofie asked as we pulled off our surgical gowns and masks and stuffed them in the hamper on that last day.

We'd just finished assisting Dr. Ingram — the grouchiest of all the grouchy surgeons — with three surgeries in a row. We'd started with an appendectomy then, after rescrubbing, gowning, and gloving, moved on to an inguinal hernia repair. Both had been straightforward. The third case, removal of a uterine tumor, was complicated simply by the size of the tumor. After taking a sample of the fluid to send to the lab, two and a half gallons of viscous fluid was drained from the mass.

"Believe what?" I joked. "That this is our last day as student nurses and we get our pins tonight? Or that, for once, you didn't break the sterile field?"

"Me break the field? Who would have

scratched her nose if I hadn't stepped on her foot?"

"Jeez, Sof, I'm still limping."

"Who are you kidding?" She nodded toward my feet. "Hurt those clodhoppers? Not possible."

The sorry state of my feet was a running joke between us. They were as gnarled and lumpy as an old tree root from Mamie training me to dance *en pointe* shortly after I started walking.

"Who else is going to put food on the table?" she had asked when I cried because my feet hurt. "Your father? He can barely hobble to the outhouse anymore. Me?" She'd always snorted at the impossibility of that suggestion. "After what you did to me?"

Tales of how my birth had "wrecked" my mother's "plumbing" were the bedtime stories I'd grown up with. The moral was always clear: she'd given her life for me and I owed her mine.

That day Sofie and I couldn't get out of the hospital and into our civvies fast enough. On the trolley, I expelled a gusty sigh of relief. "We made it."

"We made it," Sofie echoed, shaking her head in wonderment.

"I couldn't have done it without you," I said, understating the truth.

71

"Horse pucky."

"It's true."

"Says the girl who got the highest score on the nursing board exam in the entire state."

"Yeah, but that's only because you never could tell your streptococci from your spirochetes."

Sofie slugged my upper arm and I recoiled in pretend pain.

"Oops, sorry. That's what happens when you grow up with only brothers. Don't know my own strength. I needed a sister like you to practice on."

Sister.

The word made my heart ache in the same spot that peeping at families gathered around the dinner table or laughing together as they listened to Jack Benny on the radio had left tender.

But I didn't say the word back to her. In fact, I pretended I hadn't heard it. I'd learned long ago that it was dangerous to let the world know what you wanted most, since that was the thing it would always take away from you.

Sofie didn't notice, because the instant we stepped off the trolley onto Seawall Boulevard she spotted her beloved uncle Julian, whom everyone called JuJu. A well-padded, chummy guy who'd never met a stranger, JuJu was the charismatic, glad-handing front man whose handsome face was always in the papers cutting ribbons and handing giant checks to charities. While, behind the scenes, his solemn brother, Sofie's reclusive father, who'd never entirely mastered English, made and enforced the deals.

JuJu was the only Amadeo who mingled with the tourists strolling the promenade.

"Nipote," he exploded the instant he spotted his niece. He dropped the arm of the woman at his side, who had the height, beauty, bleach-blond hair, and curves of a showgirl. Sofie had told me that his wife, Aunt Patti, was a short, round Italian lady.

"Give me a sec," Sofie said.

I veered away a discreet distance in the opposite direction. For three years, we'd held fast to our promise to keep our new lives separate from our pasts.

Planted in the middle of the broad sidewalk was a scrawny, preteen newsboy holding up a paper that flapped about in the offshore breeze. In a voice splintered by puberty, the kid croaked out, "Stock market slides again. Down almost ninety percent from 1929 high.

"Read all about it!" he pleaded, but the vacationers strolling past ignored him and his bad news.

Just like the Roaring Twenties had never made it to Vinegar Hill, the economic collapse that followed the stock market crash in 1929 was simply a vague rumor here in "the Playground of the Southwest."

The Depression was a black-and-white photo in a newspaper of men shivering in a bread line somewhere up north.

Galveston, on the other hand, Galveston was bright and vibrant. A kaleidoscope of jewel-colored neon signs at night and clouds so white and cottony against a sky so blue during the day that they made your eyes ache. And, just as the Amadeos had kept Galveston floating high above Prohibition, Sofie's family had been the unbreachable seawall guarding it against the financial hurricane that had flattened the rest of the country.

On the newsboy's gaunt face was the thing so rare in Galveston that I'd had to explain it to my classmates: hunger.

"I'll take one," I said, handing the boy a couple of pennies, which he pocketed eagerly. "Actually," I added, handing him all the coins I was saving to buy a hot dog since the piece of toast I'd had for breakfast was long gone, "give me one for my friend, too." I took another paper and hurried off before he could return my change.

I skimmed the news of the world outside Galveston. None of it was good. Almost a quarter of the country was out of work. The drought shriveling up the Great Plains had gotten so bad that winds now swept tons of topsoil into dust storms that turned the day to night.

While forklifts were needed to unload the cargo of fleets of rumrunners that delivered aged Cuban rum and bonded Canadian whiskey to the docks of Galveston, in Alabama a judge fined a man fifty dollars for possession of one teaspoon of whiskey. The total of U.S. banks that had failed was nearing nine thousand. Because of malnutrition, tuberculosis was reaching epidemic levels.

International news was even drearier.

Russia had imposed rationing on flour, bread, tea, oil, and sugar. The German chancellor announced that his impoverished country could no longer repay its war debts. An unknown politician named Hitler who'd been considered a fool in 1928 when he'd predicted economic disaster was now being given serious consideration. Pundits were saying that if he'd been clever enough to predict the Depression, he might also know how to solve it.

Meanwhile, our do-nothing president, Herbert Hoover, was still against creating a government aid plan to help struggling families. Fuming, I wished that Hoover and his buddy Henry Ford, who was always preaching about how "good, hardworking Americans" didn't need handouts, they just needed to pull themselves up by their bootstraps, could actually know what it was like to be hungry and hopeless.

I stuffed the newspapers with their stories of hunger and desperation in the trash.

"Evie," Sofie called out before doing a surprising thing: she waved me over. "Come here."

I hesitated, but Uncle JuJu rushed forward, threw his arms open, and crushed me in a bear hug. "So this is the *Protestante*? Why'd Sofia keep you hidden away? Thought you had two heads or something. *Evelina,* right?"

My name, and even my supposed religion, sounded so beautiful the way JuJu almost sang it in Italian that I didn't correct him.

"Evelina, listen, you don't have to be shy around me. I'm not like my brother and the others. Some of my best friends are Protestant," he said with a good-natured bark of laughter. "I don't hold it against you. Sofia says you're okay, that's good enough for me.

"Sofia, you should bring your Protestant friend over for dinner. You finished this whole nurse thing, right?"

"Uncle JuJu, the pinning ceremony is this evening. I invited you weeks ago."

"And I'll be there," he assured her. "Better than that, we'll have a party! Next weekend. We'll fly in that band we had for your sixteenth birthday. Who was that?"

"Duke Ellington," Sofie answered in a low voice. Her family's extravagance embarrassed her. "You don't need to do that."

"For my favorite niece? And the Protestant? We gotta celebrate. Do it up right. And you know what that means?" he asked, his dark eyes gleaming. "The Hollywood Dinner Club! Whuddya say, Protestant? We'll get Guy to play."

The "Guy" JuJu referred to so casually was Guy Lombardo. He and his world-famous band had played at the opening of the Hollywood and filled the club's 500 seats for every night of their three-week run. I couldn't hide my excitement at the prospect of an evening at the crown jewel of the Amadeo empire, a place so swanky that it was rumored that Clark Gable was once seen there with Jean Harlow. It even had air-conditioning, a phenomenon I'd read about but never experienced. Reading the excitement on my face, JuJu clapped his hands together. "Okay, the Protestant is in! What about you, *nipote*?"

"We'll talk about it," Sofie said, obviously unenthused about, I suspected, this collision of her family and her new life. She nodded her chin toward the showgirl. "Hey, looks like your friend is getting impatient."

"Yeah, she's not what you'd call a sun worshiper." Walking toward the woman, he yelled back to me, "Great to finally meet the mysterious Protestant. If you ever need anything, Evelina, just give me a call at the Buccaneer." I gave a tiny nod to acknowledge all the times I'd been called into private exam rooms to deal with the cases that Sofie never heard about. Penthouse suite. Lowering his voice, he added, "The family appreciates what you've done for us."

"Appreciates what?" Sofie asked. I shrugged.

Sofie brushed off the encounter saying, "And that is Uncle JuJu," as she hurried us away. She clearly had no desire to say anything further about my first meeting with a member of her legendary family. And that was fine with me.

We quickly lost ourselves in the stream of happy tourists, faces flushed from bootleg liquor and sunburn, who strolled and staggered along the promenade, laughing and talking too loud, acting out their roles of vacationers having a grand time.

A group of boys — shirtsleeves rolled up, sea breeze ruffling their blunt country haircuts, belts tightened around thin waists, sunburned noses peeling — passed by. The shy ones acted like they didn't notice us. The bold ones gawked and grinned, showing country teeth mottled by well water. Sofie paused, struck a pose, ran a hand through her hair, and beamed a devastating smile at the boys.

The boys were dazzled.

Incidentally, Sofie had become a dazzler.

Even in her heavy-browed, lightly mustached chipmunk period, Sofie was always pretty. But back when she feared being married off and never having a life outside her family's tight orbit, she hid her beauty. Once we had a couple of years of high grades and stellar recommendations under our belts, she took to tweezing and bleaching with a vengeance and went from pretty to beautiful. And the boys noticed.

"Yeah," Sofie mused, "a party at the Hollywood. You love the idea, don't you?"

"Kind of," I admitted, already dreaming about a public celebration of the start of my new life.

"Why the hell not? The amount of time we spent on bedpan patrol, we deserve it."

"That we do," I agreed.

Joy bubbled through me like the champagne that was rumored to flow from fountains at the Hollywood. Our glorious new lives were about to start.

CHAPTER 10

May 8, 1932

"Oh my girls, oh my beloved third-year girls, this is our last day . . ." Sister T's voice quavered and broke. "This is the last time we will gather. In just a few hours you will receive the pins that will tell the world you are board-certified, registered nurses."

Her celebratory mood turned somber. "I know that talk of politics is forbidden at St. Mary's, but this election is too important for me to hold my tongue. Girls, your future is at stake. Our country is at a crossroads. In the election this November we will choose whether to pursue the path of private gain that will lead to further misery for all but the wealthiest among us. Or whether we shall unite as a people and find salvation by working for the common good.

"You, my angels, have a duty, a mission, to show your fellow citizens the way toward that salvation. Live your lives in service to

81

the common good for, as Albert Einstein tells us, 'Only a life lived for others is a life worthwhile.'

"But enough of the harsh realities. Today is a day for celebration. So, let me just say that, having had the supreme privilege of knowing you fine young women for three wonderful years, I am completely confident that each and every one of you shall find places that will bring joy and purpose to your lives and to the lives of all to whom you minister.

"All right, that's enough from me. Let us adjourn to the courtyard for our private reception before the pinning ceremony begins."

Blue and white streamers hung from the giant pecans that shaded the courtyard. A refreshment table was laden with platters of dainty sandwiches, cookies, brownies, and even several cakes. An ice mold of a dolphin leaped from a bowl of pink punch. We only saw such bounty at graduation parties.

"Well, Nurse Devlin," Sofie said, surveying the rare treats. "Shall we divide and conquer? You get the sandwiches. Pimiento cheese for me. And I'll concentrate on the goodies. What'll it be? Hummingbird cake or fudge brownies?"

"Do you even need to ask?" I answered.

"One of each for my friend with the hollow leg, coming up," Sofie said, before diving into the crowd thronging the table. Eager as I was to fill our plates, I needed a moment to absorb the fact that everything was about to change.

Sofie and I had rented rooms in a boardinghouse close to Sealy Hospital and we planned to move in that night after the ceremony. My few belongings were already packed in the battered suitcase I'd carried from Vinegar Hill. I'd been astonished to see that the three years that had transformed me into a nurse as capable of managing an entire ward as she was of calming a small child about to have her tonsils removed could all fit into that small case.

With a pang I realized that as much as I had griped along with my friends about the endless hours of work, the tortures of organic chemistry, the harshness of grumpy surgeons and cranky charge nurses, I didn't want to leave. St. Mary's had become the first happy home I'd known since my father died. For a moment, I felt as though I was standing on the beach with the tide going out and the sand shifting beneath my feet. The literal ground I had claimed such a firm footing on was being swept out from under me.

Sofie returned bearing two plates and handed me one. "Hey, probie, why so glum? Also, where the heck are our sandwiches? Aren't you starving? We missed lunch."

"Just savoring the moment, I guess," I said. I took a bite of cake and was suffused by its sweetness. Only then, as I relaxed into my triumph, did I become aware that, for three years, I had been walking on eggshells, bracing myself for the moment when I would be discovered, unmasked. And now it was over. I had done it. I was no longer the grimy girl from Vinegar Hill running from her past.

"We're nurses," I said, just to hear the words out loud.

Sofie was about to affirm our new identities when, without warning, a look of mild alarm replaced the delight in her expression. I turned toward the cause and found the Director standing at the edge of the exuberant gathering. My gaze met hers. She stabbed her index finger at me, crooked it, and beckoned me to her.

"What's going on now?" Sofie asked. "Can't that cow take one day off from riding you?"

Although the magic of the Amadeo name had protected me for three years, apparently the Director's petty persecutions weren't going to stop until I walked out of St. Mary's with that pin on my chest.

"No idea." Wearily, I handed Sofie my plate, stood, brushed a few crumbs from my skirt, and followed the Director, who was already disappearing into the main hall.

Inside, I noticed that Hector and Ron, two of the gate guards whom I'd known for the past three years, were sitting outside the office. Though I greeted the usually friendly guards with a smile and a small wave, neither of the men would meet my gaze.

Determined not to be intimidated on my day of triumph, the moment we were in the Director's office, I demanded briskly, "What is it?"

Ignoring my question, the Director sat behind her massive desk and ordered, "Have a seat." With unsettling emphasis, she added, "*Miss* Devlin."

I started to speak, to object, but my throat had gone dry. She had slid a file across her pristine desk, twirled it so that it faced me, and snapped open the manila cover. Inside were newspaper clippings. One glance was all it took for the past to rise up from where it had been waiting for three years and drag me back.

Back to Detroit.

Back to the National Theatre.
Back to Mamie.

CHAPTER 11

Winter 1921

"There she is," Uncle Jake said, exhaling a sigh of relief as he pulled out of the frantic Detroit traffic and slid into a parking spot directly in front of our destination, the National Theatre. Even in a district packed with some of the best vaud houses in the country — the Gayety, Liberty, Temple, and Columbia — the National stood out.

"Mamie?" Jake glanced back at my mother for her reaction. My mother was still fast asleep, sprawled out across the seat, as regal as Cleopatra floating down the Nile. Asleep or awake, my mother had the superhuman ability to tune the world out.

"We'll just let her sleep," Uncle Jake said with a conspiratorial wink. I nodded; life was always easier when Mamie was asleep.

Uncle Jake wasn't my uncle. Mamie made me call all the men who'd drifted through her life in the four years since Daddy died

"Uncle." Jake wasn't a boyfriend either. He'd been Daddy's best friend and they used to have an act together, The Dancing Devlin Brothers. Jake did what he could to look out for us. Found bookings for me. Did the driving. Worked odd jobs when we were between tours. At least he did when "the gloomies" hadn't caught him and made him drink.

"Didn't I promise you?" Jake asked, gesturing expansively toward the theater. "It's a Moorish palace."

Not all, or even most of, Jake's promises had come true, but gazing now at the National's high, arched entrance flanked by tall minarets topped by golden domes and festooned with rosettes, eagles, and sad-eyed angels, I saw he'd made good on this one.

"It's like *Ali Baba and the Forty Thieves* come to life," I said. Too loudly, as it turned out; I'd roused Mamie.

"Oh, stop showing off your damn book addiction," she griped. Mamie considered my "book addiction" to be unhealthy and the reason I'd lost the "sparkle" that had made me her most glorious creation, the Pint-Sized Pavlova, a toddler who could dance on her toes. When Daddy started losing his wind, adding me to the act was enough of a novelty that the bookings kept coming in. For a while, we even snagged some dates on the exalted Keith-Albee-Orpheum Circuit. But then I committed the unforgivable sin of growing up and, without Daddy to make me look adored and adorable, I was just another brat who'd had ballet lessons.

"That damn Marvin," Mamie cursed, massaging the space between her eyes where her "sick headaches" always started. "Hadn't been for him teaching you how to read, we'd still be playing the big houses."

I didn't bother pointing the basic facts of biology out to my mother: that reading was not the reason I had shot up. That I hadn't "chosen" to grow up simply to spite her any more than Daddy had "chosen" to die.

Jake gave me a wink. We both knew that if I opened my mouth Mamie would have silenced me with a harsh "When I want your opinion, I'll ask for it."

And she never asked for it.

Gawking at the National, Jake mused, "I think our luck's about to change."

"It better had," Mamie warned, peering into a compact to freshen her lipstick. She tilted her head one way then another to let the sunlight burnish her flawless complexion, her perfect chip of a nose, her fathomless violet eyes, then snapped the compact shut and concluded, "I've had it with these four- and five-a-days. They're killing me."

Killing *her*? It was *me,* the damn Pint-Sized Pavlova, who had to perform four and five times a day since the bookings had dried up and now could only get hired as a filler act between the scene switches.

The relentless schedule had destroyed my feet. They hurt all the time. But I knew better than to complain. If I did, Mamie, with a woebegone look of blameless suffering, would always respond that, of course, I could stop performing any time I liked. But if I did, she would be left with "no other alternative" than to surrender me to the Middlefield Home for Indigent Children.

The tears she could summon on cue would tremble in her eyes as she'd tell me, "Of course, no mother *wants* to give up her child, her own flesh and blood, but if you leave me no other choice . . ."

So, instead of complaining, I taught myself the handy trick of leaving my body. I simply abandoned everything that hurt — my feet, my heart, my growling belly — and watched from a faraway place where pain couldn't reach.

The three of us put on our happiest of happy faces and trooped into the National. It was like entering a jewel box. Tiles the color of sapphires, emeralds, rubies, even gold covered every wall. On second look, however, I noticed that, here and there, like gaps in a gleaming smile, tiles were missing. And that most of the bulbs in the ornate chandelier had burned out, leaving the lobby in a dusky gloom. All over the country, as people flocked to the pictures to see Charlie Chaplin and Mary Pickford, the lights were going out for vaudeville.

"Open call don't start for another hour," a voice on the other side of the lobby snarled at us. The manager, a husky fellow in a threadbare suit with a prominent shower of dandruff sprinkled across the shoulders, lumbered our way. The instant he caught sight of my mother, however, he put some pep in his step.

"I'm sure, however, that an exception could be made in your case," he cooed, rushing forward to take Mamie's daintily extended hand. "Perhaps you'd like to . . ." He gestured toward a distant door. ". . . step into my office? Have a drink? Or something?"

Jake shook his head at the predictability of the manager's response. Mamie was movie-star gorgeous and men melted at her feet.

"Why, I thank you, sir," Mamie said, faking a honey-drenched Southern accent.

"But, truth be told, the performer is my daughter." She snapped her fingers and flicked her hand impatiently.

I stepped forward.

The manager eyed me. His disappointment was as obvious as it was familiar.

Before he could speak, Mamie interrupted, her tone harshening with the nasal twang of the Texas Panhandle where she'd grown up. "We have a contract." She extracted the document from her handbag and waved it in the manager's face.

He batted it away. "You told me the kid was six. All the private advertising I sent out to our select clientele promised a six-year-old girl."

"And that is what you have here," Mamie bristled.

I had just turned nine. An exceptionally tall nine.

"If she's six," the manager exploded, "I'm a monkey's uncle. Deal's off. My clientele will not accept this . . . this . . ." He sputtered and waved a finger in my direction. "This giraffe!"

Jake leaned over and whispered, "Hey, Evie, why don't you go on and explore. This is just business talk. Go find Ali Baba."

Happy to escape, I raced up a winding staircase that twisted through one of the minarets. Stained glass hung in the windows and threw bolts of colored light across the stairs.

In the balcony, I peered down on the eight-hundred empty seats below as I settled into a maroon velvet seat of my own. Most of the velvet nap had been worn away and the seat smelled of sweat, hair oil, aftershave, and an odd, mushroomy odor I couldn't recall ever having smelled in any other theater.

Something else I hadn't ever encountered before was a sort of runway that extended from the center of the stage down the main aisle. Seats had been removed to accommodate this protrusion and others had been rearranged so that they faced the odd runway instead of the stage. I couldn't figure out exactly what it was, but something was off about the National.

I put that, along with my fear that this might be another day when Mamie forgot to feed me, out of my head, and pulled my favorite book in the whole world, *The Wonderful Wizard of Oz,* from my coat pocket.

I lost myself in it so thoroughly that Jake startled me when he appeared. "There you are. We've been hollering for you. Come on, Mamie's starving. How does chop suey sound?" I jumped up. Mamie must have saved the booking. Chop suey was her favorite of all our favorite cheap, filling foods.

Fat, fluffy flakes of snow were floating down when we stepped out. Bright halos of light now topped the theaters and movie palaces. We made a beeline for a place called Chop Suey Louie's. With a bowl of the house specialty warming me and filling all my empty places, I was half dozing when Mamie slapped my cheek and jolted me to attention.

"Have you heard a single word I've said," she demanded.

"Yes, ma'am," I lied.

"You better had because if you louse this up, I just don't know. I mean . . ."

I tensed up when I heard that woebegone tremor in her voice.

"Oh, for God's sake, Mame," Jake said, pulling a pint bottle from his pocket and looking away as she went on.

"It's not as if I *want* to send you to Middlefield. What kind of mother would want that? But if you choose to leave me no other alternative, well . . ."

Tears welled up in her eyes as she gazed out at the opalescent curtain of snow that now hung over the city. Lillian Gish, I thought. Even as the prickly nausea of panic rose at the mention of sending me to an orphanage, I admired how perfectly my mother imitated the actress's expression of beatific mournfulness.

"I'll be good. I'll be good. I'll be good," I promised.

And, backstage in the freezing theater, I was good. I questioned nothing and no one. I didn't ask where the Indian club jugglers and magicians, baggy-pants comics and animal acts that usually crowded the backstage area of any vaudeville show were. I didn't question why everyone behind the curtain was female and everyone in the audience was male. I didn't say a word when the ladies applying their makeup took special pains to rouge their nipples.

I raised no objection when Mamie told me that I had to walk down the runway and do my act out there. Right in the middle of the audience. Close enough that I could see the faces that were usually, mercifully, either a distant blur or entirely erased in the glare of the footlights. Now they would be near enough that they could touch me. Near enough that, for the first time, the watchers would be real people.

All I dared say when Mamie dragged out one of my old flouncy-skirted ballet dresses was, "It's too short, Mamie. My bottom will show."

"Don't speak like a guttersnipe. You know how it offends me."

Far worse, the costume's bodice that had once covered my chest now fell halfway down my chest nearly exposing the nubs of the almost-there breasts that I knew were supposed to be covered at all times.

Jake, who'd been out "rounding up some more bug juice," appeared backstage, his cheeks and nose scarlet. He took one look at me and confirmed my worst fears. "This isn't right, Mame."

"Yeah, well," Mamie sneered. "It isn't right that you can't get off the sauce long enough to find us some decent dates. Or even sober up enough to start dancing again and help me try to keep this family together because I'm doing the best I can."

"Mamie, vaudeville is dead unless you're a headliner."

"Or not a stumbling drunk."

Mamie, who'd been fluffing up my tutu, gave Jake a look of such fury that the goose bumps covering my freezing flesh rose even higher. That look contained all the hard arithmetic of our lives. We'd spent the last of our savings — which Mamie carried in the velveteen grouch bag on a cord around

96

her neck — on the chop suey. There was no way to make us add up if I didn't do the show.

Defeated, Jake hung his head and muttered, "A kid in a cooch show. You know this isn't right."

Cooch show. What was a cooch show?

Vibrating with rage, Mamie held her hands up stiffly beside her ears. "I forbid you to use such vulgarity in my presence. I specified that she would not be required to show her . . ." She gestured vaguely toward me.

"What?" Jake demanded, and my heart swelled. He was standing up to her. He would save me. "Her knish?" he said.

"Stop! Either be a man and support this family or leave. You ridiculous, *impotent* stumblebum."

At the last two words, Jake's shoulders sagged. He took his bottle and left. A chill deeper than any I'd ever felt shivered through me.

I didn't know what a cooch or a knish were and got no further clues when Mamie issued her final instructions: "Toe-walk to the end of the runway, finger in your mouth, turn at least five slow three-sixties, smile at the men, bend over, pretend to fix the strap on your toe shoe, toe-walk back to the stage

97

slow like you don't want to leave, look around over your shoulder, wave bye-bye, blow kisses, and you're out. Got it?"

I couldn't answer. None of it made sense. This wasn't dancing. A sick feeling of utter wrongness washed over me.

At my hesitation, Mamie leaned in so close that the beads of black resin she'd artfully applied to the end of each of her eyelashes tickled my cheek, and told me flatly, "I won't be allowed to visit you at Middlefield."

Even as I commanded my body to move forward on legs turned to wood, I did what I'd learned to do when things hurt too much or got too sad or hard or mean. I simply left my body.

I returned to my cozy seat far up in the balcony where Dorothy Gale and all my book pals waited. Safely nestled high above the runway, I observed the lanky girl in the skirt up to her bottom caught in the blaze of a blue light. In the audience, silver orbs glistened as the men wearing spectacles tipped their heads up to watch.

The girl looked familiar but she wasn't me. Couldn't be me because I was far away, high and safe. The silver orbs of all those hidden eyes couldn't be turned on me. I was watching. Not being watched.

The men who clustered at the edge of the runway leaned in so close that the girl could smell the peculiar need, the loneliness, the desperation throbbing off of them.

Why, she wondered, did so many of the men have newspapers spread across their laps? Why did the papers rustle when she approached? She toe-walked a stiff, puppet walk, the strings controlled by Mamie's instructions. She raised a frozen hand, put a frozen finger in her mouth, and sucked. The rustling grew louder, more fevered.

Cast away at the end of a runway in a sea waiting to pull her under, she clung to her mother's orders. They barely kept the puppet girl afloat as she pirouetted. At her feet, the orbs of glinting light tilted to the side, peering up her skirt at her underwear, her bottom.

"Spread your legs," a voice commanded.

"Spread 'em," another demanded.

Give your audience what they want had always been Mamie's first commandment. The girl had never decoded its meaning until now, when the audience told her exactly what it wanted. And, because her only other choice was Middlefield, she obeyed.

Knish. The word came to her like an entry in the dictionary and she understood.

"The undies. The undies."

The girl pulled them down. She knew it was wrong, but she still did the wrong thing, because that's what they wanted. That's what would keep her out of Middlefield. The rustling grew more furious.

"Hey, Pavlova, Pavlova, look here."

She looked.

A man, his mouth hanging open, his eyes hidden behind ovals of reflected light, held a small, squirming animal in his lap. The mole popped its round, pink head and one blind eye up out of the dark burrow of the man's hand as he rhythmically tried to choke it to death.

The girl attempted to escape, but a hand reached up from the murky depths she'd been cast adrift on, grabbed her ankle, hobbled her flight.

Evie was dragged down. Down from the balcony back onto the runway.

I snapped my head around to look over my shoulder in alarm.

A flashbulb exploded.

The screech of several whistles shrilled through the theater. A dozen policemen in double-breasted greatcoats swarmed the crowd. Another half-dozen swept in from the stage, herding shrieking girls in feathered headdresses and flouncy peignoirs and

100

underwear hardly bigger than a Band-Aid.

A policeman clamped a giant hand, wet and cold with melting snow, on my shoulder and, lifting me off my feet, shoved me forward.

More flashbulbs exploded.

CHAPTER 12

May 8, 1932

Those were the photos that stared up at me
from the Director's desk. The headline
above them blared, "Pint-Sized Pavlova
Caught in Raid at Burlesque Show."

"You did not mention this on your application," the Director informed me crisply.

"I was nine years old."

"The age of reason is seven. More important," she said, pointing a condemning
finger to the photo, "you were, obviously, a
willing participant." Damned by the title
"Burlesque Show," my wide-eyed alarm was
easy to interpret as the come-hither expression of a seductress.

Panic, guilt, and warring senses of both
absolute injustice and the complete inevitability of this reckoning overwhelmed me.
Hadn't I always known that this moment
would come?

"I wasn't. I was a child."

"A most *precocious* child, I would say."

The familiar sensation of observing myself from a spot far away opened a hollow pit in my stomach. "How did you get these?"

"My informant shall remain confidential."

"How long have you known?" I demanded with a starchiness I didn't feel.

"There were doubts from the start."

"But the photos? You've had them for a while, haven't you?"

"Our faith, excuse me, *my* faith, teaches me to allow the sinner time to confess her sins. I allowed you that time. You chose not to take it."

"I was a child. It was one time."

"Was it? Was working at a dime-a-dance hall any better?"

"What are you talking about?"

"All right, you prefer to call it the Bennett Academy of Dance."

"Uncle Jake's dance school? Yes, I worked there. As a dance instructor. I helped teach cotillion classes and debutantes and their escorts. I was a dance instructor."

"Were you?"

Seeing the futility of arguing any further, I summoned up the hard lessons in faking it that vaudeville had taught me and said firmly, "The pinning ceremony will begin in a few minutes. I'm leaving."

"Oh, rest assured, you will be leaving. And, certainly, yes, do go to the ceremony. But there will be no pin with your name on it."

The destiny that the Director had plotted for me from the beginning was there in her expression. "You never even submitted me for registration, did you?"

"What would have been the point? Putting aside the more sordid aspects of your past, the nursing board would never certify a candidate who'd falsified her application. A few phone calls confirmed that the grade schools you claimed to have attended either had never heard of you or didn't exist."

"I was the sole support of my mother. We traveled constantly. What does grade school matter? I graduated from high school. And I graduated from St. Mary's. And I earned my pin." Though my knees trembled, I rose to my feet. I had one card left to play. I didn't want to play it, but there was no other choice. Hating the words, I said, "I'll tell the Amadeos."

She heaved a weary sigh. "Yes, certainly, through whatever unhealthy influence you have exerted over our impressionable Sofia, you may seek their intervention."

Unhealthy influence. My skin crawled at her insinuation.

"I'll tell the paper."

"Indeed, do, by all means. You did attain a certain level of fame as this . . . this . . . Pint-Sized Pavlova. I'm certain that the tabloids will be eager to update the entire country about your attempt to infiltrate the nursing profession after a career in burlesque."

"It wasn't a career."

"You can certainly choose to make that case to the papers. The public has a boundless appetite for salacious stories. I'm sure that your sordid tale will receive ample coverage."

"You would ruin my life out of petty vindictiveness? Why? Because of some point you're trying to prove to Sister T? Or to your bosses in St. Louis?"

Though her nostrils flared, the Director went on as if I hadn't spoken. "I would have thought, though, you'd want to keep this matter private. That you wouldn't want your classmates, your teachers, Sofia's family, and every decent employer you might ever apply with to know about all of this." She prodded the clippings with the tip of her pencil.

I braced every muscle in my body, stood like a rock, and told her, "I am not leaving. I'm not. Yes, I want to make a scene. This is wrong. You can't do this."

Like an echo from Mamie's direst threat, the Director said, "I see you leave me no alternative." Emotionless as a robot, she picked up the receiver of her old-fashioned candlestick phone and tapped the switch hook twice. As she waited for the operator, she called out to the guards in the hall to come in.

Hector, a genial guy who liked to show me photos of his seven beautiful children, whispered, "Be better if you don't make a fuss."

"I'm not leaving," I said.

Ron, a beefy numbskull, clamped hold of my other arm.

When the operator came on the line, the Director said, "Connect me to the police."

She held the receiver away from her ear so that I could hear: "Galveston Police Department, how may I direct your call?"

"I would like to report a trespasser on the grounds of St. Mary's Hospital School for Nurses."

"We'll dispatch a squad car."

Smiling serenely, she thanked the operator and hung up.

"Who told you?" I asked.

"That shouldn't be too difficult to figure out," the Director answered in a bored voice as if I were an onerous piece of business she could finally cross off her list. "Who knew your secrets?"

The answer to that question was a punch in the gut. Sofie. She would never have told intentionally. But had she dropped enough unintentional clues to somehow lead the Director to Detroit?

The sag in my spirits must have been evident, because Ron tightened his grip on my arm.

Hector took the other one, murmuring, "I'm sorry, Evie. If I could get another job, I wouldn't do this, but you gotta let me escort you out. If I don't, she'll just fire me and find someone who will."

I shook off Ron's arm and left with Hector.

With the suddenness of a car crash, I was on the other side of the fence. Ron slammed the wrought-iron gate closed and locked it behind me.

I stood on the empty street with my suitcase at my feet and night coming on rapidly. Shock paralyzed me.

I glanced up at Mary's sorrowful face, white against the night sky, and only the awful inevitability of this moment penetrated my brain. Of course they found out who I really was. And of course I had to be cast out. I picked up my suitcase and walked, not knowing where.

"Evie!"

On the other side of the high fence, Sofie ran to me.

I dropped my suitcase and clung to the bars that separated us.

"Sister T told me what happened. You can't leave. This is ridiculous."

"She found out, Sof. About me. About all the lies."

Sofie wrapped her fingers over mine. "So what?" Her face was all shadows in the night. "Who cares that you were in vaudeville or didn't go to regular school?"

Sofie had never cared. That had been my blessing. It had allowed her to accept me. And, apparently, it had also been my curse. She hadn't thought my secrets shameful enough to keep to herself. Who knew what blabbermouth she had inadvertently spilled the beans to? What did it matter? It had been enough to put the Director on my trail.

Off in the distance I could see the graduates' families streaming onto the grounds, eager to find seats in the chapel for the pinning ceremony. Even from this far away, it was obvious when Sofie's parents arrived. The crowd froze at their appearance, then quickly parted to allow them through.

108

"You should go," I said. "The ceremony will start soon."

"Not without you, Evie. Dammit, you deserve that pin more than any of us. Come back in and get it."

"Sofie, there's no pin for me. She didn't even submit my application to the board."

"Then we'll go to Austin and talk to the board."

"Why?" I asked. "The first thing they'll do is call the Director. The instant she tells them that I falsified my school record to gain admission, my case will be closed."

"That's not fair," Sofie protested. "It's not right."

Instead of telling her that the world is never fair or right, unless you have the money or power to make it fair and right, I withdrew my hand, picked up my suitcase, and started plodding toward the train station.

Sofie, on the other side of the fence, stayed with me. "Evie, please, you promised. Don't leave."

"I'm sorry, Sof, sorrier than you will ever know."

"No, Evie, come on. You can't just give up without a fight."

" 'Just give up'?" I imitated the sound of a laugh, then told her the truest thing I could at that moment. "Sofie, I've been fighting my entire life. I'm tired. I can't do it anymore. Can't keep having my dreams jerked away. I can't keep fighting when I'm beaten."

"No," Sofie called out, as I walked away on the path that deep in my bones I'd always known I was fated to walk. I called to my friend, my sister, my unknowing betrayer, "Be a wonderful nurse, Sofie. Be that for both of us."

Minutes later, I was on the electric train, being transported back to the prison of a life I'd tried, and failed, to escape.

■ ■ ■ ■

HOUSTON

■ ■ ■ ■

Still in shock after the short train trip, I stood, blinking and disoriented, outside Houston's Union Station. After three years away, Houston was louder and jitterier and even more prosperous than I remembered. I stood rooted in place as businessmen in seersucker suits and women in cloche hats with the brims pulled seductively over one eye jostled past me.

Just like Galveston, the city had floated triumphantly above the dim and distant Depression that was hobbling most of the rest of the world. Instead of oceans of bootleg whiskey, though, Houston had bobbed along happily on gushers of oil and clouds of cotton. The lucky parts of Houston, that is. Vinegar Hill had never been lucky.

Struggling to get my bearings, I lingered by a newsstand and read the headlines. "Four Hundred Men Answer Fake Help

Wanted Ad. Riot Ensues." "Funeral Planned for Lindbergh Baby." "Commie Party Leads 'March on Hunger.' " "Capone Starts Tax Evasion Sentence." "German Nazis Assault Journalists." "13 Million Out Of Work: Hoover Orders Wages/Hours Cut for Employed."

The metal wheels of a trolley screeched and the electric line overhead sparked. The odor of scorched metal and burned oil filled the air. I hoisted up my suitcase and began the long trudge back to the only place I'd find a bed that night.

Back to Vinegar Hill.

Back to Mamie.

I tramped past the Glove-Grip Shoe Store, the Eureka Laundry, the Western Union office. I glanced at the line of phone booths inside and ached to call Sofie. I wanted to beg her to wave the magic wand of her money and family power and . . . ?

And what? Rewrite the past I'd lied about? Even on Galveston there were limits to what the Amadeos could do. *If* they even wanted to do it.

The humidity thickened as I approached Buffalo Bayou. The air dragged on me more with every step I took.

Halfway across the Capitol Avenue Bridge, I stared down into the water. The muddy churn of the bayou was caught in the reflection of the bridge lights. The familiar oily rag/rotten egg smell of the refineries wafted up. The low blat of a freighter's horn drifted in from the ship channel's turning basin.

Dread settled over me as I recalled the last time I'd crossed this bridge heading toward Vinegar Hill. It was the day I'd graduated from high school and I had run out of time. I had to tell Mamie the secret I'd managed to keep from her: that I had won the scholarship she'd told me I'd never get.

I had to tell her that I was leaving.

I remembered my hand, slick with sweat, as I turned the knob on her bedroom door.

"Mamie —" I'd started, but stopped dead when I saw that my mother was bringing a long hatpin directly toward her eye. On its tip trembled a molten drop of jet-black Beadex. She was performing that most delicate of operations, the one that transformed her from an ordinary beauty into a matinee idol.

Mamie was beading her lashes.

The scent of her Shalimar perfume, combined with the sickly odor of Beadex melting in a tiny, battered pot perched over a burning candle, filled the small room. My mother sat on an upholstered stool in front

115

of her vanity, her silk kimono printed with pink peonies, a present from the last "uncle," sliding off her creamy shoulders. Without ever looking away from her reflection, Mamie caught my eye in the mirror, and demanded, "Are you *trying* to make me put my eye out?"

My world, my future, shrank down to the minuscule globe trembling on the end of Mamie's hatpin. That globe contained all the worlds of fame, of adulation, that Mamie had ever dreamed of. The worlds that a woman as breathtaking as she deserved. She delivered the shimmering bead to the end of one single eyelash then started on the next bead for the next eyelash.

I took a seat on her bed and did the only thing allowed during this meticulous process: I watched.

The mirror was haloed by photos of Mamie. Most were head shots, each more luminously beautiful than the last, along with a few full-length portraits of Mamie in satin gowns that flowed over her like melted butter. Though she hadn't worked since I had "wrecked her plumbing," all of the images were printed with "Available for Bookings" and the name of one of the long-gone uncles.

Only one photo in the constellation orbiting her mirror wasn't of my mother. In that single photo, my father stood all alone. He was the father who visited me in my dreams. Young and handsome. White tie and tails. Top hat. Forever reaching his white-gloved hand out to a partner. A partner who had been torn away.

Of course, Mamie would have ripped out any evidence of a rival. Even one who had been part of my father's life long before she arrived.

I loved studying that photo while Mamie performed her lengthy "toilette." My father had a smile that was both showstopping and, where it could have been cocky, was only kind. His dark hair was pomaded to a soft luster, parted in the middle and slicked down with the tiniest bit of a mischievous curl at the ends. The words "Dandy Denny Devlin and . . ." were written in old-timey lettering above his head. His partner's name had been torn away. Beneath my father's gleaming patent leather shoes was printed "Headliner with the F. Andrews Traveling Vaudevil—" The rest of that name, of my father's life before Mamie, had been ripped away as well.

I had hazy memories of other photos from Dad's career. In the earliest pictures my father had posed with a woman wearing a feathered headpiece like a circus elephant. Another partner sported an old-fashioned Gibson Girl hairdo. Later ones showed him glancing up at the camera with eyes smoldering like Valentino's as he dipped his partner so low that her dark hair was a puddle of ink on the floor. There had been other partners. Other acts. There had been photos of my father holding me when I was a baby. I even vaguely recalled one of all three of us taken when I was a baby and my father was still healthy. All of us were smiling in that one. Even Mamie.

But those pictures had disappeared so long ago that I sometimes believed I'd imagined the handsome, kind, funny father that Mamie had forbidden me from ever mentioning. I think the only reason she allowed even that one torn photo to be displayed was so she could disparage him as "selfish" and "unreliable" for abandoning her. As though dying of congestive heart failure was like hopping a tramp steamer to Bora Bora.

Mamie finished beading the last lash and, facing me, her other, even truer mirror demanded, "Well?"

She batted eyelashes so long and luxuriant they grazed her eyebrows. When I didn't answer, she prompted, more sharply,

"Well?" and waited for what she wanted from me, from the world: naked adulation.

"Beautiful," I obliged with a frosty crispness before adding, "I graduated today."

Those spidery appendages blinked, semaphoring her bewilderment, asking what that could possibly have to do with her. And then, brightening, she remembered, "Oh, yes, right. Marvelous, marvelous. You can go to work full-time now. They adore you in that lunchroom, don't they?"

"I am not going to keep working in a lunchroom," I informed her.

She surprised me by agreeing. "Hell, no, between that and babysitting, we'll never get out of this dump. Surely you can do better. Have a look. Go on, have a look." Impatiently, she waved a manicured hand toward a section from that day's newspaper that she'd left on the bed. The want ads.

"Lots of opportunities there," she said eagerly.

I glanced down at the jobs my mother had circled in eyebrow pencil: Waitress. Dishwasher. Maid. Laundry worker. Manicurist.

Pressing face powder onto her porcelain cheeks, she glanced at my look of dismay in the mirror and chirped, "Times are hard. Even in Houston employment is down. But don't worry. A strapping young woman like

119

yourself, willing to roll up her sleeves and work hard, should be able to find something fast. The faster, the better."

I felt as though I were being held under-water.

"Of course, the easiest thing, in the short term, would be for you to keep on working in that lunchroom."

"No."

Like a drowning victim pushing off from the bottom in one last desperate attempt to reach the surface, I sprang to my feet. "No, absolutely not."

Steadying my voice, I went on, "I am not going to waste my life scrubbing pots and pressing shirts. I'm smart. Maybe really smart. I got that nursing school scholarship I applied for. I am going to train as a nurse. I'm going to start with the summer proba-tioners."

I braced myself for histrionics. Hysteria. Instead, Mamie sneered dismissively, "You can't be serious. You? Leave? You don't actu-ally think you can survive without me, do you?" She snorted a condescending laugh at the thought and returned to surveying her beauty from various angles.

I went into the other room, which con-tained a sink, a hot plate, two chairs with springs ripping through the threadbare upholstery, and my cot. Only when I knelt down, pulled my old suitcase out from under the metal cot, and started packing did she believe me. That's when the theatrics started.

"You're abandoning me?" she asked, already choking back the tears she could summon at will.

Though my hands trembled, I continued shoving things into the suitcase that had once been stuffed with tutus and pointe shoes.

"You're leaving me here to starve? Your own mother? How will I survive?"

This time, when I didn't answer, she grabbed my hands and gripped them tightly, stopping me the way someone would stop the jerking of their own palsied limb.

"How will I survive?" she demanded again.

"You'll either go back to Litchfield and live with your mother up in the Panhandle. Or you'll find some new sucker to support you."

She slapped my face hard. Once, twice, three times, her fury building. Usually, when she beat me, I simply left my body. This time I didn't. This time I rose up and, almost surprised, observed that I was taller than her and, after years of nonstop physical labor, a good deal stronger. I lifted my hand to block her blows, and then I simply kept raising my clenched fist.

At the sight of my fist raised to her, Mamie went dangerously still. "You are just like your father. You have betrayed me. Go. Leave." She spat the words out with a viperous intensity. "I won't have a traitor in my home."

Those were the last words my mother spoke to me. I had claimed my life by ripping it away from her. I swore I would never go back.

Now, however, as I stared at the brown muck of the bayou swirling far below, something inexplicable twisted within me.

Longing.

I ached to go again into that overheated room, to perch once more on the edge of her bed, and to drown in her suffocating scent of Beadex and Shalimar. I knew it wouldn't be easy; it never was. But Mamie was still the only mother I had. The only family. Also, I had no place else to go that night.

Swearing I'd only stay for the one night, I was on the verge of continuing to cross the bridge back to Vinegar Hill when a cattle egret, white wings spread wide, came sailing down the bayou. The immaculate bird glided above the dirty water. I watched it rise, soar into the darkness, and vanish.

Into that moment of serenity came a memory I'd buried along with all the others too painful to hold on to, and I remembered the last words that my mother had actually spoken to me.

What my mother had said to me as I left, my face still red from her slaps, was, "You'll be back. Mark my words. No one ever chooses to leave me. No one. One way or another, you'll be back."

One way or another.

Of course it was Mamie.

Mamie had sent the Director the clippings.

I shifted my suitcase to my other hand, crossed back over Buffalo Bayou, and put Vinegar Hill behind me for the last time.

CHAPTER 14

"Evie. Baby!" Uncle Jake exclaimed, dropping the metal trash can he was hefting with a clang that echoed through the alley. "What on God's green earth are you doing back here?"

"Back here" was the Bennett Academy of Dance. Specifically, the alley that ran behind the studio. I had thought that there was no point in going around to the front since Jake always closed at six. Consequently, we were both surprised to see each other at that late hour.

I tried to give a jaunty answer, but an unexpected swell of emotion rose through me and my face squirmed with the effort of holding back tears.

"Oh, bubbeleh," Jake crooned, using a snippet of the Yiddish that was the universal language of old vaudevillians, even for a Methodist boy from Indiana like Jake. Yiddish words always crept into Jake's speech when he was feeling tender or drunk or both.

"Come to your uncle Jake." He opened his arms to me just as he'd done hundreds of times before when we were demonstrating a foxtrot or a waltz.

I fell into them. Jake smelled both exactly like he had when I'd worked for him and also completely different. Always meticulously clean, washing up even if it meant using the men's room at the train station, he used to smell like soap and aftershave. Now he smelled grimy. What was the same, though much stronger, was the smell of booze. I caught a whiff of the sweetish odor that used to waft off of my alcoholic patients: the smell of a hard drinker whose liver was shutting down.

"Let me get a look at you," he said, holding me at arm's length.

Uncle Jake was no longer the dapper man who'd modeled himself on Fred Astaire and hardly ever appeared without an ascot and his toupee. Both ascot and toupee were long gone. The bald dome of his head made his high forehead seem even higher and the hollows shadowing his cheeks and eyes even deeper. None of that mattered. Even though it pained Jake too much to talk about him, he had been my father's best friend and he had done what he could to look out for me when no one else had.

Imitating a baggy-pants comic, he asked, "You want I should call a nurse? Hold the phone. You *are* a nurse."

"Sort of." I shrugged.

"Evie, tell your uncle Jake what's going on."

I told him about the photos, about being denied the pin I'd worked so hard for, about having no job, no place to stay. I told him about my suspicions.

"Mamie." He shook his head with sad resignation. "What Mamie wants, Mamie gets. I guess she wanted you back. Hey, kid, I'm sorry. Even for Mamie that is low. But listen, tell you what, you got a place to stay here for as long as I can keep the joint open. You want to be a nurse. I'll get you a job as a nurse."

"Jake, that's not funny. I just told you, I'm not registered."

"Registered, schmegistered. Look at you, you already got the outfit. Stick a Girl Scout pin on it and no one's the wiser. Because if you look the part —"

"You *book* the part." I finished the old vaud saying with him.

"Seriously, kid, I can get you a job as a nurse, no sweat."

126

"You're kidding," I said, not particularly amused.

"Would I kid a kidder? There's a job for you right here."

"But why would a dance studio need a nurse?"

He waved my question away. "Long story."

I recalled the Director's insinuations that Jake was running a dime-a-dance hall.

"So?" Jake asked. "You want a job as a nurse or not?"

"More than anything."

"Well, all right then." He opened the side door into the dance school with an elegant sweep of his hand. "Come on in, 'cause have I got a job for you."

Suddenly, I was in the side hall of what had once been my sanctuary. The entire studio had started life as a gymnasium, and we were now in the long hallway that led out to what had once been a full-sized basketball court complete with tiers of bleachers.

A set of swinging doors separated the hallway from the dance floor. Though the thick doors at the end of the hall were shut, the unmistakable sound of a raucous band playing a frenzied version of "Hold That Tiger" leaked into the hallway.

I couldn't imagine what lonely guy would

127

pay a dime to dance to such a hectic song.

Other things had changed as well. Handwritten signs were taped to the doors that led to the boys' and girls' locker rooms branching off on either side of the hallway. "No Spitting On Premises!! That means YOU!!" "Pick Up Your Trash." "No Smoking on My Floor!!"

Back when I'd helped out, Uncle Jake would have tossed a student out for bringing so much as a pretzel onto "his" floor. Spitting? Littering? Smoking? The old dance school seemed more like a rent-a-girl operation by the minute. On the door to what once had been Uncle Jake's office a sign now hung that read, "Pops Wyatt Promotions."

At the swinging doors that led to the dance floor, Jake paused and asked, "You ready?"

I nodded and Jake pushed the doors open.

Instead of a seedy, sad dance hall, with a few lonely customers groping a few girls as they both pretended to dance, I was greeted by the sight of a packed arena.

In the old days, I'd never seen more than a few white-gloved mothers or a chauffeur or two sitting on the bleachers. Now they were packed with a noisy, milling audience. Shouted conversations ricocheted and crashed around the old gym. Kids pounded up and down the stairs. Vendors wove through the chaos, hawking popcorn, soda, and hot dogs in booming shouts.

I recognized a few of my old neighbors from Vinegar Hill. This wasn't the Houston that the Depression had bypassed. This was the Houston of hard-timers and no-hopers. This was the Houston that had never known anything other than economic depression.

A pretty decent band — Mel and His Melody Makers, according to the name emblazoned on the bass drum — was playing on a low stage constructed beneath the spot where a basketball hoop had once stood.

Spectators crowded the edge of the floor, blocking my view. By elbowing a few aside, I managed to catch a glimpse of several couples circling the gym. They all had numbers pinned onto the back of shirts or blouses. And they were all haggard with exhaustion.

I stated the obvious: "You're running a dance marathon."

Jake shrugged and quoted the vaudeville trouper's credo. "You gotta do what you gotta do, right?"

I answered with another vaudeville standby, "Absotively."

As any old trouper would have, Jake grinned and shot back, "Posilutely."

CHAPTER 15

Signs hung from every available wall.

POPS WYATT'S HOUSTON DANCE SPECTACULAR. THE POOR MAN'S NIGHT CLUB.

THIS IS A PLACE OF REFINED AMUSEMENT. WHISTLING, STOMPING, AND CATCALLS WILL NOT BE TOLERATED.

DO NOT TOUCH CONTESTANTS.
DO NOT FEED CONTESTANTS.

Bring the whole family to the matinee. 2 bits for up to 5 people. Ringside seats, 25¢ extra.

But, dwarfing them all, was a board with hooks to change the numbers hanging there that announced:

COUPLES STARTED: 52.
COUPLES LEFT: 18.
HOURS DANCED: 697.

HOW LONG CAN THEY LAST?

"Can that be right?" I asked Jake. Nearly seven hundred hours?" "They've been dancing for almost a month?"

He brushed off my question. "A month? That's nothing. Barely even the start for a decent run. Pops's last show? In Santa Monica? Thing lasted two thousand six hundred hours. Then there was that guy up in Massachusetts, Callum DeVillier. Him and his partner, Vonnie Kuchinski, they went for three thousand seven hundred and eighty hours."

"No," I gasped, quickly doing the math. "That's more than *five* months?"

"You're the one went to school."

I pointed to the couples. "They haven't actually been on their feet for five hundred hours?"

"Naw. Ten- or fifteen-minute break every hour."

"But they can't get enough sleep that way."

"They sleep. On their feet. In the wee hours when the joint is empty."

Before I could ask how that was possible, the band struck up a jazzy version of "Shine on Harvest Moon."

I studied the floor. Where I had once taught girls with bows in their hair and boys with the comb marks still wet in theirs, were eighteen couples with numbers pinned on their backs. For a moment, they were a blur. Then a few of the pairs started to stand out. Amid the dreary duos barely shuffling along, five or so were actually dancing. Still giving it their all. Their do-or-die effort to please an audience made them as comfortingly familiar to me as members of a big, extended family lost long ago. A family that had always hidden pain and exhaustion behind a layer of greasepaint and a happy face.

Onstage, sitting behind a microphone, a suave, tuxedoed gent with his hair parted down the middle like Rudy Vallee called out, "Yowza. Yowza. Yowza. Give these kids a big round of applause to show them that you're out there rootin' for them."

"That's Alonzo," Jake yelled in my ear. "The emcee."

"Come on now," Alonzo implored. "These brave kids are knocking themselves out to give you the best show they got in 'em. Let's cheer 'em on with some good old Houston whoopin' and hollerin'."

A few of the dancers perked up at the applause. The hammier ones grinned and waved to the crowd.

"Those are the horses," Jake explained.

"Horses?"

"The regulars. Professionals, you might say. The promoter, Pops Wyatt, wires his favorites train fare to come to the shows that he sets up all over the country. Those two over there? They're horses."

He pointed to a pair of stocky dancers who looked enough alike to be —

"Brother and sister," Jake finished my thought. "Gerta and Fritz. The Krauts. This is their fifty-second show."

Though they were both built like linebackers, Gerta had a cute overbite and big, wide blue eyes that made her seem less formidable than her muscle-bound brother.

"Let's see. We got . . ." Jake did a quick count. "Four pairs of horses left. They're the only ones whose names you need to bother learning. The rest . . ." He waved away the other eight couples. "Amateurs. Pops's been letting them hang on just to give the locals someone to cheer for."

"So amateurs and horses," I repeated.

"Yeah, and stars."

"Who are the stars?"

134

"Stars? Evie Grace Devlin, come on. You know that no one needs to point out a star. You know a star when you see one, right? You see a star out there?"

I searched the faces for what Mamie would have called the It Factor. As in, she, Mamie, had It, and I'd been assured by everyone who'd ever known him that my father had It in spades. The Pint-Sized Pavlova had It for a brief moment before I outgrew even the tiny bit of audience appeal I'd once possessed. Before I could complete my search for the "stars," the band launched into a double-time rendition of "Five Foot Two, Eyes of Blue."

"Hey, watch this," Jake said, elbowing me. "They're all going to be bucking for a silver shower now."

"A silver what?"

"You'll see," Jake shouted over the music. The horses poured it on. Whether they were good dancers or not, they were lively and able to connect with the audience in a way that the amateurs couldn't. The crowd started singing along, almost shouting out the question, "Has anybody seen my gal?"

An unsmiling, sharp-boned girl, her mousy brown hair worn in a bowl cut, wearing the number "11" pinned to the back of her threadbare cotton dress, took the center of the floor with her strapping plowboy of a partner. Arms and legs windmilling frenetically, she danced with such wild abandon that, like Galveston, she made us feel for just a moment that we had all been part of the delirious Roaring Twenties and that they'd never ended. When her partner spun her, however, her dress swirled up and exposed a pair of badly bowed legs.

She almost smiled when the audience applauded but then quickly covered her mouth with her hand.

"The Delta Darlings," Jake told me, raising his voice over the noise of the band and the crowd. "Minnie and DeWitt. Couple of Pops's best horses. Audiences love 'em. Pops sees to it that they always make at least the final five."

He pointed out a gangly guy with flat feet and pop-eyes and said, "That's Patsy 'Won't Steer You Wrong' Wright. Not much of a dancer. More of a comic relief. Audiences love him."

"What's up, suckers?" Patsy brayed out, unloosing a cavalcade of laughter.

"That's his trademark line," Jake said.

"Who's he dancing with?" I asked, pointing to his petite partner.

"Cousin, I think. Lynette, Yvette, Babette. Can't ever remember her name."

A mismatched couple, him a stumpy fireplug, her a willowy swan type, passed by and Jake yelled "Ace and Lily!" in my ear. "They're an interesting pair." He shook his head and added, "To say the least."

He mentioned a few other names, but I quickly lost track of them as the crowd shouted along joyfully, "Could she love? Could she woo? Could she? Could she? Could she coo?"

The emcee, Alonzo, directed the crowd to "Look at Minnie and DeWitt down there. Our Delta Darlings are dancing their hearts out for you. Times sure have been tough for this couple. The bank took their farm and they're here fighting, just like every one of you is fighting, to win back the lives that this cruel Depression has stolen from them. Stolen from all of us. Come on now, every single one of us needs a little help these days, so open up your pockets. Who's going to start the silver shower?"

"Watch this," Jake said, tilting his head up toward the bleachers. I followed his gaze to a short fellow with a bum left arm wearing a white uniform with a black bowtie and "Trainer" embroidered on the back making his way to the top of the bleachers behind the rest of the crowd.

"The little guy in the milkman getup,"

Jake explained. "Name's Suits. He's a ringer. Works for Pops. Watch this. He's going to prime the pump."

The trainer hurled a handful of dimes down onto the floor. And, just as if he had actually primed a pump, fans started tossing down their own coins.

Minnie and DeWitt scrambled to collect the tributes. A few additional coins pattered down. Pennies and nickels mostly. All in all, it was more of a silver drizzle, maybe a heavy fog, than an actual shower. Still, every coin was scooped up eagerly by the couple, who carefully transferred them into a small drawstring bag worn on a cord around Minnie's neck then hidden back under her dress.

It was a grouch bag. Just like the one Mamie and all the vaud troupers used to keep their money in.

The Melody Makers kept speeding up the tempo, and the pros, angling for their own silver showers, obliged by picking up the pace. They too were rewarded with a splattering of change.

"How long do they have to keep this up?" I asked.

Jake checked the large clock that hung above the bandstand. "Ten more seconds."

The instant the sweep hand hit twelve, Alonzo cranked an earsplitting shriek from the siren screwed onto his table. And every dancer on the floor drooped like puppets whose strings had been cut.

"Folks, you know what that means," Alonzo announced. "It's time for the fifteen-minute break our kids get every hour. But don't go anywhere. Mel and his mesmerizing Melody Makers will keep on playing just for you. So grab a hot dog and get an ice-cold Nehi Grape from Claude right down there."

The emcee made a sweeping gesture toward a vendor in a red-and-white-striped vest and white paper cap with a sloshing tub of ice and soda pop at his feet. Claude gave a cheery salute in return.

"Stay exactly where you are," Alonzo advised. "Because Pops Wyatt's Dance Spectacular will be right back!"

The contestants stampeded toward the door behind us.

"The locker rooms are crammed with cots," Jake explained as we stepped aside to let the herd pass.

With the floor cleared, I saw that directly in front of the stage were three cots. Only one was occupied. The sign above them read "Hospital." A chunky woman in a nurse's uniform that was so soiled she constituted her own one-person infectious ward waited

139

for the pair of contestants who were limping toward her.

Disappointed, I stated the obvious. "Jake, they already have a nurse."

"Yeah," he answered. "That's Agnes. You're gonna have to steal her job."

CHAPTER 16

"I am not going to 'steal' that poor woman's job away."

"We'll see about that," Jake responded smugly. "Check the 'poor woman' out, though, before you decide."

I watched as Agnes's first patient, the Delta Darling, Minnie, wincing with pain, limped to a cot. I imagined how agonizing that furious Charleston must have been on her bowed legs. She sagged onto the first cot. With the theatricality of a magician pulling a rabbit from a hat, Agnes held a thermometer aloft then proceeded to stick it directly into Minnie's barely open mouth.

"She's not even going to sterilize it?" I protested to Jake.

With a knowing shrug, Jake indicated that I should keep watching.

With Minnie's lips clamped around the thermometer, the "nurse" manacled the skinny girl's wrist with one hand and pretended to take her pulse.

"So, what do you think about the competition so far?"

"I think she's a big, fat fake's what I think. Even without that dirty uniform, I'd know she wasn't the real McCoy. She is doing nothing to actually help that poor girl."

The surge of protectiveness I always felt when I was looking after a patient who truly needed me welled up. "What she needs is a lot of rest and a couple of knee braces. Why, look at her legs. She's got rickets, not a fever.

"And, even if she had needed her temperature taken, that big phony out there didn't shake the mercury down in the thermometer before she stuck it straight into the girl's mouth. She didn't even bother to put it under her tongue. And the way she pretended to take her pulse? Her fingers weren't anywhere near the radial pulse on her wrist."

"Yeah, Agnes is a real credit to your profession," Jake said, enjoying my outrage.

Agnes's next patient was a middle-aged fellow who limped over to a cot and hoisted his bare foot up. After the briefest of inspections, the nurse pulled out a pocketknife, grabbed the poor guy's foot, and started whittling away on the callus over his bunion.

"And look at her now," I exclaimed,

throwing a hand out toward the impostor. "She's cutting away the only protection that poor man has. He *needs* those calluses. She should be oiling them. Keeping them pliable. I want to go down there right now and yank the knife that she probably just used to pick her teeth with right out of her hand."

Agnes moved on to the third cot. Its occupant had his back to me. The number "7" was pinned on his shirt. When the fake nurse approached Number Seven the crowd came alive screaming, "Save Zave! Save Zave! Save Zave!"

Whoever Zave was, the instant Agnes touched him, he waved her away with a backhand flap.

"Bravo for him. I wouldn't let that fraud touch me either."

"So, you're good and steamed," Jake observed.

"You bet I am. It's already hard enough for nurses to get the respect we deserve without fakes like her giving us a bad name."

"So, how do you feel now about 'stealing that poor woman's job away from her'?"

"Jake, those poor kids need real help. Not someone waving a thermometer around like she's conducting an orchestra. And everyone knows how much a dancer needs their calluses."

"Well," Jake allowed, "maybe not *everyone,* but someone who spent the first eight years of her life dancing on her toes sure would. I mean, that person, that Pint-Sized Pavlova, don't you think *she* might be especially equipped to render aid and assistance to, oh, let's say, a bunch of dancers?"

I didn't answer.

"And maybe, just maybe," Jake continued, "that person just might be a tiny bit better equipped to actually help those poor kids than, oh, let's say again, Agnes out there?"

"She just might be."

Jake gave me a playful bop on the biceps. "Okay, tiger. Let's go get you a job."

CHAPTER 17

In the hallway outside what used to be his office, Jake told me, "Wait here. I'll go in and talk to Pops about you. Only don't call him Pops, okay? If he decides he can make a marathoner out of you, he'll tell you to call him Pops. Until then, he's Mr. Wyatt. Got it?"

"Sure."

Jake chucked me under the chin, and, his watery eyes going a bit waterier, whispered, "Jeez, kid, sometimes, looking at you, it's like looking at your old man. You got his eyes. Kind eyes."

He went into the head honcho's office, leaving the door open behind him. Though my view of Wyatt was blocked, he sounded like every tough-guy chiseler I'd ever met when he boomed out, "Bennett, how's Zave doing?"

I could just picture the promoter. A blunt fireplug like Edward G. Robinson with dark, greasy hair and swarthy features, who talked out of the side of his mouth. Typical chiseler.

"About that, Mr. Wyatt," Jake began. "Zave needs some actual medical attention."

"Now he tells me. Right, Kane?" Wyatt moaned to a guy who was in my line of sight. Kane looked like a bank vault in a double-breasted suit, tie, and shined shoes.

"Yeah, now he tells you," Kane echoed.

I assumed Kane was security, since his head was shaved and he had the face of a boxer: a heavy brow that had been thickened by many poundings, nose that had been redirected several times, and a puffed ear whose cartilage had endured the blunt trauma that caused cauliflower ear.

Wyatt continued blasting Uncle Jake. "Hey, Bennett, you're the one pawned that fat slobola Agnes off on me in the first place. You're supposed to be our front man here. Houston is your town. That's why I rented this dump. You promised you could turn the smart set out and fill those high-dollar box seats. I can't make any money off the cheap seats."

"What do you want me to do?" Jake demanded. "I can't advertise, because every time I do, the damn theater owners, who don't like us taking their business, get the

Baptists and the Ladies' Morality League all riled up and they go on the warpath. Also, Mr. Wyatt, listen, unless you pay me what you owe me, I can't cover the light bill. Worse than that, I won't be able to buy any more 'cooperation' from our friends on the force. You get raided for violating the Volstead Act, you're not going to have any crowd at all 'cause they'll shut you down."

"Me?" Wyatt sneered. "It's your damn hall, Bennett. Besides, cops are the worst soaks out there. They're pie-eyed half the time. Isn't that right, Kane? You ever known a flatfoot wasn't on the sauce?"

"Not a one, boss," the bank vault affirmed in a solemn tone.

"You're stiffing me, Wyatt," Jake exploded.

Kane tensed at the attack on his boss.

I heard Wyatt, whom I still hadn't caught a glimpse of, whack his hand on the desk. "How can I pay you when I'm not breaking even? No swells, no dough. No dough, no show."

"You wanted a hall," Jake protested. "You got a hall. Quit chiseling me."

"Chiseling *you*?" Wyatt demanded in an aggrieved tone. "I'm in the middle of set-ting up a show right now, a *real* show in Chicago. If word of this flop gets out to my backers, they'll shitcan the show and, who

147

knows? Maybe me too."

Lowering his voice, he added dramatically, "I'm dealing with some very serious parties up there. If you know what I mean."

He meant the mob.

"Time's ticking," Wyatt barked. "What about Zave?"

"Here's what's about Zave," Jake said, all but yanking me into the office. He threw both hands in my direction in a *ta-dah* way and announced, "Here she is, Evie Grace Devlin, a real, honest-to-God, empty-a-bedpan nurse. Isn't she perfect?"

They all stared at me.

For the second time in twenty-four hours my fate was about to be decided, and this time I'd be damned if I was going to let a bunch of small-time grifters who had nothing on me do the deciding. This time I was back in a world where I knew all the rules and didn't have to pretend to be nice or normal.

This time I was going to fight.

CHAPTER 18

Instead of the swarthy fireplug I'd imagined, Wyatt surprised me by being as tall and pale as a giant icicle. In every other way, however, from his glossy, manicured nails to the garish windowpane plaid of his suit, he was pure chiseler. A big-time chiseler, maybe, but still miles away from being a real operator, an actual power, like Mr. Amadeo or Sofie's uncle JuJu.

Making a face like he was smelling overcooked cabbage, Wyatt threw a hand out in my direction and asked Jake, "This, *this,* is your idea of perfect? Why? Because she's already got the costume? Listen, pal, I can rent a nurse's costume for six bits for the whole run. Before I even got to town I told you I wanted someone who looks like your favorite aunt to play the nurse."

Mr. Wyatt possessed a pair of unsettlingly pale hazel yellow eyes that he now turned on me as he demanded, "Is *this* what your favorite aunt looks like — Olive Oyl?"

Popeye's girlfriend? Who did this blowhard think he was? I liked this whole marathon dance setup less by every second.

"The fans come here looking for comfort," Wyatt lectured Uncle Jake. "They're getting beat up six ways to Sunday out there. Old man got fired. He's taking it out on the wife and kids. So she comes to the matinees with the kids and a coupla bologna sandwiches 'cause it's the only entertainment they can afford.

"And the old man comes to the night show with a flask in his pocket and a roving eye. They both come to forget their miseries. Watching these kids, *my* kids," he added with a maudlin note of paternalistic concern, "knock their brains out, get the stuffing beat out of them, well, it cheers them up."

"You got a pretty bleak view of humanity," Jake offered.

"Did I say I was finished?" Wyatt demanded. "Sure, they want to see someone worse off than them. But, Bennett, you better believe they want to see something else too. They want to see the other down-and-outers get comforted. They want to see a nurse who looks like their own dear ma out there patting heads and bandaging bunions.

150

Makes them feel like, maybe, just maybe, someone's watching out for them. 'Cause they know that heartless SOB in the White House don't give a flyin' fudge at a rolling doughnut whether they live or die. And they need a hero. Someone bright and shiny who gives them hope that it's still possible to win in this rigged crapshoot of a life. And that, my friend, is what marathoning is all about. You get what I'm saying, Bennett?"

"Loud and clear, boss," Jake said.

I didn't like hearing my uncle Jake, a man who'd once dazzled audiences across the country with his dancing, being bullied. Especially since it was clear that this blowhard was never going to give me a job.

"Yeah, Wyatt," I interrupted, feeling a release like I was finally taking off a tight girdle I'd had to wear for three years. "We get what you're saying. Now let me tell *you* what *you* don't get. You're treating the performers you call your 'kids' like garbage. Those contestants who are killing themselves out there so you can wear a gaudy suit and keep your dainty hands manicured need actual medical attention. Not some germ-ridden charlatan pretending to be a nurse who's going to butcher their feet."

Wyatt blinked and, acting as though I wasn't there, cracked to Kane, "Olive Oyl speaks."

"And another thing, cut out the Olive Oyl crap. I am not here to 'play' a nurse. I *am* a nurse. I just completed three years of training at one of the finest nursing schools in the country."

Wyatt snorted and did what all bullies do when you back them down: he acted like he was joking. "Calm down, sister, can't you take a joke? I was just kidding. But come on? You're trying to tell me that you're a real nurse? And you want to work a marathon for seventy-five cents a day?"

He brayed out another laugh. "Level with me. What are you really? A manicurist? A manicurist would be good. Pedicurist even better. Experience with feet. Very helpful."

"She's the genuine article," Uncle Jake insisted. "Top of her class. All three years."

"That true?"

"It is."

"So you're legit," Wyatt mused as he tilted his head from side to side, studying me like a painter sizing up an unpromising subject. He made a sour face and announced, "No, doesn't work. Too young. Too skinny. Way too tall. No padding. Not the least bit motherly."

The short trainer with the gimpy arm burst in.

152

"Suits," Wyatt said. "Can't ya see I'm having a conference here?"

"It's Zave," the trainer burst out breathlessly. "The break is almost over and he still can't put no weight on that bad ankle of his."

"Give him more juice," Wyatt ordered. "If he's not back on the floor when they grind that siren, Kane's gonna have to call him out."

"Pops," Suits objected, "you know we can't give him no more of that stuff. He'll pass out. Having the star of your show passed out ain't gonna help us none either."

"Can he stand?"

"He's trying to, but . . ." Suits's voice trailed off.

"Holy Christ," Wyatt burst out, pressing his temples as though a migraine was spiking through them. "I need this like a hole in the head. How much time we got till break is over?"

Using his right hand, Suits lifted his lifeless left arm and checked the watch that hung on that wrist. "We got just under nine minutes, boss."

For a second, Wyatt dropped the blustery front and admitted, "Zave is our hero. We lose Zave, we lose the show." Concern and something approaching fear creased his

153

features. Sounding for a moment like a very real, very worried father, he muttered, "My kids, what are they gonna do without a show? Where are they gonna go?"

Sighing heavily, as though I'd snookered him into a bad bet, he glared my way and growled, "Okay, Florence Nightingale, if you're really legit —"

"I am as legit as gravity, buster," I snapped back. After three years of putting up with the Director's torment, it felt great to stand up to a bully.

"Okay, here's the scoop. I got a regular with a bum ankle. It's not a setup. He is not trying to bring heat. He is —"

"Zave's the star of the show," Suits put in. "Our golden boy. Dames love him."

"And," Wyatt continued, "aside from a few bums looking for a place to flop, our daytime crowd is nothing *but* dames. Housewives, mostly. Come evening, when the mamas go home to make dinner, we get the working crowd. Secretaries, waitresses, busboys, soda jerks. The guys hoping someone will get in a fight with one of the floor judges. The dames, they all come for Zave."

"In short," I cut in, "you need someone with actual medical expertise to save your star."

"You're a mouthy broad," Wyatt observed.

Suits, still watching the clock said, "Pops, we're running out of time."

"All right. All right. Jeez, you sure ain't what I would've ordered from Central Casting, but if you can get Zave back on the floor, the job is yours."

"Uh-uh," I objected. Knowing I had Wyatt over a barrel, I said, "Not until you square up with Mr. Bennett."

"Oh for crying in a bucket," Wyatt hurled back. "Now *you're* puttin' the squeeze on me too?"

"Pops," Suits implored, holding his watch up to show the seconds ticking away.

Exhaling like a leaking tire, Wyatt pulled out a money clip, peeled off some bills, and flung them at Jake with the order, "Pay off the boys in blue and keep the damn lights on."

Jake snatched up the money, then tipped his chin toward the big clock: the seconds were ticking away.

I straightened my uniform and, more for Wyatt and Kane's benefit than Jake's, I told him, "See you soon. I'm going to go get that job."

I ran back out.

I was going to get that job.

CHAPTER 19

The PA system crackled to life and Alonzo announced breathlessly, "Folks, Pops has just given me the good news that real help has arrived for our Handsome Hoofer!"

A chorus of female shrieks interrupted the emcee.

Heads swiveled in my direction as I rushed across the brightly polished floor.

Agnes glowered as I approached.

Alonzo continued mouthing the lines Wyatt fed him. "Pops Wyatt spares no expense in providing the best of medical care for his kids. And that is why he has brought in a highly trained specialist, Nurse Evie Grace, to take over for Agnes."

Agnes reacted with shocked anger to the surprise announcement.

"So let's give a big hand and a heartfelt farewell to Agnes for all her great work."

For a moment, the burly fake nurse attempted to resist the three trainers who closed in to "escort" her off the floor. After a futile struggle, and lots of cursing, most of it directed at me, they wrangled her out the swinging doors.

"Can our highly trained specialist work a miracle?" Alonzo asked. Every eye in the house was fixed on me. "Let's watch Nurse Evie Grace perform her magic."

With the entire audience tracking my every move, I approached the fellow in the third cot, this so-called star Zave, who still had his back to me. I recalled Sister T's lectures on how important it was to make a good first impression.

"Confidence in the healer," my favorite instructor had taught us, "is the essential first step in healing."

With as much authority as I could muster, I asked my newest patient, "May I examine your ankle?"

Zave propped himself up on an elbow and glanced over his shoulder at me.

He had what Mamie always said was the basic ingredient of It. "A memorable appearance. Either memorably different or memorably good," she'd stipulated. I wouldn't say that Zave was classically good-looking, but he was striking in a memorable way. Tall and lean with broad shoulders, expressive eyes, and a world-class smile.

Though the parts were all fairly unremarkable on their own, somehow they fit together in a remarkable way. Even wracked with pain, he was, unequivocally, a star.

"Let's just have a look first, shall we?" I asked gently. After Agnes's "care" he was justifiably skeptical.

"You're the boss," he hissed through a tight smile, playing to the gaggle of twittering girls massed at the edge of the floor. Though I knew the effort cost him, he joked loudly, "Just wrap it up to go, Nurse."

He shot the girls a cocky grin and a wink and they dissolved into squeals.

As carefully as I could, I slipped off his shoe and sock and pushed up the leg of his trouser. The crowd gasped. Zave's ankle resembled a blue-and-purple python. His ankle and foot were swollen so badly that they made his toes appear dwarfed and stubby next to the distended flesh above them.

"It looks a lot worse than it is," Zave assured his distraught fans. The effort of his charade of nonchalance exacted a toll. Sweat sheeted his face and the color continued to drain until it approached an alarming pallor dangerously close to the grayish white of a patient going into shock. His eyelids drooped. I checked his pupils: they were suspiciously shrunken.

"How's our boy doing?"

I started at Pops's booming question. Standing right behind me, he asked, "You out of Ace bandages? 'Cause our star needs to be out on that floor in . . ." He checked the clock. "Seven minutes and thirty seconds. That's when this break is over, and if he's not dancing by then, the judges will have to eliminate him."

With all the urgent authority I could muster, I said, "This man cannot put any weight on that foot. Not in eight minutes. Not in eight hours. If you're lucky and the injury is treated correctly, my patient *might* be back on his feet in eight *days.*"

"Look, sister," Wyatt said. "He isn't *your patient* because you're not *my* nurse. The deal is, you're not anybody's nurse unless you get Zave on his feet and dancing or hobbling or whatever. Cleo can carry him for a few periods."

I assumed Cleo was his partner, still resting in the girls' quarters until the break ended.

Zave struggled to prop himself up on his elbow. "Sure," he agreed. "Cleo and I have done it before. She'll carry me and I'll hardly have to put any weight on it. Tell Suits that I need another jolt of happy juice.

159

Suits?" he asked, glancing around. "Where's Suits?"

"No," I stated firmly. "You already have way too much juice in your system."

Blinking as though he'd just noticed me, Zave asked, "And who are you again?"

"I'm your nurse and I'm telling you that you cannot go on dulling the pain enough to dance. You have to stay off that ankle. End of discussion. Period."

"Period?" he repeated, smiling. The no-nonsense manner that I'd used to quell the veterans of the Great War on my rotation through what we called the "mustard-gas ward" merely amused him.

And then he told me something that no one had told me since I was four years old. "Nurse Evie, you're cute. Help me up. Cleo'll be back soon. I gotta get on the floor."

"You can't," I argued, even as he levered himself into a sitting position.

Suits jumped forward, ready to help him to his feet.

"Stop," I ordered. "Just hold it right there. If you're determined to do this . . ."

My voice trailed off and, pointing at the soda vendor, I hollered at a couple of trainers, "Bring that tub of ice over here."

The trainers hesitated, until I barked

160

"Now!" They snapped to then, and, with the vendor's help, fetched the sloshing tub. I cradled Zave's swollen foot and guided it toward the tub. His eyes popped wide open and he sucked in air through his clenched back teeth when I plunged his foot into the freezing water.

"I'm sorry," I said, impressed that he was able to hide what had to be agonizing pain and keep on smiling, even if it was through gritted teeth. "This isn't how I'd choose to treat you, but if you're determined to continue, we have to get the swelling down so that I can wrap your injury properly."

"No problem, Nurse," Zave said. "Frozen solid beats throbbing any day. Ain't that right?" he called up to his concerned fans. "Can't feel a thing. Ready to dance all night."

The girls cheered.

Wyatt, one eye on the clock, the other on me as I knelt beside the tub, carefully monitoring Zave's ankle, called out, "You got two and a half minutes, Nurse. Start wrapping him up."

"The swelling hasn't gone down enough."

"Yeah, well, he'll have plenty of time for that when he's sleeping on a park bench after he gets eliminated. Him along with all my other horses who'll be living on the

161

street when the show closes. Because of you."

As dumb and unfounded as that pronouncement was, the responsibility for all the regulars' shaky futures still suddenly landed squarely on my shoulders. As carefully as I could, I lifted Zave's dripping foot from the freezing water.

"How's it look?" Zave asked.

"Better," I answered. "But can you stand another minute in the ice water?"

"Nurse, I grew up on the Upper Peninsula of Michigan. This feels like bathwater to me." He plunged his foot back in.

Onstage, Alonzo hoisted up a bell, rang it, and announced, "All right, folks, there it is, your two-minute warning. Our trainers are rushing into the locker rooms right now to wake up those sleepy kids, tie on their shoes, and get them back on the floor before I have to sound the elimination siren at nine o'clock. You all know the rules; any contestant who is not on the floor, dancing with his or her partner when that siren goes off, will be eliminated."

"Wrap it," Wyatt ordered.

"One more minute," I begged.

"You got no more minutes," the promoter rasped. "Get my boy back on that floor or you're fired."

"As you already pointed out, Mr. Wyatt, I don't work for you," I answered. "And this man's health is my responsibility."

Zave put his hand on my shoulder and whispered, "Thanks for looking out for me, Nurse. But, seriously, I am so blotto, I won't feel a thing."

"That's what I'm worried about. You could end up with a permanent injury."

"Ninety seconds left," Alonzo called out. "And, *oh-oh,* folks, there he is. You know him, you hate him, His Obnoxiousness, the meanest judge in the business, a man so heartless he makes Herbert Hoover —"

A cascade of boos for the president who refused to help starving citizens interrupted the emcee.

"— look like a sweetheart of a fellow. I give you our own head judge, making his first appearance tonight. Say hello to 'King Kong' Kane."

It was the bank vault from Pops's office. The boos rose to a crescendo when Kane stomped to the center of the floor holding a steel yardstick that he flicked about like a riding crop.

The doors swung open and the contestants shuffled in. The guys were bleary-eyed and rumpled, their hair sticking out every which way. The girls hid their exhaustion better, with fresh makeup, neatly combed hair, and big smiles. A couple of trainers dragged in a lanky guy I recognized as the wise guy, Patsy. He remained fast asleep even as the trainers put him on his feet and dumped him into the arms of his mousy partner, who, though wobbling beneath his weight, somehow managed to hold him upright.

All the other pros — Minnie and DeWitt, Ace and Lily, Gerta and Fritz — no matter how played out they were, brightened the instant they stepped in front of the audience. But no one outshone the last contestant to appear on the floor. She was a Kewpie doll of a girl with a headful of peroxided curls and the face of a shopworn angel. She strutted in with hands held high, grinning into the blazing overhead lights, waving for all she was worth.

"And here she is," Alonzo announced. "Zave's partner, our very own Cleo." The applause thundered as she beelined straight over to Zave, who still had his foot in the icy water.

Kane made a theatrical show of counting the dancers on the floor. Scowling with fiendish glee and rubbing his hands like the villain in a melodrama, he pantomimed that there were only seventeen couples.

164

"Oh no, folks," Alonzo warned. "King Kong is on the warpath now. We're missing one couple and we've only got seventy seconds left on the clock. His Obnoxiousness just can't wait to eliminate the latecomers. Who's missing?"

The crowd screamed as one, "Zave." Feet stomped on bleachers in time with the chant, "Zave! Zave! Save Zave!"

"Less than one minute. Will our sweethearts make it back onto the floor?"

"Can you get it wrapped in under a minute?" Zave asked, pulling his foot from the water.

"Just watch me," I answered, already drying his foot. I'd wrapped enough ankles during three seasons of South Texas football that I could do it blindfolded. Which was good since Kane was now breathing down my neck and yelling that time was running out.

The crowd booed the floor judge's attempt to rattle me.

"You all know how much King Kong hates what he calls the Pretty Boy," Alonzo said. "He is dying to eliminate Zave. Can our Angel of Mercy work fast enough to save him? Can she save Zave?"

The chant started up again.

"Save Zave! Save Zave!"

165

Working swiftly, I took two wraps to secure the bandage, and then started figure-eighting up Zave's ankle. I was just about to secure the clasps when Kane purposely bumped into me and the remaining bandage rolled free.

The crowd groaned.

I snatched the roll up before much could spiral loose.

"Oh no," Alonzo moaned. "We are running out of time." He stood and put his hand on the crank handle of the siren.

"Get a move on," Cleo commanded.

"We gonna make it?" Zave asked with an offhanded bravado I had to admire.

"You can bet on it," I assured him as, keeping the bandage smooth and just taut enough to maintain a solid pressure, but not enough to impede circulation, I twirled the rest of the wrap on. I scrambled to hook the two silver clips on to hold the stretchy bandage in place and was attaching the last one when Alonzo started cranking the handle hard as a German butcher grinding sausage. The siren shrieked. Cleo grabbed Zave and hauled him up as I shoved his shoe back onto his foot. At the exact instant that the siren fell silent, Zave was officially on his feet.

Kane growled with frustrated rage.

166

With Cleo bearing much of his weight, she and Zave joined the dancers rotating around the floor. After a couple of sedate orbits, Zave did something that, given the state of his ankle, bordered on the miraculous. He actually danced.

Knowing the pain he was in, I wouldn't have believed the transformation if I hadn't seen it with my own eyes. He straightened his spine, lifted his shoulders up and back, snapped to attention, twirled Cleo out, and rock-stepped her back into place.

Zave was a good dancer. An *exceptionally* good dancer.

An eerie sense of déjà vu swept over me when Zave lifted his head with a triumphant smile and the spotlight bathed him in its adoring glow. He was suddenly so familiar that I wracked my brain trying to remember when I'd seen him before, because I was absolutely certain that I had.

"Our nurse has done it," Alonzo exulted. "Nurse Evie has saved Zave."

The audience burst into applause and began shouting, "Nurse Evie! Nurse Evie!" and I was thrust back into the thing I'd despised since Detroit: the full glare of an audience's attention.

Once again I was the Pint-Sized Pavlova and I had pleased the frightening creature that was an audience. The long-dormant performer's instincts that Mamie had beaten into me awoke and I gave the crowd what they were calling for. With Zave directing the applause my way, I grinned. I waved. I took a bow. I didn't know if I was falling back into a dream or a nightmare when Wyatt yelled out over the din, "Come on back to the office. Oh, and one other thing."

"What?" I yelled back.

"Call me Pops."

CHAPTER 20

"We put on twelve feeds a day for the dancers," Pops, sitting now behind Jake's desk, instructed me. "Three meals and snacks. Staff only gets fed three times. You choose when. Smart ones pick the big feeds. Pays four bits a day. No laundry included."

"Fifty cents?" I balked. "No dice. You said the pay was seventy-five cents. I need at least a buck a day, or I walk."

"A dollar a day? Hasn't anybody told you there's a Depression on? I'll go seventy-five cents and you're robbing me. We'll talk raise if you keep Zave on his feet. You start as soon as Suits shows you around. Suits, show the greenhorn around."

"This civilian?" Suits sneered, jerking a thumb in my direction. "Where do I start? Telling her what a two-a-day is?"

"Don't bother," I said. "Last few years I worked the vaud circuit I was doing *five*-a-days."

To their skeptical stares, I affirmed, "That's right, houses we played, they turned the audience over five, *six* times a day. And there were some mighty hard days when I worked every single scene switch."

For one second, neither of the men spoke, then, disbelieving, Pops asked, "You saying you came out of vaud?"

"Born in a trunk."

Eyes narrowing, he asked, "What's your last name?"

"Devlin."

"I thought so," Pops burst out, slamming his palms down on the desk. His expression shifted from that of a chiseler always looking to get the jump to an unabashed fan as he waved at my face and asked Suits, "See the resemblance?"

"To what?"

"Denny Devlin, greatest hoofer ever lived, you moron. That's right, isn't it?" he asked me. "You're Dandy Denny Devlin's kid?"

I nodded.

"Well, for crying out loud," Pops exploded. "Why in Sam Hill didn't you say so in the first place? Suits, she's genuine vaud. In his prime, Denny made Astaire look like a lummox. Christ on a cracker, kid, this is gonna be old home week for you. Half my regulars come out of vaudeville."

"Was Zave on the circuit?" I asked.

"Was he ever," Pops answered. "Zave was —"

Uncle Jake, out of breath and grim-faced, burst in before Pops could answer.

"What the hell are you doing back? I sent you out to get right with our friends in blue."

"It's already too late," Jake answered glumly. "I only made it as far as the corner when the beat cop on patrol there — who, very, very lucky for you, is a buddy of mine — put me wise. Pops, you're gonna get raided tonight. It's a done deal. The fix is in."

"So undo the deal. Take the fix out. Pay the bastards off like I told you to."

"No dice. Theater owners have got the Ladies' Morality League up in arms. Someone's husband is an editor at the paper. Another one's married to a councilman. Theater owners have them all in their pocket. They got the ladies in a lather about the evils of dancing and 'exploiting misery.' "

"Rich white ladies," Pops hissed. "Bunch of brass-plated phonies. It's not like any of them are gonna give my kids jobs. Feed them. Give them a bed to sleep on instead of a park bench. They just want all the suffering done out of sight where it won't offend their fine sensibilities. Stick 'em in a Hooverville way out on the edge of town where no one can see them. Hypocrites. Worse than that gee-dee Hoover."

Jake shrugged in agreement. I couldn't argue either.

Pops ranted on, "And that is exactly why they need pictures for the papers of people in handcuffs getting pulled out of this den of iniquity we're running and hauled off in a paddy wagon. So all the gee-dee hypocrites can go back to feeling superior."

"Fudge. Fudge. Fudge," Pops muttered. Not one, apparently, to cry over spilled milk, he shifted gears and, calm as a charge nurse, said, "Oh well, it was time for me and the pros to head to Chicago anyway. When's the raid?"

"Ten. Straight up," Jake answered. "The cops got it scheduled with a photographer from the paper."

"Suits," Pops ordered, "spread the word. Horses and staff only. Tell the trainers and the sloppers first. Act natural. Don't tip off the locals or the civilians. We gotta leave 'em something to take pictures of."

Suits nodded and was hurrying away when Pops called after him, "Tell Zave to take a dive at half past nine. That way we can work in a good farewell. Give him a chance at a decent silver shower. God knows he won't be taking much else away from this disaster."

With a pointed look at Jake, he added, "None of us will."

Chapter 21

"Well," I told Uncle Jake when we were back on the floor, "this is the shortest job I've ever had."

On the bandstand, Suits was whispering in the ear of each player and the emcee. They all gave nonchalant nods in response to the news about the impending raid; they'd obviously been through this drill before.

Jake sighed. "Easy come, easy go. Listen, if you need a place to stay, you're always welcome here. Unless you're planning to head up to Litchfield."

"Why would I go to Litchfield?" I asked, naming Mamie's podunk hometown way the hell up in the Panhandle that she despised and I had never visited.

"Doesn't your mother tell you anything? She's staying up there with your grandmother Vonda Kay. Last time she wrote — asking for money, big surprise, right? — she

174

said that all the dust storms they been having had given her the new . . . ? The new . . . ?"

"Dust pneumonia," I supplied, recalling with a shudder what we'd learned in class about the life-threatening affliction. The drought that had dried up the Great Plains was causing storms that whirled the dry earth into a choking cloud of dust so fine and so thick that it could suffocate a person caught outside. Sister T had told us about a cow that was autopsied to reveal that the poor animal's lungs were clogged with mud.

"Right, right. Dust pneumonia. I sent her what I could, so that she could get to the hospital in Lubbock."

I didn't say anything and, after a moment, Jake said, "Evie, you've got that look on your face."

"What look?"

"That I-Gotta-Rescue-Mamie look."

"Jake, she's my mother."

"Evie, she stabbed you in the back."

"I'm not a hundred percent certain that she was the one who sent the photos."

"You're not? Evie, she's your mother and all, but, honestly, who else would do something that rotten? Plus, who else even had those clippings?"

His questions were too painful to consider.

Instead, I said, "Jake, dust pneumonia is a life-threatening illness. I have to go to her."

He asked the question I'd never been able to find a good answer to. "Why?"

The only answer I had to give him was "I don't think I could live with the guilt if she died. She's my obligation."

Jake shrugged and, following the old trouper's rule about never dwelling on the sad stuff, nodded at Zave and said, "Now there is a guy who can dance."

That was an understatement. Without ever putting any weight on his injured ankle, Zave was as fluid and precise as any act I'd ever seen. The unsettling sense of déjà vu hit me again and I figured that I must have seen him perform sometime when I was on the circuit. Still, as I watched, I had the oddest feeling, not of simple recognition, but of being whirled back in time. Back to a time I desperately wanted to remember but was not able to.

As I studied him, trying to puzzle out why he seemed so eerily familiar, Pops slid in next to me and moaned, "Oh brother, not you too."

"Me too what?"

"You're gaga for Zave," the promoter said.

"What are you talking about? I am not gaga for anyone. I am not the gaga type."

176

It was true. I'd never been a girl who put much stock in boys being "cute" or having "animal magnetism" or any of the other dopey excuses normal girls used for turning into ninnies. There had been a few dates back at St. Mary's, but I couldn't allow them to go beyond hand-holding and a bit of necking. I was fighting for my future and wasn't about to be derailed by some ridiculous crush.

"Is that so?" Pops challenged me.

"Is what so?" asked Suits, who had finished warning all the pros, floor judges, and trainers.

"She says she's not gaga for Zave," Pops answered.

The little trainer hooted. "You're not? Well, then, why have you been tracking him like he was a little bunny and you're a hungry wolf. I could see it from across the floor."

"You need to get your eyes checked, buddy. It's just that I am sure I know him from somewhere."

Pops and Suit *hoo-haa*-ed at that. Suits batted eyelashes he didn't have, and trilled out, "*Ooo,* hey handsome, don't I know you from somewhere?"

"Nurse, you'd better get some better lines," Pops said. "That one was old when

177

Moses was floating in the bulrushes."

Pops left. Suits continued snickering.

"Aw, go soak your head," I told the trainer.

"Truth hurts," he said, walking away. "Also, keep out of the way when the real marathoners scram out of this two-bit joint. Been nice knowing ya."

I checked the clock: 9:28. My time with the Pops Wyatt's Dance Spectacular would be up in two minutes when my patient took his dive. Over by the stage, Pops caught Kane's eye and gave him a decisive nod: time to put the plan into action. That nod was telegraphed to the other two judges and three trainers.

When it reached Mel, the bandleader raised his baton and broke into a zippy "Puttin' on the Ritz." Like an old warhorse champing to enter the fray when he hears the bugles blow, Zave picked up his tempo to a dangerous level. He looked so much like the great dance men of my youth that he seemed naked without a top hat, tails, and a cane to tap.

Zave lit up the rafters with a smile so blissful that, for a second, I believed I was a miracle worker and I had actually cured him. In the next moment, he stepped down on his bad leg. Pain curdled his fine features as he wobbled, clinging desperately to Cleo.

The crowd sucked in its breath.

I sucked in *my* breath.

It was 9:30 straight up. Right on time.

Even though the timing might have been fake, Zave's pain was absolutely real. Jaws clenched, he attempted to move. The instant he put an ounce of weight on his injured leg, however, he froze, his face gripped in a rictus of pain.

"I got you, I got you," Cleo cooed.

"Oh, boy, folks, this looks bad," Alonzo whispered into the mic. "Can Zave keep on going? Can he stay in motion?"

"Come on now," Cleo coaxed, loudly enough for the crowd to hear. "We gotta move or that big goon of a judge's gonna kick us out."

The audience chanted encouragement. Zave, leaning all his weight on Cleo, made a tentative hop forward on his good leg. For a split second, it appeared the maneuver would work. That Zave was going to please his fans screaming for him to stay in the competition instead of taking the dive Pops had ordered.

The instant his hurt foot touched down, however, the pain caused him to lurch off-balance. Flailing, he tried to grab on to Cleo. But it was too late. Cleo tilted for a moment beneath his weight, then he slid from her arms.

Cleo wailed theatrically while attempting to haul Zave back up before Kane could see him. In the bleachers, the men groaned and the women shrieked. Pops lowered his forehead into his palm, pantomiming defeated frustration. On the other side of the floor, Kane faked not being aware of Zave sprawled on the floor.

In spite of being in on the charade, I leaned forward, ready to help my patient, but Pops grabbed my arm and ordered, "Let him bring some heat."

Kane glanced at Pops and Pops gave him one solemn nod.

For a split second, I saw sadness flash across the floor judge's face. Instead of a scowling brute, in that moment, Kane resembled a preacher or a poet, a sensitive soul saddened by the injustices of the world. When he pivoted back around, however, he wore his familiar expression of mustache-twirling villainy as he descended upon Zave.

The crowd was on its feet, booing and hissing.

Kane delighted in the vitriol. Milking the moment for all it was worth, he loomed over Zave. With officious self-importance, Kane began counting Zave out. His arm a cleaver hitting a chopping block, he counted off with an agonizing slowness, slamming his hand on the floor with each number.

"One. Two. Three."

With one, final, resounding slap, Kane crowed, "Ten. You're out, Pretty Boy."

CHAPTER 22

Pops, his arms lifted to the heavens like a Roman emperor in the Colosseum calling for silence, strode to his downed gladiator. He knelt down and made a show of talking to Zave. Then, wearing his most serious, most judicious face, he pretended to reach the foregone verdict, snapped his fingers, and a couple of the male trainers sprung forward, lifted Zave onto a cot, and hoisted him above their heads like Cleopatra on a palanquin.

A collective sigh of mourning went up from the crowd. Solemn as a preacher at a funeral, Alonzo intoned the words "Zave, everyone's favorite, is leaving us. But don't worry, folks," he assured the wailing crowd while the trainers and I slowly bore the fallen hero away. "Your golden boy will be coming right back out to thank you for the support you have shown him over these past weeks just as soon as our highly trained team of medical experts looks him over."

"Team of medical experts." I guessed that was me.

The instant the door swung shut behind us, the trainers put the cot down in the hallway.

"You need to take him to a hospital," I told Pops.

"Yeah, and we 'need' a new president, but neither of those things are gonna happen tonight."

"Mr. Wyatt," I said in my best head nurse voice, "Zave's ankle could very well be broken. It has to be x-rayed."

"Zave," Pops asked his star. "Whudda ya choose? An x-ray or a silver shower?"

"Nurse," he started, attempting to focus on me, but his pupils, constricted before, were pinpoints now. I bent down closer. Zave's breath smelled of licorice, the telltale scent of paregoric, a liquid tincture of opium heavily flavored with anise to hide its bitter taste. Mothers rubbed a tiny amount of the stuff on their babies' gums to ease the pain of teething. Addicts drank it by the bottleful to ease the pain of living.

I tried to break through the opiate haze that had allowed Zave to continue dancing so long and stated slowly, "Zave, you might have a broken ankle that could leave you with a permanent limp if it is not treated."

"Nurse," Zave answered, smiling and slurring his words like a cocky drunk. "What I have for sure, no 'might' about it, is some empty pockets. If I don't do that farewell, I'm gonna starve to death a hell of a lot faster than I am ever going to die of a limp."

The trainers huddled around us laughed. From the gym area, Alonzo's amplified voice rang out. "I've just been told that Zave is back there right now arguing with the team of doctors that Pops brought in. And do you know why?"

The crowd's answer echoed back to us. "Why?"

"Because all those pointy-head know-it-alls with all their 'scientific knowledge' —"

To my astonishment the audience interrupted Alonzo to boo "scientific knowledge."

"Well, those so-called experts are trying to tell Zave that he can't come back out and say good-bye to all of you."

Pausing only to let the audience jeer on cue, Alonzo continued to whip them into a frenzy. "But Zave told them to stick their fancy degrees where the sun don't shine. He told them that nothing and no one was going to stop him from coming back out and saying thanks to all of you generous souls who have shown him so much friendship. So much support. So, well, dang it, I'll just come right out and say it, so much love."

The emcee's voice trembled with a mawkish belligerence. "That's right, you heard me, 'love.' I am not embarrassed to say that what you folks have shown that kid is love. You're like the family he never had. And now, like all the rest of us who weren't born with a silver spoon in our mouths or an oil well in our backyard, he is facing the toughest times he has ever had to face."

Since it was clear that Zave wouldn't be going to a hospital or anywhere else other than back to his fans, I cupped his toes in my hand. In spite of the heat, they were chilly. I loosened the wrap on his ankle to ensure good circulation.

"You know," Zave told me, propping himself up on his elbows, "I don't really need a pedicure, but I sure could use a little help with my hair before I go back out there. Anybody got a comb?"

Suits handed one over.

Zave took the comb and held it out to me. "No mirror, you mind? Just smooth it down a little? If I go out there looking like a hobo, that silver isn't gonna rain down the way it should."

His black hair glinted blue beneath the hall lights and was so thick that the part I cut into it showed up as the finest of white lines. I combed the flicks and flips down into neat furrows, patting the most rebellious hanks into place with my hand.

"Let's get this show on the road," Pops ordered impatiently, and the trainers hoisted the cot up. I stepped back. This was the end of the marathon road for me. Like Uncle Jake, I, too, would now have to disappear into the night.

But Zave reached his hand down and took mine. His hand felt so inexplicably right in mine that it was as though I had held it before. "Nurse, I need you. Come with us."

"Go, go, go," Pops commanded, shooing me into the procession. "The more medical this looks, the better."

A wave of applause and foot stomping bludgeoned us as we stepped through the doors. An armchair draped with a blanket to resemble a throne waited on the free-throw line. The trainers lowered Zave onto it. I stood by and looked as primly "medical" as I could.

"There he is, folks," Alonzo announced. "Your favorite. Your champion. Like all the rest of us, our pal Zave has hit a bit of a rough patch, a little oil skid on the road of life. Every one of us here knows what that's like. But he's a fighter, gang, that much I can guarantee you. Zave's a scrapper just like all of us. Ain't nothin' and no one's gonna hold Zave down for long. Or any of the rest us, for that matter. Am I right?"

The crowd of down-but-never-outers roared out its conviction that every single one of them would also be back up and swinging again in no time and I understood what Pops had said about a hero who could give them hope.

Sounding as though he was fighting back tears, Alonzo went on, "We don't want to do it, Zave doesn't want to do it, but our team of doctors gives us no choice. We've got to say good-bye tonight to this brave man. So, let's make darn sure that we don't turn him out into the night with nothing to show for all the hours he worked so hard to bring some joy and happiness into our lives. Let's make doggone certain that our hero Zave gets the classy send-off he deserves. To help us, Zave's beloved partner Cleo has a special song."

When Cleo took the stage, her cheeks were slick with tears and she looked as woebegone as Mamie ever had when she was playing a tragic Lillian Gish silent movie heroine.

The Melody Makers edged into a lugubrious version of "The Sunny Side of the Street" with a schmaltzy sax dragging them through an intro so soppily funereal, I would have laughed if, in spite of knowing exactly how the strings were being pulled, I wasn't swallowing back a hot pool of tears.

Cleo and Zave stared at each other with a bond that made every one of us ache for the love we'd lost. The love we'd never had. The love we never would have. Their eyes locked and Cleo began to sing for her fallen partner. For all of us.

Cleo's voice might not have been the greatest, but for that song, that moment singing about a man who pulled her out of the shade and into the sun, it was the best in the world. Cleo had something better than perfect pitch or a world-class voice. She had something that no amount of training or talent could ever give a person. Onstage, behind a mic, Cleo had It. Cleo could connect. She had the magic power to unlock and touch the secret, yearning heart in every single one of us.

The throb of pain in her voice was so real that it stabbed me in a place in my own heart that I was certain I'd managed to lock away long, long ago.

I don't know why I started crying then

except that everyone else was and no one was watching me and it had been a hell of a day and the night was going to be a lot worse once I was out on the street with nowhere to go. But at that moment, with Cleo singing about some faraway, impossible sunny side of the street and the fans broken up about Zave leaving and how generally rotten everything was and the show moving on and me never going to be a nurse and never even getting to ask Zave about dancing with my father and no one paying attention to me, the tears poured straight out of me.

Pops handed me his monogrammed handkerchief and put his arm over my shoulders in what almost felt like a fatherly hug. "You're okay, kid. If I have a show, you'll always have a job. Shoot me a wire at Mann's Rainbo Gardens in Chicago and I'll shoot you the fare."

Cleo's voice throbbed as she swore that even if she never had a cent, she'd be rich as Rockefeller.

Rich? With the coins, even the pennies, gleaming gold in the bright lights as they pirouetted through the air, we were all as rich as Rockefeller. So rich that we could laugh and sing and throw money at the poor stiffs who had it even tougher than we did because, in that moment, with our hero smiling, we all believed Cleo. Believed that life was going to be sweet for all of us.

On the sunny side of the street.

CHAPTER 23

"Look alive," Pops barked at the trainers who were carefully loading Zave into the front passenger seat of a big Buick parked in the dark alley. "Those paddy wagons are coming."

The marathon insiders — the horses, the trainers, the judges, the sloppers, the band — were all hightailing it out of the hall by the time the siren signaling the fifteen-minute break stopped shrieking.

"Shoot me a wire at Mann's Rainbo Garden in Chicago," Pops shouted after the crew fleeing in the night. "And I'll shoot you the fare."

"Careful," Pops yelled at the trainer who was helping Zave get settled in the front seat of the Buick. "That's precious cargo. Hey, nurse, wanna go take care of your patient?" he growled at me as if I were neglecting my duty.

Anxious to check on Zave one last time, I

191

opened the door, and, as gently as possible, I elevated his foot onto the dashboard.

"How does that feel?"

"Better," he answered in the goofy drawl of a happy drunk, still high as a kite. "You're nice. You're nice to me. I like you, Evie Gravy. Gravy," he repeated with a silly-me laugh. "I called you Gravy. You know why Gravy is the perfect name for you?"

Sad that I'd never see him again, I played along. "No, Zave, I don't know. Why is Gravy the perfect name for me?"

"Because everything goes better with Gravy."

"Bye, Zave," I whispered. "It was nice meeting you."

I gently shut the door. Jake appeared beside me in the dark alley, gripping a suitcase so hastily packed that a shirtsleeve trailed out.

"I got a friend in town," he told me. "Want to see if he'll put us up for a few nights?"

"I can't, Jake," I said.

"I get it, Mamie." He heaved a sigh, then nodded toward the car where Zave waited while Cleo and Suits shoved cases into the trunk. "Too bad you couldn't have spent more time with Zave. You two woulda had a lot to talk about."

Already heading off down the alley, I called after Jake, "Wait, what would we have had to talk about?"

Jake stopped, furrowed his brow, and said, "Didn't I tell you? Thought I told you. Your father trained Zave. Couldn't you see it? He dances just like Denny." Jake blew me a kiss before he disappeared.

Zave knew my father. Zave had danced with father.

"Snap out of it, sister," Pops barked at me. We don't got all day here. Get in the car and hit the road."

Before I could object, a Cadillac pulled up. Kane was driving. Pops jumped in the passenger seat. The faint wail of sirens came from several blocks away. Leaning out the window, Pops handed me money for "gas and eats" and warned, "Nurse, you'd better make tracks. Pronto. Otherwise, only ride you'll be taking tonight will be in a paddy wagon. See you at the Rainbo Gardens in Chicago."

He slapped his hand on the roof of the car and ordered King Kong, "Give it the gas."

"Wait," I protested. "I can't go to Chicago. My mother is sick, I have to —"

My words were lost in the roar of the Cadillac blasting out of the alley, tires spitting gravel. The blare of sirens drew closer. I had one second to decide: my mother, or a stranger who knew my father. I hurriedly opened the back door of the Buick.

"What are you doing?" Suits, seated in the back beside an already-sleeping Cleo demanded irritably. "Get up front." He held his good arm out to the driver's seat.

"Me?"

"Who else you think's gonna drive? Me?" Suits gestured at his useless arm. "Or her?" He yanked a thumb in Cleo's direction. "She's dead to the world."

"But I can't drive."

"Can't? As in won't or don't know how."

"Don't know how. Never learned."

Suits rubbed his face like he was cleaning it with a big rag. "Jeez-o-pete. That's a monkey wrench in the works."

"Hey," Zave said with casual nonchalance. "Quit sweatin' it. I'll drive."

"No," I ordered. "The pressure would be terrible on your ankle. Plus, you're blasted out of your mind. You'll kill them all."

"Maybe," Zave agreed. "But getting thrown in the slammer ain't gonna be too good for anyone's health either."

The ululating wail rose to a shriek as the police cars closed in. I searched the alley for help. Everyone had vanished.

194

"Zave," Suits squealed. "They're coming. I can't go back in the can, Zave" — the trainer was nearly hysterical — "you know I can't go back. You know what they did to me last time."

"Don't worry, buddy," Zave told him. "I promised you I'd never let anyone hurt you again."

"They about killed me last time," he said, waving his good hand toward the one hanging limp. "Sure enough killed my arm."

Gripping his hurt leg in both hands, Zave tried to slide over to the driver's seat.

His face crumpled in pain and, in that moment, I made my decision. "Stop," I insisted, getting in behind the wheel. "I'll drive."

The echoes of the sirens caromed off the buildings along Main Street, just a block away.

"What do I do?" I asked, my hands slick with sweat on the wheel.

"Take it easy, Gravy," Zave answered dreamily. "All you gotta do is steer and hit the pedals. Simple as ABC. Accelerator. Brake. Clutch. Got it?"

"Not really."

"Piece of cake for a smart girl like you."

One siren stopped in front of the dance academy and the other continued shrilling its way around the corner toward the back alley. Toward us.

"Zave!" Suits said in a panicked falsetto.

"Shall we?" Zave inquired as if he was asking me for a dance. "Clutch."

I hit a roaring acceleration then a thudding brake before finally depressing the clutch. Zave worked the gearshift. "I got you in reverse, Gravy. Ease off on the clutch and give us some gas."

With a horrible grinding sound, the engine died.

"Christ on a crutch," Suits cursed.

"Don't listen to him," Zave said. "That was just your engine asking you to let the clutch out a bit more slowly."

I tried again as he coaxed me along. "That's it, baby. Find your friction point. There it is. You got it. Ease it out now, nice and slow."

The car lurched and hopped backward. With a horrendous clatter, I mowed down most of the trash cans in the alley and slammed on the brakes so hard that Zave nearly went through the windshield.

Beaming, Zave said, "Gravy, you're a natural. Okay, clutch."

Working together, we got the Buick into drive. Zave reached across and switched off the headlights. "Better if we go out dark."

A second later the darkness was abruptly

broken when the high beams of a squad car tilted crazily into the alley behind us.

"Hit it, Gravy," Zave ordered with a sudden sharpness. "Hard."

I tromped down on the gas pedal and we bunny-hopped away.

Zave twisted around to look behind and headlights striped his face. "Take a right."

I swerved wildly into the lane. A pair of oncoming headlights jerked away, the car barely missing us.

"You nutty broad," Suits screamed. "You trying to kill us?"

"Relax, Suits," Zave said, turning the headlights back on. "Nurse Gravy is doing swell. She can sign on as my getaway driver any day of the week."

The siren grew louder and a pair of intense high beams drilled through the Buick.

"They're right behind us. For the love of God, goose it," Suits shrieked.

"Don't," Zave advised with calm command. "Can't risk a gear shift now. Slow and steady's the ticket. Slow and steady. You're just a normal citizen out for a little drive."

Zave was calm and steady and encouraging. Just the way my father had been.

The cops' lights glared on the rearview

mirror. I crept along the mercifully empty street. A few moments later, sirens blasting, the two squad cars roared past us.

"Guess those jamokes weren't too happy that there weren't any big fish to catch back there at the hall," Zave observed casually. "Hit the clutch, Nurse."

I did, and Zave maneuvered the car into second gear. "What a team we make, Gravy. You're one hell of a wheel man."

Pride warmed me with the glow of being part of a team. Even if it was a criminal gang.

We maneuvered into second, then third, and cruised down city streets that were mostly dark and mostly empty. Gradually, the space between businesses widened and traffic all but disappeared. The lights faded, before finally blinking out altogether.

CHAPTER 24

We were in the country. The smell of the land cooling down after a hot day filled the car.

Zave inhaled, then sighed out a deep breath. "The open road," he said, sounding like a pilgrim naming the shrine he most venerated. "You've got a cool head, Gravy. Most girls fall apart under pressure."

"They don't allow falling apart in nurse's training."

As I was wondering if I should wait until Zave wasn't high to tell him that Denny Devlin was my father, Zave pulled a silver flask from his pocket, hoisted it high, and toasted, "Here's to you, Nurse Gravy. You saved my bacon. Without you, my life would have gotten a whole hell of a lot more complicated." He gulped down a healthy slug then handed the flask to me.

I hadn't had any hooch since Vinegar Hill, and Zave's stuff hit me like a jolt of kerosene. I swallowed it down without gasping or choking, acting as cool as if I ended every evening of my life motoring down an unknown highway with a man I barely knew, a couple of strangers in the back seat, chugging down bootleg whiskey in direct violation of the Volstead Act.

"No one for miles," Zave said with deep satisfaction. "You can open it up, sweetheart. Just stay on 10 until you hit the junction at 47, then head north on up to Dallas. Keep your eye out for signs. If you get lost . . ."

He paused to dig through the glove box until he found a road map that he nestled in my lap. ". . . just consult this. Or wake me up if I'm not in the morgue."

"The morgue? Not sure I like the sound of that."

Zave laughed. "The morgue's where dancers go after they've been on their feet for hundreds, maybe thousands, of hours. It's like they're unconscious. Impossible to wake up. Hurricane, fire alarm, bursting bladder — me and Cleo, we've slept through them all. And Suits, guy's even worse than a dancer since he almost never sleeps during a show. But you're not going to get lost, are you, Gravy?"

"Nope," I assured him.

"You're a cool customer, Gravy," he said, stuffing his folded-up jacket between his head and the window. "I like that."

Realizing that Zave was about to conk out, I rushed to tell him, "I never really told you my last name, but it's . . ." I took a deep breath before pronouncing the name that connected us. "Devlin."

When Zave said nothing, I clarified, "Jake said you knew my father. Denny? Denny Devlin? That he taught you how to —"

A snore from the passenger seat stopped me. I was too late. Zave was already in the morgue. I drove on. There would be time. It was a long way to Chicago.

All three of my passengers were out so cold that nothing roused them. They didn't flinch when we hit a series of potholes large enough to swallow up a raccoon. A few hours later, when I had to stop and wake the owner of a gas station to fill up the tank, no one turned a hair.

When we stopped at a railroad crossing and a locomotive, lights flashing and whistle shrieking, sped past and they didn't so much as twitch, I realized that I was utterly, completely alone and in charge. The same tenderness I always felt toward my patients when I was on night duty overtook me then. At night, when my patients slept, even the

201

orneriest ones became helpless creatures, innocent beings that needed my protection.

With nothing but the sound of tires humming against the asphalt and the snoring of the souls in my care to keep me company, I had time to appreciate the astounding fact that I was driving.

Me, Evie Grace Devlin from Vinegar Hill, I was the one powering this magnificent beast of a machine through the darkness. The hours flew by. I liked being behind the wheel, being the one in charge the way I was on night duty, safeguarding an entire ward.

I cruised along, north to Dallas, just as Zave had instructed, all thoughts of rushing to Mamie's aid cast aside. The road spooled out before me, an endless ribbon of adventures as vivid as any Dorothy had encountered on the Yellow Brick Road. Uncle Jake was right: What did I have to feel guilty about? I hit the gas. It was not as if Mamie had ever looked out for me.

A dozen or so happy miles on, a sign loomed up that marked the turnoff to "Lubbock, Hub of the Panhandle."

Beneath that was a much smaller sign, one I would have missed had I blinked. It was nothing but a listing of all the smaller towns up ahead, along the road to Lubbock.

At the very bottom was Litchfield.

No. I wouldn't do it. I wouldn't take a gigantic detour up into the Panhandle. I wouldn't help Mamie. Not this time. Not after what she had done. Besides, if I added one minute to their trip, Cleo would be furious and Suits would be apoplectic. And Zave? Zave who had trusted me? Zave would feel betrayed.

But what if my mother died? Could I live with myself?

Screw it. I was going to Chicago. It was the best, maybe only, stab I had at working as a nurse. And Zave, I had to find out what Zave knew about my father.

Screw Mamie. I hit the accelerator. A thrill ran through me as the Buick surged forward. For two glorious miles, I reveled in the speed, the adventure, the choice of freedom. And then I came to the junction. Dallas and Chicago lay straight ahead. A sharp turn to the left led west to Lubbock and all the small towns along the way.

That was when I realized that I was the one who'd been in the morgue, so deeply asleep that I had believed my dreams were real.

I turned west, toward Lubbock.
Toward Litchfield.

I never had a choice.
Not really.

■ ■ ■ ■

WEST TEXAS

■ ■ ■ ■

CHAPTER 25

A couple of hours later, dawn poured the pink lemonade of a new day over the plains that stretched out flat as a ballroom floor as far as the eye could see. It was hard to imagine such a bleak and unpromising country producing my flamboyant mother.

The rising sun reminded me that my opportunity to make time was running out. No matter how far in the morgue my passengers were, they would wake soon and they would not be happy.

As light flooded over the impossibly flat land with the impossibly straight road slicing through it, I floored it and the speedometer crept over eighty.

A windmill would appear far in the distance, as striking as the Eiffel Tower against the featureless landscape. For long minutes we'd inch toward it, seeming to make no progress against the vastness of the land. Then, in an instant, I'd blow past it fast as a rocket.

The Burma Shave ads took forever to read.

Bachelor's quarters.
Dog on the rug.
Whiskers to blame.

The punch lines, though, they whisked by in a millisecond.

No one to hug. Burma Shave.

Late that morning, Cleo's voice, a sleep-dried croak, startled me. "Hey, Nurse, pull over. I gotta piss like a racehorse."

Blinking against the harsh light, Cleo's face rose in the rearview mirror. Her swollen eyes were raccooned with mascara, her peroxided curls haystacked around her head. She peered out the window and her slitted eyes narrowed even further.

"Where the holy hell are we? Zave. Zave! Wake up, Zave."

"Hmmm?" Zave inquired casually, as if he'd been fully awake the entire time. "Is there a problem?"

"Look out the window," Cleo said. "See for yourself. Where the jumpin' Jesus are we? This looks like the moon in a dry spell."

208

Zave took a long, slow gander at the scenery and asked in a voice as calm and controlled as Cleo's was furious, "Evie, would you mind telling us where we are?"

"The Panhandle of Texas."

"Are you fuggin' kiddin' me?" Cleo demanded.

With admirable gentleness, Zave asked, "Evie, sweetheart, please tell me that there is another Panhandle? One that might be along the very easy, very clear route I asked you to follow? And *not* one that is way the hell off in the wrong direction?"

My throat was dry and the answer squeaked out. "There's not."

"Evie, did you get lost?" Zave asked patiently. "Is that why, instead of sailing along Route 66 halfway to Chicago like we should be doing at this very moment, we're in the middle of this godforsaken wasteland?"

Another squeak. "No. Sorry. I need to visit my mother."

Zave winced and lowered his forehead to rest on the tips of his fingers. I was certain his hangover headache had just gotten worse. A lot worse.

Outraged, Suits piped up from the back, "She pulled a fast one on us."

The hostility was so palpable that I became highly aware that I was trapped in the middle of nowhere with three strangers I knew nothing about. Still, if I'd learned nothing else on Vinegar Hill, I'd learned that, when you're in a tight spot, it's deadly to show fear.

So, acting as if the three of them were the bad guys, I snarled, "My mother's sick. Probably close to dying. Sorry for the *minor detour*. Sorry for taking you a *little, tiny bit* out of your way so that I could visit my dying mother, but, in case you forgot, I am the one who was driving all night. Without me, you'd all be sitting in a jail cell in Houston."

Cleo was not buying my act and, in a disturbingly flat tone, said, "Kick this lying bitch out."

"Yeah, ditch the bitch," Suits echoed.

When Zave didn't chime in, Cleo demanded, "Zave? Zave, what are you looking at a map for? I'll drive now. Give the word to kick her out."

"Seriously, Zave," Suits said. "We gotta kick her out. Marathoners don't do each other that way. We gotta stick together. Like you always say, we're family. We gotta look out for each other 'cause no else is gonna. Right, Zave? Zave? Say something, Zave."

Zave crumpled the map up and commanded, "Okay, everyone shut up. You," he pointed at me, "pull in at that Mobil up there."

I caught sight of a red Pegasus flying high above a lone service station. A bell chimed with discordant gaiety as I drove over the red hose running across the driveway. The instant I stopped, the aroma of meat smoking over a mesquite fire filled the car. A sign advertising "BBQ for sale" was propped against a brick barbecue pit. My stomach growled.

"Well, boys and girls," Zave said, slapping his knees. "I don't know about anyone else, but before we figure this mess out, I urgently need to go iron my shoelaces. Also what Cleo said about the racehorse."

Suits helped Zave hobble off behind the service station. Cleo stomped away in the opposite direction.

When the attendant, a tall, middle-aged man with white-blond hair, wearing a coin dispenser around the waist of his overalls, hustled out, I gave him a wad of Pops's money and ordered a fill-up of gas, four brisket sandwiches, and eight bottles of Howdy orange soda.

The attendant used the red rag in his pocket to unscrew the top of the radiator with pecking motions, darting his hand back and forth to let the steam hiss out.

I found a lonely clump of Russian thistle to pee behind, and lingered long after I finished, watching the other three as they made their way to a picnic table set in the shade of a tall pecan tree. On his way to the table, Zave stopped to wash up using the station's thin red water hose.

Balancing on his good leg, he thumbed his suspenders and shirt off so that they hung from the waist of his pants. His abdominal structure could have been used for an anatomy lesson.

The bones of his iliac crest above the pelvis were a shallow vase from which pronounced ridges of abdominal muscles flowered. Leaning forward, he ran a stream of water over his dark hair, scrubbing his neck and face. A rooster tail of water arced through the air when he stood and flipped his hair back.

Though I had spent the past three years studying and caring for bodies — young, old, male, female, in every state of undress — none had ever riveted me in quite the way that Zave's did. A way that had nothing to do with him knowing my father. I was so riveted, in fact, that I didn't notice the spider prickles of being watched until I glanced up and found Cleo staring at me. I couldn't quite decipher the look on her face, but it lay somewhere between jealousy and pity.

couldn't figure. decipher the look on her face
but if it's somewhere between jealousy and
pity

CHAPTER 26

The wife of the station owner, her Mother Hubbard apron flapping in the dry wind, brought our sandwiches and sodas to the picnic table. I hung back until Zave waved me over, then I handed him the keys to the Buick and he passed me a sandwich.

A lot had happened since the mouthful of hummingbird cake I'd eaten at the graduates' reception in the St. Mary's courtyard, and I inhaled that mesquite-smoked brisket sandwich on soft white bread with a smear of barbecue sauce. Cleo and Suits glared at me as I ate, as though I were stealing the food out of their mouths.

I pretended to be absorbed in the station owner gassing up the Buick and kept my gaze trained on the clear glass tank of fuel atop the pump that he cranked by hand. After he washed the windows and aired up the tires, he ambled over to the picnic table.

"Say, friend," Zave greeted him. "I came

through here with a tent show about twenty years back and didn't all this," he said, sweeping his hand out to indicate the miles of wheat sprouts wilting in the sun, "used to be grass?"

The man pushed his cap back, revealing a strip of white forehead above his red, sunburned face, propped his foot up on the picnic bench, leaned forward, rested his arms on his knee, and in a high-pitched, nasal twang answered, "Yessir, it sure enough was. Finest grassland the good Lord ever bestowed upon man.

"Then come the Great War and, boy howdy, it all went haywire. Price of wheat got up to thirty dollar a bushel. Sodbusters couldn't plow that grass under fast enough. I hear it's nothing but wheat now from here purt near up to the border of Canada. Too damn much wheat. Can't hardly get five dollar a bushel for it these days."

"Been having a dry spell, have you?"

"Dry ain't the half of it, pard. We're pure dee parched. All them sprouts out there gonna be nothing but straw 'fore long. And now that we ain't got all that grass holding the dirt down, them dusters come blowing in and dump half of Kansas and most of Oklahoma on us."

The man grinned, pleased to have all the

answers for the city slicker. "Where you folks headed?"

"Chicago," Suits replied with a sour glance my way.

"Chicago, Illinois?" the man asked. "Y'all are heading in the wrong direction."

"Tell it to this one," Suits said, jerking a thumb toward me.

Zave broke the tense silence by asking, "How far is it to Litchfield?"

The gas station attendant answered, "Seventy-nine mile. From there it's a straight shot up 85, that'll run you right into Route 66, and you're back on the road to Chicago."

Zave shrugged and asked the others, "Why not drop the kid off? It's on our way and I sure the hell am not gonna backtrack out of spite."

The attendant held his hand up and backed away as they went on loudly and at length about what a crumb I was. Cleo concluded, "No, absolutely not. I am not doing this dame any favors."

"No favors for this dame," Suits echoed.

"What?" Zave asked. "You want to turn her out?" He motioned at the road. Not a single car had passed in the entire time we'd been sitting there. "In the middle of this wasteland?"

216

Suits and Cleo seamed their mouths shut even tighter.

"So your minds are made up?" Zave asked. Cleo and Suits nodded. "Fair's fair," he said. "Majority rules. Here, catch." He tossed Cleo the car keys. "You drive Suits to Chicago. As for me, I'm taking Evie to see her dying mother."

Zave hobbled up to the road and stuck his thumb out.

Cleo and Suits stomped to the car. Cleo got in behind the wheel and fired up the engine.

I ran to Zave and told him to go with them. "Don't worry about me. I've done a lot of traveling by thumb and I'm always fine."

"Yeah," Zave said, peering down the road. "We're all always fine right up to the moment when we aren't."

Revving up the Buick's big engine, Cleo peeled out, pelting Zave and me with a stinging shower of pebbles.

Zave calmly studied the Buick shrinking into the distance. When it had almost disappeared, the car stopped moving. Zave gave me a knowing nod as Cleo executed a careening turn, sped back in our direction, slammed on the brakes, and hollered at us,

"Get your asses in this car before I have one more second to come to my senses."

CHAPTER 27

Cleo gripped the wheel with furious determination. Even from the back seat, I could see her jaw grind as she blasted through the dry prairie. We slowed down for the one isolated town we passed through only long enough to register the sense of desolation that hung over it. Businesses were boarded up, windows soaped over. Bank doors were hung with "Closed Until Further Notice" signs.

The pinched, haunted faces of the few citizens who trudged about were as stunted and dried up as the infant wheat crop blistering in the dry fields. They watched with desperate longing as we escaped their sad town. Hard times were pretty much the only kind I'd ever known, but these formerly prosperous citizens of formerly prosperous communities that had once sold wheat to the entire world appeared stunned by the calamitous downturn in their fortunes.

Back in the country, we passed sign after sign announcing farms to be sold at foreclosure auctions. We passed hitchhikers who plodded forward with their backs to traffic and listless thumbs held out. These were the men who had grown the wheat that had helped Europe defeat the Germans. They had owned land and led good lives. They were so beat down now, though, that they no longer expected even so much as a lift and barely glanced our way as we sped past.

Their sorrow made me feel like I was reading *The Wonderful Wizard of Oz* in reverse. Instead of Dorothy being whirled into a magical kingdom — the way I had felt when I arrived in vibrant, thriving Galveston — I had gone backward and landed in a gray, desiccated world of shriveled crops and dried-up hopes.

We came upon an old Model A truck lumbering down the road. The vehicle was so overloaded, with a coop of chickens and a rocking chair hanging off one side and a wheelbarrow and a plow strapped to the other, that it blocked the narrow road and we couldn't pass.

"Damn hayseeds," Cleo fumed, leaning on the horn. "Pull over."

Even Cleo fell silent, though, when we pulled up behind the family. Three hollow-eyed, grimy children perching atop a stained mattress stared back at us. A pair of twin girls about six or so clung to a black dog as bony and miserable as they were. Our eyes met. I wanted to jump out of the car and feed them, clean them, hug them, save them.

Their stares followed me long after the road widened and Cleo blasted past.

We had truly entered the Depression.

CHAPTER 28

"God all Friday," Cleo cursed a short time later. "Where did these rubes get their driver's licenses? Out of a Cracker Jack box?"

The road ahead was completely blocked by dozens of cars and trucks parked haphazardly across it. A throng of excited locals were clumped along the shoulder and in the road itself. They clustered behind a temporary fence of chicken wire that stretched out in an immense semicircle. Oblivious to Cleo's honking, they gazed fixedly at the empty prairie. Suddenly, all the spectators came to life, yelling and pointing to a rise off in the far distance.

Shouts of "Here they come!" rang out and the men and boys and even a few of the women picked up clubs, ax handles, and wagon spokes.

Cleo yelled out the window, "Goddammit, hayseeds, you're blocking the damn road. Move those rattletraps." Though Cleo had a set of leather lungs, she couldn't be heard over the din. She laid on the horn and a few faces, contorted by excitement, by anger, swiveled her way.

In a calm, mildly amused tone, Zave pointed out, "Uh, Cleo, word to the wise: Don't honk at an angry mob. Especially not an angry mob of farmers armed with clubs."

"What?" Cleo demanded. "So we're just going to sit here?"

"I don't know," Zave answered with unperturbed casualness. "You have another idea? You want to try vehicular homicide, be my guest. Hit the gas. Plow right over them."

Cleo switched off the engine and folded her arms across her chest. "Thanks a ton. Nurse."

Wanting to escape the chill of Cleo's hostility, I got out of the car and joined the crowd. Everyone was craning their necks and standing on tiptoes to get a better view. The afternoon sun slanted into our eyes, making whatever it was that had riveted everyone's attention even harder for me to discern. All I could make out were some puffs of dust rising up from behind the hill they all gaped at.

And then that hill came alive. I blinked

my eyes hard, but the dun-colored hill refused to stop shifting. It was a volcano that had erupted, spewing streams of brown and gray and white lava that flowed down, heading for the fenced-in enclosure directly in front of us. As it flowed, the lava leapt high into the air. The men, hoisting up their clubs, stepped over the low fence, ran forward, and began batting at the flare-ups. I finally made out what they were clubbing.

Jackrabbits.

Hundreds, thousands, of jackrabbits.

More poured over the hill every second, driven toward us by the long line of dogs and men with clubs that appeared behind the vast herd. The rabbits resembled small kangaroos when they tried to spring out of the way of the clubs. Airborne by their powerful rear legs, their long ears glowed orange as the sun shone through them They drew close enough that I could make out the white bull's-eye of fur around their eyes.

Suits, who had taken a spot beside me, shouted, "It's a rabbit drive. They're getting all the jacks that's eating up what crops they have. I heard them jacks'll eat anything. They'll eat the bark right off a cedar fence post."

The advancing men drove the terrified herd into the chicken wire semicircle and the boys and a few of the women hopped over the low fence as the rabbits came within range of their clubs.

I tried to leave, but the crowd kept me packed tight against the fence.

The fear-maddened animals churned and jumped in frantic, futile swirling patterns, trying to escape. But the club-wielders snatched them up by the legs, by the ears. They ripped them from the air. They trapped them as they cowered on the ground.

And they brought the clubs down.

The crowd pressed harder in on me. I managed to turn my back to the slaughter. The horrible sight was gone, but I could not escape the sounds.

The frenzied yelping of the dogs. The bellows and grunts of the men. The sickening thuds of their clubs. And, worst of all, the shrieks of the rabbits. I clapped my hands over my ears, but the shrieks would not stop. I shoved through the crowd. My only destination was away from the cries.

"It's okay." A pair of strong arms wrapped around me. "I've got you, Gravy. You're okay. We'll get you out of here."

As the horrific sound faded behind us, embarrassment set in. I pulled myself together and muttered, "Sorry, I'm fine.

Sorry for acting ridiculous and making a scene. I'm fine. Fine."

"Kid," Zave said. "Don't be so hard on yourself. Anyone who wouldn't find that scene back there upsetting needs to check his pulse 'cause he is missing a heart."

And then, because he was holding me, taking care of me, the words popped out.

"Denny Devlin was my father."

Chapter 29

"What?"

"Denny Devlin was my father."

"*The* Denny Devlin? The original Handsome Hoofer? You're his daughter?"

"I am. I was."

Zave's mouth gaped in astonishment and he clapped a hand over his chest. "Why didn't you say something? Are you serious? You're Denny Devlin's daughter?"

"So, it's true? You knew my father? You danced with him?"

" 'With' him? Your father made me a dancer. Taught me everything I know. Taught me how to dance. How to survive. He gave me everything. My life. I wish . . . ." Freighted with emotion, Zave's voice faltered for a second before he finished. "I wish we hadn't fallen out of touch."

He fell silent for a moment, then said, "I'm sorry. I heard that he had passed. I really do wish . . . . Jesus, I wish so many things. Never mind. So you must be a dancer, right?"

"Sort of. Not really. I did some toe-dancing when I was little. Later on I taught at Jake's studio."

"Yeah, where the Houston show was. Jake, what a great guy. Great dancer too until the, you know, personal problems ended his career. Of course, there wasn't much left of vaudeville by that time."

"He tried to tell that to Mamie," I said. Hesitantly, I asked, "Did you know my mother? Mamie?"

Zave's fond nostalgia abruptly curdled and, too quickly, he cut me off with a curt "No, sorry, never met the woman."

"Zave," Cleo, standing beside the open door on the driver's side, bawled out. "This train is leaving. With you or without you."

"Damn," he marveled, shaking his head fondly. "Denny Devlin. The stories I could tell you."

"I want to hear them," I said, trying and failing to keep the pleading out of my voice. "I want to hear them all."

Cleo laid on the horn. We ran to the car and hopped in.

"Let's test out the shocks on this thing," Cleo cried as she drove off the road, onto the prairie, and around the bottleneck of parked cars. Though packed down hard, the fields were riddled with prairie dog holes and gaping crevices where the long drought had dried the soil and cracked it open. The car bounced and jolted like a bucking bronco until we got back on the smooth, empty road.

As soon as we escaped the snarl of cars and were sailing down the highway, Zave started to tell me, "There was this one time, St. Louie I think it was, that Denny —" But Cleo slammed on the brakes beside a sign marking the turnoff for Litchfield and announced, "End of the line, buttercup."

"Hey, come on," Zave said. "At least take her into town."

"Not on your life, buddy," Cleo answered as she switched off the engine and folded her arms over her chest. "We've taken enough detours already for your freeloader friend. Those clodhoppers back there will be passing this way just as soon as their little bunny festival is over. She can stick her thumb out like she should have been doing from the start and hitch a ride with one of them."

"Cleo's right," I said, getting out.

Zave limped over and joined me by the side of the road. "Hey, sorry about Cleo, but once her mind is set, she'll make a mule look wishy-washy."

"No, she's right. I took you way out of your way. Thanks for getting me this far."

"Are you kidding? You're Denny Devlin's daughter. That practically makes you my sister." Zave grinned straight into a sun that was just starting to dip below the horizon.

Though I smiled at his joke, that word, "sister," hit me hard. Just as I'd done with Sofie, though, I hid my true reaction.

"Listen, Gravy, we have to stay in touch. There's so much I have to —"

A sharp honk interrupted Zave. "Wrap it up back there," Cleo yelled. "We gotta hit Amarillo before the gas stations close."

"Take it easy," Zave hollered back. "I'm not leaving Evie alone on the side of the road with night coming on."

"Oh, for the love of Pete," Cleo groaned.

"Keep your shirt on," Zave yelled. "Look, here come the clodhoppers now. I'll catch one going into Litchfield."

The sun had set and most of the rattletrap vehicles had chugged past before an ancient black Model T truck signaled a turn onto the Litchfield road. Zave flagged it down and stuck his head in to talk to the farmer at the wheel. A moment later, Zave waved me over.

The driver, a shy, taciturn man with a

farmer's work-hardened hands, gave me a nod of greeting then moved aside the bucket of eggs cushioned in hay that was occupying the passenger side of the bench seat and I got in. Zave shut the door, leaned in the window, and told me, "Take real good care of Denny Devlin's daughter for me." The farmer let the clutch out, the gears ground, and the truck pulled away.

I craned around in my seat. If Zave so much as waved, I was ready to jump out and beg Cleo to take me along. But Cleo barely gave him time to hop back in the Buick before she careened away. I gazed across the flat, empty land and followed the smooth comet streak of their taillights until they disappeared.

Only then did I recall that I'd left my suitcase in the trunk.

CHAPTER 30

The farmer steadied the bucket of eggs and, eyes never meeting mine, asked, "You headed to Vonda Kay's?"

Startled to hear this stranger speak the name of a grandmother I'd never met, I asked, "How did you know?"

Nodding at the "For Sale" sign hanging on the gate of the abandoned farm we were passing, he answered, "She's pretty much the only one left living out this way. I was on my way to deliver these to her." He patted the eggs with a shy pride.

It was dark when the old truck creaked and groaned onto a lane even narrower and rockier than the road we'd been on. The desolate, desiccated land that opened up for miles all around was eerily luminous in the light of a pale, cloud-whipped moon. The mournful songs of whippoorwills filled the dry air. They fit my bleak mood. I dreaded the prospect of seeing Mamie again.

Brakes shrieking, the farmer stopped in front of a ramshackle house, with its rusty tin roof a patchwork of odd sheets of metal, its siding weathered to a ghostly gray, and the chimney little more than a pile of bricks slumping into the weeds. The place appeared deserted. Surely, the farmer had made a mistake. This couldn't be where my glamorous mother, who would have been a movie star if the breaks had gone her way, had grown up.

Twisting his big, calloused hands on the steering wheel, the farmer peered nervously at the house and, his voice tense with alarm, muttered, "That's not like Vonda Kay not to come out when she hears the truck." He tapped a sharp blast on the horn. When there was no response, all his diffidence fell away.

"Vonda Kay needs help," he said, springing from the truck.

I followed him inside the pitch-dark house.

"Vonda Kay," the farmer called into the gloom. "It's me, Dub."

I heard the weakest of wheezes and rushed to my grandmother, who lay on the floor, unconscious and fighting for breath.

"Granma." I whispered the name as naturally as if I'd been saying it all my life. "It's Evie Grace, Mamie's daughter. I'm going to take care of you."

She didn't open her eyes, responding only with a terrifyingly feeble moan.

A lantern flared to life. With exquisite tenderness, Dub scooped my grandmother up and laid her on the sofa.

Kneeling beside my grandmother, I could feel the fever burning off of her as I pressed my ear against her chest. Her breathing was shallow and rapid. Her lungs crackled with every labored inhalation. The sound made me remember the cows with mud in their lungs that Sister had told us about.

My grandmother, not Mamie, was the one who had dust pneumonia. And Mamie had abandoned her.

"How far's the nearest hospital?"

"Lubbock."

"She won't last that long. Find a quilt, a blanket, something," I instructed Dub as I rushed to the kitchen.

Fortunately, there were live embers banked at the back of the cast-iron stove and I had a fire built and the kettle boiling in no time. Dub tented a quilt over us and I held a steaming pan of water close enough to my grandmother that she could inhale the moist, warm vapor.

Through the night, Dub brought me fresh water and I coaxed the healing steam into my grandmother's congested lungs. Gradually, her breathing eased. Near dawn, she opened her eyes. She had Mamie's eyes, a startling, gentian blue. In her unadorned face, though, they looked gentle and a little scared instead of calculatingly feline.

"I'm Evelyn Grace," I explained again. "Your granddaughter. I'm a nurse. I'm going to take care of you."

She managed to put her hand, light and papery, atop mine. On her face a wave of wrinkles rose and crested in a beatific smile even as her eyelids drooped shut.

Dub returned with another steaming pan.

"She's stable now," I told him.

Dub's big, hard-muscled body sagged with relief at the news. He turned his gaze upward, touched the tips of his calloused hands together, and whispered, "Thank you. Thank you."

Daylight came. Large beams shot through holes in the roof and the chinks riddling the walls. Clouds of dust floated through the sunlight. Drifts of the powder-fine sand that the dry land puffed up with every breeze formed humps beneath all the windows and doors.

I fashioned a mask from a tea towel and placed it over Granma's mouth and nose. "That should help. At least until we get her to the hospital."

"Is she fit to travel?" Dub asked.

"We don't have a choice. The emergency is past, but she won't really get any better until she's on oxygen."

"Let me go fetch in the eggs and check on Daisy."

"Daisy?"

"Her goat. She'll be needing milking. Vonda Kay would never forgive me if I didn't see to her. That goat and the groceries I bring been about the only things keeping her alive. Do we have time?"

"Her fever has broken and her lung sounds are a bit better, so yes, we have a little time. But not much." At the pump in the back, I filled a bucket. The vast fields behind Granma's house that must have once swayed with limitless acres of wheat were now a desert humped with sand dunes and riven with deep crevices that split the barren land. Off beneath the shade of a tall cedar elm, the only tree for miles, Dub milked Daisy, Granma's floppy-eared goat.

For some reason, then, in that brief moment of calm, I thought of Marvin the Man of Marvels, telling me that a person could do anything they put their mind to. Even claim a nursing pin that had been wrongfully withheld. As if blessing my insight, a

236

cooling breeze blew across my flushed face.

The moment didn't last long.

Across the field, Dub started hollering, "Whoa. Whoa, Daisy!" The pretty goat had suddenly gone crazy. Kicking and bleating, she butted Dub away and yanked at her tether. With a sudden jerk, she snapped the rope and bounded off. I ran over to intercept her.

Daisy was fast, but after a short chase, Dub managed to haze her toward me, and I grabbed the rope trailing from her neck. Her capture didn't seem to please Dub, though. Instead, his face fell as he looked off to the north and, his tone grim and tight, he said, "That's what Daisy was trying to escape."

Across the entire northern horizon, thunderheads unlike any I had ever seen before rose in a solid black wall. They surged up, dense and angry. This strange, swift-moving bank of clouds boiled ever higher into the sky until the sun was blotted out entirely.

"We gotta get back," Dub said. "Now."

Only then did I realize how far Daisy had led us. The house seemed small and fragile and far away in the darkening distance. Dub grabbed my hand and, leading Daisy behind us, we hurried toward safety.

Frantic with fear, Daisy tripped on a deep

crack. As Dub paused to gather her into his arms, a silence as complete as the darkness fell. A second later, it was broken by the frantic calls of thousands of birds. The desperate flock filled the sky, all flapping madly to escape the storm that was bearing down on them.

A roar loud as a freight train shattered the silence and we were engulfed in a dust storm that turned the day blacker than any night I'd ever known. Tumbleweeds cartwheeled crazily past. The corrugated tin roof of the shed was ripped free and went swirling past. The sand blasted against every inch of my exposed skin, slicing into it with a thousand razor edges.

The air crackled with static electricity that made the hair on my arm stand on end and the barbed-wire fence hum and glow blue. The wind knocked me to my knees and lashed stinging needles into my eyes. Blinded by the black fog of swirling dirt that hid the house from view, I crawled on all fours.

"Follow the fence!" Dub bellowed at me, pointing to the sputtering blue line glowing through the choking cloud. It led us to the house. The three of us scrambled inside only to find that the dust swirled nearly as thick inside as it did out. The small house creaked and shuddered. Terrifying whomping sounds made me fear that the roof would be ripped away.

Following Dub's lead, I grabbed every towel, sheet, and blanket in the house, wet them all, and tacked them over the windows and doors. Then we soaked newspapers and stuffed them into every crack we could find. And still the wind drove the devilishly fine particles in. Dub gathered Granma and me together on the sofa and we held each other through the endless, dark night while the wind howled and pounded and Dub muttered that we would all be fine.

Just fine.

Chapter 31

It was dark as a cave the next morning, but at least Granma, sleeping in Dub's arms, was still breathing.

"We have to get her to the hospital," I whispered to Dub, who nodded in silent agreement.

Tiptoeing across the drifts of dust, I peeked out the blanketed window and was stunned to find the sky an achingly clear blue. I pushed open the door to go outside.

At least, I tried to go outside. The door would not budge. It was held fast from the outside. Dub helped me shove it open. A foot-high drift of dirt encircled the entire house. Bodies of birds that had suffocated in the storm littered the yard.

Cradling her as carefully as a newborn, Dub carried Granma to the truck and, head cushioned on my lap, snuggled her in. Whenever he wasn't shifting gears, he held her hand as we sped through the vast land that had kept us imprisoned.

At the West Texas Sanitarium in downtown Lubbock, a nurse settled Granma in beneath a crackly tent of thick, clear cellophane. With calm efficiency, she twisted the valve on the tank beside the bed and the enclosure filled with oxygen. Gradually, my grandmother's cheeks lost the alarming grape tint they'd had. Her eyes fluttered open. When her gaze settled on me, joy suffused her expression.

"Hi, Granma."

My grandmother lifted her hand and placed it on the curtain. I pressed mine against it and a feeling I didn't have a name for coursed through me.

The nurse, Bettye Jo, according to her name tag, asked, "Who is the family member here?"

I hesitated to claim such a grand award, but Dub nodded at me and said, "She is. She's Vonda Kay's granddaughter."

"Can we talk?" Bettye Jo asked, motioning me to join her as she stepped away from the bed.

Bettye Jo quickly confirmed what I suspected: Granma would require a lengthy hospital stay before she'd be ready to return to life on a remote farm. I asked how much it would cost to keep her in this private room.

Though I didn't say anything when she answered, Bettye Jo read my expression and offered gently, "Listen, even if we have to move her to the charity ward, I'll make sure she gets excellent care."

"Thank you, but I can't allow that to happen. I've seen country people in crowded wards. They don't adjust well." I don't mention that, as isolated as she'd been, she'd have zero immunity to every germ the city patients brought in. Including tuberculosis.

"Dog it," Bettye Jo went on, her voice tight. "I hate to have to say this, and only would because this hospital is fixing to go broke, but I can only give you one free night. After that, administration is going to make me move her. I'm sorry. I truly am."

I inquired about jobs.

"Doing what?" Bettye Jo asked.

"I trained as a nurse."

"Trained?" she asked. "Are you registered?"

I shook my head.

"Couple, three years ago I'd have sent you upstairs to fill out an application whether you had a pin or not. But now? Way the economy is? We have nurses *with* pins scrubbing out toilets."

242

Dub joined us. "I overheard you talking," he said, holding out a few wadded bills and some change on his leathery palm. "This is all I have right now. I can try to sell my farm. At least the equipment. But that'll take time. I know Vonda Kay had put some savings aside, but well, Mamie, she . . ." His voice trailed off. He didn't need to explain. Mamie had cleaned her mother out. It was what Mamie did.

I curled his fingers around the money. "Don't worry. I'll take care of it. Take care of her," I said, because I knew then exactly what I had to do. I gave Bettye Jo the little cash I had left and told her I'd get the rest. Soon. "Just don't move my grandmother to the charity ward, okay? Please."

"Don't worry, you have my word on it," she promised. "One nurse to another."

"One nurse to another."

I asked Dub if he could bring me a change of clothes. "Anything my grandmother has will be fine."

Distress creased his expression when he answered, "I might not be able to make it back for a few days. I've got livestock to see to. Pump's going out on the windmill. Animals won't have any water if I don't fix it."

I told Dub that I'd be fine. I was in a

hospital. It's where I belonged. Dub gazed for a long moment at my sleeping grandmother with equal parts fondness and fear and then he left.

I was marching upstairs to beg Administration for a job, any job, when Bettye Jo intercepted me and said, "Hey, I found something for you. It's not much, but it pays."

She brushed off my thanks, and led me to the hospital laundry down in the basement. Soon I was feeding a load of the sheets I'd just washed through an iron mangle nearly as tall as I was. The giant wringer pressed the water out and they emerged as thin and as dry as a slice of deli meat.

That night, the charge nurse, a good-hearted country woman named Darla, looked the other way when she found me sitting vigil beside my grandmother's bed. The tray she brought the next day held enough food for a couple of lumberjacks. "Bettye Jo said you were a good kid," she said, placing the tray in front of me.

My grandmother opened her eyes and gave me a beatific smile that vanished when she said in a voice so soft that I read her lips more than heard her, "Forgive me."

"Forgive you? For what? I don't have anything to forgive you for."

Each word cost her, yet in a raspy whisper she managed to answer, "For Mamie. I should have come. Should have saved you. Should have —"

A hacking cough interrupted her regrets. "Rest, Granma, rest. Let your lungs heal. It's all right. Everything will be fine now. I promise." I reached under the crinkling barrier to bring a glass of water to her lips. As she sipped, she stroked my hand. After a few bites of egg, she drifted off again.

At the start of her shift, Bettye Jo appeared with a simple day dress and a clean, crisply starched, and ironed uniform. "It's an extra," she said, shoving it at me and waving away my objections. "Patients' bath is down the hall. Take your time. You've earned a nice long soak."

Never had a bath felt so luxurious.

For the next five days, I blended seamlessly back into the life of a hospital. When I wasn't shoveling loads of soiled linen into the hospital's giant washers, I was tending to my grandmother. When I could I did everything possible to help Bettye Jo and Darla with the mindless chores around the floor as a way of trying to thank them for their kindness.

Late on the afternoon of the sixth day, Dub reappeared. He was gaunt, his face drawn with exhaustion. Fresh cuts and bloodstained bandages on his hands attested to the hard battle he'd fought with the broken windmill.

Without a word, he went to my grandmother. Her eyes swimming with tremulous joy, she put her hand on the cellophane curtain. The cellophane crinkled as he closed his raised hand around my grandmother's.

Giving them privacy, I went upstairs, collected my pay, and handed almost all of it right back, with instructions to put it toward Vonda Kay Cooper's bill and a promise that I'd send more in a few days. A week at the most.

Granma was sleeping again when I returned. Dub handed me a handsome, nearly new suitcase. It was heavy and stuffed full to near bursting. I half joked, "I hope you didn't clean out Granma's closet."

"Didn't touch Vonda Kay's closet," he said, a hard set to his jaw. "Cleaned out Mamie's. Packed up all the nice things she squandered your grandparents' money on when she was growing up. Her father . . ." Dub shook his head. "It's not good to let your child believe she is the center of the universe. Anyhow, you should have them. And a whole lot more."

I asked him to tell Granma good-bye for me. Dub said he would and then, after an awkward moment of indecision, he hugged me. His voice sodden with unshed tears, he said, "Thank you. You saved her. I don't know what I'd have done if . . ." He stopped, unable to speak the unspeakable. "Thank you. That's all. Just thank you."

At the train station, I bought a ticket to Amarillo and a transfer to the Rock Island's Golden State Route that ran between Los Angeles and my destination.

The train pulled up to the platform. I boarded.

We chugged through a landscape that could have come straight out of a *National Geographic* story about the Gobi Desert. Sand dunes, rippled with wave patterns, seemed to roll on forever. All that was missing were the camels.

I found the ladies' room and crammed myself and my suitcase in. The smell of Shalimar and Beadex wafted out when I cracked the case open. Though it was the faintest of fragrances, my heart throttled at the first whiff, and I had to slam the lid shut for a moment. When I opened it again, I saw that, though all the clothes were out of fashion, they were still the loveliest garments I'd ever had in my possession.

I changed quickly into a smart traveling suit. Though I didn't fill it out as well as Mamie must have in her prime, my height brought the skirt up to a more fashionable length.

I needed to look good.

I was going to Chicago.

■ ■ ■ ■

CHICAGO

■ ■ ■ ■

CHAPTER 32

June 1, 1932

After bouncing across the country during the vaud days then settling in Houston, I thought I knew a thing or two about big cities. I didn't. Not Chicago big. The moment I stepped off the train into the cavernous Union Station, Chicago made me feel like an ant that had been swallowed by a titanic, bustling machine.

A wave of lonely anonymity and insignificance overwhelmed me. I wished I'd held back just enough to call Sofie. I ached to talk to my friend. To tell her everything I'd been through since we parted. Though Mamie and vaudeville had taught me never to get attached, to accept that I was always just passing through, I was attached to Sofie and missed her like a phantom limb.

I sternly reminded myself that I had no time to waste feeling sorry for myself and ducked into the ladies' room. Mamie's traveling suit had been perfect for the trip, but I wasn't in Chicago to sightsee. I was here to get a job.

I freshened up as well as I could and changed into the clean uniform Bettye Jo had given me. Throwing a lightweight coat of camel gabardine over it, I left the station and entered a canyon of skyscraping towers that sucked in and spewed out gleaming, elegant people.

Horns shrilled with a hostile Yankee impatience. A trolley clattered past. A bus backfired. A motorcycle startled me as it roared past. A traffic cop blasted out a distinct one-long-and-one-short whistle sound. This cacophony was overlaid by a screeching rattle that descended from above. I glanced up. A train soared by on a track elevated high over the traffic.

"Tourist," a woman hissed when she bumped into me. With one hand she held her hat on. With the other she gripped a clutch purse tightly beneath her arm. The wind whipped the tails of her coat around behind her as she passed. I hustled out of the way.

Though I'd never flagged down a taxi in my life, I raised my arm and one screeched to the curb. "Mann's Rainbo Gardens," I told the driver, a bushy-haired, middle-aged guy whose cab smelled like old leather, hair oil, and sweat. He flipped on the meter and, without a backward glance, nosed into the traffic.

Sheltered within the cab, I was free to gape at the kaleidoscope of marvels that Chicago twirled past my window. The variety of humanity astonished me. Every face was its own distinct wonderment, but the hats — the hats alone were worth the trip. Cloche hats that hugged impeccable bobs. Small, smart fedoras with brims that swooped down to cover one eye. Turbans with beaded veils. Not to mention the parade of white gloves, spectator pumps, and stoles, mink and fox, slung over one shoulder or sewn on the collars of trim, tight-fighting suits. There were even women in trousers. The way those pants-wearing women strode through the throngs of skirted women riveted me. One hand stuck in a pocket, the other holding a cigarette between thumb and forefinger, they were as decisive and defiant as the men. As for the men, you didn't see men like these in Texas. They looked wised up and always ready with a light for the nearest lady's cigarette.

They reminded me of Zave, and I pulled the compact Sofie had given me for a birthday present when I turned nineteen out of my bag. I angled my head from side to side, studying myself in the mirror. My complexion had a nice peachy glow from the Panhandle sun. I imagined Zave looking at me.

"You got nuthin' to worry about, doll," the driver said.

I caught him watching me in the rearview mirror and snapped the compact shut.

"You look like a million bucks," he said. "Tell your fella from me that he is one lucky guy."

My fella.

I nodded and returned my gaze to the mesmerizing world outside the window.

As we headed north, though, we emerged from another world beneath the city's glittering exterior, and Chicago became one of those kids' picture puzzles with a menagerie of animals hidden in the foliage. At first, all you saw was a lovely, leafy jungle scene, but then the hidden wolves and tigers jumped out at you.

Instead of wolves, however, what I spotted were clumps of desolate men gathering in shadowed alleys. Displaced farmers in patched overalls wandering aimlessly from park benches to street corners. Dejected businessmen in suits that hadn't been cleaned or pressed in far too long trying to sell apples to passersby who wouldn't meet their gaze. Rail-thin boys scrambling through the crowds hawking newspapers with a desperation I knew only too well.

Even more miserable and defeated than all the rest, however, were the slump-shouldered men lined up in front of a sign that promised "Free Coffee and Doughnuts and Soup for the Unemployed." A handwritten note taped below it read, "Thank you, Al Capone."

"Yeah," the cabbie piped up as though continuing a conversation we'd been having. "Can you believe they put Al away for some cooked-up tax rap? After all the good he's done for this city? He's the only one looking out for the little guy. That high-hat in the White House don't give a rat's ass, pardon my French, about us.

"Don't worry, though," he assured me, even though I hadn't said a word. "The Feds may have Capone locked up on some punk tax charge, but him and his boys are still running Chicago."

"Is that so?" I said, wishing he'd shut up so I could soak in the city.

"It is indeed," he shot back sharply. "Hey, you're not one of them, are you?"

"One of who?"

"A Republican?"

"Heck, no. I can't wait until Hoover gets booted out."

"Attagirl. There it is. The Rainbo Gardens."

The cabbie pulled up in front of a titanic two-story redbrick building that sprawled beneath six frosted-glass spires and covered most of a large city block. It resembled the nightmare vision of Mamie's mythical Middlefield. He got out of the cab and set the borrowed suitcase filled with Mamie's borrowed clothes on the sidewalk next to me.

"Hey," he called out before hopping back into his taxi. "Look me up if that guy of yours don't treat you right." Then, tootling his horn in response to my generous tip, he drove off.

Feeling as if I had an ally, I plucked up my courage, grabbed my case, and rushed up the stairs to meet my destiny.

CHAPTER 33

CLOSED FOR VIOLATION OF NATIONAL
PROHIBITION ACT BY ORDER OF UNITED
STATES DISTRICT COURT.

That's what the notice pasted across the heavy wooden double doors read. A chain was wrapped around the handles and secured in place by an outsized padlock.

My suitcase dropped from my hand.

I was penniless in a giant city where I didn't know a single soul.

In one single bite the Depression swallowed me whole. And it was a dark and scary place. I thought of the men — all men, only men — waiting in line for a doughnut, a piece of bread, a cup of soup and wondered: Where did the hungry *women* go? The homeless ones? What did they do? Who helped them?

Images flashed through my mind. Of the men who had paid to look at me, touch me.

257

Of the women whose children I tended while they serviced men in flophouses if they were lucky. Alleyways if they weren't.

Mamie's clothes, I thought and exhaled with relief.

I could sell Mamie's clothes.

I picked up the case and stumbled down the steps while a set of dire calculations ran through my mind. How long would it take me to find a decent pawnshop? How long would the bag of peanuts I'd eaten on the train last? How long before hunger sapped my energy and afflicted me with sick headaches? How long before night fell?

Night.

Dread drenched me. The faces bustling past now all seemed to be male, hard, and predatory. In my adrenaline-choked state, I almost didn't notice the flock of middle-aged women, a few dragging young children, beeline past in their rush for the bus that was wheezing to a stop down the block. Housewives, I guessed, hurrying home to fix dinner for their husbands.

The housewives waited impatiently while a group of the kind of worker who brought their lunch from home in a paper bag — clerks, secretaries, office boys — got off that same bus. As soon as the workers' feet hit the sidewalk, they took off in the same direction the housewives had just come from.

As they did, I heard Pops's voice as clear as if he were standing next to me. "Aside from a few bums looking for a place to flop, our daytime crowd is nothing *but* dames. Housewives, mostly. Come evening, when the mamas go home to make dinner, we get the working crowd. Secretaries, waitresses, busboys, soda jerks."

A dance marathon crowd.

I hurried after the group. They led me to a cavernous edifice behind the main building. The inscription "Rainbo Garden Jai Alai Arena" was chiseled into its high stone wall. A huge banner partially covered that earlier identity. To my deep relief, the banner proclaimed:

POPS WYATT'S DANCE DERBY OF THE
CENTURY!!
THE POOR MAN'S NIGHT CLUB!!
BUNIONS, CORNS, BLISTERS, FALLEN
ARCHES!!
THRILLS! CHILLS! SPILLS!
DANCERS. SINGERS. COMEDIANS!
100 ATHLETIC ENTERTAINERS!

HOW LONG CAN THEY LAST?!?!

I paid my quarter and entered the multi-story stadium. The steeply pitched rows of seats funneled down to a brightly lighted dance floor gleaming far below, where, praise the Lord, contestants circled the floor.

"Popcorn! Hot dogs! Getcher peanuts right here!"

The familiar aroma of hot dogs, roasted peanuts, and popcorn being hawked by a vendor with a tray hanging around his neck greeted me like the smell of home cooking. Families that couldn't afford to buy hot dogs had picnics spread out on the bleacher beside them. Rat cheese, saltines, Mason jars of water. Kids ran wild up here, chasing each other through the far reaches of the arena while their mothers clustered together to gossip, smoke, and occasionally glance down and comment on the dancers.

Scattered here and there, out-of-work businessmen in rumpled suits perused newspapers already limp from previous readings, worked crossword puzzles, or, ashamed of being unemployed, they simply worked at avoiding anyone's gaze. Off in the far shadowed reaches, other men, arms folded across their chests, hats pulled down over their eyes, too exhausted for shame, slept.

Even farther away, I spotted a few solitary women. They mostly slept sitting up, rigidly clutching a bag or two of belongings like they were life preservers. Here, then, I thought, is where the women, at least some of them, went.

Far down on the arena floor an amplified Victrola played "Ain't She Sweet?" Though I was too far away to make out faces, the sight of contestants circling the floor was deeply reassuring.

A huge, freestanding time board announced:

100 COUPLES STARTED
ONLY 26 LEFT

HOW LONG CAN THEY LAST?

Some of Pops's guys ran up and down the stairs hawking bulletins. "Get your *Daily Dance News* right here!" they yelled. "Read the real story behind the story of all your favorites!! Attention, girls!! We have a red-hot feature for you. Read all about the Handsome Hoofer himself!!"

He's here. Zave's here.

I hurried down the stairs, straining to catch a glimpse of Zave's face, but the floor was still too far away. Although this show was a hundred times bigger than the one at Uncle Jake's, except for the massive concrete wall behind the stage where jai alai games must have once been played, the setup was basically the same as it had been in Houston.

There was a low stage where the daytime emcee sat behind a table with a microphone and a Victrola on it, along with a siren to grind and a bell to clang to signal rest break. Though they hadn't started playing yet, the drum kit announcing Mel and His Melody Makers waited behind the emcee.

As I searched for Zave, I caught sight of some familiar faces. Most of the horses Jake had pointed out back in Houston were there. The Delta Darlings, Minnie and De-Witt. The Pauper and the Princess. Ace and Lily. Thick-shouldered Fritz and his equally burly sister Gerta. The rubber-faced, flat-footed Patsy and his partner, Lynette.

Suits was weaving among them, rubbing a shoulder here, tossing a towel around a sweaty neck there. The surly head floor judge, King Kong Kane, and the nighttime emcee, Alonzo, dressed to the nines for the evening show, waited on the sidelines.

A goofy grin spread across my face. Though I hadn't even officially met most of the horses, in that huge stadium in the middle of a huge city where I knew no one and had feared I'd be sleeping on the street, those dancers felt as close as the way I imagined that family did.

But where was Zave?

He had to be down there if Pops was selling stories about him. I caught sight of Pops then, off on the sidelines where he had been cornered by three beefy men in suits and fedoras. They were poking thick fingers into his chest and giving him an earful. Pops's "backers." They couldn't have looked any more like the mob guys we all saw on the newsreels if they'd been holding Tommy guns. I suddenly worried about the job Pops had promised me. If he was already on the outs with these guys, would he even be able to hire anyone else?

Even worse, I hadn't spotted Zave. I rushed down to the edge of the floor but still couldn't find him. My knees almost gave out as I considered the prospect that he had been eliminated. Could I have come all this way and neither Zave *nor* a job was here? What would happen to my grandmother? What would happen to me?

And then, in the very middle of the pack, looking dejected, completely exhausted, and, oddly, dancing alone, there he was.

Zave.

My heart fluttered. I tried to tell myself I was excited because he knew my father, but I knew that wasn't it. Not all of it.

Zave was limping badly. Obviously, the sprained ankle was giving him trouble, and, without a partner to lean on, he had to be in awful pain.

Where was Cleo? Had she been eliminated?

The daytime announcer, a local boy with a thick Chicago accent, provided the answer. "Oh boy, folks, our hero ain't lookin' so hot. He has been dancin' solo ever since Cleo took sick. Rules say that he has exactly one day for either Cleo to get back on the floor or for Zave to find a new partner. And, folks, those twenty-four hours end this period when that elimination siren sounds. If Zave doesn't have a partner by then, King Kong will be only too happy to eliminate —"

The crowd drowned out the word "eliminate" with a full-throated roar designed to banish the possibility that their hero would be taken from them, and I saw that, once again, Zave might be my way into the show.

If I acted fast.

I shoved my way to the front of the crowd ringing the dance floor and, with a lot of elbowing, finally broke through. Though

Zave had his back to me, a connection crackled between us so strongly that, without a word being spoken, he pivoted around as surely as if I had tapped him on the shoulder.

The instant he saw me, weariness dropped from him like melting snow sliding off a roof. Grinning and holding his arms out, Zave hobbled toward me. The dance floor cleared to let the show's golden boy pass. I stepped forward and Zave embraced me.

"Gravy, I thought you'd never make it."

"What the H E double hockey sticks is going on?" the announcer demanded hotly. "Judges, we got us a civilian on the floor. Judges, you gonna do something about this?"

The two fellows wearing matching white sweaters with "Judge" embroidered in black across their chests looked to their boss, Kane, for guidance. Scowling, King Kong studied me from the sidelines. We both turned our gazes to Pops. The promoter, still wrapped in a heated discussion, didn't notice us. Kane gestured at his underlings to remove me.

The instant, however, that one of the judges put his hand on my shoulder, every fighting instinct in me flared up and I recalled Mamie's advice: "Play to the rafters." As both judges started to yank me away from Zave, I howled as though they were breaking my arms, slipped out of my coat, and, uniform blinding white under the spotlight, threw my arms to the heavens.

The crowd loved it.

"What is going on down there?" the announcer babbled. "Why is a nurse on the floor?"

"Sell it, sister," Zave whispered, grinning with appreciative enthusiasm. "Bring the heat."

The crowd hooted and cheered. Apparently, I had stepped directly into an ongoing marathon drama, and I knew that if I wanted a job, I'd better write myself into it. And fast. I flailed around, jabbing my elbow into the judge holding me. He grabbed me around the waist and I turned into a whirling dervish in his arms.

The audience screamed its delight at this unexpected bit of histrionics. Zave egged them on, hamming it up himself.

The other judge gripped me like a python and commenced to carry me off the floor. Zave, holding his arms out to me as if the judge had torn the love of his life from him, staggered after me.

The commotion caused Pops to take notice. The instant he saw me, he rushed over to Alonzo standing on the sidelines and gave him his marching orders. The emcee flew up the stage stairs and shoved the daytime guy out of the way before the judge could manage to drag me even halfway across the floor.

"Hold it right there, boys!" Alonzo commanded, his suave, professional voice ringing authoritatively through the stadium.

The judges stopped.

"Why, that's our very own Nurse Evie Grace from the Houston show that you've got there. She's an official member of the marathon family, so turn her loose."

Pops gave the judges holding me one decisive nod and they released me. Zave lunged forward onto his bad leg and wobbled as if he were about to go down. I raced to save him. He hung on to me like a shipwreck survivor clutching the last piece of timber floating past.

The applause was deafening.

Clinging to me with one arm, Zave waved at his fans with the other.

"Well, how about that, folks?" Alonzo boomed over the mic. "Looks like Nurse Evie is just the medicine our boy needs."

The applause was a warm wave of approval that lofted us way up high.

"Appears they like you," Zave said, his

voice a deep rumble against my chest. "Actually," he quickly amended, "they appear to like *us*." Still waving and beaming, he told me out of the corner of his mouth, "Play it like Denny would have."

Remembering my father's photo, I raised my head, found the spotlight, and grinned into it just as he had. Zave was right; the audience *did* like us. The air filled with coins that popped back up when they landed on the floor, like fat raindrops hitting a puddle.

We almost danced then. Which was to say that I supported him as he hobbled around the big, oval floor. "Oh God, Gravy," he whispered into my hair. "You're a lifesaver. It's heaven getting the weight off that bad ankle."

"I guess I also saved you from elimination," I said.

"Naw, Pops was never going to let that happen. He'd see to it that Cleo got her fanny back out here before then."

"Is she hurt?"

"Kind of. No. Who knows with Cleo? She runs so hot and so cold. Are you okay? Am I too heavy?"

"Not at all," I answered, because it was true. I liked holding him. I liked it so much that I could have carried him all night. After a moment, I stated the astonishing fact:

"I'm dancing with the boy who my father taught to dance."

"Well, shuffling around the floor, but yes, yes, you are."

For a while after that, he rested in my arms, we swayed back and forth, and I almost felt as if I were exactly where I belonged.

CHAPTER 34

Even before the break siren had finished blaring, Suits appeared and shouldered Zave's weight. "I'll take him from here," he said, guiding Zave toward the side hall with a sign posted above it: "Contestant Rest Quarters."

"The cavalry has arrived," Pops exclaimed, rushing toward me as the contestants cleared the floor.

"Nurse Devlin, I tell you what, you've got the timing of Fred Astaire popping up at exactly this moment. That reunion bit you pulled off out there went over like gangbusters. I had my doubts about you, didn't think you had the stuff to be a real marathoner, but the way you brought the heat. Hot dang. Fighting the judges like a wildcat. You even wore the costume."

"Not a costume," I reminded him.

Ignoring me, he raved on, "The way you swanned in here. That look on your face?

270

The one on Zave's? Either you're one heck of an actress or that little road trip the two of you took must have made a detour through the Tunnel of Love. No wonder Cleo strayed."

"Strayed? How has Cleo 'strayed'?"

He answered with a sharp yap of laughter. "Doesn't matter. The only thing that matters is what the boys think." He nodded over his shoulder to the trio of tough guys now parked in a box seat at the edge of the floor. "And it appears that they like you."

"So that means . . . ?" I prompted him.

"Means you got the job. Now go. Be a nurse. Ham it up."

"I am a nurse."

"Right, right. Go see if Cleo's alive and do that special wrap on Zave like you did in Houston. The trainers wrap it like they're putting on a diaper. Doesn't help Zave a damn bit. Why are you still standing here? Scoot."

Already walking toward "the boys," he shooed me away. "Go earn your sixty cents a day."

Insulted that he'd try to stiff me again, I hollered after him, "A dollar or I walk."

Pops snapped a finger pistol at me, pretended to shoot, and said, "Can't blame a guy for trying. Okay, six bits, but you're killing me," and hustled over to the tough guys.

The infirmary was a makeshift structure with canvas walls and a canvas top. Two of its three cots were occupied. At the closest cot, a trainer with a shock of carroty-red hair, a face full of rust-colored freckles, and the name "Red" embroidered on his pocket was beating a charley horse out of a fellow's calf.

The cot against the far wall was occupied by Cleo who was a) deeply unconscious and b) now a raven-haired vamp instead of a blond Kewpie doll. As I checked her breathing and took her pulse, Red informed me, "That little moth's been flappin' around the wrong flame." He punctuated his diagnosis with a suggestive waggle of his eyebrows.

I shook Cleo's shoulder. When she responded by trying to bat my hand away without ever truly waking up, I knew that she was not in any immediate danger.

"I suppose you wanna know who she's been cozying up with," Red said as I tried to take Cleo's pulse.

Though I didn't answer, Red continued conspiratorially, "Well, you didn't hear it from me, but a little bird told me it was Salvy Capone."

Though I was concentrating on the faint beat of Cleo's pulse at her spindly wrist, the name "Capone" caught my attention.

"Salvy is Al's favorite nephew. That would be Al Capone," Red elaborated. Eager to show what an insider he was, he leaned in close enough that I could smell the coffee on his breath and told me out of the side of his mouth, "Word is, the two of them's been takin' rest breaks together. But they ain't been restin'. If ya know what I mean. Huh? Huh?"

"Yeah, I think I might be able to puzzle it out," I answered drily.

"Salvy's the one got Cleo to change her hair. Salvy likes his women hot-blooded and dark-haired." More salacious eyebrow-bouncing. He would have made the world's worst charge nurse. His patient summary was useless.

"Right," I said sharply, "but why is she unconscious?"

"Oh, that. Salvy's wife paid off one of the amateurs to slip her a Mickey."

"And Cleo's been out now for almost twenty-four hours?"

The trainer nodded.

"So she's got to be back on the floor at the end of this period," I clarified. "Or she *and* Zave are both out?"

"Yep," Red said. "At least, that's what the rules say."

273

"Well, it's obvious that Cleo's not going to be on her feet in the next fifteen minutes."

Red snorted at my ignorance. "Rules is for the rubes, the locals. When it comes to the stars, rules are whatever Pops says they are."

Suits entered. Zave, dead to the world, was draped over the short trainer's shoulder. "He blinked out soon as he drained the main vein," Suits said. Red helped him guide Zave to an empty cot. Without ever opening his eyes, Zave shuffled along obediently. He was sleepwalking. I watched in fascination as, snoring the whole time, Zave settled himself onto the cot. As soon as he was horizontal, I quickly unwrapped the dirty bandage drooping from his ankle. Once it had been cleaned, Zave's ankle didn't look quite so bad, and he didn't wince when I manipulated the joint. In spite of him not resting it properly, the swelling and bruising were almost gone and, though obviously a bit weak, it seemed to have almost healed.

Zave, desperately in need of sleep after so many hours without a partner, didn't stir as I wrapped his ankle with a new bandage that still had enough stretch left in it to actually give him some support.

The amplified clanging of the bell that

signaled the break would be over in two minutes echoed through the stadium as I hurriedly fastened the silver clips onto the elastic bandage. Pops swept in, snapped his fingers, and Suits and Red rushed to put Zave's shoes back on and lift him to his feet.

"Wait," I said as Pops followed them out.

"What now?" Pops asked.

I pointed to Cleo. "She'll need some help getting back onto the floor."

"She's not going back to the floor for a while," Pops said. "I talked to the boys. They love the bit I worked out."

"What bit?"

"Don't worry. You'll love it, too. Just something to bring a little heat. Get those damn box seats filled. Heat," Pops all but yelled at me. "We have to bring some heat to this operation or my backers are going to start getting very nervous. Very, *very* nervous. And that is not going to be good for my health. You follow me?"

Pops was in over his head. He reeked of desperation. I tensed. I didn't like the things that people did when they were desperate. "What's that got to do with me?"

"Evie, you're in the family now, and everyone in the family's got to do what they can to pitch in and help the family."

"Like what?"

275

"Like you're Zave's partner now."

"No. No dice," I answered, the chill that had never entirely left me after the Detroit show icing my veins again. "I am not a dancer," I lied.

Suits, who was obviously still put out at me about the Litchfield detour, snorted a snide laugh. "Beanpole thinks we want her to dance. She'd cripple Zave with them two big left feet of hers."

"Don't sweat it, Nurse," Pops assured me. "We're not asking you to be Ginger Rogers. All you gotta do is drag Zave around long enough to set up the bit before we bring Cleo back. No one's expecting you to dance. Some people are dancers and some aren't. Some people were meant to shine in the spotlight and some weren't. No offense, but it's pretty obvious that you didn't exactly inherit Dandy Denny Devlin's star power. No, we just need you to be a, you know, foil. The beige that makes the bright red even brighter. The boring and normal that makes the audience miss Cleo's glamour and crazy sex appeal."

"Thanks a ton," I said.

"Don't take it personal, it's just a setup. You know, a role. And you get to play the Angel of Mercy," Pops commanded more than asked. "And lug Zave around until

276

Cleo gets back on her feet."

I studied Zave, still fast asleep, sagging between the two trainers. His face was gaunt with exhaustion. He needed rest. He needed help. He needed me. And, frankly, I needed him. If he was eliminated, my job prospects would be too.

I nodded and the trainers transferred Zave's weight into my arms.

CHAPTER 35

"We've got less than a minute and a half left on the clock," Alonzo announced from the stage, watching the second hand tick down the time left in the fifteen-minute break.

I barely had to tug on Zave to make him walk in his sleep. He staggered forward as we made our way into the dark hall, staying out of the audience's sight until Pops gave me the high sign.

"Hey, Tex," Minnie greeted me enthusiastically. "Welcome back. Look, y'all," she alerted the others. "It's Evie, she's a for-real actual nurse. You gonna carry him?" she asked, nodding her chin at Zave, who was curled up against me, head on my shoulder, snoring lightly as a kitten. "You're lucky. Zave's the best sleeper on the floor. De-Witt's a terrible lug, aincha, DeWitt."

"That's the God's honest truth," DeWitt admitted, grinning shyly as though being a terrible lug was something to be proud of. "I flail and thrash. Minnie says it's like trying to fight a wildcat."

"Will your favorite return?" Alonzo baited the crowd, adding in a teasing tone, "And I think all you girls out there know who I'm talking about."

"Zave!!" The name echoed through the arena like a battle cry.

"Will our prize solo boy make it out?" Alonzo asked in a spooky voice. "He's been on his own now for almost twenty-four long, grueling hours. If he fell asleep on the rest break there's no telling whether even a team of trainers will be able to get him back on his feet."

The crowd wailed a collective "Nooo!"

"The seconds are ticking away," Alonzo continued urgently. "And the questions keep piling up. First off, what's the story on the fair-haired Florence Nightingale who swept in here right before the break and got such a warm welcome from the Handsome Hoofer?"

I listened carefully as Alonzo essentially described the role I would be playing. The female fans were already buying it, hook, line, and sinker, and a round of *ooh*s and *aah*s gusted through the arena.

"Is our mystery nurse here to keep Zave

warm while Cleo is out cold?" Alonzo asked bawdily.

A muted round of boos from Cleo's fans greeted that ridiculous storyline.

"And, get this, folks." Alonzo leaned into the mic and added in a confiding tone, "I was told that Zave has a nickname for the Honey-Haired Homewrecker."

Honey-Haired Homewrecker? This was the lamest bit I'd ever heard. And there had been tons of lame bits on the vaud circuit.

"Zave calls her Nurse Gravy because, according to Zave, everything goes better with gravy!"

Ah, well, I told myself, I guess that sounded better than "Zave calls her Nurse Gravy because he was too high to say Evie Grace."

"But the biggest question on everyone's mind is: Will Zave return? Time is ticking, folks, and here they come now."

"We best get on out there," Minnie said to the other horses. "That King Kong'd love to cut us if we're not on that floor 'fore the siren, and we can't have that."

She grabbed De Witt's hand, held it high, and they took the floor to a roar of applause.

"Let's give a big Windy City welcome to our Delta Darlings, Skinny Minnie and her husband, DeWitt. They're desperate to win that five-hundred-dollar grand prize so they can get the family farm out of hock."

As the other pros joined the locals already on the floor, Minnie did her out-of-control version of the Charleston to acknowledge the applause.

"And, of course, our indestructibles, those crazy Krauts, brother and sister Gerta and Fritz Mueller are back."

Fritz puffed out his chest, held up both arms, and flexed his biceps like a prizefighter while his sister stood impassively beside him.

"Keep your eye on this pair of hungry Huns. It's their twenty-third marathon, so they know every trick in the book."

Twenty-three?

"And look who else is gracing us with her presence. Why, if it isn't the Park Avenue Princess herself, Lily Gotbucks. Lily's family won't allow their little black sheep to use their name because, well, marathons are too low-class for those stuck-up swells."

The crowd booed the stuck-up swells.

Lily, a vacant look in her eyes, waved and smiled the blank smile of a baby doll. Her partner, the grizzled Ace, had a lifetime of hard living written all over his face. He gently took Lily's hand and guided her into the spotlight.

"The Pauper and the Park Avenue Princess, ladies and gents. Lily's partner, Ace Atkins, always steers her straight. This odd couple is a match that could only be made here on this floor. They're in love and fighting for that prize so they can settle down and get married. Give the lovebirds a hand."

As Ace acknowledged the applause and Lily seemed to study the overhead lights, Patsy, the flat-footed funnyman, gave Ace a comic bump to knock him out of the spotlight.

"And here's everyone's favorite, Patsy," Alonzo announced. "Patsy, is there anything you'd like to say to our audience?"

"What's up, suckers?" he bellowed out to guffaws even from the seats so high up that they couldn't possibly have heard him.

Alonzo briefly introduced a few of the locals, just to get the Chicago fans cheering. When everyone else had left, I started to lead Zave onto the floor, but Pops held me back.

"Listen to Alonzo," he directed. "He'll clue you in about the bit."

As the seconds ticked away, a bad case of stage fright overtook me. Even though I didn't have to do anything other than haul a sleeping Zave around long enough to keep him and Cleo in the contest, just the thought of being watched, stared at, caused me to shiver as though I were, once again, freezing in a too-small costume in the drafty wings of a seedy burlesque hall.

"Is that it?" Alonzo asked. "Are all our dancers on the floor?"

A wailing *"Nooooo!!"* rose from the crowd.

"Who's missing?" Alonzo asked, pretending to count heads.

"Zave!!" The name boomed through the auditorium.

Alonzo played along. "Why, you're right. Where *is* Zave? Oh gosh, is the Handsome Hoofer really down for the count this time? Has he finally been beaten?"

"Nooooo!!" the crowd roared as if Alonzo had asked them if *they* were down for the count. If the Depression had finally beaten *them.*

"Oh, folks, I'm just as nervous as you are. Come on, Zave. Where are you? We all know that Cleo got knocked out by a nasty flu bug. And that even though Zave, who's had to dance solo on that bum ankle of his, is dead on his feet, he has been killing himself because he'd rather die than let you, the fans he loves so much, down," Alonzo said, a weepy tremble in his voice.

"Zave has had nothing but a few short rest breaks for almost twenty-four hours. That's

283

right, while all the other contestants have been dozing most of the night away, sleeping while their patient partners led them around, Zave has been out here on this floor. Alone. Just like so many of us are alone now. With no one sticking up for us. Certainly not that hard-hearted high-hat in the White House."

That hard-hearted high-hat Hoover was booed soundly.

"That plucky kid is just like all of us. Zave is a fighter. And right now, he's fighting for you. Fighting to stay in the game and keep doing what he can to keep all our spirits up. Will he make it?"

"Zave! Zave! Zave!"

"Oh no," Alonzo wailed. "Here comes King Kong Kane. And, boy howdy, is he ever hopping mad. You know how much this ape hates 'the Pretty Boy.' He is just dying to eliminate our hero. We've only got five seconds on the clock before Kane is gonna make me start grinding this siren and then he'll count Zave out."

"Five! Four!"

Though Kane bellowed out the count, the crowd's screams of "Zave! Zave! Zave!" drowned him out.

"Two!"

Pops held me back. I didn't know what

his angle was, but if he didn't let me go he was going to get Zave, and my job, eliminated.

"One!!"

The siren ground out a low starting note that built in ferocity until it shrieked loudly enough to drown out the screams for Zave. Only then did Zave jerk his head up from my shoulder, blink twice, and pull me into dance position.

"No," I said. "We're not dancing. I can't dance."

"Can't dance?" Zave asked, as awake as I'd ever seen him. "Didn't you say you're Denny Devlin's daughter?"

"I am. But I don't want to . . . I can't dance."

Raising our arms as high as the prow of a ship about to sail, just as the siren's last note died away, he launched us onto the spotlit floor. "You're Denny's girl. Like hell you can't dance."

CHAPTER 36

There is a light some people are born with that they can turn on and off. When it is off, you'd pass them on the street and never think twice. But when they switch it on, Katie, bar the door. You can't take your eyes off them.

Some of it is beauty. But not all beautiful people have it, and a good number of flat-out ugly people do. Zave had it in spades. And the more attention he got, the brighter it shone.

As the ravenous applause drenched him, Zave switched that light on to high beam and became nothing but quicksilver charm flowing across the floor. I, on the other hand, froze into a wooden lump that Zave had to manhandle just to get me to stumble around a bit.

"Nurse Gravy to the rescue," Alonzo announced, adding with a snicker as I, literally, tripped over my own feet, "sort of."

The band started playing "Ain't She Sweet." I could have danced to that number in my sleep, since Jake and I had used it to demo the Charleston to hundreds of students. But teaching was different. In teaching, I could manage the attention and I always turned it back where it belonged: onto the student.

Now, however, all eyes were drilling into me for the first time since Detroit. I knew how ridiculous I looked. A beanpole in a nurse's uniform thinking she was good enough to take the floor with the show's golden boy. I tried to do even the elementary steps I'd taught so many times, but my feet wouldn't obey. All I could manage were a few jerky movements. Suits elbowed Red and they exchanged smirks. Titters rippled through the crowd.

Pops, standing beside the mob guys' box seat, folded his arms in satisfaction as they laughed. At me.

Alonzo played to the crowd. "No one expected this lanky lass to be Ginger Rogers and, boy oh boy, is she ever delivering."

The titters broke into full-throated, condescending belly laughs.

"But, Lord love her, looks like our Nurse Gravy wants to dance in the worst possible way," Alonzo said. Then, with perfect comic timing, he delivered the punch line: "And, holy cow, is she ever succeeding."

That brought the house down.

"Oh well," Alonzo went on. "At least Cleo has nothing to be jealous of, does she?"

The audience hooted their agreement. Embarrassment froze me so stiff that I might as well have been the sleepwalking partner being led around. I slouched down even further.

"I'm sorry," I whispered to Zave.

"For what? You've got nothing to be sorry about. Without you I'd have been out on my ass. I owe you." Then as gently as I'd once coaxed a terrified first grader onto the floor, he asked, "Come on, whudda ya say, let's give it a whirl?"

"Zave, I can't dance."

"Can't dance? Gravy, you *taught* dance."

"That's different. That's not performing. An audience wasn't staring at me."

"Those dopes?" He flapped his hand at the gawkers. "Forget those dopes. Let's just do one for you and me."

At that point, I actually wanted to try, but when he started to lead, my joints locked and I hobbled around stiff as a mannequin. Even then Zave still beamed at the crowd like he was twirling Ginger Rogers around.

Alonzo continued, "I was told that our

sweet Nurse Gravy had such a mad crush on Zave that she hitchhiked and rode the rails like a hobo all the way from Houston, Texas, just for the romantic reunion you're witnessing right here tonight.

"So, girls, don't give up hope. If even someone like poor Nurse Evie can end up in a dreamboat's arms, you might have a chance after all!"

I tensed even more at being turned into such a pathetic figure of fun.

Zave felt me stiffen and murmured, "Relax, kid. It's all make-believe. Just play along. It'll pay off."

He was right, because a shower of coins followed this fairy tale and, remembering that I had to make enough to pay for my grandmother's care, I even managed to fake a smile.

In the midst of the clamor, however, I became aware of a low buzz rippling through the audience and noticed alarmed spectators pointing to something behind me. Before I had a chance to see what was causing the furor, a hand clawed at my shoulder, ripping me from Zave's arms, and I confronted a wild-eyed Cleo crouched in a stance that I recognized from Vinegar Hill: Cleo wanted to fight. Feeling as though I had been horribly miscast in a very bad melodrama, I backed away, holding my hands up to indicate that I was ceding whatever field of battle she imagined we were on. Cleo closed in on me.

"Look at that! Look at that!" Alonzo raved. "Seems we've got us a catfight on our hands!"

I glared at Alonzo. Everything in my expression ordered him to shut up, because under no circumstances was I going to fight Cleo. But the emcee was a trouper and a trouper always delivered what his audience wanted, and this audience wanted more of what he was dishing up.

"Who are we rooting for?" he asked the audience. "The bashful blond good girl who risked her life to come to Zave's rescue? Or the raven-haired vamp who left Zave high and dry? Maybe it's time that Cleo, our very own Queen of the Nile, got the asp?"

Boos and shouts of "The asp! The asp!" rocked the stadium as Alonzo heated up the bogus conflict between us. I was all for playing along to make a bit work, but this cheap theatrical I'd been dragged into was too much. Even as Alonzo was pumping up the applause by asking, "Who's with our fair-haired Florence Nightingale? Our hitchhiking Angel of Mercy?" I turned on my heel and started to walk away.

290

Before I could escape to the darkness at the edge of the floor, though, Cleo grabbed me again. I ripped my arm away and, my old Vinegar Hill instincts kicking in, I almost smacked her right in the chops. The audience cheered, but the suggestions they shouted — "Rip her hair out! Gouge her eyes out!" — brought me back to my senses.

I threw up my hands again and said, "Cleo, seriously, he is all yours."

"Play along," she hissed from between bared and gritted teeth as she bounced from foot to foot, hands balled into fists like a boxer about to land the knockout punch. "Act like you're jealous, mad, something. For the love of Mike, help me out here. Bring a little heat, will ya? Ham it up."

I tried to leave, but again she grabbed me and pleaded urgently, "Play along, goddammit. Didn't Pops give you the setup? Shit, he didn't, did he? Never mind. Just play along, please, or I'll be out on my ass."

Understanding nothing except Cleo's need, I pretended to grapple with her. Then, while I was busy play-acting, Cleo, the little street fighter, swept her leg behind mine, knocked me flat on my keister, and jumped on my chest. Now genuinely mad, I struggled to get up, but she had me pinned.

Leaning in close, she said, "Okay, flip me

over and I'll take a dive. Then you yell out to Alonzo that you're a nurse. That you love your patients too much to compete against them. And to, please, let you nurse and let me dance."

Since that was exactly what I wanted, I flipped Cleo off with enough force to shove her across the floor, and she threw her palms skyward in surrender. Only then did I notice how utterly, insanely wild the crowd was going. Even the mobsters were excited. Which, in the end, I supposed, was the whole point.

"Go to Alonzo," Cleo hissed at me.

As I approached, Alonzo asked the audience, "Has a truce been declared between our two hellcats? I wonder what the terms of surrender will be? I can't wait to find out who will be Zave's partner. Who will continue in the show? And who will have to leave?"

Alonzo played the crowd like a kazoo and was rewarded with a symphony of applause, whistles, and catcalls. I planted myself in front of the stage.

"And here the Honey-Haired Home-wrecker is now, folks. Let's hear what the battling broads have agreed on." He signaled for the riotous crowd to quiet down and asked, "So, Nurse Gravy, what's it gonna be?"

Speaking as loudly as I could, I stated, "I just want to be a nurse."

Alonzo put his hand over the microphone and, still grinning, leaned over and hissed down at me, "Put some heat on it, sister. No one's gonna buy the cold goulash you're serving up."

In that instant, I did what Mamie and fear of being sent to an orphanage had always driven me to do: I played to the rafters. When I tipped my head up to the lights, real, Mary Pickford tears sparkled like diamonds. I threw my arms to the heavens in supplication and, wringing my hands together in wildly dramatic prayer, I begged from my heart, "I just want to be a nurse!"

The crowd ate it up.

"Pipe down. Pipe down," Alonzo ordered them. "Our sweet Nurse Gravy has decided that her place is in the infirmary with the kids who need her most. I guess this means that the dark-haired vamp wins this round. Cleo stays."

Alonzo's last words were lost in an explosion of boos and cheers. Half the crowd hated this ruling. Half loved it.

Kane charged up the stage stairs, grabbed the microphone, and growled, "That's against the rules. Cleo didn't make it back onto the floor within the twenty-four hours allocated. Cleo and Zave are both eliminated."

The crowd hated that ruling even more. As a respecter, though not always a strict follower of rules, I had to admire Kane's integrity. He was a straight guy in a world of twists. The crowd roared out its need to keep Zave. With a nod from Pops to Mel, the Melody Makers burst into a blistering rendition of "There'll Be a Hot Time in the Old Town Tonight" and the case was closed.

Cleo stayed.

Happy to be released, I fled the floor.

The dancers, rejuvenated by the drama, blurred past as I made my way around the edge of the floor. Already on the floor with Cleo, Zave caught my eye, and behind Cleo's back, he shot me a great big thumbs-up.

The gesture was so personal, so intimate that, for just one ridiculous moment, it pulled us together into a thrilling little conspiracy and filled my head with a ridiculous thought: Zave knew my father. Cleo would never have the special bond with him that I did.

CHAPTER 37

Apparently, the whole melodrama with Zave and Cleo was my rite of passage for true acceptance into Pops's marathon family, and I had passed with flying colors. A couple of the dancers actually thanked me for saving the show. Minnie told me that I was "a bonafiddee, for-real marathoner." Even Suits managed to growl out that I was "not half bad. For a civilian. With two left feet."

I may have humiliated myself in front of a stadium full of people, but at least I was in. I was a nurse again. Pops gave me an advance on my wages. I rented a room around the corner and wired the sanitarium in Lubbock a money order to keep my grandmother in her private room for a while longer.

I wished I'd had enough left to call Sofie, but I didn't. Instead, over the next few weeks, I poured my heart out to her in long letters that I sent to the boardinghouse close

295

to Sealy Hospital where we'd planned to live.

I told her everything about how I cared for dance marathon contestants. Though it wasn't exactly caring for lepers on Molokai or anything else Sof and I had dreamed of doing when we were registered, it was still nursing.

I disinfected and bandaged blisters, gave stretching exercises for plantar fasciitis, rubbed sore arches, treated ingrown toenails, and generally attended to all the ills to which the human foot can fall prey.

I also dispensed headache powders, had a hot water bottle ready for a few minutes of relief from menstrual cramps, stirred up effervescent glasses of Bromo-Seltzer to settle stomachs that rebelled against the fare served up by the sloppers, beat charley horses out of muscles tightened into rock-hard lumps, and applied ice packs to whatever tendon was aching the most.

Though I had few actual drugs or therapeutic treatments to offer my patients, I freely dispensed the nurse's magic cure-all: a sympathetic ear. What I got in return were instant friends and stories. I'd always known that if you gave them half a chance, every single person you ever met in this life would surprise you, and that was true for marathoners. In spades.

Toward the end of my first week, DeWitt carried Minnie in and laid her slender frame gently on a cot. I asked him what was wrong, but his Southern accent was so thick that I couldn't understand a word of his answer. Doing my best to make sense of what he told me, I asked, "Are you telling me that Minnie has 'poison in her woe sock'?"

DeWitt grabbed my hand, put it on his frail wife's forehead, and carefully articulated, "She's hot as a possum in a wool sock."

I didn't know how hot a possum could get in a wool sock, but Millie's forehead was alarmingly warm. I took her temperature and peeked in her throat, where I saw white patches. "Minnie," I said gently, "sweetie, you have strep throat and should probably drop out —"

"No," she objected, her voice raspy. "Can't do that. Got nowhere to go. 'Cept the street. You heard what happens to girls on the street here?"

I had.

At least if they stayed in the show, Minnie would have a roof over her, enough to eat, and I could watch out for her. Though dancing through a case of strep wasn't ideal, it would be better for her than sleeping on a park bench. With no other option, I had her gargle with hot salt water, gave her a handful of aspirin, some mentholated throat lozenges, an ice bag, a shoulder to cry on, and told her to drink lots of fluids, lug on DeWitt as much as she could, and keep her distance from the other contestants as best she could.

The next day her temp was down and we spent the break sipping tea together. She told me that she'd never worn shoes until she started marathoning. Or set foot in a restaurant, movie house, or classroom. That she kept her hand over her mouth when she smiled because her front teeth had all "gone bad" from dipping snuff when she was young and she'd had to "git 'em yanked out."

Then there was the odd couple of the Pauper and the Park Avenue Princess. Everybody called Ace "Comrade," since the burly stevedore was the show's resident Communist. He spent the long hours on the floor lecturing anyone within earshot about how we had to vote Hoover out of office and get the blood-sucking plutocrats off our necks.

No one disagreed. Least of all me.

"Listen to these fat cats," he railed.

"Hoover and Henry Ford always lecturing us about how we just need to 'pull ourselves up by our bootstraps.' Any of you ever tried doing that? You ever tried to pull yourselves up by some little loop at the back of a boot?"

Patsy swatted away the idea, saying, "Aw, Comrade, it's just a metaphor."

"You're right," Ace exploded. "That's exactly what it is. It's a metaphor from the Civil War that literally means an impossible task. Somehow it got twisted around to make a man feel like a deadbeat and blame himself when capitalism screws him over. That's how the plutocrats keep us from organizing and rising up against their oppression."

Ace had his own personal cheering section of anarchists and Reds who were always handing out literature and singing "The Internationale." Fights broke out in the stands when the average Joes got tired of hearing the Reds tell them what chumps they were. Times were desperate and violence was in the air. It felt as if a fuse was burning down and that change had to come or the country would explode and the America we knew and loved would be lost forever.

On the other hand, Ace didn't seem to have a problem with the fact that Lily, in spite of having a screw loose, clearly seemed to have wandered in from the plutocrat world.

Lily drifted in very early one morning just as I was starting my shift. Even though her dress was ripped and stained and safety pins held the bodice together, she always carried herself as though she should be holding a champagne glass in one hand and a cigarette in a long ivory holder in the other.

She extended a limp hand, palm down, for me to shake and, her eyes never meeting mine because they were always glued to some spot above my head, asked in an accent that was stuck over the Atlantic halfway between England and America, "Evie, I am so terribly sorry to bother you, but might I trouble you for a headache powder? I seem to have completely run out of my toothache drops which are so divine for making pain absolutely disappear."

Toothache drops had been popular on the vaud circuit since the main ingredient was morphine. They used to be sold at any drugstore until huge swaths of the country ended up addicted and they were declared illegal. It was still easy, though, to get a prescription from a crooked doctor. I handed her a BC Powder and a glass of water and told her it was all I had. She gulped it down and drifted back out as

300

serenely as she'd come in.

Lily never said very much. Not about herself or, really, much of anything else other than to make extremely odd comments. She'd pop her head into my infirmary and blurt out something like, "There are eighty-five fewer spectators today at three thirty than there were yesterday." Or "I made two hundred and thirty-two revolutions of the floor last period."

On Ace's next visit, while I lanced, disinfected, and bandaged a boil in his armpit, he told me what he knew of Lily's story.

"I met her in jail in Tucson. We both got pinched for vagrancy. I seen right off," he growled in his Bronx accent, "that she was, you know, not exactly all there. She was a babe in the woods just waiting to get eaten alive by the wolves."

With a shrug like it was no big deal, he went on. "So I took her under my wing. Worked out for both of us. Thumbing a ride and putting the touch on farm wives for a handout is a lot easier with a broad. Makes you look like a family man. In exchange, I taught her how to survive in hobo jungles and Salvation Army shelters. Mostly, though, I kept the creeps and the twists from messing with her."

Ace didn't know how Lily had ended up

in jail with two black eyes and crawling with lice. "I never asked. And she never said. She likes to walk in circles around a floor and I like to eat, and we both hate the rich parasites who are bleeding this country dry. So here we are."

A few days later Patsy came in alone and, in a nervous whisper, said he'd heard the girls talking about my "secret weapon."

"So, give it to me straight, Evie," the funny man said. "What's the secret the girls are whispering about? Is it bennies? 'Cause I sure could use a pick-me-up."

"Hell no," I answered.

Bennies, Benzedrine inhalers, were the newest thing; they pepped a beat dancer up like thirty cups of coffee. I couldn't blame any of the contestants for using whatever they had to if the alternative was a soup line and a park bench, but I sure wasn't going to hand them out.

"Nope," I answered, digging into the secret stash that I'd bought at the Montgomery Ward on Michigan Avenue. There, on top of an out-of-the-way counter, I'd found the only self-service item in the store, deposited fifty-nine cents payment, and, without ever having to so much as ask a clerk, took what I needed. It was an item that had been created by the nurses who served in the Great War: Kotex pads.

I passed one to a highly skeptical Patsy and told him to slip the pad inside his shoe. He did. When he stood, all suspicion faded. "Wowzah, it's like walking on a cloud," he sighed. "Evie, you're a miracle worker. When I win this thing, I'll make sure you get your cut."

The next day, Gerta limped in supported by her partner and lookalike brother, Fritz. Gerta had a wicked splinter embedded beneath the thick calluses on the ball of her foot that she'd chosen to ignore because, as Fritz explained, "It is taking five hundred hours to build up such a callus as that. Without this callus, we are not winning."

Working carefully, I was able to remove the splinter while leaving most of the precious callus intact. Gerta stood, bounced from foot to foot like a prizefighter warming up, and her brother asked, *"Ist gut?"*

"Ja," Gerta answered, and the pair left without a word of thanks.

Everyone had stories; from Lily, the former heiress, to Minnie, who'd never worn shoes before. But they all involved hard times and hunger. They all involved the one force that had gathered us together, not just the dancers, but most everyone in the audience as well: the Depression.

The Depression took away jobs and money and, too often, it also took away drive and hope. And all it gave back was time. Time enough to care about a bunch of strangers who could almost feel like family if you watched them orbit a dance floor for days, weeks, months.

Oceans and oceans of endless time.

Enough time for me to start worrying if Sofie would answer all the letters I'd sent her. Enough time to start worrying that she might have cut me out of her life. Enough time to realize how her friendship had made me feel anchored in the world. And how unmoored and adrift I felt without it.

CHAPTER 38

Of course, of all my patients, the one whose story I was most interested in was Zave's. But he hadn't visited, and Pops had ordered me to stay off the floor, saying, "I'm working up another scenario. You know? A new angle. So I need you to lay low. Build up the suspense, see? I'll put you wise as soon as the boys say it's okay for the Angel of Mercy to reappear."

So for the next week I snuck in through the staff entrance at the back of the coliseum and, when I did peek out at the action, I was careful to stay hidden in the shadows. Which is where I was when a team of beauticians swarmed onto the floor to set the girls' hair in pin curls. It was comical watching the stylists follow the contestants around with their new handheld dryers, all of them tripping over the long extension cords snaking everywhere.

And, even though there was always a

special "hygiene break," usually during the wee hours, when everyone showered and the men shaved, Pops still brought in a crew of barbers to trim the men's hair. And, just for the sheer theatricality of it, every now and again he'd have them shave the boys.

It was a harrowing sight to watch the barbers, followed by a helper bearing a basin of hot water, lather up a contestant who had to keep moving while he was being shaved with a wicked-looking straight-edge razor. Pops never stopped dreaming up gags to keep the customers coming back.

When I worked the night shift, though, I witnessed a completely different world. There wasn't much to see during the long night hours after the band packed up. And not much of an audience to see it. The only music was provided by a scratchy Victrola, the glaring overhead lights were replaced by dim economy bulbs, the arena darkened, and the spectators who couldn't afford a bed used the far bleachers for sleep and sex.

Any time after midnight, when there wasn't a normal crowd to witness them, the sleepwalkers took over. One member of each couple would be draped over his or her waking partner, who would lead the sleeper in a slow zombie shuffle around the floor.

Around three in the morning, the crowd thinned down to the usual late-nighters. Gamblers who cleaned their fingernails with dainty little knives; bookies who worked on their lists of who owed what; bootleggers who napped or passed around free samples; owl-eyed insomniacs. My favorites were the ladies of the night who cried and laughed and drank openly from the bottles their men — customers or pimps — handed them. They always seemed a happy club, putting on their own show, even, or maybe especially, when they were fighting.

The dance marathon was a world unto itself and one, I quickly learned, where women were the true heroes. It was obvious from the start that the women were a heck of a lot tougher than the men. They were the ones who could outlast three partners, soloing until they were either eliminated or they latched on to one of the outnumbered men.

I wished every jackass I'd ever heard gassing on about "the weaker sex" would take a long hard look at Minnie and DeWitt, for example. DeWitt, the big galoot, had an easy eighty pounds on Minnie, but *she* was usually the one carrying *him* while he slept. Worst of all, like Minnie said, and like most men, DeWitt was a lugger who flailed and writhed while he slept. Watching them was like watching a tiny jungle explorer battle a writhing python.

As I'd learned, Zave was an exception to the rule. He was such a model sleeper, barely leaning on Cleo, that you'd almost have thought he was awake. Cleo, on the other hand, was a wicked lugger. She became a bony octopus with pointy elbows and fingernails on all eight arms when she slept. Zave had a job avoiding her dagger-pointed nails as she jerked from side to side.

Instead of waking her up, though, Zave would get her repositioned and go on doing what he spent most of the very late and very early hours doing — reading. Zave was a newshound with a special affection for politics and, with a lot of careful folding, he plowed through the morning and evening editions of *The Daily News, The Sun, The Times,* and as many weeklies as he could get delivered to him on the floor.

The most important fact, though, that I learned about the show as I prowled around with my eyes open and my mouth shut was that Pops was in trouble. Big trouble.

CHAPTER 39

Toward the end of my second week, Pops made the mistake so many others had: he forgot that the canvas "walls" of the infirmary weren't soundproof.

"Those goddamn guineas got my balls in a vise," Pops moaned to his trusted right-hand man, Kane. "And they're squeezing 'em so hard my eyes are popping out of my head. That greedy pipsqueak nephew wants more."

"But the crowds are good," Kane objected.

"Not the *right* crowd," Pops specified. "Not the ones'll buy the high-dollar box seats. He wants the swank set to show up the way they would've if Capone was here. That damn dago wants his picture in the papers wearing a white fedora with his overcoat draped around his shoulders like good ole Uncle Al.

"He wants the kind of publicity that only comes when important people fill the box

309

seats. How'm I supposed to get the hoity-toities in the door? The Richie Riches can go to the frickin' opera, the ballet, a bullfight if they want. Jeezum Crispum, Kane, what'm I gonna do?"

Apparently Suits was out there as well, because he chimed in, "The Frozen in Ice gimmick always brings 'em in."

"No," Pops answered emphatically. "Not after last time."

"Come on, Pops," Kane said. "Don't be so hard on yourself. Minnie was nowhere near dead when we chipped her out."

"Well, she sure looked it. Hasn't eaten ice cream since. No, I won't do that to any of my kids."

Pops cursed under his breath for a while before continuing. "Those jamokes think I can pull crowds out of my ass. I have to come up with a showstopper. A guaranteed hit. Or my unhappy investors will . . . Shit, I don't know what they'll do."

"Pops," Kane asked warily. "What kind of return did you promise them?"

"Christ, you don't want to know. More than I can deliver in this lifetime. They think I crossed them. That I'm skimming. These are people who do not like being crossed," he said in dramatic understatement. "They have made that very clear."

310

"Are those goons threatening you again?" Kane asked in a growl.

"It's getting worse," Pops lamented. "They tell me that Capone isn't happy. Fudgin' Al Capone." He spit the name out like a piece of rotten meat. "The Feds've got him locked up in Atlanta and he can still rattle cages in Chicago. And the cage he is currently rattling just happens to be mine. Cripes, if his boys thought it'd make Capone happy, they'd send him my head in a box."

Suits piped in brightly, "I heard some outfit on the South Side did exactly that thing. Club operator who was skimming. Salvy's boys decapitated him. Had to dry the head out first 'cause it was bleeding through all the, you know, wrapping."

"Suits," Kane said, "you wanna can the decapitation chatter? So, Pops, what you gonna do?"

There was an intensity to the men's discussion that reminded me of the intensity in an operating room when the docs had to make life-and-death decisions within a matter of seconds. I tensed up just as I would have back then, ready to respond to whatever orders were given to save a patient's life.

"Christ all Friday," Pops said. "I don't know. We kind of already shot our wad with

Evie and the ugly duckling stuff."

"There's always the Grinds," Suits suggested. "Zombie treadmills, circle hotshots, dynamite sprints, bombshells, horse races."

"Yeah," Kane agreed. "We can cut out all the breaks and do timed eliminations. Make everyone run all out until they drop. Maybe blindfolded. Lot of sweat. Big pileups on the curves. Kids dropping from exhaustion. That kind of heat usually pulls in the crowds."

"Open those cauliflower ears of yours," Pops said. "What am I telling you here? This ain't usual. Making all the kids duck waddle or dance backward or stand on their frigging heads. Even freezing someone alive — none of the usual crapola is gonna cut it with these bloodsuckers. Salvy ain't gonna be happy with a nice little boost in attendance. A few more bucks. Naw, he needs a gusher of dough. Or his picture in the papers so he'll look good to Uncle Al, or it is over. Maybe I should just vanish."

"And put us all out on the streets?" Suits whimpered. "Pops, this is Chicago. I can't make it out there."

I thought of all my patients turned out into the night. The vision chilled me.

Pops must have been having the same vision, because he swore, "No, goddammit.

No. They can kill me first, but I will never leave my kids in the lurch like that."

In Pops's voice, I heard the same melodramatic quaver that Mamie had always used when she was trying to manipulate me into doing what she needed me to do. The thought that this whole scenario was being played out for my benefit occurred to me, but I couldn't figure out why.

"So?" Kane asked. "What's your plan?"

Pops snorted a dry, mirthless laugh. "You tell me, Kane, 'cause I am flat out of ideas."

"Well," Kane said. "There really is only one surefire, never-fail, crowd-pleaser showstopper."

I tensed waiting to hear what this showstopper might be.

But Pops immediately vetoed it. "No dice, it'd be too expensive."

"Not as expensive as a funeral," Kane snapped back.

"Least not a good one," Suits added.

"Funny," Pops said. "You pair of jokers pick now to be funny for the first time in your lives."

Kane said, "They'd never go along with it anyway."

"At least, she wouldn't," Suits said.

I had a strong suspicion that "she" was me.

"Forget the showstopper," Pops ruled. "We gotta work with what we have. Kane, you still know that photographer at the paper?"

"Skeezix?"

"Yeah. Rattle his chain. Get him in here tonight."

"He already said he wouldn't come unless we had something new for him."

"Tell him we got a bit so new it hasn't even opened its eyes yet."

My skin prickled at this revelation, because I had the sneaking suspicion that Pop's latest brainstorm involved me.

CHAPTER 40

I was too busy that day helping my patients deal with the aftereffects of a Hungarian goulash that hadn't been entirely fresh to give any further thought to the promoter's troubles or wonder what this "showstopper" Kane had referred to was. Or how it involved me.

A few minutes before my shift was up, in the middle of a dance period, Zave appeared.

"Are you sick?" I asked. "Need some Pepto-Bismol?"

"No, I'm fine," he said, glancing around nervously. "Didn't touch that stew, but I played like I had so I could warn you."

"About what? The new scenario Pops is cooking up?"

"How do you know about it? Did Pops tell you?"

"Not exactly. What's the bit?" I asked, surprised by how genuinely interested I was.

315

"What's Pops cast me as now?" I was enjoying the feeling of being in the know.

"I'm glad you're not taking this seriously, because Pops now thinks the whole triangle deal would work better as a comedy bit. Here's how it's supposed to play. Cleo's going to leave me again for the nephew. So I'll be solo. Then I'm supposed to decide that the sweet Catholic schoolgirl is actually the one for me."

"I'm not Catholic. Or sweet."

Zave snorted a laugh at those irrelevant details. "So, once again, you come to my rescue. We dance and . . ." He dropped his gaze and studied his shoes.

"And?" I prompted after a long moment of silence.

Zave heaved a sigh. "And Pops thinks it'd be hilarious to let you stumble around while Alonzo makes wisecracks about you having two left feet."

"And then what?" I demanded sharply.

"And then the idea is, you're so humiliated, you leave. Hopefully, according to Pops's plan, in tears. One way or another, I'm solo again. This time, right before I'm eliminated, it's Cleo who comes to my rescue. The nephew, who's in on the fix, flies into a jealous rage, jumps out of his box seat, and comes down to beat my ass.

After that, who knows? All the nephew cares about is getting his picture in the papers. And all Pops cares about is making the nephew happy."

"So the big showstopper is making a fool of me and getting me to quit?"

"Pretty much."

Suddenly I felt like an intruder in the little infirmary I'd once thought of as mine, and I wondered how many more times in my life I'd be tossed out of a place where I believed I had belonged.

"Evie, don't take it to heart," Zave said. "Pops is desperate. Hell, we're all desperate. But I can promise you one thing: I will never be desperate enough to do anything that might hurt Denny Devlin's girl. You can bet your life on that, Evie. I will never hurt you."

He paused to let that sink in, then continued in a rush, "Anyway, I had to tell you. I hope you don't quit, but I wouldn't blame you if you did. I mean, I know that you really are a dancer and I know why you don't want to dance in front of an audience."

"You know? About . . . ?" My voice trailed off.

"Detroit? Yeah, there aren't many secrets on the circuit. When I heard what Mamie made you — a child, Denny's child, for

317

God's sake — do, I was furious. Wanted to come down there and give her a piece of my mind."

"Wait," I interrupted. "You know Mamie? I thought you said you didn't know her."

Zave looked away. "Let's just say that your mother isn't exactly my favorite topic of discussion. As for what happened in Detroit," he continued, anger tightening his words, "I know why you feel the way you do about dancing. About calling attention to yourself. But believe me, Evie, you have no need to feel a speck of shame about that. Mamie's the one who should be ashamed. She should have gone to jail."

Until Zave spoke those words, I hadn't realized how much I had needed to hear them. To hear someone who knew the whole story simply say that what Mamie did had been wrong. That none of it had been my fault.

Seeing how overwhelmed I was, Zave clasped me to his chest in a brotherly hug. "Families, Evie, the shit they try to make us believe about ourselves. It takes us a lifetime to stop believing it. Whatever Mamie told you about yourself, about Denny, none of it was true. Here's what is true: Denny Devlin loved you more than life itself and he would have been so proud of you. And, if he could

318

have, he would have saved you."

A place within me that I hadn't even known existed melted and came to life with a strange liquid warmth.

Kane's whistle tweeted sharply.

"Kane swore he'd eliminate me if wasn't back on the floor in three minutes."

I shooed him away. "Go. Go. Go."

Already pushing the canvas flaps open, Zave said, "Evie, you play this one however you want, I'll back you up. I just thought you ought to know. But, a long time ago, your father told me something important about fighting. He told me —"

The loudest, longest, shrillest tweet ever forced out of a whistle interrupted Zave.

"To be continued," he promised, and left.

My father had also told me something about fighting. Probably the same thing. I tried to remember what it was.

CHAPTER 41

A few minutes later, Pops hustled in wearing a woebegone expression that Mamie would have envied and plopped himself down on my examining stool with a gusty sigh. Grateful for Zave's warning, I sat down on the empty cot close to him.

"Listen, Evie, I need to tell you something." He paused and glanced around, pretending to check for spies under the cots just to let me know what a big secret he was about to let me in on. "But, Evie, this is top secret. Hush-hush. You have to keep this under your hat. Can you do that, Evie?"

"I sure can, Pops," I answered with all the wide-eyed earnestness I could muster.

"Evie," he started, using my name for the fourth time. PS: If you want to know if you're about to get chiseled, just count the number of times the chiseler uses your name.

"Yes, Pops," I prompted, leaning forward

and mirroring his hushed urgency.

"Evie, even though you haven't been part of my marathon family for long I've really come to trust you. To depend on you. You've got a real marathoner's heart. You always put what's best for the show, for the kids, first."

Another chiseler trick: tell the mark what you want them to do.

"I've tried to, Pops," I simpered.

"I know you have. I wish all my kids were like you. Especially Cleo," he gasped with a frustrated sigh.

"Oh, Pops, I can see that you're upset. Pops, tell me what's going on, Pops."

He leaned forward, lowered his voice, and confided, "Cleo just told me she's leaving the show."

"No, Pops," I gasped, pretending to believe his lie.

"Yes. Look, Evie, I hate to do this. I know you hate dancing, but Zave is gonna be solo and there are no solo girls. And if Zave gets eliminated . . ."

He winced at the prospect of such a catastrophe.

I patted his clenched hands and, though I was still puzzled about how any of these theatrics added up to a "showstopper," I finished for him. "No Zave, no show. No show, no dough. And everyone is out on the street. Oh, Pops, we can't let that happen. How can I help you?"

Pops beamed with relief. "Evie, you are aces. I knew I could count on an old trouper like you." Switching gears as seamlessly as a projectionist changing reels, he stiffened the tremulous tone in his voice and was, once again, the self-assured promoter.

"So, we've got a photographer on the hook. I told Cleo that, as soon as he shows up, she can run off with the nephew or whoever the hell else she wants to. That's where you come to the rescue."

"As a dancer?" I asked, all wide-eyed innocence.

"Well, we've all seen how you 'dance,' " he said with a patronizing chuckle.

I joined in.

"Don't worry about it. Zave will make you look good. The important thing is that Zave stays in the show. You'll be his new partner."

"But everyone knows I want to be a nurse."

"Don't worry, we'll finesse that. I've already given Alonzo the whole storyline. How Zave's found true love with a simple girl like you right out of Catholic school."

"Oh, gosh, Pops," I twittered, "I just don't know."

"I'm not supposed to say anything, Zave'll kill me, but . . ." Once again playing my confiding friend, Pops leaned forward. "But this switch was his idea. Zave wants you, Evie. As his partner."

Acting like the lovesick nitwit he clearly believed me to be, I stammered, "I guess I'd better leave now to get cleaned up. Put on something nice."

"No, no," Pops objected. "You're perfect the way you were."

The "way I was" was sallow and bedraggled in a rumpled uniform blotched with a disgusting rainbow of stains. I was perfect. The perfect butt of the callous joke he'd planned.

Pops clapped his hand like the deal was closed and jumped to his feet. Suddenly all business, he told me, "Okay, listen, Evie, I'm gonna tell you how this will play out."

I stood, looked him in the eye, and said, "Actually, Pops, I'm going to tell *you* how this will play out. I am going back to my room now to prepare. I'll be on the floor at nine sharp. Set up the split with Cleo before then and Zave and I will dance a special at the break."

Pops snorted a laugh. "Oh, sister, what are you high on? 'Cause it is some good stuff. No, I need you in the uniform."

323

"Fine," I said agreeably. "Then get yourself another girl because I'm not going out there like this."

Alarmed, he grabbed me. "Wait, wait, wait. Look, we have the whole Angel of Mercy scenario worked out."

"Great, hope you can find someone to play it."

Pops was rattled. "Come on, be a pal. This is just business. I mean, Zave and you in the nurse getup dancing together are good for . . ."

He stopped himself, but I filled in, "What? A laugh? Is that what you're saying?"

"Jeez mineez, kid, don't blow a gasket. I'm only asking if you think you can pull it off without the nurse gimmick?"

"Be here at nine," I snapped, gathering up my things. "And find out."

CHAPTER 42

"Cripes, is that you, Gravy?" Suits asked four hours later when he stuck his head into the infirmary a few minutes before nine. "You look . . ." He squinched his face. ". . . different."

Determined that if I was going to be eliminated, at least I'd go out looking good, I'd sorted through Mamie's clothes, and chosen the slinkiest item I'd found, a midnight-blue satin gown. Using cosmetics I'd picked up at Kresge's five-and-dime, I'd gone all out, copying most of Mamie's routine except for beading my eyelashes. Mascara, rouge, the works. Then I'd used pomade to slick my hair into a fashionable style with a deep side part and finger curls fluffing around my face.

Suits's reaction unsettled me. Back in my room, I'd liked the way the satin dress had slid over the new curves I'd developed since partaking of the marathon's three very solid

325

meals a day. Suddenly, though, I felt exposed and the makeup sat heavy and false on my face, reminding me of the girls backstage at the National in Detroit. I wanted to cover up. To hide.

"We gotta go," Suits said. "Pops told me to keep you under wraps till it's time for you to go on, and it's time." When I didn't move, he said, "Now."

"I'm having second thoughts," I confessed.

"Yeah? Well, have them on your own dime. Show must go on." I hesitated. Suits clapped his hands and barked, "Chop-chop."

I followed him to a spot beneath the box seats where I was hidden but had a sliver of a view of the floor. The shriek of the siren signaling the nine o'clock break startled me.

Suits ordered, "Don't get on the floor till Alonzo cues you."

"Folks," Alonzo said as the weary contestants headed off the floor toward the rest quarters, "I know you all have been following the tempestuous triangle between our very own multitalented trouper Cleo and the Handsome Hoofer, Zave —"

Female shrieks interrupted Alonzo.

"And the show's sweet little nurse who came to us straight from a Catholic nursing

326

school, where she'd planned on becoming a nun."

Despite their weariness, all the pros, sensing that the show was about to take a turn, halted long enough to learn the new plot twist.

"And you know, folks, that Nurse Gravy has refused all requests to appear since her last, uh, *performance* . . ."

He paused for the snickers he had invited.

"Well, that's about to change tonight. As you know, Cleo's heart has been stolen by Al Capone's trusted adviser and beloved nephew, Mr. Salvatore Capone. What you don't know is that only a few minutes ago, Cleo told Pops that she can no longer bear being parted from her beloved Salvy."

I craned my neck enough to catch a glimpse of Salvy in his box seat, where he had Cleo tucked under his arm. Salvy jutted his jaw out and preened at the tributes to his irresistibility. Even as he posed, Salvy kept checking the sidelines, where a photographer with a big Graflex camera and a press card tucked into his hatband was paying a lot more attention to his flask than to the new drama Pops had cooked up.

"Cleo," Alonzo instructed, "show them the little love token that's making you consider abandoning the show. Put on your sunglasses for these sparklers, folks."

Cleo held up her hand, mostly to the photographer, and displayed a glittering diamond bracelet. *Ooooh*s and *aaah*s swept through the stadium.

"But, folks, here's the catch."

While Alonzo paused to build suspense, I braced myself for whatever new angle Pops had cooked up. It was like reading a mystery novel with a plot twist on every other page. Except that I was the not-entirely-clueless heroine.

Alonzo went on, "Before Cleo leaves Zave in the lurch, she needs proof that Nurse Gravy can fill her dancing shoes. So, one time only, doing whatever dance Cleo and Mr. Capone request, I give you, the nurse who thinks she can dance!"

In the middle of the floor, Zave waited for me. I froze and couldn't step out of the shadows.

Zave came and took my hand. His eyes never leaving mine, he led me forward. I followed him to the brightly lit center of the floor where, both our arms extended now, he guided me in a slow orbit around him.

As I pirouetted in the full light, my gown became a ribbon of night shimmering with star sparkle. It swished around my ankles like a swirl of smoke. I stepped out of the shadows. The audience, expecting comic relief, was stunned into silence. Under Zave's approving gaze, I was engulfed by an entirely novel sensation: I felt beautiful.

More than that, I felt ready, eager even, to dance any style Cleo and Salvy chose, and we waited for Alonzo to announce the dance that Cleo and Salvy would request. I glanced at the box seat and found Cleo staring at me with that same unsettling mixture of jealousy and pity. She shook her head mournfully as if regretting what she had to do, then whispered in the nephew's ear. He laughed, scribbled on a scrap of paper, handed it to one of his underlings, and the junior thug raced up to the stage with Capone's request.

"That dress," Zave marveled. "I hope Capone asks for a waltz, maybe a foxtrot, something as elegant as that dress."

"With our own Cleo's guidance," Alonzo said, unfolding the paper, "the dance Mr. Capone has requested is . . ." Alonzo handed the scrap of paper to the bandleader.

Zave squeezed my hand. I basked in the certainty that he was really, truly on my side and prepared to dance, really dance. I would dance well enough to show Pops and all the rest of them. Well enough to make my father proud of his daughter.

Before Alonzo could name the song that Cleo and Salvy had selected, the band started booming out the *oompah* blats of the least glamorous, most clodhopperish tune of them all: "Beer Barrel Polka."

A flashbulb exploded and hyena shrieks of laughter erupted. My humiliation had been captured and punctuated. In the box seat, Capone and Cleo cackled away at their fine joke.

They'd all duped me. Betrayed me. Even Zave.

I tried to leave, but Zave wouldn't release my hand. Instead, he dragged me over to the stage, handed Mel a hundred-dollar bill, and called up to him, "Give me 'Ain't She Sweet.' Up tempo. Heavy on the downbeat."

As Zave, refusing to let me flee, walked me back to the center of the floor, I became aware of a pounding. Of sound waves buffeting my body. The crowd was stamping their feet on the bleachers, bellowing, "Nurse Gravy!! Nurse Gravy!! Save Zave!!"

"Zave, I don't want to do this. I can't do this."

Without turning the wattage down on his grin, he calmly told me, "You can, Evie. This isn't Detroit. You can trust me. Let's dance one for Denny."

330

The band played.

Zave pivoted to face me, held his hand out, and time slowed. Like cards that had been endlessly shuffled, every moment of my past was tapped into place, one second stacked on top of the next, until they all finally added up to this neat, new deck, waiting to be dealt.

A new game was about to start.

A flashbulb exploded, freezing the moment when I remembered what it was that my father had always said about fighting. "If you're going to fight, fight to win."

I took Zave's hand. He swung me into his arms and we constructed a dance frame that a hurricane couldn't have blown over. I lifted my head, smiled into the spotlight like a daisy drinking up sunshine, and we danced one for Denny.

CHAPTER 43

The next morning our photos — mine and Zave's — appeared on the front of the Town Topics section of the early edition of the *Chicago Daily News,* and they were even larger than the ones of Capone and Cleo. The headline read, "GOOD NIGHT, NURSE! Call An Ambulance. Angel Of Mercy Steals Capone Paramour Partner!"

I had still been unsure last night, when the Melody Makers started hammering out a zippy four-four tempo with a downbeat so heavy a deaf man could have hit it. But Zave had swung me out so that we were face-to-face and then had beamed such confidence and approval at me that I could have been with the one other person who'd ever bathed me with such adoration. My father.

Zave tapped his foot back. I tapped forward. It was 23 skiddoo and the bees' knees all over again. It was a joke version of the '20s that none of us had roared through and it made me and everyone else in the stadium feel the way that Galveston had made me feel: like we'd all finally gotten *our* invitations to the party.

In one instant all the frozen years melted away and I fell into time with Zave. My steps got looser and jazzier. I mirrored him just the way I had once mirrored my father. It had always been the best game I could imagine and I was playing it again.

As we fell further and further into sync, Zave yelled out to the crowd, "Ain't Gravy sweet? Just a-walkin' down the street. Now I ask you very confidentially: Ain't Gravy sweet?"

The fans screamed back, "Yay, Gravy!!"

I caught a glimpse of Pops, his face slack with amazement. I had surprised him, and Pops Wyatt wasn't a man who surprised easy. Happiness bubbled through me and came out as laughter. The audience joined in. They were delighted. The gawky beanpole in the stained nurse's uniform had been an act. A wonderful joke. And they had fallen for it.

"Folks," Alonzo said, "I am as surprised as you are. But it appears we've got ourselves an Angel of Mercy who can cut a rug. And how!"

With an enormous grin, Zave gathered me

333

into close dance position. Our bodies pressed together, we tilted forward then back in perfect synchronicity.

Hydraulically smooth, Zave's legs were a blur of effortless motion as we rocked forward and back smooth as a pendulum. I was so focused on Zave that, until he led me into a move that had us both leaning forward to pat the floor, I didn't notice that a veritable carpet of coins sparkled there, and more were raining down.

"It's a silver shower!" Alonzo declared. "No, wait, it's a silver thunderstorm!"

Suits came out with a push broom and made a show of sweeping up the glittering compliments the audience was showering us with.

"Friends, what do you think? Can our very own Florence Nightingale dance or what?"

The man in the lighting booth knew his stuff and raked the crowd with a spotlight. To my astonishment, people all over the stadium were on their feet, whooping and hollering.

Though not in the way Pops had intended, we had, indeed, stopped the show.

The photo that made it onto the front page of the Town Topics section captured Zave and me taking our bows and the entire stadium on its feet. The next one showed me and Cleo shaking hands. The caption read, "A truce is declared."

The deal we made was that Cleo and Zave would continue as a couple. Kane, however, added one proviso to punish Cleo: heretofore, Nurse Devlin and Zave would dance all the special audience requests.

Everyone was happy except for Salvy. And Salvy, his outsized pride wounded that instead of being the irresistible lover he had ended up the butt of the joke, was very, *very* unhappy.

CHAPTER 44

The drama accelerated rapidly after that. Especially when the Associated Press put the story on the wire and Pops found out that papers across the country were picking it up.

From then on, Pops had Zave and me dancing as many requests during the breaks as Zave, already exhausted, could stand. We never equaled our first performance simply because Zave was so worn out. But the quality of our performances was no longer the point. All we had to do was play at being a couple while Cleo fumed theatrically.

And, gads, did the crowds ever eat it up. The day after my photo appeared in the Chicago paper, a group of teen girls dressed in white blouse and skirt combos showed up. They reminded me of the suffragettes who'd protested and campaigned and marched and been jailed and finally won the right for women to vote a dozen years before. The difference was, these girls had a hankie or a napkin pinned to the tops of their heads to resemble nurses' caps and held up signs announcing that they were "Zave's Zaviors." Those girls and a dozen other clumps of "Zaviors" shrieked their heads off when Zave and I danced at the break.

"Look at that," Zave said, beaming and waving at the girls, who screamed even louder at any attention he gave them. "You've got a cheering section."

"Zave," I corrected him. "That is not *my* cheering section. They are, clearly, your fans."

"Want to bet on that?"

"Sure."

"I've got a dime that says they'll go even crazier if you wave to them."

"You're as nutty as they are. I'll take that action."

"Okay, but you got to sell it."

"And you have to lower your head so they won't just be clapping for you." As he buried his face in my shoulder, I raised my arm, switched on the highest-wattage smile I could manage, and waved my hand like I was drowning.

The applause stunned me. Of course, it rose to a deafening level when Zave lifted his handsome head.

"You owe me a dime," he said. "They love you."

"Sure they do," I joked.

"Well, they love us."

"Or they're all certifiable lunatics."

But the numbers of the coo-coo birds grew. More and more white-clad Zaviors, waving signs and cheering my brief appearances, showed up. I did my best to ignore the bizarre hubbub, since it had almost nothing to do with me and everything to do with Zave, and concentrated instead on dancing. It paid off. Every time we soloed during a break, a little bit more of the rust got knocked off of my dance instincts. Luckily, Zave was a complete pro and knew how to make his partner look good. Pretty soon, though, he didn't have to cover for me and I could follow him better than his own shadow.

Much as I came to love our moments together, I wished that Pops would stop making Zave dance through so many of his precious breaks, since the lack of rest was taking a heavy toll. By the fourth day, Zave was staggering so badly that I had to take over the lead and support him. It was during one of those moments when Zave depended on me and I took care of him that a dangerous thought first crept into my head: maybe Pops's fake romance might not be one hundred percent, entirely make-believe.

This delusion gained strength because, when we weren't doing requests or specialties during the breaks, Zave took to visiting me in the infirmary. Everyone, especially Alonzo in his daily radio broadcasts and Pops in his *Daily Dance News* newsletter, made innuendoes about the "private procedures Nurse Devlin was performing on the Handsome Hoofer when they're alone in the infirmary."

Though it would have made pretty poor copy, mostly what Zave did during the times when we weren't on the floor was sleep. In the few minutes before he passed out, though, we found out how much we had in common.

I learned that he'd had a childhood as lonely and as tough as mine. His father owned a dairy farm in a little town on the Upper Peninsula of Michigan. He and his six siblings were expected to carry their weight from the moment they were old enough to tug on a teat or muck out a barn. Like everyone else they knew, the family were staunch Lutherans.

"Yeah, Jesus and cheeses," Zave joked with a hollow laugh. "That's all they thought life was about. And there I was singing 'Shine On Harvest Moon' to an audience of Guernseys and trying to tap-dance on a milk pail."

I didn't learn much more, certainly not about what interested me the most, my father. Though his face always lit up when I mentioned him, and Zave would tell me what a great guy, "the greatest," he was, he seemed almost evasive when I pressed him for details. Especially about how they'd met. I was starting to suspect that it pained Zave to recall my father as much as it did Jake and I shouldn't press for information.

It was after one of these snooze sessions, just as a trainer was dragging Zave to his feet, that Pops entered and we both watched the trainer sleepwalk Zave back to the floor.

"Good-looking guy, huh?" Pops commented.

"Do you need something?" I asked sharply.

"Yeah, these came for you." He reached into his jacket pocket and pulled out a dozen or so letters.

My heart leapt: Sofie had finally answered. I grabbed for the letters. Pops bumped me away with a solid hip check.

"Hey, those are mine," I protested. "It's a felony to interfere with the U.S. mail."

"Yeah, but see?" He waved an envelope at me. "They're in care of me. Pops Wyatt." He fanned through the stack. "Let's see, we've got Peoria. Duluth. San Diego. Holy mackerel, the West Coast."

"What are you talking about?"

"Your fan mail, sport. It's nothing compared to the boxes of cards and letters that Zave gets, still it looks like that AP story must have been picked up all across the country." He ripped open an envelope and started to read. 'Dear Evie, My name is *blah-blah-blah*. You have shown all the girls like me that we can be career gals and still catch the eye of a real dreamboat like Zave. I never thought that an ordinary girl like me, you know, nothing special, could do either of those things.' "

While I was reeling from the idea of a stranger, even one who thought I was nothing special, would write me, Pops tore into another.

"Let's see what Mobile, Alabama, has to say." He scanned the letter, only stopping to read: " 'I love you both and am not even jealous because you give me hope that if you can get a guy like Zave anyone can. I figured I'd leave school when I finished eighth grade, but you have inspired me to be a nurse like you.' "

Pops blinked a few times then said, "Who'da thunk it? Gravy, you're an inspiration."

"Hand 'em over," I said, desperate to find out if Sofie had written.

He was passing the stack over when a return address caught his eye and, letting me snatch the others away, he jerked that one letter back and asked, "Galveston? Who do you know in Galveston?"

Sofie. She *had* written.

"Give me that."

He twisted from my grasp and read aloud, "Sofia *Amadeo*? You know the Amadeos?" he asked incredulously.

"What's it to you?"

"No, seriously, Evie, tell me. Do you know the Amadeos?"

"Could I have my letter, please?"

"Not until you answer my question."

"Why do you care?"

"Why do I care? Because I am trying to get us all out of Chicago alive. Because I have been bustin' my balls trying to set up a show in Galveston for forever. Because it's the one town in America that dodged the Depression. Because it's the only virgin town in the country worth going after."

"Virgin?"

"You know, hasn't been burned by a lousy

promoter who skips out on a bunch of bad paper. Doesn't pay off the prize money."

"You mean like you did in Houston?" I said, ripping my letter out of his hand.

"Jeez, you're a pain in the ass, Devlin. Houston was an emergency situation, okay? Would you rather we were all sitting in the can right now? Galveston, though, if I could put on a show in Galveston it would be pure class all the way. No corners cut."

Sofie's letter was burning a hole in my hand. "Well, good luck. See yourself out," I said, motioning toward the curtain and already opening the envelope.

"Evie, listen, you don't understand. The situation here is . . ." His gaze darted around. This time he didn't have to act nervous or pretend that he was confiding in me. This time when he leaned in to whisper in my ear, his fear was so real I could smell its acrid odor on him.

I leaned away. "Pops, if you want to set up a show in Galveston, set up a show in Galveston. You don't need me."

The promoter snorted a derisive laugh. "Oh, you sweet little innocent babe, if you actually knew as much about the way the real world works as you think you do, you'd crap your panties. Never mind. If you really had any connections there, you'd know that

343

Galveston is a closed town."

I bit my tongue. I was not going to tell him that I'd made a three-year study of the way the "real world" worked in Galveston, Texas.

In a low voice, Pops lectured me, "Not even the mob can get into Galveston. And believe me, everyone from Al Capone to Lucky Luciano has tried to carve out a piece of that juicy action. And they have all failed. No one gets in 'cause those son-of-a-bitching Amadeos have got that city sewed up tighter'n a nun's hooha. Shit, they even have the Texas Rangers in their pocket. So sure, waltz in, set up a show," he said in a mocking tone. "Great idea. For someone who's tired of living."

"Sorry, I can't help you."

"Naw, it ain't you, kid. It was never gonna happen anyway. Far as I know, there isn't even a hall in the whole city big enough to stage a show you can make any real dough on. Forget it. Go on. Read your letter."

A hall. Big enough to stage a show.

I didn't say another word.

Not about the Amadeos.

And not about the family's enormous white elephant.

The Starlight Palace.

CHAPTER 45

I tucked Sofie's letter into my bra, where it stayed nestled next to my heart until I could read it in the privacy of my room that night.

The instant I was alone, my hands trembling, I opened the envelope. The sight of Sofie's handwriting — the gentle forward slope of her letters, the careful precision of the cursive the nuns in grade school had taught her — overwhelmed me with a surge of homesick longing for all I'd had. All I could have had. All I'd lost.

A clipping from the Galveston paper fell out. There I was above the headline "Local Girl Saves Show."

Dear Evie,
    You're famous! Criminy, Devlin, I'm so happy you're not dead that I'm *almost* not mad you haven't written. Or called. Or sent a wire. Or anything.

345

My hands dropped to my lap. Sofie hadn't cut me off after all; she'd never gotten my letters.

I'm sending this to the arena in Chicago that the article mentioned. Sure hope you're still there. Sure hope you'll do a pal a favor and pick up a pen and write sometime.

Don't worry, considering the whirlwind you've been in, I'm really not *that* mad. Okay, I'm a *little* mad.

Oh well. Let me fill you in on my news. Evie, I LOVE my job. I'm working at the Galveston Sanatorium. That's right, the booby hatch. But it's not what you think it is. Or what I thought it was. The advances being made today in psychiatric science are astonishing. Patients who have been locked inside the prison of their own minds for years, decades, are starting to be released with some of the new treatments that are just now starting to be put into wide practice.

Oh no, look at me rambling on already. Gads, I can't help myself. The only thing the girls I work with want to talk about is whether Clark Gable or Errol Flynn is "dreamier." I miss having someone to talk with who isn't mostly interested in medicine for the "cute" interns. Shoot, Devlin, I miss *YOU!* Maybe if you'd write a pal every now and then, I wouldn't have to blurt it all out at once. But since you haven't, here it comes.

Do you remember the doc who gave a lecture during our psych rotation? Dr. Kaufman? He talked about all the latest research from Germany? Well, he is the director of my unit and he wants to bring the treatment of the mentally ill out of the Dark Ages. He even knows about this new procedure that he says is as simple as getting a wisdom tooth removed that can instantly cure mental diseases from schizophrenia to catatonia. Can you believe that?

Oh, Evie, I really wish you were here. It's so exciting to be part of this new movement. Dr. K is going to study with the leading expert on the procedure in this country, Dr. Walter Freeman, who's head of the Neuropsychiatry Department at George Washington University and has successfully performed hundreds of these simple surgeries. And, Evie, guess what? Dr. K has already asked me if I'd be interested in being part of his surgical nursing team.

Evie, it's what we always dreamed of doing. Helping — really, truly, helping. The

347

days of dunking maniacs in barrels of ice water then leaving them to freeze on a stone floor in Bedlam to calm them down are over. We can finally cure these terrible diseases.

Needless to say, my parents are horrified. They tried to bribe me with the offer of a new car — a Cadillac, no less — into not taking the job. They actually believe that, somehow, they can stuff me back into my old room where my old Flossie Flirt doll is still sitting on my bed and I'll forget all about nursing. Or having any kind of a life that they don't dictate and control.

So I moved out. Not to the boardinghouse where we were going to rent rooms, but to my own apartment. They blew another gasket about that, so I stopped even going home for Sunday dinner and only communicated with them through Uncle JuJu.

Gosh, I love JuJu. He says we're the family "black sheep." He's not, but it's great to have him on my side. Truth to tell, he owns the building I live in and he gave me a special "niece discount" on the rent so that I could afford it on my salary. Not to drop *too many* hints, but it does have two bedrooms and one of them is sitting empty.

348

Anyway, to my amazement, my parents missed me just a little bit more than I missed them, and they've actually accepted that I am a nurse and I have my own life. It doesn't hurt that they really like this fourth-year med student, Danny Reid, that I've brought home a couple of times. Don't jump to any conclusions. I'm not one of those girls we talked about who were always more interested in getting their MRS. instead of an RN. It's not serious with Danny and me. Or well, not *too* serious.

Evie, I hate the way we said good-bye. I had so many questions about why you left that I went searching for Sister T and found her crying her eyes out. She told me the whole story about the clippings and Detroit.

Which we do not give two figs about.

I stopped and reread those sentences several times until I actually believed in her blithe dismissal.

I'm not even mad that you never told me the whole story about Detroit, because, as you know, there sure are things about my family that I never mentioned to you.

Anyhow, Sister T and I went straight to

349

the Director. I wish you'd been there when that little dynamo lambasted her for blaming *you* for being used by your mother. She really gave that witch what for.

Oops, I just checked the time. Gotta scoot. I'm working double shifts because we're short-staffed. Even with the job market the way it is, we still have a hard time hiring nurses. People's thinking about mental illness is in the Dark Ages.

Oh gosh, Evie, I sure wish you were here. I miss hashing everything out with you. In general, I just miss you. Like CRAZY. I pray that this letter reaches you at the show. I didn't know where else to send it.

Your Pal 4Ever, Sofie

P.S. Come home. STAT. That's an order. Seriously, Evie, come home. I miss you. I really, REALLY miss you.

CHAPTER 46

Though I stayed up late that night writing Sofie the fattest, juiciest letter I could fit in an envelope and send to the right address, I woke the next morning long before the sun rose filled with new energy, new hope, and rushed to the arena. It would be an agonizing wait until I heard from my best friend again, but I had decided to make good use of it: I would corner Zave and make him tell me about my father.

As I expected, the place was dead. Dim economy lights cast a murky glow over the floor. The far reaches of the stadium, where sleepers and those enjoying other horizontal activities were tucked away, were completely dark. All the dancers seemed to be either unconscious or operating on automatic pilot and they barely noticed as I edged onto the floor.

Zave, reading one of his neatly folded newspapers while he managed a thrashing, snoring Cleo, offered the only spark of life. "Gravy," he greeted me with a surprising heartiness. "What a nice surprise. What are you doing here? Your shift doesn't start for a couple more hours."

Suddenly shy, I faltered. "I thought maybe this might be a good time to finally talk about my father."

"Denny," he said, savoring the name. "Yes. Great idea. Here, you take these." He handed me his papers. "And I'll get Cleo settled down." Dodging a flying elbow, he arranged his partner into a more comfortable sleeping position and, her head resting on his broad shoulder, she stopped struggling. The one judge on duty, an overweight guy sprawled on a folding chair, twirled his finger to signal a warning to Zave to keep moving and I fell into step beside him.

"Okay, where should I start?"

"At the beginning," I said eagerly. "I want to know everything. Right from the start. Don't forget a single detail."

"I couldn't if I tried. Every second of that first night I set eyes on Denny Devlin is carved in my memory."

For a moment or two, Zave stared off into the distance. His obvious affection for my father was like rain on parched earth after a childhood of listening to Mamie disparage

352

him for "unforgivable betrayals" like dying.

"It was a miracle," Zave began. "No other way to describe it. There I was marooned in Elmer, Michigan, where, from my earliest memories, I was out of place. I just didn't belong. Especially not in my own family. You know?"

"Completely," I answered.

Shaking his head as if to get rid of the memory, he went on, "Anyway, it was the summer of 1913, right after I turned ten. Not that anyone in my family noticed.

"No matter," he hurried on, brightening again. "That was the day that the miracle happened. The F. Andrews Traveling Vaudeville Show, the World's Greatest Tented Amusement Enterprise, came to town."

"Yes," I gasped, recognizing that name. "That's what was printed on the one photo Mamie kept of my father. Actually, she only kept half of that photo, because she tore the other half off. The half that showed his partner."

"Yeah, the one where he's going . . . Here." He shifted Cleo onto my shoulder and, with both hands free, Zave held an invisible top hat up and reached his other hand out to an invisible partner.

My mouth gaped as I realized, "You were on the half that was torn away. You were his partner."

"I told you," Zave said, shrugging off my amazement. "We had an act there for a while."

For a moment, both of us saw the same photo in our minds and remembered the same man. This, I thought, this must be what it was like to have a sibling.

"Yep, it was a good act until Mamie cut me out. Literally. Good ol' Mame," he mused. "She must have been a bed of roses as a mother."

"You don't know the half of it."

"Mamie," he concluded with a doleful shake of his head. "She was a real doozie."

The feeling of having a sibling came over me even more strongly then as we both pondered the woman who had had such outsized power over our young lives.

"Hey, let's go back to the part before good ole Mame entered the picture," Zave suggested, to my wholehearted agreement.

"So," he said, his tone buoyant again, "the miracle happens and a show was actually coming to our godforsaken corner of the world. I memorized the handbills pasted on every lamppost in town. Jugglers, comics, a magician, but, most wondrous of all, dancers.

"Well, everyone in five counties was in an

uproar. Not even the circus had ever made it to our desolate patch of the Upper Peninsula and now a whole vaudeville show was coming.

"I squirreled away every penny I could. And finally, on the last day of the run, I scraped together enough for a ticket. When your father twirled onstage, Evie, there I was front and center. The tails of his black tuxedo flew out behind him. His spats, shirt, and smile were all blinding white in the spotlight. And when he danced . . ."

Zave stopped, lost in a memory that he knew meant as much to me as it did to him. He shook his head and went on.

"Evie, I tell you, in that instant I knew that I'd been right all along. There had been a terrible mistake and I had been born into the wrong place, the wrong family. But now, I was certain that there was a whole other world out there waiting for me.

"I don't remember drawing another breath for the rest of the show. Comics shooting seltzer into each other's pants, dogs with cone hats jumping through hoops, two ladies boxing. But the hit of the show was a dentist, Painless Parker this guy called himself, who numbed customers up with cocaine then pulled their rotten teeth out for fifty cents a pop. I barely noticed any of it.

"When the lights finally came up at the end of the show, I hid in the mildew-smelling canvas of the big tent. But a crew led by Mr. F. Andrews himself, the flintiest bastard who ever drew breath, came through beating the canvas with bats, chasing out anyone trying to stay on for the late show without paying.

"That set all the other freeloaders running. But when he conked me, I didn't let out a peep. I'd grown up getting beaten on by experts." He gave a mirthless chuckle, pretending that his father's cruelty was a joke.

"After the late show, I threw myself on your father's mercy. Told him I was an orphan. That the farmer who'd taken me in beat me. Luckily, my old man had broken my nose recently, and I still had the bruises all green and yellow around my eyes.

"Your dad," Zave whispered, the light of a happy memory again shining in his eyes. "He had the most wonderful Irish brogue. First words he ever said to me were, 'Aw Jay-sus, boyo, that's not right.' "

In that moment, as Zave spoke, I was with my father again. His voice, his smell, his kindness, everything that Mamie had tried to take from me, they all came back. I used every word Zave spoke like bricks to rebuild the palace of memories that Mamie had tried to tear down.

"He found me a ride on the tent-and-prop truck, told the driver I was the new roust-about, and just like that I was part of the F. Andrews Traveling Vaudeville Show. An hour later Elmer, Michigan, was a bad dream I'd finally woken up from.

"Pretty soon, Denny started bringing me up onstage. I was comic relief at first. Me in my overalls and clodhoppers. Him in the tux, top hat. But the better I got, the less funny that was. From the start audiences thought I was his son. We looked that much alike."

I glanced up at Zave and the face on that torn photo melded into his.

"Can I tell you something?" he asked.

"Of course."

"I tell everyone that my birthday is August nineteenth. But that's not the day I was born. That was the day that your father surprised me with a tuxedo he'd had made for me and a pair of proper dancing shoes, and asked if I wanted to be an official part his new act, The Dancing Devlins. A father-son act. That's what he called us. And then . . ."

Zave's voice trailed off into the saddest sigh I'd ever heard.

"And then what?" I prodded gently.

He shrugged. "And then Mamie. But even worse than her was what I did later. Or failed to do later. I wasn't there when he needed me. Didn't even visit when I heard he was sick. Didn't do a goddamn thing to help the man I owe my life to. That weighs on me, Evie. It weighs heavy."

"Oh, Zave," I tried to reassure him. "If Mamie didn't want you around, there wouldn't have been any way you could have seen him."

"There are always ways, Evie. I owed him so much." Brightening a bit, he added, "But you're here now. Do you believe in fate?"

"I believe that life deals some crappy hands and we have to do the best we can to play them."

"No, I mean, do you believe that there are reasons things happen, because I believe the reason you walked onto the floor back at Jake's and fixed my ankle was so that I could try to pay back a little of what I owe your father. I think Denny wants me to help his daughter to make up for not helping him."

"I don't . . . I'm not sure. I don't know what to say."

"You don't have to say anything. My job now is to help you the way your father helped me and I should have helped him. So your pin? That's what you want most in this world, isn't it?"

I nodded.

"Okay, who do I need to talk to to get it for you? Because, believe it or not, I can be very persuasive when I want to."

I smiled at the thought of Zave attempting to sweet-talk the steely Director.

"Go ahead, laugh," Zave said.

"I'm not laughing at you. You just don't know the Director. Nothing short of a bomb going off in the middle of Galveston is ever going to change her mind."

"So we have to make a bomb go off," Zave concluded. "Metaphorically speaking."

Seeing the doubt in my expression, Zave asked, "You want to be a nurse, right?"

"More than anything."

"Okay, then, be back here tomorrow and we'll figure out a game plan."

It was almost dawn when I left the auditorium. Though I'd had hardly any sleep and would have to be back on duty in a couple of hours, I almost started skipping. I was part of a "we." Me and Zave, "we" were going to figure out how to get my pin.

Whether Zave could really help me or not,

knowing that I had someone on my side, someone looking out for me, even someone who cared enough about me to tell me lies to raise my spirits, was exhilarating. The cool early-morning air outside the arena could have been helium, I was that light and springy.

When a slovenly fellow with a bottle in the pocket of his bagged-out suit veered toward me, smiling and winking, I realized that I was grinning like an idiot.

"Hey, honey, you lookin' for company?" he asked with a leer.

On any other day since Detroit that leer would have made something inside of me shrivel away in shame. Made me feel as if, somehow, I had invited such lechery. But not today.

"Not yours, buddy," I told him with grin. "Never yours."

"Can't say as I blame you," he said.

The sun rose. I strode briskly toward it.

CHAPTER 47

Early the next morning I was back, pacing the darkened floor beside Zave and a snoring Cleo. He asked me what I intended to do about getting my pin.

After I told him he questioned me. "So, your plan is to get some kind of steady job, and save up enough to go to Austin and present your case to this nursing board? Sounds bureaucratic. Sounds like a bunch of timid rule-followers who are looking for a reason to say no. And, as soon as this Director witch tells them you faked your school records, they've got their reason, right?"

"Right. Which leaves me exactly nowhere."

"Don't say that. Tell me, who pulls the Director's strings? Who does she answer to?"

"The Bishop? The Motherhouse? God? The Virgin Mary? I don't know."

"Come on, we all answer to someone."

"Yeah, someone with power," I put in

361

dourly. "Which counts me out."

As Zave started to refute my gloomy claim, two ghostly forms materialized beside us. The light was so dim and they were so quiet that until one of them started giggling, I didn't realize that they were a couple of teenage Zaviors.

The non-giggling one, a rawboned girl with a lantern jaw whose all-white outfit included work pants that made her resemble an intern, stepped forward and said solemnly, "Hello, Nurse Devlin, I'm Clarice Allred, and this is my friend."

"Alice," her friend chirped nervously.

"We don't want to disturb you —"

"Or Zave," Alice, who appeared on the verge of swooning, interjected.

Zave bestowed one of his patented heart-melter smiles complete with a wink that caused the giggler's knees to wobble. She reached out to her friend for support.

Clarice shoved her away and continued. "But, well," she stammered before thrusting a notebook with "Class Autographs" embossed on the cover. "Would you mind?" She uncapped a pen and held it out to me.

"You want me to . . ."

Clarice blushed, her brusque front crumbled, and she explained uncertainly, "Give me your autograph? 'To Clarice.' If it's not

362

too much trouble."

Alice shoved a book at Zave and babbled, "I'd love to have yours, Zave. We come to every show, but the guards won't ever let us get close. Then this friend of mine's uncle who's the night janitor here tipped her off about coming early."

Zave took her book and pen and, directing every molecule of his attention at the giddy girl, said, "Alice, darling, it would be my pleasure."

As I signed Clarice's book, she told me, "You're my inspiration. You're doing something important with your life. That's what I want. I want my life to mean something."

Touched by her raw honesty, I shared my truth. "That's all I've ever wanted. Clarice, listen to me, if I can do it, I'm certain that you can." It was a lie, since I hadn't actually done "it." The sparkle of hope that lit up Clarice's expression, however, was as real as gravity and made me think of how my life would have changed a lot sooner if I'd ever even glimpsed a woman who looked like me wearing a nurse's uniform.

As the girls left, Zave announced, "Gravy, your problem is solved. There, right there, is your power."

"What? The power to get girls to dress up like milkmen?"

"No, the power of publicity."

I gave him a Popeye squint of incredulity.

"I'm serious. You're Nurse Gravy, the Angel of Mercy. People know you from coast to coast. Wait until they hear about you in Galveston."

I didn't interrupt to tell him about the clipping that Sofie had sent.

"Local girl makes good. Hometown papers love that stuff. They'll probably run that AP story on the front page."

I was impressed that he'd called the Galveston paper's reaction so perfectly, and joked, "You got that all wrong. They ran it on the front page of the Entertainment section."

"See? That proves what I'm telling you. Publicity gives you power in this country. You just have to know how to use it right."

"Maybe in Chicago, but not down in Galveston. The well-bred girls at school liked to say that a lady only got her name in the paper three times: when she was born, when she was married, and when she died."

"They sound like a real barrel of monkeys. All I'm saying is that we can work this hometown hero angle. It's all about getting your story out before the other side does. Trust me, Gravy, that's the way the world works now. Those well-bred girls are living in the past."

Zave tapped his lips thoughtfully as we strolled. Halfway around the floor, he said, "Obviously, we have to figure out how to get your side of the story out in Galveston. That'll give us the leverage we need."

Though I adored being a "we" with Zave, he didn't know the Director, or her grudge against me.

"Don't look so worried," Zave said. "I promise you, I will fix this for Denny Devlin's daughter. Come here." He moved Cleo over to his left shoulder and held his right arm out to me. Feeling like a shipwreck victim who's finally been fished out of a dark sea, I stepped into his embrace.

This, I thought, was what having a brother, maybe even a boyfriend, someone on my side, must feel like. I didn't want the feeling to end. Didn't want to go back to belonging nowhere and to no one. The calculations I'd made about Pops and his show shifted a bit and I saw that the promoter and I both actually wanted the same thing. I wanted the show to continue. Maybe I even wanted to be part of the next one.

As our little trio made a slow loop, me tucked under Zave's arm, Patsy plodded past and cackled, "Hot cha, Zave. One girl ain't enough for you?"

A couple other guys passed and saluted Zave with wolf whistles.

"Mind your own beeswax," he tossed back with a laugh.

"I'm glad to see you lovebirds are in such a good mood." Even before I saw him, I knew from the smell of cigar smoke that Pops had joined us.

I quickly pulled away from Zave.

Around the floor, the other dancers, who'd previously been as alert as a bunch of coma patients, were all jolted back to life at the sound of the promoter's booming voice. It was a rare occurrence for Pops to deign to actually come onto the floor except during prime evening hours when "the boys" were in attendance.

A sudden appearance like this usually meant that one of the pros was going to get warned about smoking marijuana or had been caught messing around with an underage local. It was amazing how inventive some of the guys could be about finding time and a hidden place to disappear with a willing girl.

Or, if the offender was expendable — either an amateur or a dud with the crowd — there would be no warning and Pops would simply hand the offender his walking papers. No farewell. No silver shower. Just one more empty cot in the rest area.

"Pops," Zave said, tipping his chin to greet the promoter. "Whatcha need?"

Slump-shouldered and long-faced, even among a bunch of sleepwalkers, he was the weariest-looking soul on the floor. Glumly, he answered, "A miracle."

"What variety?" Zave joked back. "Raise the dead? Or fish and loaves?"

"Naw, just the usual keep-Capone's-nephew-from-putting-my-feet-in-a-bucket-of-cement-and-dumping-me-in-the-middle-of-Lake-Michigan-type miracle."

Though the early-morning air was still cool, Pops was sweating and twitchy. "And guess what?" he asked, attempting a joking tone. "I can't swim."

No longer kidding, Zave advised, "Pops, calm down, man. Breathe."

The concern in Zave's voice undid Pops. His bluff exterior fell away, revealing the raw terror beneath it. He was breathing hard, and his eyes were wide with panic when he said, "Zave, the boys aren't happy. The lovebird bit between you two was working great there for a while. Goosed up attendance enough to get the boys off my back. But the numbers are back down. Worst of all, the swells and the photographers ain't showing up anymore."

He winced and massaged a spot right below his sternum where, I suspected, an ulcer was flaring up. Pops's fear vibrated across the floor like the first tremor of a deadly quake, and even the slumped dancers farthest from us perked up and shot glances at their boss the way scared children will look to their parents to see if they should be worried.

His fear was genuine. Also genuine was the fact that he was now using it to work me. I'd spent my life around chiselers and con artists, so it was about time I figured out what the game here was and if there was any way I could win.

In a woebegone tone that he overplayed a bit, Pops said, "I don't know how we'll save the show."

Carefully studying the two men, I cut to the chase. "Probably by asking Zave and me to put on some kind of a showstopper."

I was relieved that no glances were exchanged: Pops wasn't in cahoots with Zave. Even if Zave was in on setting me up, though, I might have gone along with the play, but since he wasn't I was almost eager when I asked, "What do you have in mind?"

"Would you two mind telling me what this showstopper you're talking about is?" Zave asked. "Because I'm telling you right now, I'm not letting you freeze Evie alive."

"No," I said. "Pops has already eliminated that possibility, haven't you, Pops."

Pops eyed me shrewdly, trying to suss out what my game was.

"Okay, then what . . . ?" Zave stopped as a light dawned on him. "No, Pops, no way. If you're thinking what I think you're thinking, we are not interested."

"Interested in what?" I asked. "Because beyond showstopper, I don't know what you're talking about."

"Should I tell her?" Pops asked.

"Go ahead," Zave answered. "Because it is never going to happen."

When neither man spoke, I prodded, "What? What is never going to happen?"

"It's ridiculous," Zave answered, waving away what he obviously thought was a crazy idea. "You'd never agree to it. Or me either."

"Agree to what?"

Silence again greeted my question.

Running out of patience, I adopted the tone I'd been forced to use when I'd done a few rotations as a charge nurse and had to deal with smart-ass orderlies and snide interns, and demanded, "Tell me exactly what you are talking about."

After a moment, Zave finally answered,

"A wedding. Specifically, a cellophane wedding."

Chapter 48

"A cellophane what?"

"Wedding," Pops supplied. "Last time we staged one, we broke attendance records at the Roseland Ballroom. With the Depression on no one can afford to get married anymore. I read where across the country, weddings are down by something like a third. That's a lot of people with dreams they're only gonna fulfill vicariously. So, watching some lucky couple start life together is a surefire draw. Plus, weddings always bring in the society crowd. And that would make Salvy happy enough that I might get out of this town alive."

"What's cellophane got to do with it?" I asked.

"That's the gimmick," Pops explained, getting excited in spite of himself. "All the gowns and tuxes are made out of cellophane."

I had questions. "Cellophane? Like see-through cellophane?"

"Just the outer stuff," Pops explained. "Everyone keeps on their regular underwear. Slips, teddies, tap pants, what have you. It's actually more than what you women wear to the beach, but the suckers get a kick out of thinking they're peeking at what they shouldn't be seeing."

"Okay," I muttered. Pretending I didn't already know that he was talking about me and Zave, I said, "And you think you can actually talk a couple of dimwits into getting married wearing candy wrappers?"

"No," Pops exclaimed. "That's the beauty of it. No one really gets married. We do the whole big buildup. Get sponsors to donate flowers and make the gowns. Then there's a raft of wedding presents. Last time we staged one the couple raked in an icebox, a suite of living room furniture, a trip to Cuba, a complete trousseau, and a year's supply of Ovaltine."

"But they didn't actually get married?" I said. "How's that fulfill anyone's vicarious dream?"

"There's a 'ceremony,' " Pops said dismissively. "But it's just some jaboni we pull in off the street, turn his collar around, and stick a copy of the wedding vows in his hands to read."

"And this ludicrous charade works?"

"Like gangbusters," Pops assured me. "Of course, we have to use the couple that's most popular with the crowd. And, to make the whole setup play, they have to leave the show after the 'wedding' and go off to start their new lives together."

"Of course," I agreed archly. "And I assume you think that Zave and I are the most popular couple."

Pops answered mournfully, "Cleo's the vamp now, so, unfortunately, yes. Which leaves us exactly nowhere, since there's no way you'd play along."

For several long, silent moments we shuffled around the floor. As Pops stared glumly at his feet I worked through all the new angles they had just very conveniently presented to me. The wheels turned and spit out one indisputable fact: Zave was right. I was never going to get my pin unless I appealed to a power higher than the Director. And Zave had given me what looked to be my only avenue to getting some of that power.

I startled them by asking, "Pops, what kind of publicity did your last wedding pull in?"

Pops shot a quick glance of surprise at Kane. But he didn't look at Zave, which

373

bolstered my hope that he wasn't in on the setup. "Huge," he answered.

"National?"

"Coast to coast."

"What happened to the couple after?"

"They headlined a couple shows for me. Brought in giant crowds until the blushing bride got pregnant by one of the locals. You probably read about them. 'Mr. and Mrs. Moonlight'?"

"So they were big enough to open a show?"

"A couple of shows."

"What was the local coverage like?"

"Wall to wall. Papers, daily radio broadcast, the works."

"Kind of like a bomb had dropped in the middle of town?"

Zave smiled at me.

"Huh?" Pops said.

I liked seeing the puzzled look on the promoter's face as *he* tried to figure out what *my* angle might be. I'm sure he thought "crazy," but I didn't care. If I was going to get played, I would call the game, because I'd be playing for a lot more than winning a marathon. I'd be playing for my pin.

Against all the rules, I halted, made the men do the same, and announced, "Okay, here's how it's going to go. I'll be the pretend bride in this pretend wedding."

"Oh, Evie, that's great. That's great." A jubilant Pops tried to hug me. I stopped him.

"What?" Zave asked, genuinely puzzled. "You're not serious, are you? You really want to do this?"

"Why not? If it's all just an act? What's the difference between that and me playing a homewrecker? I mean, if you want to? Do you?"

"Oh Lord, oh jeez, oh God." Pops pulled me into a crushing hug. "Evie, you saved my neck. You saved the whole damn show. The kids are gonna be so excited. We'll pull in a whole new crowd." Hyperventilating, Pops stumbled over his words as he rushed on, "Salvy will love giving it to Zave like this. Evie, I could just kiss you."

He crushed my head between his big mitts and almost attempted to do that, but I broke out of his hold and announced solemnly, "But first I have a few terms."

"Sure, sure, anything," Pops hurried to agree.

"First of all, don't ever con me again. If you want something ask me straight up."

"Con you?" Pops asked, feigning bewilderment.

"Save it, Pops," I said. Feeling as if I were standing at the top of a tall diving tower about to plunge into the speck of a pool far below, I sucked in a deep breath and continued, "Because I want to set up a show in Galveston. More important, I *can* set up a show there."

"In Galveston?" Kane asked dubiously.

"In Galveston, but —"

"You have 'terms,'" Pops interjected sourly.

"I do. First, all publicity goes through me. I will control every story that goes out."

"Sure, no problem," Pops agreed readily, relieved that my terms weren't financial.

"Second, you will hire a real actual nurse and I'll train her."

"Whatever you say, Evie, except you're still forgetting one thing."

"What's that?"

"There's no venue on the island big enough to make it worth the trouble."

"Oh, but there is," I purred, pleased by the novel sensation of having something on the promoter. "I know the exact place. It'll require some sprucing up, but it's huge and the owner is desperate to figure out what to do with the place."

"Sounds too good to be true," Pops said, once again the wised-up operator. "What's the catch?"

"The catch is you run a good show, don't cut any corners, and give all the contestants a fair shake."

"Done."

I was pleased at how ecstatic Pops and Kane were at the prospect of setting up a show in Galveston. In fact, the only one who wasn't excited was Zave. "Wait," I said, "Zave never actually agreed."

"You're in," Pops asked. "Aren't you?"

"It's not a real wedding," Kane, holding Zave's gaze, reminded him.

Zave didn't speak until Pops said, "Come on. It's the gimmick of the century. We'll charge a fortune for the ringside seats. Say you're in."

Looking away from Kane, Zave paused for an excruciating moment, then shrugged and answered, "Sure, I could use a year's supply of Ovaltine."

Pops, already strategizing with Kane as they walked away, paused, and called back to me, "Hey, what's the name of this dream venue?"

"The Starlight Palace."

CHAPTER 49

"The Handsome Hoofer has popped the question," Alonzo exploded that night. "And, folks, hold on to your hats, because our Angel of Mercy said yes!"

The applause could have registered on the Richter scale. Zave and I stood front and center in the middle of the floor with the circling dancers making a beautiful frame around us. Zave beamed into the rafters and I, in a crisp, new, whiter-than-white uniform, looked away with what appeared to be demureness.

Actually I was shell-shocked by how quickly the grand plans I'd set in motion had solidified around me. The instant I told Pops about the Starlight Palace he hustled me back to his office, put me on the phone, and I called the Buccaneer Hotel, where I knew JuJu was ensconced with his current mistress.

"Could you put me through to Julian

Amadeo?" I asked the hotel operator.

"Whom may I say is calling?" she purred.

"Evie Grace Devlin."

"I'll check if that guest is available at this time."

In the silence that followed, the men arched eyebrows at each other as if they were indulging my little folly though they, in all their wisdom, knew it would fail.

"Evelina," JuJu exclaimed in his familiar growl of a voice. I held the receiver up so that the three men could hear. "To what do I owe the honor? The whole town has been reading about you."

"Oh, JuJu," I said, suddenly wishing this were a friendly call to Sofie's uncle and regretting mixing business in.

"That's Uncle JuJu to you." As he corrected me, I motioned for the men to leave, snapping my fingers impatiently to hurry them along.

When they closed the door, I explained the situation, concluding, "And, well, I just thought that the Starlight Palace might be the perfect spot for a show. Sofie told me how much you and your brother wanted to reclaim a bit of the Pier's former glory, and it occurred to me that this might be a way to do it."

My heart sank when my proposal was met

with complete silence, and I cringed, thinking of how humiliating it was going to be when I told the guys I'd been refused.

Finally, JuJu said thoughtfully, "Evelina, you know what? I think I like it. A big event like that might just fit in with our plans. We've been sprucing the old place up a little. Just enough to make it presentable as the site of a gala Fourth of July fireworks extravaganza where my brother and I are going to announce our plans to renovate and reopen the Starlight Pier."

"Really? Are you serious?"

"No promises, but we might be able to work something out. Especially if the show is going to feature our local girl made good, right?"

"That's the idea."

"Good, good. My niece misses you. I'm getting a phone put in her apartment so you two can talk."

"I miss her. A lot."

"Sofia is friends with everyone, but has never had many close friends. Not a true friend like you. Everyone needs a true friend."

"I know. It'll be great to come home." Relief, nerves, hope, who knows what, but my voice wobbled on those last words.

Switching to a gruffer business mode, JuJu

asked, "So, this Wyatt guy. Is he on the level?"

After a moment's hesitation, I told him the one thing I could truthfully say about Pops. "I promise you that Pops really cares about putting on a great show."

"He's not gonna pull a fast one on us, is he?"

"Uncle JuJu, Mr. Wyatt is a lot of things, but he is not a stupid man. He fully understands and appreciates who the Amadeos are and the unique place your family occupies and how very unwise it would be not to honor that."

"Yeah, word is the nephew is squeezing him pretty hard. I'll have to square things with Salvy first, but okay, then, Evelina, if you'll vouch for this Pops character, I'll ask my brother. I know this will make Sofia very happy. Put Wyatt on the horn."

Chapter 50

I waited in the hall and prayed that Pops was closing the deal. When he burst out ten minutes later and announced, "We got a show," the electric thrill that surged through me could have lit up Coney Island.

Nearly hyperventilating, and vibrating with a manic energy, Pops declared, "Evie, I'm gonna leave for Galveston with an advance team tonight. JuJu's gonna send contracts tomorrow. I'll have Kane bring you yours."

"Contract?" I asked. "Why do I need a contract?"

"Because you're the star of the show. You and Zave. And stars always sign contracts." Already grabbing his hat, he was almost out the door before he paused, took a steadying breath, and said, "Thanks, Evie, seriously. You don't know what you've done."

"Saved your life," I reminded him. "You remember my terms, right?"

"Sure, sure. We'll work it out. Whatever you want. Gonna be great. Gonna be gangbusters. Have a great wedding. See you in Galveston."

He was gone, and that evening I was standing in the middle of an arena listening to Alonzo announce my engagement.

When the emcee went on about "the kind of real, true happy ending that will make you all believe that, no matter how tough times may be right now, everything is going to turn out all right," there were so many white hankies fluttering to mop up tears that you would have thought an army was surrendering.

Zave winked at me as though we were pulling the greatest prank ever. Still, when Alonzo talked about our "storybook romance," a bit of the electricity that crackled through the audience somehow sparked in me as well. Ticket sales shot up immediately. But what really made attendance go through the roof was when the Associated Press picked up the story and it went national. Attendance skyrocketed and sponsorships for the wedding poured in.

They started off with what some of the other dancers told me were run-of-the-mill offerings: a steak dinner at Louie's Chop House; two tickets to the Biograph ("Air

Cooled By Refrigeration") Theater to see *No Man of Her Own* with Clark Gable and Carole Lombard; a steamboat cruise around Lake Michigan aboard the U.S.S. *South American.*

As soon as the AP began carrying the story nationally, though, the offerings became much swankier. When headlines like "Marathon Medico Cures Handsome Hoofer's Heartache: She Said YES!" began appearing across the country, the big-name retailers became interested.

The Saturday after our engagement was announced, Zave twirled me under the floodlights as Alonzo revealed that Marshall Field's department store had contributed the lingerie that would be worn beneath the transparent gowns and that C.D. Peacock at the corner of State and Monroe Streets — "providing Chicago with fine jewelry since 1837" — would be designing a wedding ring "as enchanted as this couple's enchanted romance."

Zave and I were pirouetting around, grinning into each other's faces, having fun with an exaggeratedly sweeping, exaggeratedly romantic Viennese waltz when Alonzo announced that "the world-renowned Palmer Hotel has just now alerted the show that they will host our enchanted couple for a three-night stay at the Honeymoon Suite."

Zave stiffened at the word "honeymoon."

"Oh ho," Alonzo hooted. "What do we have here? Not one but *two* blushing brides? Have you ever seen two people more embarrassed in your lives?"

The crowd answered with wolf whistles and raucous laughter that rocked the arena.

Though Zave recovered quickly and began hamming it up, overplaying the role of the bashful swain, it was too late; I'd already seen the look of distaste on his face at the mention of a honeymoon. Not one to run from the truth, I realized in an instant that whatever chemistry I might have dreamed existed between us was completely one-sided. I made a feeble attempt at pretending that I too was in on all the fun while Zave waltzed me off to the sidelines so that I could return to the infirmary.

"There she goes, our blushing bride," Alonzo crowed.

At that, the pounding waves of applause melted into a syrupy sludge of cooed *Awww*s, as if I, gangly, too-tall Evie Grace were the cutest, most adorable, most beloved thing in the whole wide world. Zave's expression had confirmed that I was neither.

Though my brain knew what the score was and accepted it as a means to my end of getting my pin, my stupid heart had, apparently, fallen for the charade. At the edge of the floor, I yanked my hand away from Zave's.

"Evie," Zave called after me, "come tomorrow. Early. We have to talk."

CHAPTER 51

I stayed up most of the night. The path that only a short time ago looked so bright and shiny and clear now seemed hopelessly murky and ill-conceived.

"Hey, look, gang," Minnie shouted when she caught sight of me as I dragged in a few hours later. "It's the blushing bride."

The contestants were gathered around the high table eating scrambled eggs, toast, and orange slices, and drinking far too much coffee. As prescribed by the rules, they all stayed in motion, swaying from foot to foot like chained elephants as they ate so that King Kong or some other vigilant judge wouldn't eliminate them for not staying in constant motion. Even as they ate and swayed, they hurled good-natured jibes my way.

"Bet you're looking for your 'fiancé,' " Ace called out.

"No practicing for the honeymoon allowed," Patsy joked.

"Don't listen to those wiseacres," Minnie said. "Zave's in the rest area, taking a hygiene break."

"A fiancé's gotta shower and stay spring-time fresh for his girl, right, fellows?" Patsy asked.

Breaking through the guffaws, Lily called out in her elegant, fluting voice, "He has been gone seven minutes and," she swiveled her head to the clock, "fourteen seconds. Should he return, we shall inform him that his betrothed came calling."

As usual, no one reacted to Lily's odd outburst.

Cleo caught my eye. Her expression was unreadable, but when she gave me the barest hint of a nod it seemed almost sympathetic. I nodded back and fled to my canvas sanctuary. There, waiting for my signature atop my small, battered supply cabinet, I found the contract for the Galveston show.

I was skimming through the document that would obligate me to be in Galveston "on or before June 27th to participate in all promotional activities in preparation for the opening of The Amadeo Family's Dance Marathon in Celebration of the Grand Re-Opening of the Starlight Palace and Pier on July 1, 1932" when Zave appeared. His hair, still wet from the shower, was dark and sleek as a seal's fur. Wayward licks curled up here and there, dripping beads of water on the shoulders of his shirt.

"Oh, you got your contract, too," he said in a tone as flat as I felt. "Listen, about the show, the wedding, all that, we should probably talk."

"We probably should."

Zave peered at the canvas walls, the trainers and cleaners coming and going, and asked, "Can we do this in Pops's office?"

In the office, Zave locked the door, took a long, steadying breath, and said, "I know you caught my reaction to Alonzo talking about a honeymoon last night and that it hurt your feelings. Probably made you think that I was lying about how I feel about you."

"Look, I'm a big girl. I know the score. I never expected you to carry me over the threshold or anything. I know we're going into this as friends. You never lied. I just assumed too much. Don't worry about it. If you want to call this whole . . . Zave? Are you all right?"

Zave had suddenly gone pale, his hands trembled and an oily sweat had broken out on his ashen face.

"You don't look well. Sit. Come on. Sit right here." I helped him take a seat on

Pops's sofa, sat beside him, put my hand on his back, and suggested in my most calming nurse voice, "Why don't you put your head between your knees."

He did, and I reminded him, "Breathe."

I fetched a glass of water. He raised his head and drank. Gradually his color returned. I knew what a talented performer Zave was and how entirely capable he was of hoodwinking me, but I didn't believe he was good enough to fake a case of near shock. Whatever else we may or may not have been to each other, he was now my patient and I asked gently, "Zave, what is it?"

"The dream that I didn't think was possible?"

"Sure, we'll start anywhere you'd like," I soothed, worried now that he had had some sort of cerebral incident that had scrambled his thinking.

"A family. I never had one. Not a real one that wanted me to be a part of it. That didn't hate everything about me. I've spent my life peeking in windows and spying on families. Groups of people who were just happy to be together. Who laughed. And I always wanted that. I always wanted to belong."

He pressed his fingers to his lips until they

stopped trembling before he went on. "But I never believed I could have it. Until you came along and I got the crazy idea that it might be possible after all."

He paused for a moment before continuing with a dismissive snort. "Stupid, right? We don't know each other at all except on the floor of a dance marathon. Maybe that's why I pushed for the show in Galveston, I figured it might be the solution. Or part of one. I'd help you get your pin and, in the meantime, we could actually get to know each other. Maybe even win ourselves a little nest egg to set up house. Or an apartment. Maybe just a room somewhere. But it would be clean, and have a nice southern exposure, and it would be ours."

I was speechless with confusion. I had nothing but questions, yet I knew better than to interrupt, and he continued.

"I guess I got carried away. Being with you, talking about your father, joking about us being related, it seemed like you wanted that family connection as much as I did. I started to believe that we could give that to each other. A real family. One that accepted us for who we are.

"I mean," he asked. "Isn't that what everyone wants? Not to feel, not to be, all alone in the world? Until you came along, I didn't think it was possible. I didn't think that people like me were allowed to even want a family."

People like me.

I suppose I always knew that there had to be a catch. Something that would explain unexceptional me plus charismatic him. Because, according to the usual math, the two of us simply didn't add up. Even in the fantasy of a dance marathon.

"Oh," I said, and he knew I understood.

We sat in silence as I recalled all the boys, the men, on the vaud circuit that other performers had disdained, called "sissies." I never had. They were always my favorites. Perhaps I had intuited that they could not have cared less about peeking up my skirt and had no interest whatsoever in what I later learned was my "knish." They were also generally funnier, smarter, and more playful than the run-of-the-mill skirt-chaser.

"You can't tell anyone. Please. It'd be the end of what career I have left."

"Cleo?" I asked.

"Cleo knows. But no one else. Pops'd kick me out. The other guys'd beat the holy hell out of me."

I wanted to tell him that they were his friends; they'd never hurt him. But I also recalled how often my funny, smart, playful friends had had to wear extra layers of greasepaint to hide bruises, cuts, black eyes, and worse.

Friends like Terry.

Terry had a dog act, Terry and the Terriers. He spoke in a high, fluting voice and danced onstage with his five "babies." Late at night, after the last show was over, Terry would let me babysit his "darlings" while he roamed whatever city we were playing. I loved taking care of his puppies. Especially when all five of them snuggled in bed with me.

One night, however, Terry didn't come back from his explorations. Not that day, not the next, not ever. When I asked where he was all Mamie would tell me was that Terry had gotten "what he deserved." I begged to keep his dogs. Mamie laughed at the request, found someone to take them, and told me never to mention "that degenerate's name" again.

Later I learned that Terry had died in jail that night. Some said it had been suicide. I knew it wasn't. He never would have willingly abandoned his darlings.

"Zave, that is nobody's business but yours. Of course I won't tell anyone." His sorrow and his shame were palpable. "It's all right, Zave," I promised him. "It'll be all right."

393

"It's not," he told me. "It never will be." With a rueful sigh, he plucked the contract I was still holding from my free hand and pitched it in the trash basket. "Well, we won't be needing that anymore."

"Why not?"

"Evie, you're not an unkind person, don't be unkind now."

"No, Zave, I'm serious. Why would we cancel Galveston? Or the wedding? Or anything?"

"Because I'm . . ." In spite of all his brave words, this was one that he still couldn't say.

"Homosexual?" I supplied with all the compassion I'd learned from little Sister Theonella and none of the cruel judgment that a harsh world had burdened him with. Now all I wanted to do was alleviate his suffering. And that is when I remembered something Dr. Kaufman had mentioned during the lecture that Sofie had reminded me of. On the list of mental afflictions that the new treatments could cure — catatonia, hysteria, schizophrenia, alcoholism, epilepsy, nymphomania, feeble-mindedness. Dr. K had included "sexual inversion."

My heart raced and I had to bite my lips to keep from smiling. I had to talk to Sofie and get all the information before I could

394

tell Zave that I had the solution to his, to *our,* problem. And that it was easy and modern and would make everything we both dreamed of possible. But it was too soon. Until I could give him the thrilling news, though, I had to do what I could to alleviate Zave's suffering.

"Zave, remember how you told me I shouldn't feel a speck of shame about Detroit? Well, you shouldn't feel any shame either."

He gave me a suspicious look.

"I'm serious," I said. "We studied sexual inversion in class. All this baloney about it being a sin or a deviancy is wrong. What you have is a medical condition and it's not your fault."

His expression became even more doubtful.

"Yes," I assured him, more excited by the second as bits and pieces of that lecture came back to me. "I wish I had my notes, but I'm going to ask a friend who, I promise you, is very discreet, to do some research. She'll track down all the latest developments. Zave, new frontiers are opening all the time. Just look at smallpox. We've almost got it eradicated."

"Smallpox?" Zave repeated in a dull monotone.

"I'm just saying that there's help."

"Yeah, help, that's great, but the Galveston gimmick is still the same. We're supposed to be newlyweds trying to earn enough to start a life together."

"So let's do that."

"You still want to go ahead with this whole scheme knowing what you know? Why?"

"Why not? First of all, you're right about the power of publicity. You're even more right about not letting the world decide who I am. I want to go back to Galveston with my head held high, not hiding anything, not ashamed of anything, and get my pin. And the same goes for you, Zave. You have to make the world give you what you want. *We* have to make the world give us what we want."

"And that means . . . ?"

"Yes, that means that the ridiculous fake wedding is still on," I said with much more confidence than I felt. Of course, nothing in my life had prepared me for this moment and I had no idea how I should feel.

"And the honeymoon?"

"Look, Zave, I never expected you to carry me across the threshold or anything. I'm not some starry-eyed nitwit. You already feel like my brother. We can simply continue that way and see what happens in Galveston. Maybe there is actually a way for us to have a family."

As if to punctuate the moment, the two-minute-warning bell clanged. I stood, but Zave remained seated, studying me with a sad wistfulness that broke my heart. He looked like a little boy who'd been hurt too many times. I wanted to protect him. Heal him.

I reached my hand down. Zave took it and stood. "Evie, I feel the way I did when I first met your father. I feel as though, with you by my side, I can be a new person, a better person. I don't know where this will ultimately lead us, but I want you to know that, in my way, I truly do love you."

I nestled my face in his neck, and inhaled the odor that was his alone, a mixture of bread fresh from the oven and the ocean and warmth and life. For several delirious moments we simply stood there and he patted my back. They were brotherly pats, but there was love, real love, in them.

CHAPTER 52

"Look at the creeps packing in to see us in our undies, would ya?" Cleo snarled, lighting a new cigarette from the stub in her mouth. The house was already packed from floor to rafters, and still the crew Pops had left behind when he went to Galveston was cramming in anyone with four bits for a seat in the bleachers or five bucks for a spot up front. He planned to rake in everything he could today since this was the last time Zave and I would perform.

I was waiting with the rest of the women — all of us in our crinkly, floor-length cellophane gowns — out of sight of the audience in the hallway leading from the rest areas to the floor. For once, thanks to a special hygiene break, and to the bouquets we each clutched, we smelled of roses and lilies instead of old socks.

I tuned in to the spiel Alonzo was giving about the sponsors. "Let's give a big hand to Foster's Fine Florals, Chicago's finest florist, who supplied all the flowers for today's most special of events. When you think flowers, think Foster's."

All the girls, except for Cleo, believed that there was a normal romance, or at least the beginning of one, between me and Zave, and they treated me like a real bride at a real wedding. Lily, whom I suspected had actually been a bridesmaid at lots of fancy weddings, glided up and extended her limp hand. As we shook, she bestowed a heartfelt, if slightly confused blessing. "I wish you and yours all the very best of the season and extend to you glad tidings of joy. The house is full and eighty-nine Standing Room Only seats have been sold. It's a record for a non-sporting event in this venue."

"Thank you, Lily," I said.

Gerta approached next. The cellophane gown she wore over a delicate knee-length slip that left her meaty calves and broad shoulders exposed was as yellow and as transparent as a butterscotch wrapper. Gripping her bouquet as though it were a chicken whose neck she was about to wring, she told me solemnly in her German accent, "Maybe, someday you are really marrying Zave. I belief that you can be haffing a good life with Zave. Maybe he is too hand-

399

some, *ja*? But still a hard worker."

"Oh, Gertie," Minnie trilled, letting a rare toothless smile escape. "Don't be a killjoy. How can a fella be too handsome?" She buried her pixie face in her bouquet and inhaled the scent of her own dreams. "You're so lucky," she told me in a whisper. "Me and DeWitt could barely afford to buy a marriage license. Forget having a for-real wedding with flowers."

"Minnie," I promised her, "after the show in Galveston, you and DeWitt will be able to afford anything you want."

"You think so?"

"Absolutely. I know that city and they are going to love you."

"Evie, honest Injun, I don't know what we'd of done, you hadn't saved this show and helped Pops set up one in Galveston. I mean, after what DeWitt and me send to folks back home, we don't have a plug nickel between us."

Though I waved away her gratitude, just as I'd brushed off the thanks from the other pros, it made my heart bump. I liked being the hero. Liked it a lot.

Minnie's gaze turned to the floor, where all the men except for Zave were lined up. She sighed and asked, "Ain't they just fine as all get-out?"

They were. Instead of transparent mens-wear, all the guys wore actual tuxedos, courtesy of Joseph Fry's King for a Night, a business that offered the brand-new option of renting formal wear. They had a huge sign posted above the bandstand: "If You Want to Be Handsome. Don't Spend a King's Ransom. Rent. Don't Buy. From Joseph Fry."

All of us, in fact, looked pretty great. A team of beauty operators had donated their services and we had been groomed to within an inch of our lives. They'd circulated among the girls all night long, setting and styling freshly washed hair. Meanwhile, barbers were shaving the men, trimming their hair, and even, we'd heard, buffing their nails.

"Why don't the boys have to show off their BVDs?" Cleo groused.

"Because," Minnie answered, "no one wants to see some hairy guy in a sleeveless T-shirt with garters holding his socks up. Us gals and our undies are all that they're interested in."

And what undies they were. Marshall Field and Company had delivered towers of thin, flat boxes emblazoned in bold black with the department store's name and their iconic clock logo. Slips and bras, garter belts and hose, tap pants and chemises, all in pastel silks of peach, pale pink, and powder blue, decorated with embroidered flowers, tiny mother-of-pearl buttons, and appliqued bows.

My ankle-length slip of ivory silk could have been an evening gown. If they made evening gowns that floated over a person's frame, somehow emphasizing all the places that had, amazingly, filled out even more. I can't say if it was the abundant meals or my new alliance with Zave and hopes for not just my pin but possibly even a family, but for the first time in memory the hunger that had gnawed at me my entire life had vanished.

"Put that out before you are killing us all," Gerta exploded, slapping a cigarette from Cleo's mouth and grinding the butt beneath the sole of her Mary Jane into a black smear on the floor. With a loud crackle, Gerta waved her crinkly gown at Cleo and said, "One spark and *whoosh.* We all explode."

Cleo waved her away. "Aw, don't bust a gasket there, Helga, I need to calm my nerves. I've never been a whatchamacallit?"

"Maid of honor," I supplied. I'd asked Cleo to stand beside me as a peace offering, a way of including her in a ceremony that she might once have hoped would have been hers. She was important in Zave's life and, if Zave and I really were going to be together, I had to find a spot for her in my life as well. Also, she was the only one who knew Zave's true nature, and that was an unspoken bond between us.

"Yeah, Helga," Cleo boasted. "I'm the maid of honor."

"Cleo," Gerta said, "I am telling you again and again. Mein name is Gerta. Gerta. Gerta. Not Helga. Or Heidi. Or Gesundheit."

"God bless you," Cleo quipped.

"Cleo, quit baitin' her," Minnie ordered.

The women's squabbling faded away when the lights went down and we could all take a peek at the floor without being seen. Zave, his best man Kane by his side, stood at the center of a large riser next to an older man dressed as a minister. His groomsmen, all the horses Zave had worked with for years, plus Suits, flanked him.

A trellis threaded with long-stem pink roses and clouds of baby's breath arched above Zave's head. My breath caught. They say all men look good in a tux. But put a man like Zave, who'd look good in an old bathrobe, in one and you had an actual showstopper.

Maybe Gerta was right. Maybe a man

could be too handsome. Too far out of my league. Even a man with a secret like Zave's. Suddenly the entire proposition seemed absurd. Something shifted then crumbled within me. Feeling as if my knees were about to give way, I pushed through the crinkly pastel gowns claiming I had to visit the ladies room.

Cleo grabbed my arm and yanked me to a stop. "If you gotta pee, hold it. If you're thinking of taking a powder, forget it. Show's starting. And my feet are killing me."

"Cleo, I don't know about this. About any of it."

"It's just a gimmick," she reassured me. "Come on, you've been around long enough to know that none of it is for real. Don't take it so seriously."

She slapped a fake smile over all that was too serious and I wondered if that included her feelings for Zave. I plastered on my own imitation happiness and took her arm. "Thanks, Cleo. Seriously, thanks for everything."

"What for? It's not like the hero was ever gonna marry the vamp," she said with an offhanded insouciance that was almost believable. "Move it. Show must go on, right?"

Cleo rushed to join the line of bridesmaids

marching into the spotlights while the Melody Makers played a sweet and slow version of "When You're Smiling" and I was left all alone in the darkness.

When Cleo and all the bridesmaids were lined up on the riser, the band fell silent for a moment. My stomach dropped when I heard the first chords of "The Wedding March." Matching the music's funereal pace, I stepped forward. The instant I reached the spotlit floor, a benediction of "*ooh*s" and "*aah*s" rained down. Long rows of older women already had hankies out, blotting up leakage. Kane, standing next to Zave, nudged him, and Zave's gaze fell on me. I couldn't detect a hint of artifice in his smile as he beheld me. In that moment, my fears fell away and I all but floated up to my place next to Zave beneath the rose arbor. Cleo stood on my left. Zave was so close that I could smell his lilac vegetal aftershave. More than a dozen groomsmen, tuxedoed like Hollywood stars, and an equal number of bridesmaids, wrapped up like fruit jelly candies, flanked us on either side.

Zave took my hand and flashbulbs exploded. We were momentarily blinded as photographers from several Chicago newspapers, as well as the AP, captured the entire wedding party. We'd get the publicity Pops had promised.

I recognized "the minister" as the night janitor, an older fellow with a deep, resonant voice that fit the part and a bad drinking problem that didn't. When he reached the "I dos," Zave faced me and added a whispered word to the vow.

"I, Zave Cassidy, *will* take thee, Evelyn Grace Devlin, to be my wedded wife, to have and to hold, from this day forward, for better, for worse, for richer, for poorer, in sickness and in health, to love and to cherish, till death do us part, according to God's holy ordinance; and thereto I pledge thee myself to you."

One thing I could say for the audience, the constant partner in my relationship with Zave, was that as much as they loved a show, a staged drama, they could also faultlessly detect a true moment. And when I pledged myself, body and soul, to Zave, they registered my sincerity like a Geiger counter, and tears rained down almost as heavily as the coins, and bills, did.

The Melody Makers boomed out an exultant recessional. Zave pulled me to his side and whispered, "We can make this work. I know we can." He took my hand and, as he arched his other arm over my head to protect me from the patter of flung coins, we stepped onto the new path we would try to walk together.

I shoved aside one pesky realization: until the fake minister spoke it, I hadn't even known Zave's last name, Cassidy. I wondered if it was real.

CHAPTER 53

The wedding ended when the siren shrieked.

"That's it, folks," Alonzo announced as the floor cleared. "It's break time. Now our glamorous bridal party will have fifteen minutes to change, maybe grab a quick nap, then we'll all be back right here for more round-the-clock thrills. Cleo is a single now, so come on back and see if she picks up a new partner."

Zave and I were the last to leave the floor. Our final exit was heralded by a crescendo of applause and the sweet, fluttering kiss of wadded bills tossed from the box seats. Since Zave and I had already sent our bags ahead to the Palmer, I quickly changed out of my big crinkly wedding gown and slipped into Mamie's traveling suit. Back in the hallway, I was stunned to find all our friends waiting, squandering their precious rest time to wish us well.

"We're sure gonna miss you," Ace told me gravely. "You were a hero of the common man. You treated everyone equally. You listened to us. Cared about us. Really cared. You're a true comrade, comrade. Stay in touch. Our side will need you when the fighting starts."

Zave stood back, letting me have my moment in the sun while, one after the other, they all thanked me. Minnie was the last one. "We love you, Evie Grace. You were good to us. Real good. I wouldn't of made it without you, and that's the God's honest."

Even Cleo had a few words. "Evie, we had our differences, but I think I speak for all of us when I say you saved our bacon and you're a real marathoner."

"Yeah, Gravy," Patsy brayed. "Three cheers for Nurse Gravy."

In the midst of the cheers, I noticed out of the corner of my eye that the sax player, Tony, had sidled up next to Zave and handed him something that Zave popped in his mouth. When the sax player winked insinuatingly and gave Zave a manly thumbs-up, I was pretty certain that the pill wasn't an aspirin.

I didn't think anything more about it as we headed for the exit.

Kane stopped us at the door. Glaring at me, he warned, "Don't forget, you both signed contracts. If you aren't in Galveston by June 27, there will be trouble. And you'd better pray it's legal trouble because, no matter how buddy-buddy you think you might be with them, you definitely don't want trouble with the Amadeos."

"Don't sweat it," Zave assured him.

"And you'll be there, too. Right?" Kane asked Zave with a surprising intensity, sounding more like a concerned uncle than the raging judge he played on the floor.

"I'll be there," Zave promised. Then, taking my arm, he added, "We'll both be there."

Then "we," the two of us, stepped out of Mann's Rainbo Gardens Arena and into the real world.

CHAPTER 54

It was deliciously cool outside the arena. Zave gulped down several deep lungfuls of air that had not already been breathed by a thousand people. Air that didn't smell of cigarettes, fried onions, and body odor.

"Who needs marijuana," he asked, "when a person can get high on breathing this stuff?"

Delighting in the sensation of being uncaged, of seeing the sky over our heads instead of steel rafters and floodlights, of feeling fresh air against our cheeks, we set out. It was early evening and the sidewalk was crowded with couples heading to dinner, the movies, who knew where else? And we were one of them.

A couple.

Though the word carried a large, unexplored asterisk, it still shimmied happily through me. All I could think of were the positives of our unorthodox arrangement.

How many women had a partner who actually wanted the best for them? Who supported their desire to have a career? To be more than a housewife? A mother?

"Chicago." Zave pronounced the name as if casting a magical incantation.

" 'City of the Big Shoulders,' " I said, quoting a poem I had to memorize in a high school English class.

" 'Hog Butcher for the World,' " Zave shot back. " 'Tool Maker, Stacker of Wheat, Player with Railroads.' "

What other poems did Zave know? What memories, opinions, dreams, regrets did he have? Who had broken his heart? Whose heart had he broken? I wanted to know it all. Mostly, though, I wanted to know if we could possibly work.

As daylight faded, streetlights, signs in dizzying neon colors, and shop windows blinked on and Chicago transformed into a night creature, black and sparkling with jewels of light. Zave responded to the new excitement pulsing around us with the same feral energy.

"Hurry," Zave said, urging me forward at an alarming pace. "I don't want you to miss this." I scrambled to keep up as we dodged cars while crossing several busy streets. Finally, we emerged onto a peaceful swath of green, already darkening as the sun lowered.

"Lincoln Park," Zave announced. "Not much time left. Let's go."

We rushed past busts of Beethoven and Benjamin Franklin. Past monuments to Lincoln and Grant. Past a Viking ship with a red-and-white-striped sail, round shields lining the sides, and a majestic carved dragon at the front.

I was breathing heavily from the strain of keeping up when he halted at the edge of Lake Michigan. As boundless as the ocean, it rippled with ribbons of rose and silver all the way to the far horizon. Dozens of boats, pristine white teepees, skimmed across the Prussian blue water. A whole village of boats, they moved in perfect time with the wind, the white blades of their sails slicing across the turquoise sky.

"It's lovely," I said, exhaling away the tightness within me that loosened the way it always did when Sofie and I stood at the ocean's edge back in Galveston.

"This isn't even what I wanted to show you," Zave said, taking me by the shoulders and turning me around, away from the lake, until we were both staring at the skyline as the setting sun gilded the skyscrapers in gold.

413

"Look," he said, pointing out buildings. "There's the Mather Tower and right next to it is the Carbide and Carbon Building. And, oh, look there," he exclaimed, a manic intensity spiking through and speeding up his words. "The Lindbergh Beacon just switched on. That's the Palmolive Building. See why that whole area is called the Gold Coast? There's so much more I want to show you. Let's go."

He grabbed my hand, but I refused to move.

"We have to hurry," he pleaded, tugging on my hand.

"Zave, stop."

He stood in front of me, sweating, breathing heavily, and looking worried.

"What did Tony give you?"

"Nothing. Don't worry about Tony. We have to go."

"It was a bennie, right? Because you sure are acting like someone on Benzedrine."

"No," he started to deny it, then barked out a laugh that was too loud, too sharp, and said, "Well, that's what I get for marrying a nurse."

"Zave, we have tomorrow. Many tomorrows, I hope. But right now I am exhausted and so are you. Let's grab a cab to the hotel and get some sleep."

He glanced away. "Evie, I want to be what you need. I truly do. Tony said bennies were a bridegroom's best friend and would, you know, help me perform."

"Zave, don't worry about any of that. No 'performance' is needed. It wasn't a real marriage and this isn't a real honeymoon."

His tense shoulders drooped with relief. "I should've known you'd understand." Though a bit calmer, Zave was still jittery and restless. "Jeez, I wish I hadn't taken that damn pep pill. I feel like I'm about to jump out of my skin. Come on, let's explore the city. I'm sure not going to sleep tonight."

"Zave, I would love to, but I really am dead on my feet. How about if we just go to the hotel and head out tomorrow?"

"I'd only pace and keep you awake."

"Maybe you should walk around for a while? Wear yourself out? I'll leave the room key for you at the desk."

"I wanted tonight to be special for you. Or, at least normal."

Laughing, I said, "I think we both might have missed the turnoff for normal a long ways back."

"What's the bellboy going to think when he takes the bride to the honeymoon suite and she's all alone?"

"What's our first rule?" I asked. "That we

don't care what people think. Go, Zave, we've got loads of time ahead of us to figure this out. To figure out if we even want to be together. We've got an entire dance marathon."

When he hugged me, it was with love. Though it might not, in fact, have been everyone's idea of romantic, it was better than that. It was real. And it was more than I ever thought I'd have.

CHAPTER 55

The honeymoon suite at the Palmer took my breath away. Larger than our entire shotgun house back at the foot of Vinegar Hill, it had a sitting area with a settee, two armchairs, and a liquor cabinet gleaming with entirely illegal bottles of the finest scotch, gin, bourbon, rye, and champagne.

Determined to enjoy every second of such unimaginable luxury, I popped the bottle of bubbly, poured a frothing coupe, and, after switching off the lights, installed myself on the settee to sip it in peace. Floating high on the twenty-fifth floor, I became a traveler through outer space as the glittering pin-pricks of city light that populated my view were transformed into a constellation of stars.

Zave will love this.

I couldn't wait for him to return so we could share all this opulence. Glancing over at the canopied double bed at the far end of the room, I knew that Zave would insist I sleep there and that he would take the narrow settee.

The other person I wished I could share all this with was Sofie. My gaze fell on the black Bakelite phone. I wanted so badly to call her, but I still didn't have the number.

Though I wished Zave would hurry back, I was glad for a few rare moments alone. I had a lot to think about. Obviously, the biggest issue, maybe the only one, was sex. On that score, I'd always thought that sex was a highly overrated activity. One that women, much more than men, usually ended up paying far too steep a price for. Sure, I'd peeked at lots of happy families and dreamed of being part of one. But I'd also caught far too many glimpses of boredom, disinterest, hostility, and outright misery.

And then there were the scenes that played out behind closed shutters and drawn blinds. The evidence of those could only be seen later. On the bodies of women. Eyes blackened. Teeth knocked out. Bellies swollen with unwanted children. Perhaps passion, all those butterflies that girls talked about fluttering in their stomachs, came at too high a cost. Why wasn't an arrangement between friends preferable?

Children? I thought of adopting one of

those unwanted babies born into the wrong family, of lavishing upon it all the love that neither I nor Zave had received, and a calming sense of rightness settled over me. It seemed only minutes later when a loud pounding jerked me awake. I leaped to my feet: Zave was back.

"I'm coming." I threw open the door. After the cave-black darkness of the suite, the hall light momentarily blinded me. No one was there.

"Zave?"

Slouching, hidden in the shadows, a figure uncoiled itself and stepped forward.

"Cleo, what are you doing here? Why aren't you at the show?"

"I had to get out. If Pops wants to take me back later, he can bend a few rules."

"Where's Zave?"

Ignoring my question, she asked, "You gonna make me stand in this damn doorway all night?" She reeked of whiskey and cigarettes.

Barging in, she snapped the lights on and pronounced the suite "Snazzy. Very, very snazzy." Continuing to take in the fancy touches, she collapsed on the settee, grabbed the bottle, guzzled about half of it, burped, and concluded, "Well, Stretch, looks like you landed jelly side up."

That show of bravado appeared to exhaust her. The tough-girl act wobbled and, for a moment, she was simply a child, a very sad, very tired child, who should have been put to bed long ago. And who should have been hugged and kissed and told she was the most precious thing ever, because I saw in her the same vast hunger that I'd grown up with, and all I could feel for Cleo was pity. Pity and guilt that I'd been the cause of Zave leaving her.

"Not entirely," I answered. There was no reason to pretend with Cleo. She knew who Zave was. She was the one person in the whole world who understood exactly how I was feeling.

"So what'd you decide?" she asked.

"About what?"

"Zave told me you're engaged. Are you going to marry him for real?"

"Should I?"

"Don't ask me," she scoffed. "I'm the bitch. You're the nice girl. We need different things."

"I'm not that nice, Cleo, and I doubt that what you need is much different from what I need."

"You think so?" Her question was more sad than sneering. "Evie, don't kid yourself. You're a normal girl and you want the normal things. Like a family."

"In my whole life," I told her, "I have barely even glimpsed normal. I wouldn't know normal if it came up and bit me on the ass. I've never expected normal. Even having a family has always seemed impossible. But with Zave? Maybe it is possible. Not 'normal,' but possible."

"Sounds like you've made up your mind." She went to the liquor cart, inspected a few bottles, poured herself a tumbler of gin, and daintily added one ice cube.

"I don't know," I admitted. "He wants me to have what I want. He's going to help me get my pin. He's smart, kind, loves books, makes me laugh. He looks out for me."

"And?"

"And what?"

"And the only thing that really matters. Do you love him?"

"I love him."

"Aw, kid," she said with genuine compassion. "I'm sorry about that."

"What do you mean?"

"Nothing. Everything. It'd just be a hell of a lot easier if you didn't."

"Did he ever —"

"Ask me?" Cleo finished. "You're kidding, right? As long as I've known him, the guy has been nuts to have kids. Do I look like

421

anyone's mother to you?"

"Lots of women have kids who don't look like mothers."

"And you and I both know how *that* ends up." After a healthy swig of gin, she asked, "So whatcha gonna do?"

"I guess, for now, we'll just see what happens. We plan to get to know each other in Galveston before we decide whether or not to make the wedding real. But, seriously, Cleo, you probably know him better than anyone else in the world. What do you think I should do?"

Cleo sat down and revisited the bubbly before asking, "You're asking the woman whose partner you stole?"

"I wouldn't say that —"

"Relax. I'm kidding. In any case, you're the only person who can answer that question. What do you want to do?"

"I want to be with him. I've never felt this way about anyone else. Not even close. Cleo, it's not perfect, but it's so much more than I ever expected to have that I can't really see why not. He swears he wants to change and I am almost certain that there are now medical techniques that can help him do that."

"Change, huh?" she echoed with weary skepticism. I couldn't blame her; the general

422

public was simply not aware of all the astonishing advances being made in medicine. Plus, why *should* Zave have changed for her when she hadn't even wanted a family?

"In any case," I said, "we'll have the entire show in Galveston to really get to know each other."

"Get to know each other? During a dance marathon?" Cleo hooted as she emptied the hotel's box of cigarettes into her bag. "When you're both always under a spotlight? With people watching?"

"Is that really any more artificial than two people out on a date all gussied up and watching everything they say? Seriously, Cleo, I doubt there is any better way than a dance marathon to find out who someone really is."

"Oh, I could think of a few," she said.

Tired of being patronized, I challenged her, "Cleo, Zave and I have a bond. I know what I'm getting into." My tone was sharper than I'd intended and she jabbed right back.

"Do you? Do you really?" she asked, snapping her bag shut after stuffing in a few monogrammed cocktail napkins.

"Yes, I really do," I said sharply.

With a defeated sigh, Cleo got to her feet and announced, "Okay, if that's the way you

want to play it. That's the way we'll play it.
Come on. We're going out."

CHAPTER 56

In the cab, all Cleo would tell me about our destination was that it was Zave's favorite Chicago haunt and if he was anywhere in the city, that's where he would be. "We'll surprise him," she said, sounding far more weary than excited.

An endless river of cars flowed red through the electrified streets. The vibrancy of the city infected me with its energetic optimism. Chicago gave me courage, made me bold. Made me want to run toward adventure. Risk. Love. Gradually, though, the lights faded and the buildings grew shorter and farther apart.

"Cleo, why is this place so far out?"

"We're going to a speakeasy."

"I figured that much. But there are dozens of speaks within walking distance of the hotel and they barely bother to disguise what they are."

"Maybe they don't need to. This place

does," Cleo said with no further comment.

The cab pulled onto an unlit street and stopped outside what appeared to be a deserted warehouse. There wasn't a door or an entrance in sight. The only sign of life on the entire street was a phone booth that had been built directly onto the side of the warehouse. The driver flipped off the meter. I reached forward with several bills to pay. Cleo brusquely shoved my hand away, demanding, "What? Don't you think I can afford a lousy cab ride?"

Out of patience with Cleo and her erratic moods, I asked the driver, "Could you wait here for a minute? I need to talk to my friend."

"Take your time," he answered as he tipped his cap over his eyes and leaned back. "They say talk is cheap. Not this time, ladies." He flipped the meter back on.

On the sidewalk, a dismal light shone from a bulb inside the phone booth. Cleo seemed small and defeated in its meager glow.

"Cleo, I understand if you hate me."

"Hate you?" she asked. "For what?"

"For, in your own words, stealing Zave."

"Oh, Evie, you can't steal something from me that I never had. And, no matter what you tell yourself, what you never will have either."

"Cleo, I know who he is."

"Sure, I knew too. I always knew. And I thought I could accept it. Just like you think you can accept it. Just like you think that your love will be enough for the both of you. So you never ask for a thing and you hope. And then you start hoping that you'll stop hoping. But you never will, Evie, that's what I'm trying to tell you. You'll never stop hoping for the real thing."

"You're wrong, Cleo. You don't know what I know. Not about medicine, not about Zave, not about the connection I have with him that no one else can ever have."

"Am I?" she asked, not unkindly. "So then how about this? How about you get back in that cab, go back to the hotel, take a bubble bath, eat yourself sick on room service, and then go out and meet someone who can love you the way you will never, ever, no matter how hard you try and what you tell yourself, stop wanting."

Maybe, if I hadn't had a childhood of Mamie ripping my heart out with her theatrics and her tears, then tossing it over her shoulder as soon as I actually believed in her latest manufactured tragedy, I might have listened to Cleo. Instead, all I could think of were all the times that Cleo had reminded me of Mamie when she'd turned her face up to the lights so that the audience could see the tears glistening in her eyes.

Angry at Cleo for trying to con me, I raised my voice. "You don't know what you're talking about. He never asked you to marry him. To have a family, a life, with him."

"Oh, kid," she answered, shaking her head wearily.

"Because he asked me, Cleo. I'm sorry if he never wanted that with you, but he wants it with me."

"Screw you," Cleo said. "Don't ever say I didn't try. I just wish that you were half as tough as you think you are."

I threw another five at the driver and as Cleo and I walked to the cheerless building I told her, "You have no idea how tough I am."

CHAPTER 57

A hole opened in the wall that the phone booth had been built against and one eye examined us. "You're in the wrong place, ladies," the owner of the eye shouted gruffly through the peephole.

"No, we're not," I shouted back.

"Okay, what's the password," he demanded.

"Screw your password," I said, venting my annoyance on him.

"Josephine Baker," Cleo supplied. "Now open the frigging door before I poke my finger in your eye, you Cyclops."

A heavy door hidden by the fake phone booth creaked open and a wave of sound hit us. It was composed of equal parts hot jazz, clinking glasses, and patrons yelling to the bartenders over the noise.

"Make it a double. No, a triple!"

"Two gin rickeys and a South Side Fizz. Hold the mint!"

"Three French 75s and use the good stuff!"

As I beheld the scene, I felt like Alice after she'd gone through the looking glass. As dreary and unpromising as the outside of the club had been, the inside was just that alluring and glitzy. Deeply shadowed scenes of impossible elegance swam out of the pools of candlelight illuminating the room. Feathers and fur, creamy shoulders and swan necks emerged from the darkness. Women wore deeply plunging evening gowns snatched from a fantasy of satin and silk.

I peered into the gloom straining to find Zave, but my eyes were drawn to the only bright spot in the place, the stage. A heavy-set Negro man in white tails and white top hat sat at a white piano, pounding out a barrelhouse beat while a chorus of slender, scantily clad dancers — tall feather headpieces bouncing, spangled costumes cut high on long legs — strutted and high-kicked with military precision behind him.

"Here, toots." Cleo shoved a glass clinking with chips of ice into my hand and ordered, "Get this inside of you."

The cocktail was a syrupy lemonade concoction that burned going down but improved dramatically with every sip. "Do you see him?" I asked, raising my voice. "Is he here?"

Cleo shrugged, tipped my glass up to my lips, and ordered, "Bottoms up," before she shoved her way back to the bar for refills without answering my question.

The piano player began singing in a powerful baritone about his love for a "lowdown woman" who was doing him wrong. He flirted shamelessly with the audience, calling out to the women if they'd like to "shuck off that old man" they were with and hop up onstage and be his easy rider. " 'Cause," he promised, "I sure will treat you right."

Gales of laughter — high, warbling titters and deep, masculine guffaws — rocked the crowd. They all took such pleasure in being together that their exuberance gave the atmosphere an electric charge that promised nothing but good times. I plunged into the joyously ribald club determined both to find Zave and to show him that this wild scene, which he obviously figured I couldn't handle, didn't faze me in the least. That I was a lot more worldly than he gave me credit for.

I squinted at a table of gangster-looking toughs in rakish fedoras, huddled around a flickering candle. At another table a pair of tuxedoed gents whipped out lighters the instant their dates, a couple of heavily rouged and mascaraed society matrons, stuck cigarettes into long holders. A cluster of college boys in shawl-neck sweaters lounging against the wall eyed some young women who were ogling them back with almost cartoonish interest. Here and there the white caps of sailors bobbed like pale froth on dark waves.

As I neared the stage, I came to understand why the club was so clandestine. The lyrics that the singer was belting out with a bawdy ferocity were so blue that the club would have been shut down the instant they were reported.

We grinded all night
And the night before, baby
And I feel like I wanna grind some more
Oh, grind me honey
Shave me dry
And when you hear me holla baby
Want you to shave me dry.

The top-hatted singer stared straight at me, growled, and laughed lasciviously when I turned away. I searched the crowd for Zave, but, blinded by the bright stage lights, it was like peering into a mine shaft. I squeezed my eyes shut to help them adjust to the dark and opened them to the sight of a familiar pair of broad shoulders and the back of a familiar head. I didn't need to see his face. The particular sheen of the velvet-dark hair, even the set of the ears, I recognized them all. I was following my heart, surging forward to follow it, when other images took shape in the dark.

A pair of pale arms, delicate hands, fingers tipped with ruby-red nails, were wrapped around Zave's neck. A spill of long bleached hair cascaded over his tuxedoed arm as it cradled her head.

Their lips were pressed together so tightly that their two profiles made one tight seam. Zave was kissing her hungrily, greedily, deeply. He was kissing her the way that, no matter how I might deny it, downplay it, dismiss it, I yearned for him to kiss me. I looked away, back to the stage. The singer's booming growl suddenly sounded distant and thin, the words reaching me as a haunting echo.

I gots nipples on my titties, big as the end
   of my thumb
I gots somethin' between my legs'll make
   a dead man come
Oh, baby won't you shave 'em dry?
Now, draw it out.

Want you to grind me baby, grind me until
I cry.

The singer shot me a devilish grin. When he threw back his shoulders, it was obvious that he was not a stout man but a woman with a chest like a pouter pigeon. And the dancers behind her? I noticed the ropy muscles of the high-kicking legs that ended at crotches that weren't female.

Suddenly, the smoke was too thick, the laughter too brittle. One of the society matrons sitting with the attentive dates leaned her head back as she languidly brought her cigarette to her lips with a thick-wristed hand. A large Adam's apple protruded from the elegantly arched neck. The table of gangsters stared at me. Smooth-skinned, narrow-shouldered, and wide-hipped, the vests of their tuxedoes rounded over what could only be breasts.

The woman sitting in Zave's lap raised her head. Her face was a puddle of smudged makeup. The mane of blond hair had been pushed to the side, exposing the black mesh of a wig cap and the short hair beneath. The beautiful boy's mouth was a smear of crimson.

I had the sensation of being simultaneously hurtled backward and forward in

434

time, unable to gain a foothold on the moment I currently occupied.

The singer hit a thunderous final chord and rasped into the mic, "I'm Gladys Bentley and this is the Pansy Club, y'all. And we do what we do with whoever we want to do it with here. Police best not try to stop us!"

The force of the raw jubilation that greeted the singer's call to liberation shoved me outside. Somehow Cleo managed to stay with me as I passed back through the phone booth onto the sidewalk. The heavy door shut behind us and we were alone on an empty, silent street.

"I'm sorry," Cleo said. "More sorry than I can ever say. I just thought you deserved to know."

Unable to speak, I nodded, and Cleo did something remarkable: she put her arm around me. "Evie, I was just like you. Hell, I *am* still like you. I thought I was wised up. That I was the hip mama who didn't want the square life. That that was for civilians. But Evie, there's a world of difference between knowing something and feeling something. You deserved to know how it feels before it's too late."

When I could speak, I said, "Tell Zave . . . Just tell him good-bye."

In the cab, the driver caught my eye in

the rearview mirror as he pulled away from the curb, and muttered, "Yeah, I didn't figure that was your scene."

As we drove back into the city, the Lindbergh Beacon that Zave had pointed out to me earlier rotated leisurely, flashing out a welcome as it guided air passengers safely home through the endlessly dark night.

■ ■ ■ ■

LITCHFIELD

■ ■ ■ ■

CHAPTER 58

June 22, 1932

At first glimpse, it appeared that a strange sort of human pig was standing upright outside my grandmother's farm, tossing feed to the chickens gabbling softly at her feet. Then the creature caught sight of me walking up the long narrow road, ripped off its snout, and there was Granma, grinning and waving an enthusiastic welcome.

"It's a gas mask," she explained later as we sat on the porch and sipped lemonade. "They gave it to me at the hospital for when I was outside. So the dust won't build up in my lungs again."

"Well, it's working. You look wonderful." And she did. Cheeks glowing, eyes bright, she appeared twenty years younger than the broken, old woman I'd left at the hospital in Lubbock.

"I feel like my old self again. Evie, you saved my life."

I brushed that statement away.

"No, it's true. I'd of died you hadn't gotten me to the hospital. Well, you and Dub. Then you sent money every week so I could stay in that lovely room. And, oh my. The food. Like Thanksgiving every day. Look at me. I'm bustin' out of my britches they fed me up so good."

Though I smiled at the evidence of her recovery, she noticed the deadness in my eyes and said softly, "You must be awful tired after your trip."

"I'm fine," I answered, making an effort to perk up and beam happiness that I didn't feel.

Tilting her head from side to side like a puzzled spaniel, her kind eyes soaking me in, my grandmother inquired gently, "Are you sure?"

Determined not to cry, all I could manage in reply was a tight nod.

"Is it about that dance feller you married?"

Crap. Had the story reached even this remote outpost? I dipped my head to hide my sorrow.

"I'm sorry. I didn't mean to intrude."

"You aren't. Apparently the whole world knows. But don't worry. The wedding wasn't real. None of it . . ." My voice faltered. "Not a single bit of it was real."

She gave me a tight nod. Just like all of us, my grandmother was a product of her time and place. And people around here were, above all else, stoic. They bore their grief in private. Sharing your troubles with others was considered "burdening." Only the weak and selfish "burdened" others with their woes.

Instead, we did what we had always done. We worked. At dawn the next morning I constructed a barricade of chores that sheltered my heart and numbed my mind. However much I tried to dodge them, though, memories managed to slip past the wall of work. Unbidden, they came.

How he held a finger up before he started a story. How, no matter how much pomade he put on his hair, it broke apart into curls. How he pressed a finger against his lips when he was thinking, then patted his mouth twice when his mind was made up. How his right nostril flared a bit when he was about to say something that he knew would make me laugh. How his neck smelled. How he watched out for me. Took care of me. Made me feel, for one moment, beautiful.

On the morning of June 26, a day before I was supposed to be in Galveston per the contract I'd signed, a wagon pulled by a swayback mule with "Rural Free Delivery" written on the side stopped outside the house.

The creaking of the tack and the postman yelling, "Whoa, Ned, whoa!" startled me and my grandmother. She shot me a look of alarm at this highly unusual occurrence.

"Mail!" the postman bellowed, and we rushed outside. He was a big man wearing dusty overalls and a battered Stetson. "Vonda Kay," he hollered at my grandmother as she approached to take the stack of letters he held out to her. "You need to get you a mailbox."

"What'd I need a mailbox for?" my grandmother asked. "My granddaughter's only one sends me mail and she's here now."

"Well, you ain't gettin' none today neither," he said with a wheezy laugh at his witticism as he handed over a fat fistful of letters. "All these here are for your famous granddaughter. Look to be fan mail, I 'spec."

To the sound of the postman's geeing and hawing as he got the mules turned around, Granma passed me the stack of letters that had been forwarded from Chicago. The sight of them, evidence of the fraud I had perpetrated not just on myself but on the tender hearts of those who had believed in me and my fantasy, made me ill. I handed them all back to my grandmother.

In silence, she leafed through the letters, reading the return addresses and muttering with astonishment, "Des Moines. Newark. Fort Dade. Indianapolis. Cincinnati. Los Angeles. Why, Evie, there must be fifty letters here. All forwarded from Chicago. Spokane. Dayton —" With a quiet gasp, she stopped reeling off the names of cities. Fearing she was having breathing difficulties, I glanced over sharply to find her staring at the address of a letter resting on her lap.

The only thing printed on the return address was "Zave."

Without a word, my grandmother handed over the letter, then left me alone.

Alone. That was the supposed cure in this already isolated country for heartbreak and sorrow. That and work and never mentioning the delicate topic. It was a lonely way to be. The specter of a lifetime of loneliness was what drove me, in spite of my best intentions to never again have any contact with Zave, to open his letter.

CHAPTER 59

The sight of a full page of Zave's handwriting shook me. I felt as though I were meeting him for the first time while already knowing everything about him and everything that would happen. My hand trembled as I began to read.

Dear Evie,

Cleo told me what you saw. Told me everything.

I can never expect you to forgive me. So I won't ask for that. The most I can hope for is your understanding. I owe you more than I can ever repay. At the very least, I owe you my story. My full story.

I was born Milton Dowd, the second youngest of seven children. From my earliest memories, I was out of place. Where my father and brothers, even my sisters and mother, were oaks, sturdy, strong, and unbending, I was a willow, sickly, weak, and limp.

I had to pause and remind myself to breathe. Seeing how tender and lyrical he was on the page made me yearn again for all I could never have.

I wanted to read books, draw pictures, and play hopscotch. Real boys packed rocks inside of snowballs, jumped out of haylofts, and tied firecrackers to cats' tails. Boys, real boys, scared me. And I repelled them.

Everything about me was wrong.

The smell of hay and cow shit still reminds me of our barn, where my father tried to beat the sissy out of me. I was never quite sure what my crime was. Had I held my wrists wrong? Or laughed too much? Or spoken in a voice that was too high? Or used words that were too "fancy"? Or expressed undue admiration for a sister's new pair of shoes? Or, worst of all, danced? Even just swaying to the little tunes I hummed to myself enraged him.

And then the root of my wrongness, my sin, revealed itself: I liked boys. The world saw the evil before I saw it in myself. I tried to change. To be normal. To hide the

445

twisted thing in me. I failed. I never knew what gave me away, but my father knew long before I did. And the other boys knew. They scented me out like a wolf scents a rabbit.

I only felt safe in the dense, sunless woods. There I would take off my mittens, cap, jacket, boots, lie down on carpets of snow and pine needles and pray to Jesus to either take the wrongness, the sickness, the deviancy from me, or to let me die. That was where the boys found me that day. The first time it happened. They trapped me, beat me, used me to "practice" being married. They "gave me" what I was "asking for." Of this I will say no more.

I told you that your father saved me. Evie, he not only saved my life, he gave me a life worth living. From the moment he twirled onstage, blinding white and pure in the spotlight, all the evil urges simply went away. I was burned clean in the blaze of his glory. I became your father's shadow. Anytime I wasn't patching canvas, repainting flats, or running errands, I was studying Denny Devlin.

At first I stayed hidden, copying him in private. Mimicking every step until I could do his whole act. When he noticed me, he didn't mock me or chase me away or beat me or any of the things I expected — he praised me. He encouraged me. Told me I was the most natural dancer he'd ever seen. And then he taught me how to be a better one.

I was born again. As his son. A Dancing Devlin.

Pretty much from the start our father-son act clicked. After a few months on the hayseed circuit, your father decided that we were too good for the F. Andrews tent show. We started saving to travel east and audition for the Keith-Orpheum Circuit. Then, on the last stop of the western circuit, we set up outside Litchfield and your mother entered the picture. Mamie always had a talent for spotting a soft touch. She told Denny that her father was "interfering" with her and she begged him to save her. All she needed was a lift to Lubbock, where an aunt lived.

There was no aunt, but by that time it didn't matter. Denny was smitten and Mamie had managed to get herself pregnant. And pretty soon I was kicked out. After that, after your father left, the unnatural urges came over me again. Worse than ever. Evie, back in Houston, before I even knew that you were Denny's daughter, you were healing me exactly as he'd done. Not just my ankle, but, like your father, you gave me a reason and the strength to overcome my failing.

Though the bennie I took on that awful night did play a part, I can't completely blame it for my transgression. I was weak and I betrayed you. I don't deserve your forgiveness, but I am desperate enough to ask for it. If you give me the second chance I don't deserve, I will never be weak again. You are the one, single chance I have to be good. Not to be alone. To have what I want most. A family.

Evie, like your father, you are already more of a family to me than my own ever was. No matter what happens, that will never change. But I promise that if you will allow me to redeem myself in Galveston, I will never let you down again.

Please meet me in Galveston. Please give me another chance. We can win that competition, take the money, and start a new life together. A happy life.

That is my promise and my plea,

Zave

CHAPTER 60

June 27, 1932

"Evie, are you feeling all right?" my grandmother asked while we ate our usual lunch of beans, supplemented with the treat of a store-bought banana that we split.

"What?" I asked, pretending I was not still reeling from Zave's letter.

"I don't mean to pry. But you seem a bit puny. How are your lungs? Not getting that dust new-mony, are you?"

I plastered on a smile that never reached my eyes and answered too brightly, "I'm fine."

We finished our meal in silence. Figuring, as always, that I needed solitude, Granma went to check on Daisy. As soon as I was alone, I did what I'd been trying most to avoid doing. I thought.

No, Zave and I could never be together. Not after Chicago. Although my head had completely accepted Zave and whatever arrangement we might make, thanks to Cleo I knew that my heart never truly would. The pain would simply be too great.

Then I thought of the sad, abused little boy trapped in a world of ice and hate. I saw myself rescuing little Milton and nearly melted. I had to be strictly analytical then and accept that the powerful pull I felt was bound up with my own thwarted yearning to rescue both my father and the sad, abused little girl that I had been. I reminded myself sternly that my going to Galveston would not change a single minute of either of our wretched childhoods.

Though my mind was made up, every molecule of my body remained unconvinced, and I ached for Zave right down to the sinews holding muscle to bone.

In any event, it no longer mattered. It was already too late. The countdown had already started. All the pros and the horses were already there, staying at whatever fleabag hotel Pops could get the cheapest rate on. The paper would be full of ads. Handbills were plastered on every telephone and utility pole in town. They'd start registering locals soon. I could never make it to Galveston in time.

The dates had really lined up for Pops, though. The Fourth of July was on a Monday. That meant there would be a huge holiday crowd for the July 1 opening. And it would only get bigger over the long week-end.

In spite of myself, I yearned to be part of it again, to belong to a group that squabbled and competed, but also came together and protected each other, a group that was almost a family. But all that, even the dim possibility of what I might have had with Zave, was nothing compared to what I had truly lost: my pin.

That, too, was impossible. Now that I was welching on a deal I'd made with the Amadeos, I could never show my face in Galveston again. Sofie's friendship aside, it was not entirely out of the question that Mr. Amadeo would send one of his enforcers all the way to Litchfield to make an example of me about what happens when you cheated the Amadeos.

A loud knocking at the door startled me. They were here. The enforcers.

Before I could even think about hiding, the door flew open. My visitor marched in, took one look at me, emitted a dry laugh, and said, "Well, look who's here."

"Hello, Mamie."

CHAPTER 61

A man with a thin mustache and a weak chin, wearing a suit of black-and-yellow windowpane plaid, followed my mother in. Though he was probably only in his early thirties, the man's hair, combed straight back, was so thin that streaks of pink scalp showed through the sparse, dust-colored strands. Outside, a forest-green Packard touring car sparkled in the harsh sunlight.

Mamie glanced around as if seeing the modest house she'd grown up in for the first time. As though she'd accidentally entered the past of some other girl. Some ordinary girl not destined from birth for stardom.

Gone was the bedraggled, shopworn tarnish of Vinegar Hill. She wore a smart, dusty-rose dress with flutter sleeves that floated about her slender arms and hugged her newly toned figure. A pendant of what might actually be a real diamond on a braided gold chain rested on her delicate collarbones. Her nails were impeccably manicured and painted a tasteful seashell pink. Her hair floated in soft waves around her face.

In spite of myself and all the hard lessons she had forced me to learn, a spasm clenched my heart. She was again the great beauty of my childhood. The distant star whose light I reflected, though it never warmed me. Like an outgoing tide, I felt the gravity of the fairy-tale world she'd constructed tugging on me. The one where she had reigned as a queen as beautiful as she was blameless.

She eyed me up and down with bitterly familiar disdain and the spell was broken. Like a lens shifting in a camera, I zoomed out from the close-up, suffocating focus my mother had always required, and drew farther and farther away until I might have been observing the two of us through a telescope.

Or from the balcony of a drafty theater in Detroit.

Mamie stared pointedly at the sofa. A moment passed before her escort twigged to what was required, whipped out a large, monogrammed handkerchief, and flapped it on the cushions, raising a few puffs of dust. Mamie settled herself, folded her white-gloved hands on her lap, crossed her dainty ankles, and said airily, "I didn't expect to see you here," as if I were a distant acquaintance she'd happened to bump into at a party.

"Monty," she told the man. "This is the *baby sister* in all those newspaper stories that I showed you." She shot me a sharp glance of warning. I didn't need it. I had always been her baby sister, never her daughter, when a new man friend was around.

"Delighted to make your acquaintance." Monty gripped my hand in his doughy palm, shook it too heartily, and glancing from me to Mamie, said, "You're right, darling. There isn't much of a family resemblance."

"We had different fathers," I said, smiling at Monty more out of pity than anything else. He was trying to please my mother; I knew how lethal that was.

Mamie tugged off her gloves and beckoned the weasel-faced beau to join her. He responded like a well-trained schnauzer, plunking himself down next to her. Once settled in, he threw his arms onto the back of the sofa like he owned the place. I figured him for some well-heeled trust fund brat. A not-terribly-bright or well-liked rich boy that Mamie had managed to momentarily enchant.

I wondered what she wanted and decided to open the negotiations by telling her what she always wanted to hear. "You're looking well. *Sis.*"

"Why, thank you," she purred, taking Monty's hand and gazing at him adoringly. "It's all because of Monty. He is a very shrewd businessman. Titan of industry, to be exact. Anyhow, Monty came up with the positively inspired idea that he should represent me for both film and theatrical opportunities. It took a lot of convincing, but Monty finally got it through my silly head that anything spent on my 'upkeep' was simply a wise investment."

While Monty preened like someone had just handed him a Phi Beta Kappa key for his brilliance, Mamie opened her beaded clutch a tiny crack. I caught a glimpse of a full pack of Luckies. Immediately, she snapped the bag shut and lamented, "Oh, phooey, Monty, I'm out."

Monty was offering Mamie a cig from the gold case he whipped out of his pocket before Mamie had time to finish arranging her lips into a fetching pout. "Oh, darling, you know I can't smoke your big, strong Chesterfields. Only a man's lungs can stand up to those brutes. I have to have my ladies' Luckies." Her hand fluttered about the ivory column of her neck. "The toasted tobacco is more soothing to a girl's throat, doncha know?"

Monty was out the door and raising dust, racing back into Litchfield before Mamie's hand had left her delicate "girl's" throat.

Mamie reopened her purse and pulled a cigarette from her pack. On her first exhale, she asked, "Where's our grandmother?"

" 'Our'?" I answered, marveling that her annoyed tone had no effect on me.

"You know what I mean. I can't have Monty thinking I have a daughter as old as you *and* a mother who's a grandmother."

"So how old does Monty think you are?"

"You're only as old as you feel."

"Okay, how old does Monty think you feel?"

"Sarcasm does not become you."

Mamie turned her head away, blew out a column of smoke, and fiddled with the diamond around her neck. "You show me an actress who divulges her true age and I'll show you an unemployed bit player. Where is she?"

"You mean your mother? Probably hiding from you." I was delighted to learn that with my new sense of detachment had come a

456

courage I'd never before felt around her.

"Well, aren't you just as sweet as ever? Actually, I'm glad you're here. You're in all the papers. You must have really raked it in in Chicago."

"I am not giving you any money. Not one, single, solitary dime."

Acting as though my words had wounded her delicate sensibilities, she whimpered, "I knew that the marathon world would coarsen you. That and nursing. All those naked bodies. And the Catholics. Why, you're tough as an old boot now, aren't you?"

"Now? *Now* I'm tough?" I asked. "As if my childhood was Easy Street. As if you ever, even once, sheltered me from anything."

Mamie plucked a flake of tobacco off her tongue. "You always were so harsh and unforgiving. I could never do anything right in your book, could I?"

"I was a child, Mamie. Your child."

A bottomless chasm opened up. One that would swallow me whole if I moved one centimeter closer to Mamie. Stripping my voice of all emotion, I asked in a robotic monotone, "What do you need money for? Seems like Monty's loaded and that he's crazy for your knish."

"I beg your pardon," Mamie demanded. "When did you start talking like a guttersnipe?" She fanned herself as if my vulgar words had to be batted away.

"Maybe it was around the time you shoved me onstage at a burlesque show."

"That is a lie," she declaimed with a thunderous rage. "I would *never* stoop to appearing at a burlesque hall."

"Yet you seemed to have had no trouble forcing your child to do so."

Mamie's eyes popped open as wide as a heroine in a horror movie. Some of the shock was genuine. I'd never mentioned that nightmarish time before. Never spoken to her like this. Doing so now left me both terrified and exhilarated, as though I'd suddenly discovered a fearsome power I hadn't known I possessed: the power not to care.

She immediately shifted gears when I failed to react and, once more the wounded victim, whimpered, "There it is again. All the injustices that you *imagined* I inflicted upon you. I was always wrong, wasn't I? Never the parent that you believe your sainted father would have been. I was never good enough for you to love. Not the way you loved him."

What always confused me growing up was that, in the moment she spoke them, Mamie absolutely believed every word she uttered. The tears she shed now were real, welling up from all the injustice of my rejection. She really should have been on some screen other than the one in her head, where she never stopped starring.

Angry that I was not playing my part, she sniped, "Well, pardon me for not being the perfect mother. But who the hell do you think kept you alive after your precious father abandoned us?"

I laughed at the fathomless depths of her deluded narcissism. "Me," I answered simply. "I kept myself and you alive, and my father didn't abandon us, he died."

She waved that detail away as if death were a lover he'd chosen to cheat on her with and said, "You go ahead and tell yourself whatever story you choose about all the petty trials you imagine I inflicted upon you. The truth is you owe me. The absolute least you can do is loan me enough to get my start in Hollywood."

"If you need a stake, why don't you hock that rock around your neck?"

She slapped her hand over the gem as if she feared I'd steal it. "Monty gave this to me."

"Then get Monty to front you the dough."

"Monty's finances are rather tightly controlled by his ridiculous family."

"I bet," I said, exalting in my snide tone. "Keep your jewels, but I don't have any money, and if I did, I wouldn't give you a cent."

Mamie shot me a gimlet-eyed glance. "You are a very poor liar, my dear. Your face has positively leapt out at me from the front pages of newspapers in several cities. Even though these dance marathons are the absolute lowest form of entertainment — if they even qualify as entertainment — I know that you had sponsors for your wedding from Marshall Field's to the Palmer Hotel and that thousands of dollars in prize money were awarded. So, please, don't insult me by saying you have no money."

"Nope, no prize money. No wedding. It was all a put-up job."

"Well, obviously, I knew it was a lavender wedding."

"What's that mean?" I asked, immediately regretting that I had allowed myself to be lured back into engaging with her.

"Oh, I'm pretty sure you know. That boy, Zave or whatever Milton is calling himself now, hated me from the instant Denny fell for me. He adored Denny. The attachment was positively unhealthy."

"That's a lie."

460

"Oh, not like that. Denny had many flaws but he was the farthest thing from a deviant you could imagine. Definitely a soft touch but not a swish. Man could not keep his hands off of me." She shuddered before heaving a gusty sigh and concluding, "Oh well, leave it to you to marry a faggot."

I would have slapped her if the thought of touching her hadn't repulsed me. My eyes narrowed, the fury I refused to speak building in me.

"Oh, now you play the goody two-shoes. Too pure to know what a faggot is even after you married one. Zave is a fruit, a fairy, a nancy boy. A goddamn queer."

The question that went unasked my entire childhood bubbled out of me. "What made you so cruel?"

"Me? Cruel? Because I'm giving it to you straight? That makes *me* cruel? I suppose you think that Denny was better than me because he'd never call a spade a spade. Never say what the whole world knew about his precious little protégé. That the boy was a deviant and was poisoning the whole show with his corruption."

"So it was you," I said. "Of course it was you. You got him kicked out of the show. You forced a child out into the world alone."

After a long, elegant draw on her cigarette,

she hissed, "He was no child, believe you me."

"You tried to ruin his life just like you tried to ruin mine by sending the Director those clippings." For a fraction of a second, the truth took her by surprise and she blinked like an actress who'd forgotten her next line. That tiny hint at an admission of guilt was replaced by outrage at what a callous, vengeful, neglectful daughter I was. And how deeply, *deeply,* I had hurt her.

She watched me and waited for me to hit back. To hurl more accusations, rage anything other than the complete obliteration of the silence that I turned on her. She always needed to provoke some sort of reaction. Needed it to feed off of. To feel alive. I no longer had that to give her. And so she prodded. Taunting me with her familiar litany of laments about how I'd stolen her dreams of stardom by being born then proving to be such a disappointment.

"A bony scarecrow of a girl who couldn't even keep her own hair brushed. Too bad you weren't a boy. You should have been a son."

"And you should have been a mother," I stated with a calm finality.

"Well, I guess neither one of us was quite the prize in the Cracker Jack box that we wanted, were we?"

When I said nothing, Mamie played the wronged victim, ranting about all the hardships I'd forced upon her and how she had borne them with the patience of a saint. Even as the heat of her outrage grew hot enough to kindle actual belief in her ordeal, she seemed to slip farther and farther away. Soon her words felt as though they were being beamed to me from the distant past. From a different life. One that I had so little interest in being a part of any longer that I couldn't ignite even the smallest ember of anger to lob back at her.

No longer caring what this spluttering stranger thought, I spoke the insight that her visit had sparked. "Mamie, I'm glad you stopped by."

"Oh, again with the sarcasm," she needled.

"No, I'm serious. You've just made me realize how wrong I have been."

"I have?" she purred, perking up, waiting for me to beg her to take me back.

"You've made me realize that I was just about to act as horribly as you had."

"Oh, what are you talking about now?"

"I'm talking about you never, not for one moment, loving me for who I was. I'm talking about how I've done the exact same thing because I have someone who loves me and I'm refusing to accept him for who he is." With a sudden exhilaration I concluded, "I'm going to Galveston."

"Back to your 'husband,' " she said archly. "Why not? A girl who looks like you? A lavender wedding with a queer? You're lucky to get that."

"I am lucky," I said, surprising myself with the revelation. "There is more goodness, more kindness, more true feeling for me in Zave's little finger than there ever was in your entire body. Also," I went on, "you had better leave the instant your latest sucker returns."

"Just exactly who do you think you are? Speaking to me like that? With your filthy dance shows and your degenerate friends? I will leave when I am goddamn good and ready to —"

Gravel pinging, Monty singing, "Hi-dee, hi-dee, hi-dee ho!" along with Cab Calloway on the car radio, the big Packard came to a halt outside.

"Good, he's back," I said, standing and walking toward the door. "I think I'll just go on out and have a little chat with ol' Monty. Fill him in on a few details. You know, like, much as I wish it weren't true, I am your daughter and you are probably as old as his mother. Perhaps I'll also give him

464

a quick inventory of all the suckers who've preceded him and of all your pathetic attempts to be a star."

With a bored glance at her fingernails, Mamie said, "Go ahead. He'll never believe you. As soon as Vonda Kay comes in, I'll have her fetch the sheriff and have you removed from her property."

I watched Monty standing beside the Packard, angling his head from side to side to catch a glimpse of his reflection as he combed his hair.

"Fine," I said idly. "But you should probably know that since my grandmother is terrified of you and since you can make her do whatever you want, I had her sign the deed to the farm over to me."

Mamie jerked to attention. "What are you talking about? This farm is mine. It is my legacy."

Outside, Monty pocketed his comb and strode toward the house.

"The farm," I answered coolly. "The only thing of value that you haven't managed to steal from her, I own it now. So, technically, if we decide to call the sheriff, you would be the trespasser."

I hadn't had my grandmother sign her farm over to me, but Mamie believed me because it was what she would have done in my place. What she thought anyone who wasn't a sucker would do. Her eyes went glacier blue as she calculated the worth of making a scene and having her age revealed now that there was no possible gain.

The screen door creaked open.

Mamie stood, all expression falling from her face. Hate, love, annoyance, guilt, nothing registered. That beautiful face I had idolized was as chillingly blank as that of a rider on a crowded subway who had blotted out the unpleasant strangers around her.

"Oh, Monty, hello," I said. "I was just telling my —"

"Monty, you're back," Mamie exclaimed, drowning out my next word as she rushed forward, tears, wonderfully cinematic tears of wronged victimhood, trembling in her fathomless eyes, and threw herself into the hapless sap's arms.

"Uh-oh," he said, "did you two sisters have a little spat?"

"It's nothing, darling," Mamie purred, curling into his embrace. "Maybe just a bit of the green-eyed monster that I have such a handsome beau."

"Jealousy," Monty chuckled, pleased by his own wisdom. "Happens in every family. It's all about 'Who did Mother love the most,' right?"

Knowing that these would be the last words I would ever speak to the woman who'd given birth to me but had never let me call her Mother, I looked Mamie in the eye and answered, "Not in this case, Monty. You see, our mother was a bitch and I don't care anymore who she does or does not love."

As a plume of dust rose in the hot, still air behind the Packard, I caught a whiff of a fragrance lingering in the doorway. Before I could identify the scent, a spasm of grief squeezed my heart like a fist.

Beadex and Shalimar.

CHAPTER 62

As soon as Mamie left, I packed up. When I told my grandmother I was leaving, she made a dozen hard-boiled eggs for me to eat on the road and gave me a pair of my grandfather's pants, boots, and his old hat.

"I surely do wish I had enough put aside to buy you a ticket. But if you're bound and determined to hitchhike, keep your hair tucked up in the hat. And don't walk dainty. Walk like a man. Act like you own the place. The way men do. You'll be safer."

I had to hike through Litchfield and all the way back to the main road before I could hitch a ride. When I finally made it to Lubbock, I stopped at the Western Union office. There was no time to shoot Pops a wire and wait for him to shoot me the fare, so I sent Sofie the shortest, cheapest telegram I could. COMING HOME STOP.

I was trying to hitch a ride out of Abilene when a cop pulled over and told me he'd run me in if I didn't move on.

"On what grounds?" I asked.

" 'Less you got fifty dollars in your pocket and a home to go to, you're a vagrant."

"So being poor is illegal?" I said, feeling like Ace.

"One more word out of your smart mouth and I'm booking you. Now get out of my sight."

Furious, I stomped off toward the "Hooverville" at the edge of town. What Pops had said about the hypocrites who protested the dances because they threatened "morals" was right. They didn't give a damn about the contestants and their "morals," they just didn't want to be reminded that people were hungry and homeless. They wanted the suffering to be done conveniently out of their sight.

It was dusk by the time I reached the sprawling hobo encampment composed of dozens of clusters of homeless wanderers gathered around fires. Though most of the campers were men, there were a surprising number of women, children, and gangs of kids barely into their teens. At the center of the camp, men stirred pots of food balanced on rocks over the flames, smoked, played cards, talked and argued in raucous voices. When they started passing a bottle around, the jovial spirits brightened even more.

On the edges of the camp, though, other men sat, grim and oddly prim, wearing what had once been decent business suits. The eyes of the broke businessmen were haunted and made me think of all the stories about Wall Street brokers and big bankers jumping out of skyscrapers. Being poor was new to these gents. It frightened and shamed them and they wanted to pretend it was temporary. That they'd found their way to the dead end of a dirt road among hoboes and panhandlers because of some terrible mistake that would soon be cleared up.

Off in the shadows of several shacks and lean-tos made out of scrap lumber and old highway signs, I spotted a few rawboned women and malnourished children. It made me sad to see how resigned they seemed to be to life on the far edge of a dismal town.

I took my grandfather's hat off, shook my hair out, entered the women's camp, and handed out the hard-boiled eggs to the children and a few of their mothers by way of introduction. The women saw that I had lived a version of their hard lives, that being poor wasn't a shocking new catastrophe, and they welcomed me to share their fire.

The stories they traded were about lives that had been lived on the edge long before the stock market went sideways and about the nudge that was all it took to send them over that edge. A child falling ill. One missed payment on a mortgage. A windstorm ripping young plants from the earth. The rain that never came.

All the stories were sad. But the saddest came from the small gang of kids, many not even teens yet, who proudly announced that they were "ridin' the rails" together. A skinny brown-eyed girl, her hair in a bowl cut, told me in a matter-of-fact tone, "My parents had to turn me out 'cause I et too much. They's eleven of us and I et the most, so they had to turn me out. What else could they do?"

I didn't have an answer other than to give her the egg I had been keeping back for myself and my grandfather's hat with the advice to keep her hair tucked up in it and to walk like a boy.

CHAPTER 63

I hit the road again at dawn after a sleepless night and made good time catching rides. My luck turned bad outside of Dime Box. Darkness fell and, no matter how badly I wanted to make it to Galveston by the date specified on the contract, I couldn't risk hopping into a car when there wasn't enough light to size up the driver. I also couldn't hang out on the side of the road and risk getting picked up, since I didn't have enough cash on me to beat a vagrancy charge. I had to hike forever before I finally reached an all-night diner.

Careful to hang on to the last few coins I had so that I could send Sofie another wire and buy a ticket on the Interurban from Houston to Galveston, I ordered a cup of coffee. With cream. After I finished the first pitcher of cream and half of the sugar dispenser, the waitress, a kind soul, brought me another pitcher of cream and I finished that one as well. As nice as she was, I knew that she would have to throw me out if I dozed at her booth. So, with her supplying endless refills, I dragged myself through another sleepless night.

■ ■ ■ ■

GALVESTON

■ ■ ■ ■

CHAPTER 64

I made it to the downtown Houston train depot late the next afternoon, sent Sofie a wire saying that I was on my way, zipped into the ladies' room where I quickly cleaned up and changed into a dress, and caught the first Interurban to Galveston.

Bracing myself against the gentle sway of the train that was trying to lull me into sleep, I sat up straight and reviewed my battle plan. My thoughts, however, kept skipping from memories of dancing in Zave's arms to the image of a nursing pin, my nursing pin, glowing in a dark haze.

I wanted them both.

Could I, could any woman, have them both?

Who knew? All I was sure of was that I was going to fight like hell to get them.

My first order of business was to get the information about a cure for Zave from Sofie. After that, I would tell my story so often to any reporter who would listen that the nursing board in Austin would know it by heart. And they would be so solidly on my side that even the Director couldn't sway them.

Sofie was waiting for me at the station. The sight of her, my friend who had never doubted, undid me. We collapsed into each other's arms.

"I was so worried," Sofie said. "When you didn't show up on the date of the contract you signed . . . Well, let's just say, everyone has been worried."

I knew that meant that JuJu was furious, but I was too joyful to get into that mess and just said, "Oh, Sofie, I'm so happy to see you." Normally, I would have stopped there, but between all that had happened with Zave and Mamie I felt stripped bare, and from that moment of nakedness, the truth emerged: "You're the best friend I've ever had, Sofie. You're my sister."

"I know," she answered simply. "Ditto for me."

I'd always heard about the phenomenon of no time passing after not seeing a friend for a while, but I'd never experienced it until then. Which was why the next thing to pop out of my mouth was "You cut your hair," as if that were something she'd sneaked away to do over a lunch break.

"So?" she asked, brushing the curls framing her face.

"So? I *love* it," I said, fluffing the curls with my fingers. "You have the perfect hair for this style. It makes your eyes look huge."

"Quit talking about my stupid hair. *You're* the one with the big news. Ever since the show was announced all the paper writes about is our 'Hometown Heroine.' Everyone is wild about the big reopening of Starlight Pier. Just look!"

Handbills for the show were plastered everywhere throughout the station and they all featured Zave and me in our wedding finery. Cringing at the sight of my face on such public display, I fought the irrational desire to rip down every one of them by reminding myself of Zave's wisdom that, in this new world we inhabited, publicity was power.

"Zave! What a dreamboat," Sofie gushed. "Tell me the whole story. And don't leave out a single detail." Then, as if the realization had just struck her, she said, "Evie, you're a married woman."

"Well, engaged."

She blinked. "Engaged? But the photos? That gown?"

I glanced around the station, crowded now

479

with happy families bustling in to start the long Fourth of July weekend early, lowered my voice, and confessed, "It's a long story."

"Gotcha," Sofie said. Just as we had from the very beginning, we didn't have to explain; we simply understood each other. She leaned in close and whispered, "Sounds like this might be a story for a quiet corner booth at Gaido's. You hungry?"

"Famished."

"Why did I even bother asking?" she joked. Taking no notice of my exaltation at the small miracle of someone knowing me, knowing my habits, she hooked her arm through mine, we set out for the Seawall, and, just like that, I was home.

For one moment, the familiar soundtrack of the excited chatter of tourists, the slap of gentle waves, the low wail of a jazz horn escaping from a club, made me feel as if Sofie and I were bright-eyed probies all over again. That my dream, all of it, my pin and Zave, was still waiting if I worked hard and was bold enough to claim them.

The sun was almost down by the time we reached Gaido's. The Starlight Palace at the end of the pier was a dark silhouette against streaks of crimson and turquoise. Even from this distance, though, I could tell that the entire pier was a hive of activity. Activity that I had set in motion. The pounding of hammers and the rasp of saws rang out as teams of carpenters prepared for opening day. Though we were too far away to make out faces, I still strained to catch sight of Zave.

"Is he there?" Sofie asked as I stared. Not even trying to deny who I was looking for, I shook my head. "Do you want to check in before we eat?"

"No. Not yet. Tomorrow's soon enough. We need to talk first."

"Definitely," Sofie agreed eagerly.

I was sure she was anticipating an evening of juicy girl talk. That was an evening I couldn't deliver. Though she was the most compassionate and discreet person I knew, I suddenly became acutely aware that she also belonged to a church that considered homosexuality the *"crimen pessimum,"* the worst crime, and had a long history of burning offenders.

"That one," Sofie told the hostess, pointing to an isolated booth in the far corner.

I waited until the waitress had delivered our sixty-five-cent deluxe shrimp platters and left before, after swearing Sofie to secrecy, I told her everything. She listened with her whole heart and I saw the wise, compassionate caregiver she had become,

481

the one who would never judge, the one hundreds of lucky patients in her future would trust implicitly. Only when Sofie clasped my hands in hers did I realize that, even in the heat, they'd gone icy cold.

Her voice was a feather bed of luxuriant sympathy as she cooed, "Oh, sweetie, you've really been through the wringer, haven't you? We have to fix that." Without my saying another word, the quicksilver connection that had always existed between us lit up and she added, "Well, obviously, I have to talk to Dr. K and get all the details about the latest procedures for reversing sexual inversion."

How could I have ever doubted her?

"I know that you'll be trapped at the contest," she went on. "So I'll bring you the research as soon as I can get it. Sorry, it might be a while, though, since Dr. K has a practice in Houston and only comes into Galveston to give lectures and do rounds once a week to assess the psychiatric cases."

Relief floated the words out of me. "Oh, Sofie, you've given me such hope. I already owe you so much. And now this? I don't know how I'll ever be able to thank you."

"What are friends for?" she asked, brushing off my gratitude. "If I wasn't pulling double shifts, I'd be at the Palace cheering you on every single day. But, the very instant I get that research, no matter what I'm doing, I'll bring it to you."

It was velvety dark by the time we stepped outside. Though the Starlight Palace blazed bright as a lighthouse guiding travelers to safe harbor, I still stared at it with deep uncertainty.

"Don't worry," Sofie said. "We live in an age of medical miracles."

"We do," I agreed. "Oh, Sof—"

"Come on," she interrupted before I could try again to express the gratitude flooding me. "I can't wait to show you the apartment. Complete with a guest room that has no checkout time."

She grabbed my arm and, together, we strode down Seawall Boulevard as if we were Barbara Stanwyck and Joan Blondell playing bold career gals ready to take on the world.

CHAPTER 65

Thursday morning, though Sofie and I had stayed up until dawn talking, I was so buoyant with new hope and happy to be back in Galveston that I nearly skipped down the Starlight Pier. Even the brand-new uniform that Sofie had loaned me felt lighter than air. The fat gray-and-white gulls wheeling overhead filled the air with cries that felt like welcomes.

Workmen carrying lumber on their shoulders, painters with cans of paint and ladders, cleaners with buckets, brooms, and mops bustled about. The entire pier now shone beneath a fresh coat of white paint. The Starlight Palace, though, took my breath away. From a dowdy, woebegone tower of splintery, grayed wood it had been transformed into a Taj Mahal.

Or, at least a huge building that was so blindingly bright in the sun that, for a moment, I didn't notice a guy in a bad suit lurking around in the shadows. Holding a clipboard.

" 'Scuse me." A plump fellow who was sweating profusely and dragging his partner behind him bumped me aside in his haste to join the mass of giddy young people already gathered outside the Palace's double-door entrance. A handwritten sign read:

Registration for The Amadeo Family's Dance Marathon in Celebration of the Grand Re-Opening of the Starlight Palace. Absolutely NO ADMITTANCE Until Opening Night. 6 P.M. Friday, July 1.

I pushed through the mob, stepped up to the local guards Pops had stationed in front of the doors, and prepared to explain that I was with the show. Before I could open my mouth though, a girl in the crowd behind me shouted, "That's her. That's Nurse Gravy!"

The girl was flanked by a dozen other teens. Several held up signs that identified them as "Zaviors!!"

A lanky girl waved her sign at me. "We Love GRAVY!!" She yelled at the guard, "Let her in. That's Zave's wife."

"Who?" the guard, an old guy who cupped

his hand behind his ear to hear better, asked.

"The Handsome Hoofer and the Nurse," several of the girls screamed. "Don't you read the papers?"

The guard's mouth dropped in recognition. "You're her?" he asked, standing aside. "They been waiting for you. You better get in there. On the double."

As I moved through the crush, the girls all asked versions of the same two questions: "Where is Zave?" and "What is Zave *really* like?"

I hid my dismay at learning that, apparently, he wasn't already there, and stepped into the Starlight Palace. From every corner, painters and cleaners clattered about, moving ladders and buckets.

The mammoth old dance hall that used to be a convention center that used to be a skating rink that used to be a sports arena had been considerably freshened up. Every door and window was wide open. Light flooded in and fresh ocean air blew through, chasing away the residual odor of must and decay from the rotting wood that had been painted over rather than replaced.

At the center of the frenzied activity were Pops and his right-hand man, Kane. Both were too busy to notice my entrance. Kane was planted mid-floor, legs wide, head swiveling from one side of the arena to the other as he pointed from the highest of the three tiers of wooden bleachers, to the newly installed box seats ringing the mammoth floor, to the wooden stage and band shell.

"Check out the windows," Kane said, and Pops craned his neck to study the ceiling that rose high above the bleachers. Banks of windows circled the top. Most of them were broken. Swallows swooped in and out, soaring between nests in the rafters.

"Do you see what I'm talking about?" Kane asked. "If there's the tiniest spark all those broken windows'll act like a chimney. And those?" he asked, pointing to blackened electrical outlets with odd wires poking out. "Place is a firetrap."

"Lucky we're sitting on an ocean of water then, ain't it?" Pops shot back.

"That show up in Maine," Kane continued. "They were sitting on a *mountain* of water. Six feet of snow. That didn't stop the hall from burning to the ground in half an hour. Four dancers died."

Pops flapped his hand as if he was waving away an annoying gnat. "Well, ain't you the Gloomy Gus. I heard all about that show. Last December, right? Who puts on a show in December in Maine? That numbskull, fly-by-night promoter Doc Winthrop's who. Biggest chowderhead in the business. Nothin' like that's gonna happen here. Don't even mention it."

"Anyone looked at the wiring?" Kane probed.

Pops turned from a crew foreman who was holding a clipboard up so that the promoter could sign an invoice and growled at his head judge, "Don't start in again on the fugging wiring. We got a budget."

"Yeah," Kane shot back. "A budget for paint and cosmetic repairs. This place is fifty years old. Some of those breakers down there in the utility room are insulated with newspaper."

"So? What do you want me to do? Rebuild? Amadeos gave me a strict budget. Cosmetic only."

Kane shook his head.

"Quit being a nervous Nellie. The Amadeos are highly safety conscious. See all those fire alarms?" He gestured to the array of gleaming new red metal alarm boxes that had been installed throughout the hall. "Plus, the county's putting a fire marshal at the door to make sure we don't go over capacity."

"A sold-out house? That's optimistic," Kane scoffed.

"Jeez, look on the sunny side for once in your life, will ya, pal?"

"What about exits?" Kane asked.

"I don't have time for this. Ask *him* about the fugging exits," Pops said, waving at a passing workman. Kane started to do just that, but Pops called him back. "One other thing. The brother, JuJu, he wants to collect the take every day. At four in the morning."

"Are you kidding me?" Kane asked.

"Do I look like I'm kidding?"

"So that means I have to close out and deliver the night's take to him at four in the A friggin' M? That makes no goddamn sense."

"Tell me about it," Pops lamented. "But, hey, pal, on this island, only thing that makes sense is what the Amadeos say makes sense. In Galveston, you play by Amadeo rules or you don't play at all."

"Yeah, sure, Pops. But every night? What kind of haul are those wops expecting to pull in? I mean, what'd you and the boys talk about when I wasn't around?"

Kane fell silent when he caught sight of me.

Pops, following Kane's gaze, boomed out, "Well, would you look at who finally decided to grace us with her presence? Where the hell you been? Amadeos have been riding

489

my ass. Hard. You were supposed to be here early to fulfill publicity obligations as per the contract you signed."

Kane, clearly not happy to see me, dove in before I could answer. "All the other pros are already here and registered. They're not going to like us playing favorites. Rules state that —"

"Stuff your damn rules," Pops ordered. "Since when have we ever made our stars stick to the rules. She's here. That's all that matters. The locals want her. The Amadeos *really* want her. She's in the show. Hell, at this point, she *is* the show. End of story.

"You," he said, jabbing an angry finger into my chest. "Get set up in the girls' quarters." The Pops who'd been snivelingly grateful for me saving him and his show back in Chicago was gone and the old Pops was back. "And hurry it up, then meet me back at the entrance. All the kids are going to help register locals."

He clapped his hands and bawled out to everyone around him, "Back to work. We got a show to open in one day."

"Pops?" I asked.

He glanced back. "Why are you still here?"

"Zave?"

"What about Zave? You tell me about Zave."

490

"Is he here?"

"Does it look like he's here?" he sneered. "Yeah, he's in town. Somewhere. Checked in, then vanished. I don't know what kind of good-bye you two had in Chicago and I don't care, but he has been on the bender to end all benders ever since. All I care about is that you two had damn well better be the happiest married couple ever to step out of a honeymoon suite or, mark my words, there will be hell to pay."

Buoyed by Sofie's optimism, I promised him, "That won't be a problem. Zave and I are together now. For real."

"Evelina!" a familiar voice boomed out. Uncle JuJu hustled toward me, arms outstretched. "A little late, but you're here now and that's all that matters." Clasping me in a one-armed hug while gesturing at the transformation of the Starlight Palace with the other, he asked, "What do you think?"

"It looks great. *You* look great." And he did. Always an ebullient person, he now seemed positively giddy.

"Oh, Evelina," he all but crooned, "I am *so* glad that you told Wyatt to call. None of this would have happened without you. Not this," he said, gesturing expansively at the renovations. "And certainly not this." Grinning, he extended a hand toward an elegant woman wearing an enormous sun hat that swooped down rakishly, hiding her face.

"Lamb chop," JuJu called to her, "come over here."

She approached at a languorous pace, silk beach pyjamas flowing about her as she moved. She reached us and peeked up from beneath the hat.

"Cleo?"

"You rang," she answered jauntily.

JuJu turned me loose and Cleo filled his arms. She looked rested and restored from our Chicago ordeal. But there was something else, something more than just the golden tan and diamond earrings she sported. I couldn't put my finger on it other than to say that, for the first time since I'd known her, she wasn't a buzzing spring of sullen, coiled energy.

"Without you, Evelina," JuJu continued, "Cleopatra and I might never have met." He pronounced it "Clay-oh-pat-trah" and Cleo cuddled in a bit closer to him.

"Yeah," Cleo said. "Thanks, Evie." She held my eyes. "Seriously. I owe you. Come on, I'll walk you to the girls' quarters."

As soon as we were out of JuJu's earshot, she asked, "So?"

"So what do I think of you and JuJu? Or so? You can't believe I'm here?"

"Both."

"You and JuJu? Is it —"

"Real? It's a hell of a lot more real than the 'diamonds' the nephew gave me in Chicago. Which turned out to be paste. The only thing real about Salvy was his god-damn wife."

"The one who slipped you a Mickey?"

"The same. He swore from the start that he was leaving her. That lie was even faker than that damn bracelet. Cheap bastard. JuJu wants to buy me a house. Make our 'arrangement' permanent."

"Cleo, that's great. Listen, about Chicago. About leaving you the way I did, I'm sorry."

"Evie, stop. You don't have a goddamn thing to be sorry for. Thanks to you, I'm the one finally landed jelly side up for once in her life."

"Cleo. Doll," JuJu cried from the stage where he was consulting with the band-leader, Mel. "Could you help us out up here?"

"Be right there, hon," she purred back. "He asks me about everything. I've been in on all the planning. He really wants to put on a quality show. Isn't that cute?"

"Adorable," I answered. I was going to tell her about me and Zave, but Cleo was already halfway across the floor, the pyjamas billowing around her like a vivid, striped cloud she was floating away on.

Chapter 66

The rest area, deserted now, was filled with cots crammed in between a row of sinks and showers. The horses had already claimed the best spots along the edges and stowed their footlockers, secured against thieves with heavy padlocks, under the cots.

Their clothes hung on pegs beside the cots. I recognized Minnie's flour sack dress printed with pink and purple pansies, Gerta's maroon dress, half-moons bleached under the armpits from sweat, and Lily's moth-eaten, monogrammed bathrobe, a souvenir of her past.

I slid my suitcase under the cot next to Minnie's, ran a comb through my hair, swiped on some lipstick, and headed back out. Signs advertising the sponsors Pops had already lined up were being hoisted above the bandstand. "Piedmont Cigarettes." "Murdoch's Bath House." "Verkin Photo Company." "Gaido's Seafood Restaurant."

"Star Drug Store."

Though none of the family's dozens of betting parlors were mentioned, every Amadeo club, bar, and restaurant was: The Turf Athletic Club. The Studio Lounge. The Western. Murdoch's Bingo. The Sui Jen Cafe. The star of the show, however, was "The Hollywood Dinner Club: The Southwest's Most Elegant Nightclub."

With a twinge, I thought of the graduation party Sofie and I almost had there. A tremendous squawk jolted me out of my moment of regret. The sound system came to life, followed by Alonzo's amplified voice. "Testing. Testing. One. Two." *Thunk. Thunk.* The emcee thumped a finger against the microphone.

Back at the entrance, several card tables were being set up directly in front of the big glass double doors. Striding down the pier to man them were most of the old gang. Fresh and rested from their hotel stay, they all looked like younger versions of the exhausted zombies I'd last seen in Chicago.

Zave wasn't with them.

Minnie caught sight of me and her face lit up. She raised a scrawny arm and waved me over, announcing to the others, "Hey, shove over. Make room for Evie. She's one of us now."

Grabbing a chair for me, Patsy said with a grin, "Welcome to the club. So, you're just a regular marathon poop now?"

"Looks that way," I answered.

"Who's gonna plaster our corns?" Ace wailed.

"Corns?" Patsy shot back, pulling his rubbery face into a cartoon expression of surprise. "I was working up to asking for an enema."

Being packed in next to my friends reminded me of all the families I'd peeked at, crowded around a dinner table, talking and laughing, and just being together.

Minnie passed me a stack of legal-size documents with the instructions, "All you gotta do is ask these questions and write down the answers. If anyone seems buggy, you know, lice or something, take them back there for a check." She jerked a thumb back toward a couple of standing screens set up behind us.

"Minnie," DeWitt interrupted, "you forgot the most important thing."

Minnie covered her toothless "oh" of surprise and hurried to add, "Yeah, sorry, Pops said he only wants the cream of the crop for this one."

"Yep," Patsy chimed in. "He said to be extra selective. Only people who are pretty

497

to look at."

"I guess that counts you out," Ace quipped.

Patsy cocked his fist in pretend anger before continuing, "Anyway, no losers, deadbeats, leeches, mooches. No baldies or fatties. Crossed eyes are out. You get my drift?"

I nodded and that was the end of my training because the guards let the crowd in and hopeful locals swarmed the tables.

"Can I bring Mr. Beans with me?" asked my first candidate, a stout middle-aged woman wearing a wide-legged jumpsuit printed with enormous red and yellow hibiscuses, who thrust her bug-eyed Chihuahua into my face. The dog bared his tiny, sharp teeth. I told her absolutely not and she stormed off.

After that the questioning went smoothly. I asked the contestants what medical conditions they had. If they'd ever had a serious contagious disease, were subject to fits, wore a truss, or if they or anyone in their family had ever been in a mental asylum.

It was a little awkward to ask couples wearing patched trousers, threadbare dresses, and shoes with knots holding the laces together this required question: "Do you have sufficient wearing apparel to appear clean and neat at all times?" I wanted to pass these hard-luck duos on so that, at least, they'd get fed and sheltered and have something to hope for as long as they lasted. But Pops's rule about wanting all the contestants to be attractive ruled most of them out.

The most important question and the only one no one was allowed to fudge on was, "Do you have lice?"

"You calling me lousy?" demanded a horse-faced man in high-waisted trousers when I made that inquiry.

"No, sir," I answered calmly. "This is for your safety as much as anyone else's. You will be in very tight quarters and an infestation of any kind would spread like wildfire."

I stood up and started to ask him to step behind the screen so that I could comb through his hair, but he stomped away before I could finish. The waiting crowd hooted when, halfway down the pier and thinking he was out of sight, he scratched his hindquarters vigorously.

We worked until the sun went down, and every moment of those long hours I spent in a state of high alert, straining for a glimpse of Zave coming through the crowd.

But he never appeared.

CHAPTER 67

Friday, July 1, 1932

After registrations closed for the day, I stayed on with most of the horses, working late into the night to get the Palace ready in time. When I finally dragged back to the apartment, Sofie and I started gabbing and didn't stop until dawn. For the fourth night in a row, I hardly shut my eyes.

By the time I reached the pier on Friday morning, I was running on nervous energy and fumes and kicking myself for being stupid enough to start a dance marathon in a state of exhaustion. I swore that, as soon as Zave showed up, I'd have him teach me the fine art of sleeping on my feet.

If he showed up.

I studied the long line of hopefuls waiting to register. Zave wasn't among them. When I reached the card tables where my friends were already weeding through the applicants, I was greeted with a hail of increas-

500

ingly urgent questions about Zave's where-abouts.

Before I could open my mouth, Pops was there, assuring all in a loud voice intended for the locals to hear that "Zave is on his way. I just got off the phone with him."

"Is that true?" I whispered to Pops.

"You better hope it is. And you better *pretend* it is in front of the civilians."

Before I could take my seat, several technicians hustled past, carrying crates labeled "KTRH Radio Houston."

"Set up on the stage," Pops directed them.

"KTRH?" I asked in amazement. "You got the biggest radio station in Houston to come out?"

"Well, your pal in Houston did."

"Uncle Jake? Uncle Jake is working for you?"

"He's my ground man in Houston so he got this pissant lunchtime show to come out."

"Not *Niles at Noon*?" I asked.

"Yeah, yeah," Pops said dismissively. "Something like that."

"Pops, *Niles at Noon* is the biggest show in Houston, and Jake was a genius if he convinced them to come all the way out here for a remote broadcast. Everyone in Houston listens to Niles. The whole town

501

shuts down. I remember walking for blocks and blocks and never missing a single word because everyone had their windows open and everyone had Niles tuned in."

"Okay," Pops said. "I get it. Jake did *something* right."

I was elated to hear that Jake was working, but before I could sing his praises any further, Pops thrust a couple of sheets of paper at me. "Here's the run of the show." His voice harshened as he warned, "And don't ever be late again. You're on Pops Wyatt's dime now. Got it?"

"Got it," I said to his retreating back. I took my seat and Patsy informed me, "Pops said we need more talent. If they say they can dance or play an instrument, we're supposed to send them over to Mel to do their bits. Cleo's gonna work with the singers. If they're not completely hopeless, that is. And I'm the guy," he went on, stabbing a thumb in his chest, "who gets to decide if someone's funny or not. Got it?"

"Like a bad case of mumps," I shot back.

The comforting familiarity of snappy patter. The language of vaudeville troupers, the language of my childhood, eased my jittery nerves and the next few hours zoomed by. We sent the dancers and players in to Mel, where they auditioned for him. Soon we were being "serenaded" by a third-rate Bing Crosby imitator singing an off-key version of "Just a Gigolo" and a girl with a bit too much cutesy *boop-boop-de-boop* attempting "I Wanna Be Loved by You."

Mel was always kind and professional. The bandleader even managed to salvage a couple of dancers who tapped away to "I've Got Rhythm" with such a colossal *lack* of rhythm that he signaled the saxophonist to add a few blats in the right places and turned the fiasco into a comedy bit.

It was near noon when a scrawny local girl with dark circles under her eyes took a stab at "Ten Cents a Dance." Though it didn't go well, she had enough native talent that Mel called out to Cleo, who was off in a corner, snuggled up with JuJu, "Cleo, come on up here. This kid's got something, but she needs you to show her how to sell a song so that the clouds'll open up and rain those silver drops down."

Onstage, Cleo, Mel, and the local girl huddled up briefly before Cleo stepped up to the mic, said, "Try it this way," and sang about selling herself to "fighters and sailors and bowlegged tailors" for ten cents a dance. From the first note, there was a throbbing edge to Cleo's voice that had almost, but never quite, been there before, and it was riveting. She sang now as if she was confessing not only her own life story but telling ours as well. All the jostling and chattering stopped and the sort of electricity that only the absolutely real and absolutely true can spark shot through the Palace. Cleaners put their mops aside and painters their brushes. Motion ceased at the registration table. Though we'd all heard Cleo sing before, we'd never heard her sing like this as she bemoaned her life with rough guys and tough guys who tore her gown and crushed her toes.

Beside me, Minnie's chin quivered. Ace chewed his bottom lip when it started to tremble. We all thought we knew Cleo, tough as an old boot and twice as ready to kick your ass. We didn't, though, because she wasn't singing about a dime-a-dance girl, she was singing about herself, about us. About every one of us that this damn Depression was kicking around and using hard and making do things we didn't necessarily want to do.

And then, perfectly on cue, a commotion on the pier caught my attention, and as Cleo warbled that sometimes she thought she'd found her hero, the crowd parted and there, luminous in the blazing coastal sun, was Zave.

CHAPTER 68

Friday, July 1, 1932
11:50 a.m.

Like the others, after a week of rest Zave, too, was a younger, more innocent version of himself. He was attacked by a mob of Zaviors. He leaned down to sign a shy, withdrawn girl's autograph book, and for a second, as he peered gently into her adoring face, I saw the abused boy that my father had saved. Then Zave lifted his head. The beach sun washed over his face, his smile, and he was again a matinee idol. Or, at least as close as the girls on the pier would ever get to one. As close as I would ever get.

Minnie, Lily, and Gerta glanced at me, gauging my reaction. I was certain they all noticed the flush that rose from my neck to my cheeks as my heart galloped. Not wanting my reunion with Zave to be scrutinized, I fled the crowded pier, and ducked inside the Palace. Hidden in the shadows, I watched him enter the cavernous hall.

"Evie?" he called.

The high windows threw crisscrossing beams of light across the floor. Motes floated as thick as a cloud of gold dust around him as he searched the building.

"Evie?"

I waited until his face fell, until I saw genuine disappointment when I didn't answer, before I found the courage to speak his name.

"Zave."

"Evie, you're here."

I stepped toward him. "I'm here."

When we were close enough to touch, Zave halted. An uncharacteristic tentativeness gripped him. The silence between us lengthened until I became aware of the sound of Pops arguing with a vendor. Of locals squealing outside when they were admitted as contestants. Of my heart thudding. It was a silence that preceded an important statement and I did not break it. Quietly, he said, "You read my letter."

"I read your letter," I confirmed.

Zave lowered his head.

His defeated gesture made me angry at all the cruel, stupid idiots who had piled on the shame he now bowed beneath.

"Zave. Look at me."

He did.

"I understand."

"Do you?"

"I'm trying to. I'm here. Do you still want the same things I do?"

"More than you can imagine," he answered.

I started to speak, but Pops barged in. "Good, good. You're all made up, right? You're married, right?" He stared meaningfully at us, making sure that we were going to play along.

Zave waited for me to answer.

"Yes," I answered, taking Zave's hand. "We're together."

Pops exhaled a gusty sigh of relief. "Aw, jeez, I was sweating this. You have no idea the hell you two have put me through. Mr. Amadeo made it clear as vodka that he was not going to be happy if our star attractions, especially the hometown girl, weren't both here being the blissful newlyweds they signed on to be. Not happy at all. And, after Chicago, I am done with unhappy investors."

"We're here," I affirmed.

"Great, great. Now, go get on that stage. The broadcast goes live in five minutes and Niles wants both of you.

"I need you to hook those listeners fast

and reel 'em in hard. If we don't make a bundle this weekend with the Fourth of July holiday, we'll never make it. I've never put on a show this expensive. We need crowds. Big crowds. Right out of the gate."

That sounded odd since I'd heard Pops say more than once that his philosophy was to build slow and let word of mouth bring in the crowds.

"No sweat," Zave assured Pops.

"You," he told me, "hit the struggling newlywed angle hard. Got it?"

"We got this one in the bag," Zave, the old pro, promised both me and Pops, and we took our places beside the host, who greeted us with a wordless smile.

The radio technician raised his right hand, pointed his left at Niles, and called out, "Fifteen seconds to air. Stand by."

Zave whispered, "Tell your story."

"Now?" I muttered, blindsided by his request. "I can't."

"Okay, then," he said blithely. "I will."

I started to tell him not to say a word, but the second hand hit twelve, the radio tech pointed emphatically at Niles, and in mellifluous tones he announced, "Hello, friends, this is *Niles at Noon* on a beautiful Friday on the first day of July. You're listening to KTRH, Houston's radio giant.

"We're broadcasting remote today, direct from the newly reopened Starlight Palace on the historic Starlight Pier here in the Playground of the Southwest, Galveston, Texas, where The Amadeo Family's Dance Marathon will open tonight at six P.M. sharp. The Amadeo family name is synonymous with fine entertainment and they told me that this will be a real dance competition, not one of those cheap walkathons. They guarantee all dancing, all entertainment, all the time.

"So don't wait. Come on down to the Starlight Palace for an evening you won't forget. Right after the noontime news, we'll have more about the marathon from America's sweethearts, the Handsome Hoofer and the Never-Naughty Nurse."

Though I winced at my latest nickname, I was pleased to have my status as a nurse reaffirmed in Galveston, where it mattered most.

Niles's voice was sharper as he read the news. "Sorry to start with some bad news, but word is that the Dow Jones Industrial Average has plummeted to an all-time low of forty-one points and the post office has raised the price of a first-class stamp to three cents. And, get this, folks, those Germans have invented a whole new way of campaigning. By airplane! A candidate for president, Adolf Hitler, staged twenty-three rallies in only seven days. Now that's what I call barnstorming.

"But the candidate we're all wondering about on this side of the Atlantic is the one that the Democratic Convention is selecting right now in Chicago to run against President Hoover in the election this November." With increasing urgency, Niles went on. "The last time our nation saw the kind of hardship we are currently suffering was during the Civil War. With our country's future hanging in the balance, anticipation is running high as we wait to learn who the candidate to run against the Republican nominee, President Hoover, will be. Sadly, however, the Democratic delegates remain deadlocked. None of the three top candidates, not even the popular Democratic governor of New York, Franklin Roosevelt, has managed to secure the seven hundred and seventy votes necessary to win their party's nomination."

A collective "Aw" of disappointment rose through the Palace and from the Pier.

"But, friends," Niles continued in a bouncy, upbeat tone, "no matter who you're rooting for, you are guaranteed to forget all your troubles tonight at the grand opening

510

of The Amadeo Family's Dance Marathon on the Starlight Pier. Right now, I'm going to hand the microphone over to the man I know you're all waiting to hear from. You've seen his photo in all the papers, you've read about how this Handsome Hoofer lost his heart to the show's nurse. I give you the man himself, Zave Cassidy."

"Well, howdy out there," Zave said with a perfect Texas accent. "I just want to say to all you proud Texans, your state should get a lot more stars than just that lone one. Texas deserves its own galaxy. It's just that dang purty.

"Folks, Evie and I are just so excited to be here and hope that every one of you listening will turn out to cheer us on. Especially Evie, because she deserves it more than anyone. She loves Galveston even though, and I'm not supposed to tell you this, but I will."

I held my breath.

"Folks," he continued, his bouncy, country tone turning maudlin, "I hate to tell y'all this, but a terrible wrong was done to this wonderful woman by my side here, and we've come back to Galveston to put it right. Evie's only dream in life is to be a nurse. Now, she's a lot smarter than I am, but she worked her rear end off for three years and she aced every test they put in front of her. But do you know what, Niles?"

"What, Zave?" Niles asked, eager for whatever twist Zave was putting on the typical promotional spiel. Pops, on the other hand, was apoplectic.

"Because of some stupid technicality, the director of Evie's nursing school refused to give her the nurse's pin that she had poured her heart and soul into earning."

Technicality.

"Now I ask you," Zave implored, "is that right? Evie is just like all of us who are getting kicked around by the fat cats and big bosses. So, folks, if you're as tired as I am of seeing the little guy, or gal, get a raw deal, come on down tonight and cheer on the woman who will steal your heart just as sure as she stole mine, my own sweet Evie Grace."

I sat speechless as Niles went down the long list of show sponsors. I couldn't believe how Zave had managed to make my story belong to every listener who'd ever gotten a bad break. The campaign to get my side out had begun. I squeezed his hand under the table. He squeezed back and, just like that, we were a team again. He was on my side and that was all that mattered.

Niles, shooting us a big *okay* sign as we

left, leaned in to say, "If you love you a good love story, come on out tonight at six and cheer on Zave and Nurse Evie and all the other incredible contestants."

As we walked back outside, Zave held my hand up in his like a referee declaring the winner of a prizefight, and the crowd gathered on the Starlight Pier applauded.

CHAPTER 69

Friday, July 1, 1932
4:00 p.m.

At four that afternoon, Pops herded us all into the girls' quarters with the order, "Everybody lay low in here until I give you the high sign. We're gonna open the doors soon and I don't want anyone getting a peek at you until the grand entrance. Gotta preserve the mystery, right?"

For the next two hours the mirrors above the five sinks were crowded with contestants fluffing up or patting down hair, brushing on swipes of mascara and rouge, tilting their heads to check themselves from different angles. The amateurs peeked back over their shoulders to straighten a hosiery seam and slip on fancy pumps. We pros chuckled knowingly at the newcomers. We were all barelegged and wore comfy socks under our ground-gripper shoes. I liked being on the inside. Knowing the score.

"Hey, Stretch," Cleo said, approaching me with a pot of rouge. "You look like death warmed over. Come here." As JuJu's girl-friend, she'd taken on the role of den mother looking after the Amadeo family's interests. Tentatively, I leaned down. Cleo smelled of Beeman's clove gum, tobacco, and a deeply human animal odor that was all her own. Half expecting that she would smear me with great dots of clown makeup, I was relieved when, with the gentlest of touches, she stroked what had to be subtle brushes of color onto my cheeks.

Popping her gum, she tipped her head from side to side to check the effect. "Well, you don't look like they just pulled you out of the morgue anymore, but you sure don't look too peppy either. Did you get any sleep last night?"

"A bit," I answered, not adding that I couldn't recall the last time I'd had a full night's rest. "Thanks for sprucing me up."

Cleo shrugged. "Can't have the rubes worrying that their hometown heroine is about to keel over. That'd be bad for the show."

Patsy poked his head in and the locals, who weren't yet used to random guys appearing in our quarters, shrieked and squealed. "Aw, can it, girls. None of you got anything I haven't seen before. Listen, I got a news flash for you. Pops is charging a dollar a head. And, get this, he's asking five whole bucks for box seats. He is even getting fifty cents for seats up in the rafters and a dime for kids. Can you believe that?"

Incredulous, Minnie said, "No show charges that much. Not even a quarter of that."

Glumly, Gerta predicted, "That is too much. The seats will be staying empty. This I am promising you. No one is having such money in times like these. Pops will be losing his shirt. And then the gangsters are unhappy. And then the show closes and then again we must run like frightened chickens with our heads cut off into the night. Perhaps this time we are starving to death."

"Clam up, Helga," Cleo snarled. "You don't know shit from schnitzel. And don't ever, *ever,* use the word 'gangster' again when referring to the Amadeo family. Also, it wasn't Pops who set the prices. And I should know. I was in on all the planning. High-level stuff. Signor Amadeo himself decided what to charge. And I am pretty sure that Mr. Amadeo knows this town just a little bit better than you do, Heidi."

The blare of an air horn startled us.

516

"What's that?" Minnie demanded, covering her ears.

"That's called an air horn, Corn Pone," Cleo answered with a casualness that emphasized her insider status. "The Amadeos said no bells or sirens. They thought it would disturb the crowd. Make them think of a fire alarm. Only air horns will be allowed."

"But it still means two minutes till showtime, right?" Minnie asked.

"Obviously," Cleo answered.

"How do I look?" Minnie asked me.

"Like a dream walking."

Minnie squeezed my hand. Hers was icy cold from nerves.

"All of you, out," Cleo ordered. "Into the hallway."

We crowded into the dark hallway where, not only couldn't the audience see us or hear us, but we couldn't see or hear the audience. Provided one was actually there. Because, though we craned to catch a glimpse of a crowd, all we could see was a bit of bare floor illuminated by the high-intensity lights once used for prizefights.

Mel and His Melody Makers were playing a rousing version of FDR's campaign song, "Happy Days Are Here Again," since Roosevelt was far and away the people's favorite candidate and our only hope for pulling out of the economic pit we were in.

"Partner up," Cleo ordered. "Partner up. Zave and Evie, you're leading, of course."

We all shuffled around in the darkness, unable to see anything except the glare of the empty floor. Without a word Zave slipped in beside me. The band stopped playing and an ominous, echoing silence fell.

"That is the sound of an empty hall," Ace pointed out in a whisper.

"Ah well," Patsy cracked, lowering his foghorn voice as much as he could. "At least we won't have to worry about getting beaned by one of those downpours of quarters that we all hate so much."

A few of the pros laughed gamely.

The public address system crackled to life and Alonzo announced, "Welcome, welcome, welcome to The Amadeo Family's Dance Marathon, celebrating the reopening of the historic Starlight Palace. Before we get started, though, I would be remiss if I didn't mention the family that created the Galveston we all know and love, the Playground of the Southwest. You know who I'm talking about, folks. They brought you the fabulous Hollywood Dinner Club, the Sport Lounge, the Sui Jen Cafe with plans to transform it into the even more luxurious

Balinese Room, and too many others to mention.

"This family single-handedly put Galveston on the map and has kept it there. While the rest of the country may have fallen on hard times, one family kept the wolf away from the door here in Galveston. These generous folks and community leaders have made Galveston a nationwide destination for beachside amusement that has all the class and elegance of the Stork Club in New York City. A place where every single one of us, bankers and bank tellers alike, can forget our worries. Ladies and gentlemen, I give you Amadeo Family Enterprises."

The name "Amadeo" brought the house down. Even if only a dozen people were in the audience, they whooped and hollered as if the place was packed.

Alonzo continued exuberantly, "And the new highlight of that empire is our fantastic venue tonight, the Starlight Palace, crown jewel of the newly reopened and painstakingly restored historic Starlight Pier."

Painstakingly restored? A few coats of paint and some cleanup?

"As we've promised, this is not going to be like any other show before and, I promise you, folks, there won't ever be another one like it. The Amadeo name is synonymous with quality entertainment and that is precisely what they insisted we provide. Twenty-four hours a day. Every day. This won't be some mopey walkathon. No siree, Bob. There will be no sleeping allowed on the floor. Our plucky contestants will be dancing nonstop around the clock."

Gasps of astonished dismay erupted from the pros.

"That's right," Alonzo continued. "There will be no sleeping allowed on the floor. So come on over when the clubs close. No matter how late or how early, our brave kids will be knocking themselves out to entertain you. And they will be doing it with their eyes wide open. Most shows have a fifteen-minute rest break every hour. Not this show. This is going to be a fast show with lots of eliminations. So there will only be one break every *two* hours. For exactly fifteen strictly timed minutes."

"What?" Ace exploded in the darkness. "A break every *other* hour? *And* we can't sleep on the floor? Is Pops trying to kill us? None of us is gonna last a single day. Kane, where are you? I can't see a goddamn thing. Kane, you there? What gives?"

"What gives," Kane's baritone rumbled back, "is what our investors say gives. They're the guys who made the rules. But you better believe I'm the guy's gonna enforce them. So quitcher bellyachin' or hit the road. This ain't the army. You can leave anytime you want."

Lowering his voice, Patsy asked, "What's the deal? Are they *trying* to put on the shortest show on record? Whoever heard of that? Idea is to run a show for as long as it lasts. Milk it for as long as possible. They're gonna break us down in a few days. This makes no sense."

As Alonzo thanked the sponsors, my confidence drained away. I had been depending on being able to sleep on the floor. I could barely have survived a *regular* marathon. These new rules would kill me. Fast. Far from being a triumphant winner whose cause would be championed by the people, I would be a loser deserving of her fate.

"And now," Alonzo declared, "without further ado, let's bring out the stars of our show, starting with America's sweetheart couple. You know them as the Handsome Hoofer and the Never-Naughty Nurse, I give you . . ."

As an endless drumroll spiked my anxiety, I gave Zave the bad news: "I can't do this."

"Zave and Evie!" Alonzo exploded.

Zave took my sweaty hand and surged

forward. But my feet wouldn't move. "Evie?"

When we didn't appear, Alonzo vamped, saying, "Zave and Evie, and all our contestants, will be dancing their hearts out in hopes of going home with the reward that will change their lives. A grand prize of, hold on to your hats, folks, because you are not going to believe this. Two thousand dollars!"

My jaw dropped open. Behind me all the grumbling about the harsh new rules dissolved into gasps of delighted disbelief. Two thousand dollars. That was enough to change everything. Enough to hire a lawyer to present my case to the nursing board. Enough to give Zave and me a start on the kind of life we wanted. The life *I* wanted.

I straightened up, threw back my shoulders, and, as I had done so often before, I plastered over fear, pain, exhaustion, and heartache with a smile.

In the darkness, Zave asked me, "Are you ready to win a dance marathon?"

"Just watch me," I answered, grabbing his hand and leading him forward into the blinding lights.

CHAPTER 70

Friday, July 1, 1932
6:12 p.m.

The shoes.

At first, coming out of the dark hall, blinded by the dazzling light, that's all I could make out. The shoes of the occupants of the raised box seats that ringed the floor were nearly at eye level. Fancy shoes. Burgundy pumps with Cuban heels. Black-and-white spectator wingtips. High-heeled Mary Janes. Pink heels with rhinestone ankle straps. White bucks that only a wealthy man could have kept clean.

And all the box seats were filled. Clearly the Amadeo name was enough to get the high rollers to turn out. At least for opening night. I squinted up into the blinding light, dreading the sight of the rows of empty seats. At first all I could make out were gigantic American flags and huge swoops of red, white, and blue bunting scalloping the top tiers of seats that stair-stepped up to the high windows.

Before my eyes could adjust, Minnie gasped. "Oh my Lord, the place is packed."

Lily, gazing around with a fixed stare, concurred. "She is correct. Every seat is taken."

They were right. Every single solitary seat in the house, from the fifty-cent nosebleed section, down through the dollar bleacher seats, all the way to the five-dollar ringside box seats, was filled with spectators grinning and clapping and waving flasks around like it was New Year's Eve. We'd all seen full houses before. But none like this.

After expecting an empty house, we looked like kids seeing a heap of presents beyond any of our wildest dreams piled beneath the Christmas tree. The blast of an air horn startled us. It wasn't any shriller than the siren the announcer usually cranked, but it was unnervingly different.

Alonzo held the horn over his head, unloosed another blast, and announced, "Let the first-ever Galveston all-dance spectacular begin."

"May I have the honor?" Zave asked, whirling me into dance position. He clasped me close and the crowd whooped as we christened the empty floor with a loping foxtrot. In an instant, all my jitters — about the contest, about Zave, about my pin — vanished.

One by one, the couples were introduced and the floor around us filled up. I doubted that any of us except for Lily had ever been to a deb ball and most, like me, hadn't even made it to our junior-senior prom. But this made up for all the special evenings we might have ever missed.

Tonight this wasn't a "poor man's" nightclub. This was the real thing. The crowd had paid nightclub prices for their tickets, the swells were drinking real nightclub booze, and everyone was on vacation. They were loose and free. With money, applause, and laughs. And we soaked up every bit of it.

Photographers from the Galveston, Houston, and Dallas papers, along with the AP guy, stood on the edge of the floor and blasted flashbulbs in our faces every time Zave and I passed. The bulbs stopped popping as soon as we were out of range.

"You're grinning like we've already won," Zave said as we glided away from the photographers. "Did Pops tell you the fix was in for us? What's the secret?"

I did have a secret. I wanted to tell him that, at this moment, Sofie was chasing down the key to our future, but I couldn't risk getting either of our hopes up prematurely. "I can't tell you now," I said. "But I will."

"Hey, get a load of that," he said, gesturing into the stands. Through the glaring lights, I caught sight of a growing number of Zaviors dressed all in white. But now, lots of them were holding signs demanding, "Give Evie Her Pin."

My pin. Zave's campaign was already working.

"There's no way you won't be able to get your story out now," Zave said. "All that's left is for us to win this hoedown and collect our two thousand."

In that moment of jubilation, I almost told Zave that, at any minute, Sofie was going to appear with information worth a lot more than any amount of money. But the excited crowd raised such a ruckus when Patsy stepped forward, mugging wildly, that I didn't.

"Here's our funny man, Patsy 'Won't Steer You Wrong' Wright. And it looks like Patsy's trying to tell me something."

Patsy hollered a few lines to the emcee, which he repeated into the microphone. "Why, Patsy, you say you just got back from a pleasure trip?" Alonzo asked. "Where did you go, Patsy? Did you visit the Grand

Canyon?"

Patsy folded his arms and mimed an emphatic "No."

"Well, where did you go, Pats? Did you go see the pyramids of Egypt and float on the Nile like Cleopatra?"

Another cartoonish "No."

Pretending to lose patience, Alonzo blurted out, "Well, gosh dang it, Pats, don't keep us in suspense. Where the heck *did* you go on this pleasure trip of yours?"

Waggling his eyebrows ferociously, Patsy unloosed his foghorn of a voice and bellowed loudly enough to be heard in the rafters, "I took my mother-in-law to the train station!"

The throngs in the cheap seats, the ones who had to scrimp and save for a few days at the beach, who had to think twice about spending half a buck on a night out, they ate up Patsy's routine like it was hot stew. Nothing fancy, been reheated dozens of times, none of the ingredients were fresh, but who cared? It was warm and familiar. And, for the moment, that was all it took to fill them up and make them forget about foreclosures and bread lines. Even the high rollers whose oil and cotton fortunes had kept them as immune from the Depression as they were from Prohibition howled.

I laughed more from the exciting secret fizzing away inside of me than from anything Patsy said. Sofie was right, we *did* live in an age of miracles. And she would bring us, me and Zave, ours.

CHAPTER 71

Buoyed by the crowd's enthusiasm and the prospect of a two-thousand-dollar prize, the next six hours vanished. Before we knew it the air horn was blasting to signal the midnight break.

"Here's where the magic ends," Ace predicted as we all rushed to get off our feet for fifteen minutes. "When we come back from break, this place will be a ghost town and the seconds will become hours. Guaranteed."

"Ah well," Patsy said wistfully. "It was nice while it lasted."

I'd been too keyed up to sleep during the first rest break, but this time I conked out the instant my head hit the pillow, only to jerk awake to the piercing shriek of the air horn what seemed like seconds later.

To our surprise, though, when we filed

529

back onto the floor, far from being a ghost town, the house was still packed. As Pops had promised, there was a fire marshal posted at the door, and he'd monitored capacity limits fiercely. Those who hadn't been admitted earlier had waited outside and, every time someone left, another paying customer filled the empty seat.

During the break, the sloppers had set up the tall tables, and the typical midnight snack awaited us when we returned. But, instead of the usual doughnuts and coffee, like everything else in Galveston, even the snacks were first class. There was a gorgeous spread of pastries, melon balls, papaya, oranges, and bananas.

JuJu had also sent a generous wad of cash up to the Melody Makers to keep playing as long as the house was full. This meant that, instead of throttling back when the bright house lights were lowered, we all had to keep on performing and stay in perfect dance position. We weren't even allowed to slouch.

My feet and eyes were on fire by the time the air horn shrieked for the 2 A.M. break. When we dragged ourselves back onto the floor after that, we found that the crowd had started to thin out. Only then did JuJu release the Melody Makers, who packed up their instruments and headed wearily out the big double doors. To our relief, the phonograph recordings that replaced the band didn't skip and weren't scratched like the ones in Chicago.

Though lots of the box seats had emptied out, Cleo and JuJu stayed put. They chatted, and swilled bonded liquor from a silver flask that never seemed to run dry, but mostly they laughed. I tried to recall another time when I'd seen Cleo truly laugh the way JuJu made her laugh and I couldn't.

"They seem happy together," I said to Zave.

He studied the couple with avuncular amusement. "They do, don't they? I hear they clicked right from the first meeting. I hope it works out. She deserves a good guy."

"So Cleo was in on setting up the entire show?"

"That's what she says, and the way those two are joined at the hip, I don't doubt it."

"Were you at the meetings?"

"No, thank God," Zave scoffed. "I've had enough sponsor meetings to last a lifetime. I don't need to ever listen to Pops try to bamboozle the local marks again. Especially not the Amadeos. Pulling one over on that crew would not be good for a person's health.

"In any event, I wasn't in any shape for much of anything when I got here. After Chicago . . ." He paused, his fluid gait stiffened, and our rhythm was thrown off. "After Chicago," he continued with an effort, "things were pretty dark."

"Zave, it's okay. You explained. You said that nothing like that will ever happen again. Let's put all that behind us."

"We will. I will," he said with strained determination. "I swear that part of my life is in the past. It has to be. Evie, you don't know what it's like. People like me get beaten, arrested, killed all the time. Just look at Suits."

"Suits is . . ."

"Yeah, he was arrested for indecent advances in St. Louis and, just for the fun of it, the cops beat the hell out of him."

"And that's how he lost the use of his arm?"

Zave nodded. "After you left Chicago, I went back to the hotel and drank up most everything they had in that swanky suite. I don't remember much of the next few weeks. Not even the train ride down here. Kane just loaded me onto the train like a sack of oats."

He gave a rasp of a laugh and concluded, "So, no, I was not exactly in the best shape for meetings with a bunch of con men trying to con each other."

Though he attempted to put a bounce in his words, they were still flattened by a pain that I wanted desperately to assuage. "Zave, it is all going to be so much simpler than you think. It really, truly is. You just have to trust me."

"You sound mighty confident," he said with slight suspicion. "Does this have to do with your big secret?"

"Forget it. I shouldn't have said anything until I had all the information about the procedure."

" 'Procedure'?" Zave echoed. "Not sure I like the sound of that."

"Don't worry," I assured him. "It's good news, I promise you. Probably the best news you'll ever get."

He held me, my heart against his, and we moved together in perfect, unspoken synchronization, harmonized now not just in movement, but in our commitment to a future together. I thought again that even if this calm, sibling affection was all we would ever have, it was enough. I was snug in a boat, heading, at long last, to a safe harbor.

With the lights dim and the music dull, horses like Gerta and Fritz tried to catch a few winks even as they ambled around the floor maintaining a perfect dance position. But Kane, who was putting in a double shift for opening night, was vigilance itself. He flew across the floor to deliver stinging smacks to their shins with his metal ruler that were so loud that the drunks partying in the uppermost seats howled with laughter at Gerta's hearty German curses.

For the next few hours Zave and I sailed along, content simply to be together until a gunshot rang out and Kane hollered, "Get off my floor!"

His fury was directed at a local couple who'd drifted off. He shouted at them and pointed to the doors with dramatic fury worthy of an Old Testament God driving Adam and Eve out of the Garden of Eden.

"But I barely shut my eyes," the local boy, a brawny farm kid taller than Kane, protested.

"I gave you a ten count," Kane hollered back.

"But we didn't hear. Please, sir, please, we have to win this money," the young woman pleaded. "We have three little ones at home and they're hungry."

"No sleeping on the floor," Kane thundered back, eliciting a storm of boos and hisses from the suddenly lively crowd.

"Go on. Get off my floor. We're not running some crummy walkathon here," Kane ordered with more furious finger-pointing. Now people were on their feet, hurling popcorn boxes, balled-up programs, and even a few soda bottles as they cursed their new villain.

"That is so unfair," I said as the young man led his weeping wife off the floor.

"I can't argue with you," Zave agreed. "Pops probably told Kane to bring enough heat to give the late-night crowd something to tell their night owl friends about. Give them a reason to buy tickets. Hey, should we give them something to tell their friends about?"

With that, Zave twirled me around, spinning me faster and faster until the faces in the stands and the other couples still on the floor and the pain in my feet and the ache in my back all blurred together and disappeared.

CHAPTER 72

At a quarter of four the clock froze. Though it made the time go even slower, I couldn't tear my eyes away from that cruel device with its hands that seemed to have stopped ticking forward. I was counting the seconds until the 4 A.M. break when I could get prone for a blessed fifteen minutes. Amazingly, the house was still more than half full.

At five minutes before four, exactly as the Amadeos had ordered, Kane and JuJu emerged. Kane was carrying a metal box with a heavy lock. I guessed they'd done the count. Given what Pops was charging for tickets and how many times he'd managed to turn the full house over in one night, that case had to contain a small fortune.

JuJu snapped his fingers and two of his men leaped over the box seat railing onto the floor. As Kane handed over the box, his

536

jacket flapped open, revealing a shoulder holster. The gun it held was not the starter pistol he used to signal eliminations.

CHAPTER 73

Saturday, July 2, 1932
6:13 a.m.

"Get up, dearie," the stout female trainer ordered as she hauled me to a sitting position and stuffed my feet back into my shoes. Minus the time it had taken to get to my cot, stuff a pillow over my head, try and fail to block out the incessant chatter, yell at everybody to shut the hell up, and finally drop off, I'd been asleep for a grand total of three minutes.

"Didn't you hear the horn?" the trainer snarled, dragging me forcefully to my feet. "Shake a leg, lazybones, you've got ninety seconds to get back on the floor." All trainers, I concluded, were sadists.

Bleary as a boxer reeling from a roundhouse punch, I watched Minnie on the cot next to me wobble to her feet. "Gosh awmighty," she moaned, grimacing as she stood. "Feels like I been on my feet for a

538

month 'stead of only twelve hours. Not being able to sleep on the floor is murder."

I counted up how many nights I'd already gone without any real rest. What was today? Friday? Given the nights I'd spent traveling, I was heading into my fifth day with virtually no sleep. I wondered how long I could last.

"Never am I being in a show like this," Gerta put in, stretching her back. "There is no rest. Always dance position. Always dance tempo. One day of this is *worse* than a month in a regular contest. Look, already so many cots empty."

She gestured at the locals' area where, only four hours before, all the amateur girls were sleeping double. Kane had been firing off his starter pistol like a Wild West gunslinger so often that each girl now had a cot to herself.

"They're dropping like flies, ain't they?" Minnie asked as we all shuffled back onto the floor.

Zave approached with a mug of coffee. It had a thick slice of buttered toast balanced on top. "I thought you might need this," Zave said, handing me the steaming mug.

I sipped the coffee. Zave had remembered how I liked it, and extra cream swirled through the dark brew. By the time the air horn shrilled, I'd finished the toast and coffee, and we were in correct dance position on the floor.

The early-morning crowd was still surprisingly large. The late-late-nighters had been augmented by shift workers either stopping in before their workday began or the night crews dropping by to unwind and see what all the hubbub was about.

A familiar radiance was pouring in through the windows ringing the high ceiling and the double doors at the entrance. The glorious splendor of a Galveston sunrise, like those that had greeted me every morning at St. Mary's, warmed the cavernous hall with a hopeful blush of color. The sun, the coffee, and remembering that I was competing for two thousand dollars, a chance at a life with Zave, and my pin perked me up enormously.

"You seem bright-eyed and bushy-tailed," Zave said, stifling a yawn with the back of his hand. He'd used his break to shower. His hair was wet and his breath smelled of minty tooth powder. "That's good, because I am dragging. You're going to have to keep *me* awake this period."

"Will do," I answered with all the pep I could muster.

"Talk to me," he said. "I need to keep my

brain occupied."

"Sure. Any particular subject?"

"Mmm. How was Litchfield?"

"A bustling metropolis," I joked. "I especially enjoyed the Litchfield Philharmonic Orchestra."

"Dry," he commented. "Your father had a dry wit too. It was lost on your mother. I bet if good ole Mamie was there in Litchfield that she gave you an earful about me."

I cringed recalling my mother's hateful words. I didn't want them — want her — to contaminate what Zave and I were building together. "As you know," I answered, "Mamie was never shy about sharing her opinions."

"Opinions about me, no doubt."

"Why should you be any different from anyone else?" I attempted to joke. "Me, for example. Her own daughter. She always had a lot of opinions about me."

Zave wasn't put off. "Go ahead, tell me what she said."

"Oh, you know," I said with studied casualness. "She was utterly gleeful about telling me about your . . ." I stalled out. The straight-talking, unflappable nurse's manner I was so proud of had abandoned me.

"My preferences?" Zave filled in.

"Yes."

His reaction wasn't what I had expected. In fact, all his concern was for me as he asked, "Did it make her happy to hurt you?"

Though the answer obviously was yes, I was still unable to put the idea of a mother together with the idea of a person who was not only willing but happy to hurt her own child. Words bottled up in me, but, as usual, Zave and I didn't need them.

"That's what tore me up the most," he said. "The realization that my father liked hurting me. That he searched for reasons to hurt me. That there would never be anything I could do to make him stop hating me. I have no doubt that he would have killed me if your father hadn't saved me."

At last, face-to-face, he was speaking the words he'd written, telling me the truth of his life. He already knew the truth of mine and still he was holding me, claiming me.

"Zave, what happened to you should never have happened to any child. Reading your letter broke my heart."

Like the perfect brother, Zave answered, "And what you endured with Mamie broke mine. But what you have to remember, Evie, is that Mamie didn't love you, because she couldn't. No matter how perfect you were or how much you did for her, she was never going to love you. Because she couldn't. Because your mother was never capable of loving anyone except herself."

Though I knew all this in my head, sometimes it takes a voice outside that head to reach your heart, and Zave's words washed over me like an absolution. I laid my cheek on his shoulder and snuggled further into the realization that, though our love wasn't the kind that made teen girls sigh at the movies, it was the kind that I needed. The kind that rescues a person.

Just as I was nestling into that cozy fantasy, the morning newsboy entered, yelling, "Extra. Extra." We all held our breath, eager for the news that Roosevelt had won the contested nomination and would be our candidate.

"The second ballot has been cast at the Democratic Convention in Chicago," he yelled, and then paused for several torturous moments before announcing, "FDR falls short of nomination by one hundred and four votes. Read all about it."

"No," I gasped.

"Don't worry," Zave assured me. "There will be another vote. FDR just has to do a little horse trading. He'll get those votes."

"Will he?" I pleaded more than asked. "Honestly, the thought of having to endure

Hoover for another four years is more than I can stomach. I know lots of people say Hoover is a decent man, but misguided decent men have done some terrible damage in this world, and Hoover is terribly, terribly misguided."

"I promise you," Zave said. "FDR will win, he'll be our president, he'll end this goddamn depression, and he'll save our country."

"How do you know? Hoover's got all the money and all the money men behind him."

"He has to. There won't be any America left to save if Hoover gets four more years. All that damn plutocrat cares about is helping his friends in big business. But it's the little man who needs help."

Zave sounded like Ace. More than that, though, he sounded like exactly the man I wanted to be with.

After several long moments, he went on in a soft voice, "We can make this work, Evie. *I* can make this work. I swear there will never ever ever be another night like Chicago. I'll be good."

Shame and guilt burdened his words. "Zave, it's not a matter of good or bad. You aren't, you never were, bad or evil or wicked. You have a medical issue."

"Is this more about the 'procedure' you

mentioned?"

"Don't say it like that. It's a very minor surgery."

"Surgery? It's surgery now, is it?"

I had to squelch Zave's skepticism. Calmly, I told him, "So many advances are being made in medicine that it's impossible to keep up with all of them. Hundreds of thousands of children who would have died from diphtheria and scarlet fever will now live because of a simple vaccination. We can prevent rickets with cod liver oil."

Unable to control my enthusiasm, I went on breathlessly, "In one of the last lectures I attended, we learned about a new antibiotic that researchers are working on. It's called penicillin and it will save millions of lives."

"But that's a pill you swallow? Or a shot, right? What you're talking about is surgery. About cutting. Into what exactly?"

"Zave, honestly, I shouldn't have started talking about this until I had all the information in my hands, because I don't know all the specifics. But Sofie is going to bring the latest data as soon as she can. I do recall Dr. Kaufman saying that the procedure is no more complicated than removing a wisdom tooth."

"So we're back to 'procedure' now?"

"Call it whatever you like, okay. What does

it matter, if it cures you? If it means you can be normal."

"And what, exactly, do you consider me now?"

"You know that's not what I meant. Is a person with rickets normal? What you have is a disease. It's not something you chose. And now it can be cured. Zave, it's a miracle."

"Right, right," he answered too hurriedly. "A miracle."

"I thought you'd be happy."

"I am, Evie, sure. Sounds great," Zave said, but I could feel the sag of his spirits in every increasingly labored step he took as we shuffled around the floor in silence to Gertrude Lawrence warbling "Someone to Watch Over Me" on a phonograph recording.

Zave's melancholy was contagious. The bone-deep weariness that nerves and adrenaline were holding off now swamped me. We rotated in silence for a dozen or so more songs before I apologized again. "I'm sorry. I really shouldn't have mentioned any of this until I had all the facts. I was just so excited. So certain that you'd be as happy as I am."

"I am," he said, sounding about as happy as a rainy Sunday. "But why can't we have a

546

life together without completely changing me?"

"I'm not talking about completely changing you. Zave, this is medical science. You'll still be you. You'll still be the man I love who was the boy my father loved. All that will change is one thing. The one thing that's stopping us from really being together."

He had no answer and, in the silence that followed, though our bodies remained in constant contact, as we made our endless orbits around the endless floor, he completely withdrew.

Clearly, I had already said too much, so I retreated as well. For the next six hours as my mind deadened, my feet swelled, and my head, eyes, and every joint in my body throbbed with pain, I did what I'd done through endless night shifts, through going to high school while working two or three jobs, through dancing on bloodied toes five times a day: I simply hung on.

Faint though it may have been, I'd always clung to the flicker of hope for better days. And with absolutely no other choice I clung to that glimmer now.

CHAPTER 74

Saturday, July 2, 1932
2:32 p.m.
For all of the next very long, very hot day,
Zave and I couldn't seem to mesh. We were
at odds, wasting energy we didn't have to
spare. Even as we remained fixed together, I
could feel him drifting farther and farther
away. Farther from me. Farther from the
dream of us making a life together. I was
certain that if I did not produce proof
within the next few hours that medicine
could really allow us to have a truly happy
life together that I would lose Zave.

I watched anxiously for Sofie, willing her
to appear. The heat was atrocious. The
bleachers, already filling up for the evening
show, could have taken flight with so many
people fanning themselves. The men had
their sleeves rolled up, shirts wilted around
sweaty necks. Women pressed cold green
bottles of Coca-Cola to flushed cheeks.

"They think *they're* hot," said Cleo, who fell into step alongside us as she was walking from couple to couple, passing out salt tablets and paper cups of water. "Try staying in constant motion down here with your body pressed against someone else's, right?"

"As rain," Zave responded brightly to his old partner. After he popped the salt pill in and slugged down the cup of water and Cleo had moved on, he didn't open his mouth again for the rest of the period. We parted without a word when the break came around.

The girls' quarters were an oven. I put a damp cloth over my eyes to block out as much light as I could. Still, sleep was impossible in the heat. The two-minute-warning horn blasted. We all hauled ourselves upright, grabbed a handful of the aspirin Cleo was handing around, and shambled back out.

On the way, Minnie and I ducked into the ladies' room for a quick pee and a swallow of water to get the aspirin down. "Don't make no sense to me," Minnie said as I bent over to slurp down a drink from my cupped hand.

"What?" I asked, wiping my mouth.

"The Amadeos wanting the show to run so fast. They're burning us out."

"I think," I answered, "their main concern has always been to get publicity for the reopening of the Starlight Pier."

"Then why don't they keep the show going as long as they can? They're making gobs of money *and* getting everyone talking about this place."

"Oh well," I said, drying my hands on my skirt instead of the dingy towel hanging limply from a nail. "Every show's different, I guess. We'd better get out there or this one is going to end real soon. For us."

Zave emerged from the boys' quarters soaking wet. He'd stepped, fully clothed, into the shower. The instant we were on the floor, Kane raced over and, jabbing his finger in Zave's chest, hollered about how we were "disrespecting *his* floor" by dripping water on it.

"Aw, leave him alone," a man in the riled-up crowd yelled. "He's just trying to cool off."

But Kane continued haranguing us. His fury, however, was so ferocious that it stopped feeling like a put-up job. The finger-jabs threatened to poke right into Zave's chest and he had a murderous gleam in his eye. A gleam that I had no doubt many of his boxing opponents had seen. Right before they were pounded to tripe.

Finally, Zave grabbed the judge's hand, held it, stared into Kane's eyes, and said in an utterly calm and utterly commanding tone, "That is enough."

Touching a judge was grounds for automatic elimination, but Kane had no reaction. To the crowd's furious boos, Kane, his big boxer's shoulders rolling from side to side with each heavy step, plodded up the stage stairs and conducted a heated caucus with Pops and Alonzo. Alonzo — who, instead of his usual evening shift, was putting in twelve hours a day — covered the microphone as Kane gesticulated wildly.

Removing his hand, Alonzo purred into the mic, "Well, it sure doesn't pay to make King Kong mad. For Zave's unforgivable sin of dripping water on 'his' floor, Raging Kane Kong is going to punish all the contestants. He has decreed that there will be no rest break at six P.M."

This time the boos started on the floor. As one, in defiance of the dance position rule, we all raised our hands and shook them at Kane, causing him to run around the floor, tweeting his whistle maniacally in our faces while flat-footed Patsy crept around behind him making faces and thumbing his nose.

Not only did the crowd love it, showering

all of us with applause and coins, but the too-real fakery broke the ice between me and Zave. Laughing, we gathered up the change and filled Minnie and DeWitt's pockets with it.

That burst of adrenaline buoyed me for a short while. By the time the clock hands crawled their way to six, however, when we should have had at least the bad joke of a fifteen-minute break, I again felt beaten to a pulp.

A series of eliminations jolted us back to attention. Three times, nearly one after the other, Kane fired his starter pistol into the rafters. In all three cases, it was the boys' knees that hit the floor first. The girls could have continued as singles, but all three chose to exit with their partners, and the floor was emptier by half a dozen dancers.

Next, a couple from Minnesota, veterans of dozens of shows up north in cooler climes, achieved a first of some kind by both passing out and hitting the floor like a pair of dead flounders at the exact same moment.

Even the horses, the real pros, were suffering. Though Ace and Lily were barely shuffling, their mouths hung open and they panted like dogs. Patsy squeegeed sweat from his brow and flicked it toward a laughing crowd.

Fortunately, King Sammie, Samuel Bert, had brought his new invention down from Dallas. He called his treat sno-cones and was selling the balls of ice bejeweled with ruby-red and sapphire-blue syrup as fast as he could crank the handle on his ice-crushing machine. Audience members passed the chilly treats down to us while, surprisingly, Kane pretended not to notice. Zave and I collected so many that we supplied all the amateurs who didn't have their own cheering sections.

The sweet, icy crystals provided instant relief. Zave's cone turned his lips a blue so frosty that it cooled me just to look at him. I was sure that my red cone had stained my lips as cherry red as Snow White's. Or Sleeping Beauty's. I wanted to press my lips against Zave's and kiss them until his blue and my red blended and turned both our lips purple. I wanted to kiss him until he awoke and wanted to kiss me back.

"How long can they last, folks?" Alonzo asked, swabbing the back of his neck with a handkerchief.

How long could *I* last?

Purple, I thought, as I stared at the open doors, willing Sofie to appear and hand me the keys that would unlock my happiness.

The color we made together.
Purple.

CHAPTER 75

Saturday, July 2, 1932
6:01 p.m.

It was a huge letdown for us all when the six o'clock break came and went without the air horn sounding. Fortunately, the Saturday-evening crowd in the ringside box seats arrived early and was glamourous enough to take our minds off our aching feet. And backs. And heads.

The Houston oil executives and the slumming bankers joked, smoked cigars, and drank openly from bottles of bonded whiskey while their mistresses or the women they'd rented for the evening fanned themselves and pressed dainty hankies to their upper lips.

Two large parties of women in the sheerest, whitest cotton dresses and men in crisp seersucker suits had brought maids who carried large hampers of food into their row of adjoining box seats. Imagining themselves

555

cutting-edge wits, they laughed at the gay fun of eating squab and cucumber sand-wiches amidst the hoi polloi.

Their adult children, the trust fund heirs and oil heiresses, were even drunker, louder, and freer with the smart remarks. Asking one of the poor maids to "Peel me a grape" was a guaranteed side-splitter. The slum-mers acted as if they'd been set loose in a foreign country filled with natives who couldn't understand English and whose opinions didn't count anyway. They com-peted to see who could curse the loudest and make the most outrageous joke. Even the girls were throwing around eff yous. They didn't care about the honest folk behind them eating jelly sandwiches on day-old bread who were shielding their chil-dren's ears from the blue language.

A few of the young swells, in addition to being drunk, were also high. Even if they hadn't been joking loudly about being "vipers," I'd have known they were smoking marijuana just from the odor of burnt rope and roast beef that wafted off of them. As we glided past these gilded darlings, Zave pinched his thumb and forefinger together and pretended to suck. They howled with laughter and held out joints. Which he ac-cepted.

The reefer made Zave even more distant. I figured he had every right to be. I had wounded him and couldn't repair the hurt until I was fully armed with the facts. So, in spite of the happy, holiday atmosphere that soared as the sun set and evening breezes blew through the Palace, lowering temperatures, a numb haze imprisoned me. Even when Zave and I performed a couple of specials barely sprightly enough to net us a miserly sprinkling of coins, I merely moved forward in a robotic stupor brought on by a combination of sheer exhaustion and my sadness about my fading hopes for Zave and me.

My doldrums were only pierced when, later that evening, I felt an odd sort of electricity ripple through the audience. A message passed from one enthralled spectator to the next until a clamor of voices drowned out the recorded music.

"What is it?" I asked Zave.

He shrugged and nodded his chin toward the entrance, where a newsboy was selling special editions of the paper as fast as the crowd around him could rip them from his hand.

"Whatever it is," I said, trying to pique his interest, "the bigwigs don't look too happy."

Up front, as soon as the news reached the

men in suits, they folded their arms and sour looks creased their faces.

"Let's go investigate," I suggested, steering us toward the newsboy. Before we could get close enough to read the huge headline, however, the news reached the stage and the Melody Makers broke into a spirited rendition of "Happy Days Are Here Again."

"FDR won the Democratic nomination!" I exploded.

Waves of jubilation swept through the cheap seats as the average Joes realized that Roosevelt would be our candidate.

"Thank God," Zave said.

"Thank God," I echoed.

In the crowd, when word spread that, for the first time ever, a presidential candidate was going to broadcast his acceptance speech, a chant started, "Turn on the radio. Turn on the radio." Soon the united voices rose above the band. "Let FDR speak."

Alonzo's smooth chuckle was amplified through the Palace. "We hear you, folks, we hear you," he placated, shooting a nervous glance at Pops, who stood at the edge of the stage. Pops's nervous glances were reserved for the high-dollar donors in the box seats, who were shaking their heads sternly and giving scowling thumbs-downs. Ultimately, though, the only vote that counted in

Galveston was the Amadeos'. Pops fixed his gaze on Uncle JuJu and waited.

Cleo, curled up beside him, whispered in his ear as she gestured toward the cheap seats. JuJu swiveled around, taking in the immense crowd of FDR supporters who looked perilously close to devolving into an angry mob if they didn't get their wish, and he gave Pops a slow nod of approval. Pops shot a finger at Alonzo, the emcee switched on the radio, and Franklin Roosevelt's voice filled the hall.

I'd never heard FDR speak before and, after reading so much about his plans to help the common man, his voice surprised me. "He sounds like a snobbish Yankee."

Zave answered, "Yeah, well, he sure doesn't think or act like one. And that's all I care about. Just listen."

I did.

FDR started his address by pointing out that no other nominee had ever spoken to the convention before. "Let it be symbolic, therefore," he said, "that I break tradition. I will break foolish traditions and leave it to the Republican leadership, far more skilled in that art, to break promises!"

There was a moment of stunned silence at hearing such harsh honesty, then the Palace erupted in cheers. Mine among them. After only a few sentences, I had come to love that snobbish Yankee voice.

When the furor subsided enough that I could hear FDR again, he was talking about the Depression. "There are two ways of viewing the government's duty in matters affecting economic and social life," he said in a sonorous voice that built in intensity. "The first sees to it that a favored few are helped and hopes that some of their prosperity will leak through, sift through, to the laborer, to the farmer, to the small business man. But that is not and never will be the theory of the Democratic Party!"

There was whooping and hollering for that thundering proclamation. Caps and fists were thrown into the air in a mighty hallelujah. The only grumps in the whole place were the bankers and oil bigwigs, who muttered darkly about the "rise of Communism" and "the end of individual liberty as we know it."

When the furor died down again, Roosevelt was speaking about Prohibition. "This convention wants repeal," he stated unequivocally. "Your candidate wants repeal. And I am confident that the United States of America wants repeal."

Repeal Prohibition? Did that get them on their feet? You bet it did. I thought the bleachers would collapse under the foot stomping. It took a while for the ecstatic audience to calm down enough that we could again hear the man that every one of us except the box seaters fervently, desperately hoped would be our next president.

FDR said, "The main issue of this campaign should revolve about a depression so deep that it is without precedent in modern history. This is no time for fear, for reaction, or for timidity. It will not do, as Republican leaders do, to explain their broken promises of continued inaction, that the depression is worldwide.

"One word more: out of every crisis, every tribulation, every disaster, mankind rose with some share of greater knowledge, of higher decency, of purer purpose. Today we have come through a period of loose thinking, descending morals, an era of selfishness, among individual men and women and among nations. Blame not governments alone for this. Blame ourselves in equal share. Let us be frank in acknowledgment of the truth that the profits of speculation, the easy road without toil, has lured us from the old barricades."

At that a few of the high rollers, the profiteers of speculation, actually appeared ashamed.

FDR railed on, "Never before in modern history have the essential differences between the two major American parties stood out in such striking contrast as they do today. Republican leaders not only have failed in material things, they have failed in national vision, because in disaster they have held out no hope, they have pointed out no path for the people below to climb back to places of security and of safety in our American life."

"He understands," Zave whispered, his voice thick with unshed tears. "None of us is asking for a handout, we just want a way out. That rich bastard, he really understands."

In the stands, the chins of strong men who'd slogged on in spite of hardship and hunger trembled the way any victim's does when, after years of being ignored or even blamed for their tragedy, someone listens. Someone hears them and offers help. Skinny wives clutched their husbands' sinewy hands. Ropy-muscled fathers lifted up a child to hear the words of the man who would save them.

Finishing as powerfully as he had begun, FDR promised that if we gave him not just our votes but our help, that we would "win in this crusade to restore America to her own people."

Alonzo switched off the radio, and for one second the only sound that could be heard was sniffling. Then thunderous applause rolled down from the bleachers and boomed throughout the Palace. In reaction, the Richie Rich Hoover supporters began booing loudly and calling them "Bolsheviks" and "freeloaders." Men in crumpled shirts and suspenders got to their feet and screamed back. Vicious, snarling expressions of rage contorted their faces.

The incendiary whiff of violence hung in the air. One spark and the powder keg of fury would have erupted.

Pops signaled Mel and the band broke into a lively tune.

Most of the smart set relaxed and pretended to take the news of Roosevelt's victory the way they took all the news that leaked into their enchanted world, as a joke. They called each other comrade, laughed too loudly, and continued to drink too much.

One wag, a stylish fellow in a white cotton tennis sweater, stood up, reached into the pocket of his trousers, hauled up a handful of change, and, to the giddy delight of his set, yelled, "Distribute the wealth!" as he flung the coins directly at Zave and me.

A silver dollar hit Zave's forehead and anger flashed across his face. Breaking dance position, he scooped up a handful of the heavy coins and flung them with all his might directly at the jerk's face.

Ace, Patsy, DeWitt, and several of the other pros left their partners and scrambled to grab coins and pelt the rich dope, who was now cowering in his seat, hands protecting his face, as he yelled that he was "only joking." The plebes in the stands behind the jerk also began peppering him with coins and hurling vicious insults; it was worth a few precious coins to the men to make the brat squirm.

I was certain we'd all be eliminated, and braced myself for a series of ear-piercing tweets then a deafening gunshot from Kane. But the hawk-eyed judge had his back determinedly turned to the melee, pretending to be giving a stern lecture to a local couple. Before he turned around, ever so slowly, Kane discharged several short, sharp blasts on his whistle to give all us misbehaving dancers time to regain proper position.

When Zave pulled me into his arms again, we did a slow, triumphant waltz that was rewarded with coins and even a few bills. Zave, ever the performer, perked up like a wilted daisy in an actual shower. He grinned at the crowd and waved. A roof-rattling cheer arose.

He was their hero. He was mine. But I was losing him. Though he was still in my arms, the link that had pumped joy and hope into my life had become so weak that all I had left was his reluctant physical presence. Tired as I was, a shuddering dread lurched through me as I imagined my life when even that was taken from me. Our future had become a critically ill patient hanging on by the barest of threads. Our time was running out. If I didn't show him proof of the medical miracles I'd promised, he would be gone. His mind, his heart, would be forever shut off to the life we might have had and I would have lost the two things I cared about: my pin and Zave.

I was already in mourning for what might have been when, like the cavalry in a Western movie, far off, on the other side of the vast hall, silhouetted in the double doors, her white uniform glowing a luminescent pale blue in the moonlight, there she was.

Sofie.

CHAPTER 76

And she carried a manila envelope. Unfortunately, the fire marshal wouldn't let her in because the house was full. I searched for JuJu to come and rescue his niece. But it was far too early for him to make an appearance. I started to head toward her, but the band suddenly stopped playing and Alonzo froze all motion with a strange request.

"I need everyone's attention. That means everyone. Dancers, even you need to stop and listen. That's right, King Kong is giving everyone a break so you all can hear this important announcement."

The dancers froze and I was trapped in place as the emcee made his announcement.

"Oh boy, oh boy, folks, this is the best ever. Thanks again to the generosity and community spirit of the Amadeo family,

Galveston will be treated to a Fourth of July fireworks spectacle that they don't want anyone to miss. Not even our dancers. So mark your calendars, friends. Because in two nights, on the Fourth of July, we are going to be taking the whole darn show outside for a spectacular display of pyrotechnics!"

All around me dancers' mouths opened in astonished delight.

"That's right, contestants," Alonzo went on. "You heard me. For the first time in any show, anywhere, you'll be allowed outside during the competition." He paused for dramatic effect then concluded, "Because you'll be dancing on the sand!"

I was so intent upon Sofie that the announcement barely registered. All I cared about was the manila envelope tucked under her arm, its flap held closed by a red string wrapped between two cardboard buttons. Excitement surged through exhaustion when I told Zave, "Sofie's here and she has it. She brought the information we need."

Zave peered across the eerily still floor to the entrance, where Sofie was arguing with the fire marshal. Of course, she wouldn't even think of dropping her last name, the one that opened every door on the island.

The marshal folded his arms and motioned for her to move away from the exit he'd been ordered to keep cleared. As Alonzo hyped the fireworks display, my fear grew that Sofie would simply leave. The instant Alonzo finally finished his spiel and the dancers were unfrozen, I dropped any pretense at dancing and steered Zave toward the exit as rapidly as I could. Unfortunately, Kane was planted right in the middle of the floor, whistle stuffed in the grim line of his mouth, hand gripping the elimination pistol, cocked and held at the ready. I couldn't afford to catch Kane's attention; not with the information that would change mine and Zave's lives almost within our grasp.

Bobbing and weaving through clots of dancers, we made our way to the open doors of the exit. Just in time to see the fire marshal turn Sof away.

"She'll be back," I told Zave, not believing my own cheery words. Sofie hated calling attention to herself, to her last name, and that's what would be required to get in.

Deflated again, I was dragging around the floor in a daze when, from the corner of my eye, I caught sight of a blur of white: Sofie. And she was flat-out barreling past the fire marshal.

"Sofie!" I screamed, even breaking dance

position to wave frantically at her.

"I have it," she cried, holding the envelope aloft.

Dodging some couples and nearly plowing over others, I tugged Zave toward her. An uproar arose as contestants objected both to the intruder and to me and Zave breaking dance position.

"Sofie," I yelled, all my happiness at seeing her and hopes for a miracle compressed into that name.

As we closed the distance between us, Sofie called above the ruckus, "Dr. K loaned me the entire journal. He said the article you need is in it. My shift isn't over yet, but I came as soon as I could. I didn't even take time to look at the article."

Only one couple and a few yards stood between us. My focus narrowed down to the envelope in Sofie's outstretched hand. I was close enough to see how fatigue had reddened her usually luminous eyes when a great mitt of a hand intruded into my field of vision and clamped itself onto the envelope.

"I'll take that," Kane said, ripping the envelope away from Sofie. "What have you got in there? Bennies? Cocaine?"

"Kane," I moaned at the ridiculous possibility. "Come on."

"It's only a medical journal," Sofie yelled.

"A magazine," I explained to the ex-boxer.

"What? You think this is the Reading Guild now?"

"Give it to her," Sofie demanded.

"Get this intruder off my floor," Kane bellowed, and two trainers immediately appeared. Sofie, already embarrassed by the attention, left without another word.

"Please," I begged. Tears of frustration, exhaustion, and anger stung my eyes. "Let me have it."

"Oh, I'll let you have it, all right," Kane roared, balling up his fist as though he were going to clobber me. The crowd, thinking it was a bit, cackled.

"But it *is* just a magazine," I pleaded.

" 'Just a magazine,' " he taunted. "A magazine with a hole cut into it to hide your goofballs. Your bennies. Your jazz cigarettes. This is going straight into evidence."

The crowd, enlivened by the sight of my pleading, my tears, booed Kane. They thought it was all an act. Maybe it was. Who knew anymore? I was more exhausted than I'd ever been in my life.

I tried to rip the envelope from Kane's hand. I didn't need to pretend that I was close to hysterics. Every dream that had been stolen, every promise broken, every

570

sad Christmas and ignored birthday, every night I'd gone to bed hungry, they were all there in Kane's spitefulness.

I lunged at him, ready to claw his face off. Kane, still the deft boxer, pivoted, and I fell harmlessly upon his broad back. Though Zave reached for and held me, I remained rooted, glaring hatred at Kane as he stomped away with what I was certain was Zave's and my passport to a better life.

"Come on," Zave urged, after I resisted his efforts to get us moving again. "It won't help if we get eliminated."

"That was the information I've been telling you about. Aren't you even the tiniest bit upset?" I demanded.

"Sure."

"You don't act like it."

"Evie, come on, you know the score. Kane's just doing his job. We'll get the journal from him at the next break."

As I scowled at his retreating back, Kane did something he never did during prime show hours. He handed his gun and whistle to the other floor judge and, taking Sofie's envelope with him, he disappeared down the hall that led to the rest quarters and Pops's office.

"Why is Kane leaving?" I asked.

Before Zane could answer, the alternate

judge fired the starter gun. The blast reverberated throughout the Palace, startling me and the swallows in the rafters. I gasped along with the crowd when I saw who had been eliminated: Gerta and her brother, Fritz. They had stumbled and were sprawled on the floor, too tired to get up. The judge hovered above them.

They lay there frozen, disbelieving, smoke still curling from the pistol. The rest of us, all the pros, were just as stunned. Gerta and Fritz were the two horses we considered indestructible. Kane would never have eliminated them. Not until the very end. The show had to have a few horses like that stolid pair. Not to win; they never won. But to come close enough to give every hard-luck plodder in the bleachers hope that they could, if not triumph, at least survive through sheer animal endurance alone to see another, maybe even a brighter day.

All the regulars exchanged nervous glances. This show wasn't like any other they'd ever been in. If Gerta and Fritz could go down, any of us could go down.

The air horn blasted, signaling the ten o'clock break.

Feathers from the startled swallows were still floating down on the empty floor as we trudged to our rest quarters.

CHAPTER 77

Buoyed by FDR's nomination and an ocean of liquor, both bonded and bathtub, the Saturday night crowd was in such a state of giddy intoxication that even the big-city bankers were joining in the toasts. When they weren't, that is, cursing him and his "buck-toothed, do-gooder, Commie wife" to everlasting damnation. In the end, though, this golden crowd didn't truly believe that anything could possibly, seriously threaten their gilded lives.

For a while, as footsore and fatigued as we all were, the arguing, laughing, and lambasting of either FDR or Hoover kept us energized. By midnight, however, I was nearly catatonic with exhaustion. It was the end of my sixth day with little more than a few catnaps. Still, I believed I was holding my own. Then, with no warning, I slipped

573

directly into a waking dream.

Instead of circling a dance floor, I was back on night duty. In the children's ward. A familiar sense of contentment filled me as I tended a little one suffering from croup by the faint orange glow of a night-light. A mentholated mist from a vaporizer daubed with Vick's enfolded us in a cozy cloud. With a joyous lift, I realized that the child was mine. Mine and Zave's.

A guttural howl yanked me back into reality. The source of the scream was Durwood, a buck-toothed local kid who'd entered with his wife Irma. Durwood, fists churning in the air, shouted at an imaginary foe, "Come on out here, you sidewindin' son uh bitch. I'ma drop you like an ox. Cheatin' with my wedded wife. Come on. I'ma clean your plow, you cheap bastard."

"Shut up, Durwood," Irma yelled, slapping him hard across the face.

Instantly, he swiveled and threw a punch that would have knocked his petite wife into tomorrow if she hadn't ducked. Still tossing wild punches, Durwood railed at his imaginary foe, "I'ma learn you good 'bout prowlin' where you oughten be aprowlin'." Abruptly, he fell silent and his whirling fists sagged to his sides. Weeping openly, he lamented, "Irma's my wedded wife. She ain't yours to lay up with."

Everyone laughed. Everyone except Irma who, though she hadn't been eliminated, scuttled out of the open doors as quickly as she could, leading her still-thrashing husband behind her.

"Squirrelly," DeWitt said, diagnosing the man's waking hallucinations.

Lily, taking care of Ace, surreptitiously sleeping on her shoulder, added offhandedly, "That is the first time I've ever seen anyone take leave of their senses this early in a show. Usually no one loses their wits like that until a few weeks in. Of course, in a regular show we'd all be sleepwalking now and this would be just one, long bad dream."

She trilled a strange laugh and added with a chilling flatness, "Who knows? Maybe it is."

CHAPTER 78

"Welcome to the Dead Zone," Ace greeted me after the 2 A.M. break. His voice came from far away.

Zave had been required to physically drag me off the cot and onto the floor where, try as I might, I could barely stagger forward. I noted with distant detachment that the stands were still nearly full. Spectators carried on celebrating FDR's win. Men in shirtsleeves passed bottles around. Mothers gossiped with friends while their children slept beside them. Everyone was on vacation and no one wanted to leave the party.

I felt like a deep-sea diver wearing lead-weighted boots, my head enclosed in a dome of metal trapped far, far below the surface. With each step, I sank further down, further from the noise, the pain. Time this far down was marked only by the

576

shift in illumination as we moved out of the glaring overhead lights and into the shadows at the edges of the floor.

Lily stared either at me or through me and droned, "Given tonight's attendance, the show's net — not accounting for pilfering and skimming — was four thousand, eight hundred, and eighty-three dollars."

It seemed urgent to me that I assemble a response to her perplexing mathematical message, but even as I attempted to stammer out that I didn't understand, Lily was drifting away. Everyone was drifting. I was drifting. I was drifting. The realization that I was losing my mind sent a bolt of adrenaline through my body. That surge of blind terror was quickly blanketed by a stultifying mental fog. The floor grew soggy beneath my feet. The hot vapor of my own breath choked me. Like urgent communications from a faraway battlefield, I sent myself frantic alerts that I had to get the journal from Kane. I caught a glimpse of the judge ducking behind the stage and tried to chase after him. The best I could manage was a sodden trudge.

Even that momentum was halted when Mamie grabbed me. I tried to bat her away, but she clawed at me, pulling me back. Back to her. Forever. I punched out even as some distant part of my brain sent the message that my mother wasn't really there with me. That I was flailing at a phantom. That blip of knowledge vanished when the Director joined Mamie. Though I was dimly aware that they were both phantoms, I still had to fight them or I would die. I clawed and punched. From far away, a distant voice commanded, "Evie, stop. Stop."

"Look at her," a voice shouted from the crowd. "The nurse. She's cracking up."

"Did you see that?" another voice asked. "She tried to paste Zave."

Who were they talking about? Who tried to hit Zave?

I looked around frantically for him. Finally, in the reflection from the double doors, I found Zave. But I couldn't recognize the person he had wrapped in his arms. I knew that it was supposed to be me. But it wasn't me. The person he was holding with such heartbreaking tenderness was Mamie. Then Cleo. Then the beautiful boy from the Pansy Club. Not me. Never me.

And then I felt his arms. Felt him holding me. Protecting me, and my racing heart slowed. I knew what was happening: I had gone squirrelly. But I didn't know how to stop it. Or if it ever would stop. Or that it would be so terrifying. With an enormous effort, I formed the words "Something. Bad."

I felt more than heard Zave's words as they rumbled against my chest. "It's okay, Evie. I've got you. I've got you. You'll be fine." He guided me to a shadowed spot. "You're just a little squirrelly. Happens to everyone. It just hit you early because you're a greenhorn and you came in exhausted. Nothing to worry about. Just hang on to me. It'll pass. I'll take care of you."

I was panting and could feel my eyes pushing out of their sockets. "Lost. Everything. Lost. Pin. You. Everything."

"No, sweetie, I promise, you haven't lost anything. You're with me. I'll take care of you. Just rest your head, okay?"

I did.

"Now, close your eyes."

"Scared."

"I've got you, baby. I won't let anything happen to you. Not to Denny Devlin's daughter. Close those beautiful peepers. The fix is in for us. You're the local girl making good, you're Nurse Gravy. Get some sleep." He held me tighter and began swaying gently from side to side as he softly crooned, "Hush little baby, don't say a word, Papa's gonna buy you a mockingbird."

I wanted to tell him that my father used

to sing that lullaby to me, but my mouth wouldn't work. The leaden deep-sea diver boots pulled me down. I fought to return to the surface but my struggle only made me sink even faster. I was being pulled to a destination I'd been meant to arrive at all along. I somehow knew that a reckoning awaited me far beneath the surface of my consciousness and I surrendered to it.

They were all down there. The girl from the hobo camp whose family had turned her out for eating too much. The emaciated twins clinging to their emaciated dog on the back of the Model A truck heading west. The prostitutes sitting in the steam cabinet, dying of syphilis. The kid with croup. The veterans of the Great War destroyed by mustard gas. The hungry newsboy. Marvin the Man of Marvels. They all waited for me. They had all needed me. They'd been sick and hurting and I'd yearned to help them. To make them well. And now, amazingly, they were.

Marvin stood on two strong legs and waved to me. The prostitutes fanned themselves and gossiped happily. The veterans gave me snappy salutes. The children were plump-cheeked. Even the dog was healthy. They had all been healed. They were whole again.

Then, like a scene shift onstage, the spotlight blinked out. When it blinked on again, my father — tuxedoed, grinning, pomaded, and luminous with life — was dancing within its radiant embrace. So, I thought, losing my mind was the price for being with my father again; I wish I'd known sooner how easy it was.

My father rainbowed the cane in his hand over his head while he danced beneath its silvery arch until, stopping abruptly, he extended the cane out, drawing my attention to another part of the stage. The spotlight blazed on and there was Terry, my friend who'd left one night and never returned. Terry's darlings, his beloved dogs, scampered around him.

Terry conducted them as if they were his own personal orchestra. With the barest tilt of a finger or flash of his palm, they twirled, they spun arabesques, they pranced about on their hind legs, front paws held up like dainty dowagers extending genteel hands. Terry, aglow with the excellence of the moment, was their rhapsodic maestro.

"Perfect," I whispered.

Then, as if he'd always been there, Zave, the gangly, ten-year-old Zave still growing into his front teeth, appeared beside my father. I saw the fine, confident man which that boy, protected and guided by my father, would have grown into if Mamie hadn't betrayed him. Zave gazed at my father with fathomless admiration as he mirrored his every movement so impeccably that again I gasped, "Perfect."

Before the words were out of my mouth, Zave vanished. The stage went dark, my father was gone, and I was left with that one word: perfect. Whole and complete, the realization dawned on me: Zave had always been perfect, but I'd wanted him to be perfect for me. And so I'd made him into a person that I could change. A person who needed to be healed. A sick person.

The verdict was swift: I had been wrong and I had wronged.

After seeing Mamie again in Litchfield, I believed I was correcting her horrible wrong. I believed I was accepting Zave in a way that Mamie had never accepted me. But I hadn't. That is what my father had shown me. Hiding behind the shield of science and medicine, I was insisting that Zave "fix" himself. I shuddered thinking of all the times and all the ways that I'd told him that he was a broken thing that could only be made right and normal with a surgery that I still knew nothing about beyond a half-remembered lecture.

All these thoughts sputtered and flashed across a brain so exhausted that only a new jolt of adrenaline kept it from shutting down entirely. I had one last critical mission before I could sleep: I had to tell Zave that I was wrong. That he was now and had always been . . . Perfect.

First, though, I needed to pull myself out of the muck of half-conscious delirium that had swallowed me. I had to open my eyes, my mouth, and form words coherent enough to tell Zave that medicine was wrong and that he was right. Exactly as he was. That there was nothing to be fixed or cured or healed. There never had been.

I struggled toward the surface, toward the small pearl of light that was consciousness gleaming in the darkness. I had to wake up, and I had to do it now. There wasn't a moment to lose. I had already inflicted too much damage, but the lead boots kept dragging me down. Finally, I managed to rouse myself enough that I heard whispered words, angry words. Though it was painful, I forced my shut-down mind to make sense of the words.

"Have you seen this?" a harsh voice demanded.

If there was an answer, I couldn't summon the energy to attend to the soft syllables.

"Is this what you want?" the angry voice demanded. The question was accompanied by the intrusive sound of papers being rustled next to my ear.

Again, any answer was too soft for me to hear, though I did detect a rumbling against my chest which made me remember that Zave was holding me. So, yes, I concluded dimly, Zave was giving the inaudible answers spoken in a voice so soothing that, in spite of the adrenaline, in spite of the terrible wrong I had to put right, I slipped again into the exquisite blackness.

Only the jarring anger of the other man's voice could shock me back into consciousness as it asked, "Goddammit, Zave, how much more do you need to see?"

I couldn't recognize the speaker's voice. If only I could open my eyes. I tried, but my body was as far away and beyond my command as it had been on the stage of the National Theatre when I'd observed myself from the balcony.

"You have to decide. Now. Before it's too late."

"I can't." It was Zave and he was in pain. I had to stop his pain. Everything depended on me reaching him in time.

It took several minutes, but I finally forced my eyes open. I gazed at Zave, but my fractured mind scrambled his face into all the paintings and statues at St. Mary's. He became all the saints porcupined with arrows. Jesus on the cross. Mary holding her dead son. He became sorrow.

I tried to tell him not to be sad. That there was nothing to be sad about. Nothing to cure. Nothing to change. But my feet were icepicks stabbing pain through every cell in my body. And my brain was a wad of scorched wires that refused to communicate with my mouth and continued to feed me bizarre images instead.

I thought I caught a glimpse of Kane, bent beneath the weight of an enormous duffel bag, slide unnoticed through the shadows, toward the rest area. My brain wanted me to believe that snakes, thick black pythons, writhed from the open top of the bag.

Stop hallucinating, I ordered myself. But the black snakes wouldn't go away. Kane punched the black snakes back into the bag and hurried away.

"Whuh . . . ?" I asked in a dry croak. But the snakes were already gone.

"Go back to sleep, Evie," Zave told me. "Everything will be fine."

"No," I said, the word standing for everything I had to tell him. That I was wrong, that whatever was in Sofie's envelope was wrong. But he was rocking me again and singing that Papa was gonna buy me a mockingbird and the waves of black velvet closed over me again and I sank back down to where the seaweed swayed and pain and heartbreak, loneliness and regret, didn't exist.

CHAPTER 79

Sunday, July 3, 1932
3:19 a.m.

"Evie, stand up," Zave ordered.

I tried to obey, but my legs had turned to licorice twists that buckled beneath me.

Zave grabbed at my shifting weight as I slid down his chest, unwieldy as a sack of grain.

"Evie, wake up. You have to wake up."

I opened my eyes. Though nothing seemed entirely normal, at least there were no black snakes

"Are you awake?" Zave asked.

I glanced at the clock. 3:19. An hour had passed and I still hadn't given Zave the message from my father. I had to tell him I was wrong.

"Zay—" I said on a long exhale that left me withered.

"Don't try to talk. Just wake up. Now, Evie. Evie. Open your eyes. I need you to be awake. Wide awake. Are you awake?"

With great effort I nodded.

"You need air," he said, and began forcefully lugging me over to the open doors.

"Staw—" I tried to tell him to stop, that I had to deliver the most important message he would ever receive. That he didn't need to change. I needed to change. The world needed to change. Medicine needed to change. But he ignored my dry, croaking attempts at speech.

We passed a heavyset woman wearing a ratty coat with a collar of beady-eyed minks biting each other's tails. Leaning over the railing she yelled, "Hey, Evie. I pray a rosary for you and Zave every night."

Was she real?

At the doors, a breeze blew in from the Gulf that was almost cool against my skin. I breathed in air that smelled of the ocean instead of boiled hot dogs, disinfectant, and armpits.

"Okay, Evie," Zave said as we rocked in place. "I need you to listen and remember. Are you listening?"

I told him I was, then noticed that no words were coming out of my mouth.

"Evie, here's what you have to know. Just two things. No matter what happens —"

"Way —" I muttered, believing I was telling him to wait, that I had something urgent to tell him first.

"Just listen, please, and remember, first of all, remember that I truly do love you."

Love you. I told him that I loved him too, but the words remained locked in my shriveled throat.

"And two, that whatever happens, it's not your fault."

Happens? Fault?

And then, Zave let me go. I wobbled, unable to imagine how I would ever stand again without his support. I staggered after him as he retreated toward the rest area, but he was already gone.

Was I hallucinating? I had to be. Otherwise, Kane's whistle would be shrieking.

"Zave," I called.

But before his name was out of my mouth, a clanging like an earthquake in a sheet metal factory exploded. A fire alarm. The shriek of the siren we hadn't been allowed to use joined it, creating an ear-piercing alert.

For a split second, every single soul in the Palace froze. Women and children covered their ears. Belligerent annoyance curdled the men's faces as they looked around for whoever was in charge to shut off the damn racket. Every head swiveled, searching for the prankster who had pulled the handle on the red fire alarm.

But it was not a prank. Kane was on the stage cranking the handle on the siren for all he was worth.

An acrid smell assaulted me. A woman shrieked, "Fire!"

At the far end of the floor, dense plumes of black smoke billowed from the hall that led to the rest areas. The fire alarm howled as the audience, now a roiling mob, rose. All sound was blocked by the alarm and the scene became a pantomime of silent shrieks.

Mothers screamed wide-mouthed for their children. The aisles clogged with panicked spectators. Men climbed over the railing, dangled down until they could drop onto the floor, then held their arms up to catch the children the women handed to them.

The boards beneath my feet bounced as if cannonballs were being dropped on the floor. A human stampede thundered my way. Leading the charge were the dancers.

Zave was not with them.

"Where's Zave?" I shouted at the churning mob storming toward me. But panic had deafened them.

"Where is Zave?" I screamed again. All I got for an answer were freak-show close-ups of eyes bulging with fright. No one paused.

No one even heard me.

I battled against the tide of the stampede that was rushing out through the double doors and trying to sweep me into its undertow.

A society matron wielding her heavy purse like a battering ram shoved me aside. A little girl with leg braces who'd lost her crutches was passed above the heads of the mob. A burly guy was knocked down at the door. Someone stumbled and went down. Then someone else. There was a bottleneck at the door. The black thunderhead of smoke pouring from the rest area closed in.

"This place is a tinderbox!" a man bellowed. "It's gonna blow!"

Panic rippled through the trapped mass and they went wild-eyed with terror. A shrieking woman clawed at the face of a man blocking her way. A couple of teenage boys crawled over the heads of the blocked crowd as if they were cobblestones in a road.

My eyes streamed with tears from the acrid smoke. I brawled my way through the mob, trying to get back to the floor. To Zave.

A storm wave composed of elbows, shoulders, knees battered me. A trombone slide punched me in the shoulder as the player bludgeoned his way through.

With a last, herculean shove, I burst from

the shrieking bedlam. Through the smoke and tears, I caught a glimpse of a pair of broad shoulders and shrieked, "Zave!"

The black haze engulfed him until, suddenly, his hands reached out from the choking cloud and grabbed me. Only it wasn't Zave.

"Kane?"

"You have to leave," the judge roared above the pandemonium.

"Zave," I yelled back. "I have to save Zave. He went back to the rest area. Back to where the fire is."

Kane, immobile as a bank vault, wouldn't move and he wouldn't allow me to move either.

In a frenzy, I screamed at the bullheaded judge, "Do something. Get Zave. Stop him. Please, Kane, for God's sake, save him."

Instead of going to Zave's rescue, though, Kane wrapped me in a grip so tight he crushed my lungs and I went light-headed.

"Let me go." I kicked, I flailed, I screamed the horrible words: "Zave is trying to kill himself."

The arms tightened even further around me.

Powered by a burst of adrenalized energy, I freed my right hand and raked a trail of bloody nail marks across Kane's cheek.

In an eerily calm tone, he said, "I'm sorry, Evie," and with something approaching gentleness, he balled up his boxer's fist and delivered a swift bop to my jaw.

My head popped back and the lights went out.

CHAPTER 80

Sunday, July 3, 1932

Someone is screaming Zave's name.

It's me.

But when I come to, shivering on the dark beach, I realize that the cries have only been audible in my nightmares.

I can't tell how long I've been out. It couldn't have been long though. It's still night and the fire seems freshly unleashed. The Palace is a macabre jack-o'-lantern. Flames leer out of the open door. They poke lurid tongues from every crack in the old building and paint the ring of windows at the top a fiery orange. With a violent shattering, the glass in the few intact windows explodes and the beast escapes. The fire devours the Palace and rolls, bright and orange as a wave of lava, down the pier, igniting everything in its path.

I ask Minnie, DeWitt, Ace, everyone still there if they've seen Zave. They shake their heads no and stare at their feet. I ask if he might have gotten away. Patsy shrugs and says it's possible. Anything is possible. No one will meet my gaze.

A Coast Guard fireboat appears and maneuvers in alongside the blazing pier. It blasts the fire with its water cannon. A cloud of sizzling white steam billows toward us. Choking, wiping stinging ash from their eyes, most of the remaining gawkers amble away and then, finally, all the dancers leave. Except for Minnie and DeWitt. Minnie pulls me close. "Your teeth are chattering. You were laid out on that cold sand for more'n an hour."

"What are you talking about?" I ask. "That's not possible. I could only have been out for a few minutes. The fire was raging when I came to."

"I don't know what to tell you about all that, darlin'," Minnie explains softly, speaking gently, the way I would to a fever-addled child. "But it's been more than an hour since Kane carried you out."

I touch my jaw. It is sore from being whipped back when he hit me.

"Kane barely popped you," Minnie says. "Didn't need to since you were already half-unconscious. A little tap's all it took and you were in the morgue so heavy that you didn't turn a hair even with all the hul-labaloo going on. Firemen dragging hoses right past your head and all. I figured you'd be out for at least a day. Two maybe. I can't believe that you're awake now."

I don't feel awake. I feel trapped in a chaotic dream. "But the fire? All that smoke? It was already roaring when Kane pulled the alarm."

Minnie told me, "There was just moun-tains of black smoke pouring out, nothing else, for the longest time before it really caught."

As if to show how distorted my sense of time is, the flat, gray light of dawn reveals the blackened stumps of what was once the Starlight Pier and Palace poking up from the waves lapping onto the beach. Bits of charred wood litter the sand.

"Did everyone else — ?"

"Get out?" Minnie finishes for me. "Can't be sure, it appears so."

"Pops? Suits? Alonzo?" I ask, but the name I most want to speak remains frozen on my tongue.

DeWitt gives a dry laugh. "They led the charge. Soon as the police showed up askin' questions, they hightailed it outta here like kerosened cats."

"The police?"

"Oh, yeah," Minnie confirms. "They was crawling all over here. They wanted to talk to you, but you was dead to the world."

"Cleo and JuJu?"

"They was long gone," Minnie says, "before the siren even went off."

One final, distant hope glimmered and, voice trembling, I ask, "Kane?"

Minnie tells me, "Soon as he brought you out and laid you down, he lit out. Didn't say a word to no one. Kind of surprised me he didn't head out with Pops and them, seeing's how tight they all are."

The sun starts to rise. The pastels brightening the sky are a gross intrusion. In the early-morning light I notice that Minnie, gazing nearly hypnotized by the rising sun, is clutching something to her side, half hiding it.

A manila envelope with red strings.

"Is that . . . ?" I point to the envelope. "Did Cleo give you that?"

Minnie hides it behind her back.

"Did she tell you about . . . ?"

"About you and Zave? And the operation you wanted him to have?" She looks down at her feet and nods her head. "She purty much told everyone. And showed them the pictures."

Without a word, I struggle to my feet and

597

take the envelope from her.

As she lets the envelope slip from her hands, Minnie says, "I know you were trying to help, but, Lord, Evie, if I'd of seen what's in there, I'd of killed myself too."

I don't have the strength to tell her that I have no real idea of what's in the envelope. I unwind the red strings and lift the journal out. There is a note tucked into the center. *Here is the article with the information your friend needs. Dr. K*

I open to the marked page. Before my brain can absorb the images — a patient, head strapped down, eyes held open by a gloved nurse, an icepick — every fiber of my being is already recoiling in horror. I drop to my knees and pray that I am still hallucinating. That the grotesque photos are a nightmare.

Procedure.

The word is now an abomination.

I am an abomination.

Minnie whispers something that fails to penetrate my shock. She hugs me then leaves and I am alone on the damp sand.

Time passes. I don't know how much. Suddenly Sofie is beside me. "I came as soon as I heard about —"

Her gaze falls on the unspeakable photos and she speaks only one word before her hand covers her mouth: "No."

"Sofie," I moan. "Zave thought I wanted to do that to him. He thought I knew. That I wanted that monstrosity for him. That it was his only choice."

I face the best friend who helped me commit this unspeakable act and speak a truth that is as clear and unyielding as the sun rising in the east. "I killed him."

CHAPTER 81

Sunday, July 3, 1932
7:03 a.m.

"You're in shock," Sofie tells me back at her apartment as she slides a mug of tea across her kitchen table. "Drink this."

"Sofie," I beg, "how could I have advised that, that . . ." I am so horrified by the memory of the barbaric photos that I can't go on.

"You didn't know," Sofie answers calmly as she presses the warm mug into my hands. "Neither of us knew."

"Why couldn't I have accepted him as he is?" I beg Sofie, beg myself. "As God made him? I was worse than Mamie. Than his father. I was worse because I should have known, Sofie. I should have known. I should have known."

My chant gushes forth in an inchoate flood as if I were casting a spell that could wash away the terrible wrong I had done.

600

That could take me back in time, so that I would have known more than I had. Been kinder than I had been. Understood more and blindly trusted less. If only I had known as much as I thought I did.

"Evie, stop," Sofie tells me in her strictest head nurse voice. "Drink the tea."

I babble on, unable to get hold of myself.

"Now," she orders, lifting the mug to my lips until I take a sip.

The tea is bitter. Acrid. It is the punishment I deserve. I swallow.

The instant I stop babbling, images from that journal flap through my mind on leathery, black bat wings. A patient. Strapped down. Nurse restraining him. A doctor. An icepick. An open eyeball. The images run like scenes from a mad scientist movie that I can't turn off.

I grab Sofie's hand and hang on. She is my last tether to sanity.

"Evie, listen to me. Can you do that? Can you listen?"

I recognize her tone. It is the one we always used with disoriented patients who'd had a head injury or a stroke. We had no tone for the wicked. For the unforgivable.

"Evie, you didn't know. I didn't know. We were doing what we thought was best. What the experts told us was best. Zave's death is

601

not your fault. You're not to blame. Do you understand? Nod if you understand."

I nod because I *am* to blame. Zave killed himself because of me.

Sofie sees my anguish. "Evie, you are not in your right mind. You need sleep. You are having a nervous breakdown brought on by a lack of sleep and shock. Drink the tea."

Mechanically, I swallow the bitter brew.

Sofie, my unwitting accomplice, blameless sharer of my guilt, squeezes my hands even harder and offers her own plea. "We didn't know. We did the best we could. We wanted to help."

At the word "help" her professional demeanor dissolves in tears and she pleads, "How can a person be expected to know what they don't know? Tell me that. We didn't know, Evie, we just didn't know. It's that simple."

I nod, pretending to agree that anything will ever be simple again.

An odd warmth seeps down from my brain, melting everything in its path. When it reaches my eyelids, I ask in a slur, "The tea? What did you put — ?"

"Just something to help you sleep," Sofie admits. "You have to sleep."

CHAPTER 82

Monday, July 4, 1932
Twenty-four hours later, I wake, understanding perfectly what I must do. I tiptoe into the kitchen and select a knife. A fish-boning knife with a dagger-slender, arched blade.

Sofie must have been listening because, as quiet as I've tried to be, she enters a second later. I hide the knife in the folds of the nightgown she had wrestled me into.

"You're up," she says tentatively. "How are you feeling?"

Too sad to live.

"Better," I lie.

"Hey," she says in the too-peppy voice she uses when she's pretending a plan she has all worked out in advance has just popped into her head. "How about if I call in to work and tell them I can't make it today? We can go out? Take the ferry to Bolivar Island maybe?"

She handles me with kid gloves. Sofie, my friend, my sister, I wish I didn't have to do what I have to in her apartment. But there is no other choice. I cannot endure the unendurable. I cannot live with what I've done.

"No, no," I say with as much animation as I can muster. "Go to work. To be honest, I'd like to be alone."

"Are you sure?" she asks, eying me as if I'm a psychiatric patient who's just told her that I'm really Princess Anastasia, last survivor of the Romanov dynasty.

"I am completely sure," I answer.

After some more reassuring, she is about to leave when she pauses, reaches in under the neck of her uniform, draws out a small maroon leather bag on a cord, and hands it over. "I almost forgot. This is for you."

Zave's grouch bag. My knees start to buckle. I right myself before Sofie notices and asks casually, "Where did that come from?"

"It was around your neck," she answers, confused.

I don't want to tell Sofie about grouch bags and how, for all my young life, and for Zave's as well, they had held what was needed to go on living. "Oh, right, right," I say, giving my forehead a "silly me" tap.

"Forgot I was wearing it."

"Not like you to forget three hundred dollars," Sofie jokes, taken in by the breezy manner I am just barely managing to fake.

Zave had given me his savings, what *he'd* needed to go on living. He must have strung it around my neck when I was sleeping on his shoulder. I bite the inside of my mouth to stanch the tears and hand the bag back. "You hang on to it," I say. "Put it toward rent."

Sofie appraises me. I know my act isn't working; she's doing a "patient evaluation" and she's noting several "danger flags," as we'd learned to call disturbing symptoms of mental unrest. "Hey," she says with manufactured cheer, "I feel like taking the day off. Why don't I just call in to work and —"

I take the phone receiver from her hand and, in the calmest, most level tone I can fake, tell her, "Sofie, you're a true friend. The only one I've ever had, and I appreciate you looking out for me. But, honestly, I just need to be alone for a while, okay? I have a lot to think about."

"Don't think, Evie, okay? No thinking. Not today."

"You're right," I lie again, eager for the conversation to be over. Eager to stop the horrific images that drove Zave to his death from flashing incessantly through my mind. "I'll be fine. Really."

"You don't have to be fine, Evie. You just have to hang on for a while. Will you do that for me?"

"I will, Sofie. I promise. There's nothing to worry about. Really."

The instant Sofie leaves, I draw the hottest bath I can stand and step in. The shock of the heat halts the images for a few blessed seconds. By the time I am seated, however, they have returned. I cannot live with them. With what I have done. It is that simple. As though I were reading how-to instructions, a few words from a long-ago lecture guide me. "Fatal exsanguination is most likely if the arteries are slit open lengthwise."

The blade of Sofie's knife has been professionally sharpened. The bone handle is easy to grip. The tip of the knife might as well have been a scalpel. It slides into the radial artery as easily as any surgical implement.

A flower of crimson blood blossoms from the small entry wound, unfurling and swirling through the water. At the moment I realize how easy this will be, how infinitely preferable this is to living another moment with the knowledge of what I've done, an odd sound startles me.

Someone is speaking.

"Sofie?" I say, even though the voice is male. It continues. I can't make out words, but the timbre, the rhythm, are as familiar as my own heartbeat. They comfort me. The voice has a lilting roughness about it. It is a sound from the time before I understood words. The sounds tell me that I am the moon and the stars and the sun of his world. That I am the most wondrous baby girl ever born and that, no matter what happens, he will always love me. His daughter. His child. The sounds tell me that I will do great things. Things that only I can do. Things that I must do.

The inchoate sounds stop and are replaced by knowledge. The knowledge of what it is I must do. This knowing comes from my bones, from my blood. I cannot yet articulate the new certainty. Only that it has been my destiny all along. And every step and every misstep I have taken was required for me to arrive at it.

I put the knife down and rise from the bath. I dry myself and bandage the small wound on my wrist. No amount of my blood can wash away what I've done. My sin will not be absolved that easily. More, much more, is required of me. My life, my whole, entire life, every second I have left, is what is required.

I made a tragic mistake and a man died as a result, and my small, meaningless death could never atone for that. All I can do now is try to keep others from making that same tragic mistake.

■ ■ ■ ■

Four Months Later

■ ■ ■ ■

CHAPTER 83

November 2, 1932
All Souls' Day

I get a job shelving books at the Moody Medical Library. There I learn that the hideous medical atrocity that was supposed to "cure" Zave is called a "lobotomy." Because this, and the ignorance behind it, is the enemy I will fight, I force myself to look at the photos. The bald, bespectacled Dr. Freeman, wearing neither gloves nor mask, but an inexplicably sleeveless tunic that exposes his hairy forearms, blithely hammers an icepick into a man's eye socket in front of a crowd of unmasked, ungloved reporters and doctors who crush in around him and the wretched patient who has been rendered unconscious by electroshock.

Freeman, I learn, has no surgical training. He is a showman who travels the country performing his "painless, ten-minute procedure."

611

The gut-wrenching revulsion I feel is inde-scribable.

Cocooned within a shroud of guilt, I grieve for Zave. America, seeming as close to suicide as I am, grieves with me. Five thousand banks have gone out of business, taking the life savings of hundreds of thou-sands with them. The dust storms up in the Great Plains are getting so bad that some-times the red dust of Oklahoma covers the sky above Galveston with a hellish haze.

Henry Ford, who'd once been our hero for inventing the assembly line and giving us Model Ts, tells us on the radio that we should vote for Hoover. That government relief will kill the American spirit. We know he is an idiot because hunger and despair are already killing the American spirit.

I don't see much of Sofie these days. Danny Reid, the fourth-year she's been dat-ing, takes up most of her free time. Danny grew up in Galveston and has had a crush on Sofie since he was an altar boy. Sofie did make time to talk to me about her momen-tous decision: she's decided to get a medi-cal degree.

I am even more excited about the idea than she is and promise I'll help her every step of the way.

"You bet you will," she laughs. "Because

you'll be going with me."

I smile and say in a wistful tone that we'll talk about that later. Sofie doesn't push me. She knows that a wistful tone means that I'm just barely holding it together.

When she's home, Sofie answers calls from newspapers around the country begging to speak to the Handsome Hoofer's widow. She takes messages and adds them to the album she is making with all my press clippings, promising that "Someday you'll want these." I find that a dubious prospect.

Every few weeks, she receives a postcard from JuJu. The first one comes a month after the fire. On the front is a trolley car ascending a steep hill in San Francisco. Other cards arrive with greetings from Toronto, Saratoga, Pensacola, and, finally, Sicily. I don't know if the Galveston police would have ever dared to haul JuJu Amadeo or his paramour in for questioning, but their extended holiday seems to have helped everyone avoid the issue altogether and no one ever comes to question me.

At least no one from the police department.

The insurance investigator, that guy in the bad suit with a clipboard, is another story. He hounded me for weeks after the fire, popping up at the apartment at odd hours.

I would peer down at him on the front porch from our second-story window and tell Sofie not to answer. Each time, he scrawled his phone number and "Call me! Urgent!" across his business card and left it in the mailbox.

J. ARNOLD WINSLOW, EXAMINER
AETNA FIRE INSURANCE COMPANY
HARTFORD, CONNECTICUT

After he'd left eleven cards, Sofie called the police department and reported him. She used her last name and, a few minutes later, a patrol car was parked outside our apartment. J. Arnold drove by once after that, caught sight of the car, the visits stopped, and I let my guard down.

But months later, a few minutes after Sofie leaves with Danny, there's a knock. Thinking she's forgotten her key again, I open the door.

It's Winslow. He carries his clipboard in one hand and a case about the size of a hatbox in the other.

"About time," Winslow says, sticking his foot in the crack so that I can't shut the door on him. Up close, he is younger than I'd thought, though an older man's air of sour disappointment still hangs over him.

"Mind if I come in? Ask a few questions? Or, if you'd prefer, I can get a warrant."

Though I know that if Winslow had been able to get a warrant, he would have, I let him in.

It's time. I've buried the truth long enough.

In the living room, he sets down his case and places a file labeled "Starlight Pier" on the coffee table between us, picks up his clipboard, plucks the pencil resting atop his ear, taps the sharpened point on the form he is waiting to fill in, and says curtly, "You were the last person to speak to Milton Dowd, aka Xavier Francis Mathews, aka Zave Cassidy, aka Little Denny Devlin, aka the Handsome Hoofer, is that correct?"

"It is."

"Can you explain why Milton chose to go toward the fire rather than fleeing from it?"

Again I see Zave walking away. Choosing death over the choice I'd given him. Though I ache to tell the whole story, this part of it isn't mine to reveal. It's Zave's. I make myself breathe and finally answer. "That's a personal matter."

"I've been informed that you two had a fight."

"By whom?"

Instead of answering, Winslow informs

me, "I was told that you two had a fight because he wouldn't have a surgery you insisted he have. What was the surgery for?"

I see that I can never have the release of confession. Zave's truth is not mine to tell. I make my face a blank and say, "I don't know what you're talking about."

He pulls two photos from beneath the papers clasped by his clipboard and places them on the coffee table facing me.

I barely stifle a gasp: they are mug shots. Of Zave. Though he has been beaten so badly I almost don't recognize him.

I bite my lip to keep from betraying my rage and sorrow and Winslow tells me, "Arrested for indecent advances. So, Miss Devlin, this is all a matter of public record. If you could just confirm what I've been told."

"And what might that be?"

"That you demanded that Milton Dowd undergo a lobotomy to correct his sexual deviancy."

Though I've accused myself of that precise crime a million times, hearing it spoken aloud is a punch to the gut. Because I will not reveal what Zave chose to hide, I pass my shock off as outrage and say, "Someone's been lying to you."

A long, tense moment passes in which I

gird myself for his counterattack. It never comes.

Instead, he pronounces, "My conclusion exactly."

I scramble to figure out what angle he is playing.

"So tell me," he asks, "why would Miss Evans spread around this story that Milton Dowd committed suicide rather than undergo a lobotomy?"

"Who is Miss Evans?"

"Mabel Evans. You know her as Cleo."

I know that Cleo hated me for what she believed I had wanted to inflict upon Zave. Still, I can't see her ratting on anyone. Even me.

Winslow spreads several more photos on the coffee table and my head jerks away from them. I can't. I'm not ready.

Winslow registers my reaction and asks confidently, "Look at these and tell me what you know about them."

When I don't move my head, he gives me the penance I must perform. "Miss Devlin, look at this photo."

I accept my punishment, look at the black-and-white photo, and exhale with relief. Though I can't identify the charred mass, it is, clearly, not human remains.

"What can you tell me about this photo?"

he asks, tapping it with the point of his pencil.

"It looks like a scorched furnace boiler surrounded by blackened debris."

"And this?" he asks, indicating the next photo, which shows a charred clump of black sludge pooled on the bottom of the huge boiler.

"I don't know."

He peers at me, as suspicious as the police detective I suspect he once was. "What was in the boiler, Miss Devlin?" he asks again.

Bright, shining pieces of a puzzle I didn't know I was solving fall into place. This piece is labeled "Black snakes in a duffel bag."

"I'm sure I wouldn't know," I lie.

"Really? And what about the sum of, roughly, four thousand and eight hundred dollars? Does that ring any bells?"

I have to slap on my best poker face because bells are not just ringing, they are clanging as though it's Armistice Day in France, and ask, "Should it?"

Winslow expels a hissing sigh of exasperation. "Look, Miss Devlin, you can drop the wide-eyed innocent act any time you want. I'm thorough. Checked you out. Asked around. Found an excellent source. Quite a history you have. Vinegar Hill by way of the strip shows."

I can imagine who his "source" was and the glee the Director must have taken in sharing her insinuations, but I remain as impassive as a plaster saint.

"Thick as thieves with the Amadeos, aren't you?" he goes on. "Living here with the daughter, aren't you?" He glances around. "Nice place. Not something a library worker could afford, though, is it?"

He doesn't expect an answer and I don't give him one.

"Look, I don't care how tight you are with this little island's ruling family. You could be a sister, for all I care. That cuts no ice with me. Mobsters are mobsters in my book. Unlike everyone else in this crooked town, I don't work for them."

I stand and inform him, "We're done here, Mr. Winslow. You can let yourself out." As I'm leaving the room, Winslow hisses, "Devlin, I'm on to you."

Fortunately, my back is turned to the investigator. Otherwise, he would have seen me break into the biggest smile that has cracked my stony face in weeks.

For the next few hours, I pace the floor waiting for Sofie to return from her date. Finally, Danny's car pulls up, doors slam, there is the indecipherable rumble of Danny's voice, and Sofie's answering laughter.

Hovering in the darkened foyer, I count the approaching footsteps, waiting for the knob to turn. It doesn't. Instead, there is more chatting and laughing, then silence.

For the long minutes of their farewell, I nearly burst with eagerness to tell Sofie the news. I'm about to flash the porch light on and off like an overprotective father when she finally comes in.

"Evie, you startled me," she says when she finds me hovering inside the door. Alarmed by my unusual expression she asks, "What happened? What's wrong? Why are you smiling?"

"Zave," I answer. "He's alive."

CHAPTER 84

Sitting at the kitchen table with mugs of hot cocoa, I jabber nonstop, connecting the dots of good news that the investigator had inadvertently sprinkled about. At least the ones that are safe to reveal to Sofie. Tempering my enthusiasm, I conclude, "There's very good reason to believe that Zave might be alive."

Her brows furrowed, she asks, "Go back to the part about the snakes and the boiler."

"That's the point," I say. "They weren't ever snakes. I was squirrelly. Hallucinating. From the look of that black sludge in the photo, I'd guess that they were strips of old tire."

"Strips of tire?" Sofie repeats, hiding her skepticism behind professional patience.

"Right. Lots of them. Kane probably had a huge stash hidden away. He burned them in the boiler. That's what caused the smoke."

"And Kane wanted smoke because?" she prompts.

"To warn everyone. To make certain that the Palace was cleared out before they started the real fire."

"And you think Zave might have survived because of the smoke?" Sofie asks doubtfully.

My nod of agreement is only half a lie covering the truth of what I can't figure out and the lie of what I have. I believe that Zave might have survived because of Kane. Because Kane is strong and tough and does the right thing. I believe that he showed Zave the barbaric photos he had confiscated. And that Zave, instead of committing suicide, had escaped with him.

"Why on earth would Kane want to burn down the Palace?"

The answer "to do it before your family did" remains unspoken. As always, Sofie's family is off-limits. Maybe I'm right and the Amadeos intended from the start to torch the place and the marathon was just a convenient cover to make it look as though they truly wanted to revive the white elephant they had squatting on some of the island's priciest real estate. Maybe I'm wrong. In the end, it doesn't matter because Kane beat them to it. And Kane did it for the money.

The instant the examiner told me the number written on the paper, I'd known immediately what it was and where it had come from. Just as Lily had calculated, it was the total receipt for that day's box office, minus a few pilfered dollars.

Sofie interrupts my calculations. "Evie, talk to me. You're smiling again."

"Am I?" I say, touching my lips.

"You really believe that Zave survived a fire that burned everything down to the pier pilings?"

"I think he was long gone before the fire ever started," I answer.

Like the superb caregiver she is, Sofie asks gently, "Are you getting enough sleep?"

"Plenty," I answer, even though I've almost forgotten what real sleep feels like. "Sofia Amadeo, you are the best. I love that you worry about me, but honestly, you don't have to anymore. He might be alive. He really might be."

Sofie pats my hand. "I'll pray for that."

In bed that night, I can't shut my mind off. Every piece of information the examiner gave me snaps into place alongside other pieces of the puzzle.

It's clear to me now that, from the start, the Amadeos intended to torch the Palace.

That's why, other than slapping on some paint, adding the bare essentials for a marathon, and doing just enough to give the appearance that they were serious about honoring their pledge to reopen the historic Palace, they didn't do any actual restoration.

The Aetna Fire Insurance Company must have had the same suspicions, which is why they had Winslow and his men patrolling the Palace around the clock. They would have been there every second.

Except for the Amadeos' Fourth of July fireworks spectacular, when everyone, even the dancers, would have been outside.

What a perfect cover. Not only would the Palace have been completely emptied out, but who could possibly blame the Amadeos if, during a selfless display of patriotism and community spirit, a random spark were to land on the splintery, sun-baked timbers of the Starlight Palace and burn the old money pit to the ground leaving behind only the extremely valuable shoreline real estate it had occupied?

The one hitch was that someone beat the Amadeos to the punch. And that someone was Kane, who'd figured out early on that something was off about the show. And then it was Kane who'd seen the fate that awaited his friend. And it was Kane who, when the acting stopped, did the right thing, saved Zave, and covered both their tracks with his own fire.

A few of the pieces still aren't clicking together, but each clue that adds up to Zave being alive is another weight lifted off my heart. Dampening my joy, however, is the knowledge that, if he is indeed alive, Zave is out in the world somewhere, contaminated with the belief that I wished the abomination of a lobotomy upon him.

Still, if Zave is alive, I might yet have an opportunity to explain. But how, I wonder, will I find him?

That is my last thought before I fall into the truest, deepest sleep I've enjoyed for months.

CHAPTER 85

November 3, 1932

I am still grappling with that question as I shake Post Toasties into a bowl and Sofie, who'd been in the other room chattering away on the phone to a cousin, hangs up, comes into the kitchen and asks, "Guess what?"

My mouth full of cornflake mush, I grunt, "Whuh?"

"Cleo and JuJu are back in town. And, get this, he's divorcing Aunt Patti. Turns out she's been cheating on him and is thrilled about the split."

Skipping right over the divorce bulletin, I swallow hard and ask with too much urgency, "Where are they staying?"

"What bee is in your bonnet now?"

"Sofie, if Zave is alive, I'm sure Cleo knows where he is and how to get in touch with him. I have to talk to him. I have to explain."

"Yeah, but Cleo isn't exactly eager to see you."

"You know I have to see her."

"She doesn't get up before noon."

"She's going to today. Where's she staying? The Buccaneer?"

Her eyes dart away from mine.

"The penthouse suite?"

They dart even farther.

"Oh, Sofie, never play poker," I tease.

A few minutes later, I am on Seawall Boulevard and nearly running to the Buccaneer.

"Just leave the cart in the hall," Cleo croaks out when I knock.

In response, I hammer louder and cover the peephole.

"What the holy hell is the problem with you — ?"

Cleo, or rather, a person who used to be Cleo, swings open the door, stopping dead when she sees me.

"You," she says with disgust.

I hurl myself in front of the door she is slamming shut and burst out, "I know that Zave is alive."

For a moment, she freezes, this new version of Cleo. This new Cleo who wears no makeup. Whose hair, once brittle from bleach and dye, has been cut short, and is the dark honey of her natural color. Who is softened and filled out instead of jagged and empty. This new Cleo who, instead of haunted and jittery, seems, of all things, contented.

At least she is until the shock wears off and she snarls, "Who have you been talking to?"

Her reaction makes me so happy, I would have kissed her if I wasn't pinioned between the door and the jamb.

"So he is alive?"

She pushes harder.

"Listen, Cleo, I don't care anything about the fire or the insurance money or the take from the show, or any deal you might have with the Amadeos. That is completely between you and them. Just, please, please, tell me, is he all right?"

The pressure eases.

"Who have you been talking to?" she demands again, this time with deadly intent.

"I haven't talked to anyone and, Cleo, I never will. I don't care about the fire. Or who started it. Or why. Or what an incredibly convenient cover story Zave's supposed suicide was. Or why you spread the story about me driving him to suicide. I don't care. I honest to God don't care. All I care about is Zave. So, just tell me, is he alive?"

"Why the hell should I tell you a goddamn thing. You and your miserable 'procedure.' Was Zave so disgusting to you that you'd turn him into a vegetable? He shared a secret with you and you tried to use it to destroy him."

Again, it's a relief to hear the words I've battered myself with for months, to hear the truth, finally spoken aloud. I surprise her by saying, "You're right. More right than you will ever know. You accepted Zave for who he is and I didn't. But, Cleo, you have to believe this: I didn't know what was in that journal. Neither Sofie nor I set eyes on that article and those hideous photos until after the fire."

"Yeah, right," she says with withering skepticism. "From what I hear you sure were selling something you didn't know anything about awfully hard."

"I was," I admit. "I was trusting and stupid and wrong. But Cleo, I loved Zave. I always will. I thought we could have everything we dreamed of."

Her voice is slightly softer, slightly less accusing when she says, "Everything the world told him he *should* dream of. We're not all born with the same dreams."

"I know that, Cleo. Now. And I'm going to spend the rest of my life making certain that as many other people as possible know it too. Just tell him, okay? You helped me once before. Back in Chicago when you showed me what I needed to see. Help me again. Please."

"Look," she says, a bit of the anger easing out of her rigid posture. "I can't help you. Don't know that I want to, but I could almost forgive you because I understand you so well. Better than you understand yourself."

She stopped pushing.

"We don't expect anyone to actually, truly love us, do we?" she asked without expecting an answer. "It doesn't feel right. It's not what we're used to. We don't trust it. Loving someone who can't love us back feels like the real thing. And I should know. I went down that dead-end road for more years than I care to count. But, Evie, word to the wise, it's not the real thing. I promise you, the real thing feels like the real thing. You just have to believe that you deserve it."

She's talking about her and JuJu and I'm happy for her. I should leave, but I can't keep myself from asking one last time. "Tell me, Cleo, please. He's alive, isn't he? I need to know. I really, *really* need to know."

She is almost the old Cleo, tough as nails

again when she answers, "I already told you what you really, *really* need to know," and slams the door shut.

CHAPTER 86

By the time I step onto Seawall Boulevard, the pain of Cleo's denunciation has given way to jubilation. Her reaction confirmed my hope: Zave is alive.

That certainty reveals the obvious next step I must take in order to do everything within my power to stop the destruction of minds and souls that so-called medical science has unloosed upon the world and to make sure that no one else makes the same tragic mistake that I almost did. I have to get my pin because no one is going to listen to a wannabe nurse who couldn't even get registered.

I make a brief stop at the apartment to pick up the ammunition that Sofie helped me gather — the album of newspaper clippings — before I stride back down Seawall. Back to St. Mary's.

This time, when I pass beneath Mary's sorrowful gaze, I want to tell Jesus' mom to

632

cheer up; it's all going to work out. Inside the hospital, the smells of floor wax, carbolic acid antiseptic, and Flit mosquito spray hit me the way some people say the scent of apple pie and coffee affect them and I feel as if I'm home.

I'm just passing the children's ward when a familiar voice cries out, "Jesus, Mary, and Joseph, you're back." Sister Theonella claps her hands together in prayer position and raises them above her head saying, "Thank you, Blessed Virgin, for answering my prayers," and then she wraps me in a hug. "I was wondering when you'd get around to visiting your old teacher."

"I wanted to," I answer. "But I've been kind of a mess since I got back."

"I've heard bits and pieces," she admits. "Tittle-tattle that I've not paid much mind to. I've been waiting to hear the whole story from you. Care to tell me about it?"

For the next hour, we sit in the sanctuary of the hospital chapel and I tell Sister T everything. She listens thoughtfully, bows her head, and when I've finished she doesn't speak for so long that I'm certain I've exceeded even the limits of her ability to forgive.

There is a beatific glow about her, though, when she raises her head, muttering, " 'Indecent advances.' How could I have been so blind? All the men I've seen in the emergency room who've been beaten within an inch of their lives, yet they acted as though *they* were the ones at fault? Refusing to press charges? Begging me not to put the visit in their records? And I simply acquiesced. Pretended not to see what I'd seen. Not to understand what I understood."

Anguished, she confesses, "Evie, I've stood by in silent approval as Kaufman recommended the very procedure you've spoken of." With a sudden fierceness she declares, "Oh, this must stop. As long as the Director is in charge, I won't be allowed to invite you to speak to my classes on this topic, but I'm certain that the more progressive instructors at the Sealy College of Nursing will want you to address their classes immediately." Then, wincing, she adds, "There is just one thing . . ."

"My pin," I supply.

"Right," she confirms.

"So, I'd better get my pin," I conclude.

Sister T accompanies me to the reception desk and calms the poor probie who explains frantically that "The Director is busy. She's left very strict orders that she's not to be disturbed," while I enter the Director's office without knocking and lock the door behind me.

The Director tips her head up and, again, the lenses of her glasses become the two blank silver orbs that once filled me with shame.

Not today.

The Director's mouth, squeezed between starched white linen, pleats into a severe frown as she orders, "Leave or I shall have you removed."

"No," I correct her, amused that I could ever have let this small-minded martinet bully me. "You are not going to do that."

I allow her a second to funnel steely disgust at me. She reaches for her phone. I take the receiver firmly out of her hand and hang it up. "You're not going to call any-one." My tone is as flat and even as it was the last time I spoke to Mamie.

She rises. For the first time, we both notice that I am a tall, strong, young woman and she is a short, doughy, old woman and we are alone together in a locked room.

"What do you want?"

"My pin."

Her laugh is a rusty, bitter thing. "Oh, the cheek of your kind. You really have no shame, do you?"

"And what is it, exactly, you believe I should be ashamed of?"

635

"Don't play the innocent with me, my girl. You know I have photographic proof of your depravity."

"Photographic proof," I echo. "I'm glad you brought that up because I would like you to take a seat and examine *my* photographic proof."

This time, I am the one to slide clippings across her desk, an album full of them. "Please, do sit down and have a look."

She snorts a raspy, belittling laugh, but she sits. With a bored sigh, she flips through a few pages before slamming the album shut. "Such a tawdry masquerade," she pronounces. "Impersonating a nurse. All this proves is your complete unfitness to be certified."

"And yet," I say, turning the pages slowly back to stories that appeared in Chicago, Cleveland, Philadelphia, New York, Dallas, Houston, St. Louis, and a dozen other cities, "in all these photos and press accounts, I am the very embodiment of fitness.

"It also appears," I say, slowing down at the clippings from the Galveston paper, featuring photos of the "Hometown Heroine," "that the editors right here have taken a particular interest in my story. How do you think those same editors would react now if I were to share with them the details of how my time at St. Mary's was cut short?"

"I shall not submit to this vile attempt at blackmail. If you won't leave, I shall."

"I'm sorry to hear that," I say, closing the album and standing. "I thought you cared about the reputation of St. Mary's. You leave me no choice now but to agree to the interview requests I've received from papers around the country curious as to why, exactly, I have been denied my pin."

"Why should I care about the sordid tales you tell?"

"Yes, elements of the story of my girlhood are sordid, aren't they? Imagine then if I were to tell that girl's entire story to the sympathetic reporters, whose readers already know her as the Angel of Mercy?"

"I knew from the second I laid eyes on you that you were no good."

I lean forward, my hands resting on her desk as I hold her gaze and answer, "Is that so? Because I knew from the second I laid eyes on *you* that you were a bully. Turned out we were both right.

"So here is what you're going to do. As soon as I leave, you will call the Texas Board of Nursing in Austin and explain your terrible error in not submitting me for registration earlier."

She snorts an infuriatingly dismissive laugh.

I snatch a pencil from the cup on her desk and scrawl Sofie's number on the first piece of paper I can stab the lead into. "It is now eight fifty-three. You have until noon to correct your error. If you haven't called the board by then, I will begin alerting the papers."

I storm out of her office. For the next three hours, as I pace the apartment, I feel as if I'm back on the marathon floor wishing the clock would hurry up.

Noon comes and goes and the phone remains silent.

By two, I know that the Director has called my bluff.

And won.

Battling with a nun in the tabloids is not how I want to get my message out. I sink onto the sofa and take stock of my situation. I'll probably have to go back to nursing school at Sealy Hospital. I accept that my path will be hard.

When, though, had it ever been easy?

CHAPTER 87

Election Day dawns as bright and breezy as Sofie and I feel: we're going to vote in a presidential election for the very first time. I count all the buttons with FDR's face and slogans like "A Big Man For A Big Job" and "Vote For A New Deal" and announce gleefully, "Not a single one for Hoover in the lot."

"Promise me again that FDR is going to win," Sofie pleads.

"Of course he's going to win," I assure her. "There won't be any America left to save if Hoover gets four more years."

Sofie waves her hands in front of her face as if to erase the nightmarish possibility of Herbert Hoover being reelected. "Change to a happier topic? What are you planning to wear tonight?"

"Not sure. Maybe a bulletproof vest?"

"Stop," Sofie insists. "I told you Cleo's

639

feelings about you have softened. JuJu says she wants to bury the hatchet."

"In my skull?"

"No, she really wants you to come to this soiree she's hosting."

"Are you sure?"

"Trust me," Sofie promises. "I explained your whole mission and swore that neither of us had seen that damn journal until after the fire. I mean, if she's going to hate anyone, it should be me. So?"

"So what?"

"So what are you going to wear?"

"Sofie, thanks for putting in a good word for me, but I'm still not quite ready to go out."

"But Danny is going to bring that class-mate of his that I told you about."

"The one that you maintain wants to meet me?"

"Don't say it like I'm lying to you. You have quite a few secret admirers."

"Yeah, I'll bet."

"If you're going to be Miss Modesty, look at it this way. There aren't a heck of a lot of girls hanging out at the Sealy library. Let's just say, you have been noticed."

I start to scoff at that, but Cleo's advice about feeling like I might deserve the real thing comes back and I listen instead.

"It's true, Evie, for the guy smart enough to see it, you are a real head-turner. Plus, it doesn't hurt that you've been in the papers. What med student *wouldn't* want to date the country's most famous nurse."

"Most famous *unregistered* nurse," I correct her.

"Oh, come on," Sofie insists. "That's just a matter of time. As for tonight, it's an election party. Much as you go on about your hero FDR, you have to come."

"But what if he loses?" I moan. "I won't be able to stand it if Hoover wins."

"In that case, you'll be at the perfect place. Cleo's arranging everything and you know what that means? Plenty of alcohol to drown our sorrow. Plus, it's going to be at the Hollywood Dinner Club. And they're going to serve Baked Alaska. How swanky is that?"

The past few months have stripped away so much of the tough shell I'd had to develop with Mamie that tears now seep through at the memory of the party JuJu was going to have if everything hadn't gone wrong. I blink hard, swallow the lump in my throat, and admit in a soft voice, "I don't think I'm ready to go out."

"I'll be with you," Sofie promises. "I'll always be with you."

My vision blurs. I hide the gush of emotion behind a lame wisecrack. "Wow, you really want that Baked Alaska."

"I really do. And, for your information, it's Baked Amadeo in Galveston."

I notice a gap has opened up in front of us and announce brightly, "Come on, let's go in there and get FDR elected."

Sofie takes my arm and my best friend and I step forward, ready to do our part to end the Depression.

CHAPTER 88

That evening, our cab can barely crawl along Seawall Boulevard, it is so jammed with hopeful revelers. Sofie sticks her arm out the window and raises her flask in solidarity to the carousers getting drunk either to celebrate FDR's election or to anesthetize themselves against the nightmarish possibility of his loss. The chaos of neon, happy shrieks from the roller coaster, and the velvet feel of the night air make me grow sentimental as Galveston once again vanquishes dreariness.

"I'm glad you talked me into coming."

"When have I ever steered you wrong?" Sofie asks.

"Never."

We take a right off of Seawall at Sixty-First Street. A few blocks later I spot the stunning Spanish-style architecture and red-tiled roof of the Hollywood Dinner Club.

Inside, though the club is appropriately

dim, what I can make out takes my breath away. It is a combination of an ornate Arabian fantasy and New York sophistication with golden chandeliers, an enormous dance floor, and what seems to be an acre of tables. The one jarring note is that not a single one of those tables is occupied.

"Where is everybody?"

"I think I see them," Sofie says, darting away.

As I pivot around, trying to locate her in the gloom, all the lights are switched on and dozens of Cleo's guests spring into view. For reasons that I cannot fathom, they all commence yelling, "Surprise."

I join in shouting "Surprise" and am searching for the honoree when I start to recognize faces in the crowd.

I understand why Cleo might have invited Sister T, as well as our old chums from St. Mary's and Sofie's new friends from Sealy Hospital. But what on earth are my grandmother, Uncle Jake, Minnie and DeWitt, Ace and Lily, Gerta and Fritz, and Patsy and Lynette doing at Cleo's party?

As the guests close in, an elevator-drop sense of lurching unreality causes me to fear that I might throw up or pass out. My gaze travels from one face to another as I scramble to comprehend. For a horrible moment,

I'm certain that I have gone squirrelly again and am creating this vision out of my own longing.

My grandmother, healthier than ever, Dub by her side, steps forward and clasps my hand. "Evie Grace, are you all right?"

"Why are you here?" is all I can mumble.

"For you, darlin'," she answers. "We're all here for you."

"But why?" I ask, still too stunned to make sense of what is happening.

Sister T steps forward and answers with brisk good humor, "To correct a terrible wrong." Tucking my arm under hers, she says, "Come along," and leads me to the bandstand where Sofie and our St. Mary's chums, each holding a candle, are already assembled in a line across the front. All the guests gather on the dance floor in front of the stage.

Taking her place at the center, Sister T directs, "Lights, please." As the house lights are again dimmed, Sister T, who is holding a small porcelain re-creation of Florence Nightingale's Lamp of Knowledge with a candle wick poking from the spout, asks, "Evelyn Grace Devlin, if you will join me."

On the stage, I search the faces for Zave. Surely, if Cleo has somehow managed to round up all the others, Zave would have come as well. Unless he truly does hate me.

"Welcome, all," Sister T starts, and the crowd falls silent. "To Evie Grace's long-overdue pinning ceremony."

The crowd chuckles at my stunned reaction.

In response to the dumbfounded expression I turn on her, Sister whispers. "The Motherhouse simply had to be apprised of a few irregularities and they recalled the Director for a much-needed retirement. Then I did what should have been done long ago and submitted your application to the board along with your stellar record and exam scores, and, presto-change-o, here we are."

She claps her hands and commands, "Nurses, please, begin."

The girls at each end of the line light their candles then pass the flame onto the candle held by the girl next to them until the two closest to Sister T both press their flames into the Lamp of Knowledge, and it blazes to life.

Sister T hands the candle to me with this invocation, "May this flame give your hands skill and tenderness. May it give your lips words of comfort. May it give your ears the ability to hear what is not spoken. May this lamp light the way to understanding and compassion in the special mission that you have been chosen for. And now your pin."

With that, Sister fastens a silver pin emblazoned with the letters "RN" to my gown, whirls me around, and announces, "I give you Nurse Devlin."

CHAPTER 89

The lights go back on and my friends crowd in. Dinner is served, but I feel like a bride at her wedding, too excited to eat, hungry only to talk to everyone. There is one person I have to speak to first though.

"Where's Cleo?" I ask Sofie.

She takes my arm and leads me through the crowd. Cleo is seated regally beside JuJu at the head of a long table. She cuts me off as I start babbling out thanks.

"Don't mention it. Least I could do after being so crappy to you."

"I deserved it," I say.

She waves my comment away. "Naw, the only thing you were guilty of was being a wide-eyed sucker for the medical con."

JuJu calls me to his side and whispers, "Good work with that insurance stooge. The family is grateful. You wanna drop by for dinner this Sunday?"

I glance at Sofie for her approval.

Without a moment of hesitation, she gushes, "Evie would love it. *I* would love it." Stopping abruptly, she asks me, "That is, if you want to?"

"Yes, I do," I answer. I want to say more, but I feel as though I'm whirling around in a snow globe that has been decisively shaken up.

"Go on," Cleo says, a new gentleness rounding her words. "The gang is dying to talk to you."

Ace, Lily, Minnie, DeWitt, Gerta, Fritz, Patsy, and Lynette crowd in, all talking over each other in answer to my questions: "How have you been? Where did you go after the fire?"

"It was pretty tough sledding for a while," Ace answers.

"Then we found a show in Omaha," Patsy interrupts.

"What a debacle that was," Lily says, speaking to a twinkling chandelier. "Attendance never surpassed one hundred and fifty-three paid admissions."

"I've fed hogs better'n the slop they give us there," DeWitt elaborates.

"We just got a lead on a show up in Cleveland," Ace says. "Saw the notice in *Billboard.* Promoter's name is Sanford, Doc Sanford." Out of the corner of his mouth, he stage-whispers, "I'm pretty sure Doc Sanford is Pops, but you didn't hear it from me. Anyhow, he already wired us the fare."

"I'm so happy you all came," I exult.

"Oh, we wouldna missed this for nothin'," Minnie puts in. "Not for all the silver showers in the world." Then, for the first time, she gives me a huge smile that isn't hidden behind her hand. A huge, *toothy* smile.

"Minnie, your teeth."

"I know," she answers, touching the gleaming choppers. "I can smile again. For real."

They toast me with the French 75 champagne cocktails that Cleo has designated the drink of the evening. After a couple healthy slugs, I dare to ask, "Has anybody heard from Alonzo? Or Suits? Or Kane?"

"Not a peep," Ace answers. "Those boys took it on the lam before we were even out of the Palace."

"Yeah, they been laying so low," Patsy interjects, "the moles is charging them rent."

With laughter covering up my intensity, I ask the question burning inside me with studied casualness: "And Zave?"

The frivolity stops dead. I try to interpret the glances that ping-pong from face to face. Before I can decide if they all know as much as Cleo or if they think I've lost my marbles, a loud trumpet fanfare halts all conversation.

"Mel," I cry out as the bandleader and his combo take the stage. Written across the bass drum head is "Mel and His Melody Makers, House Band of the Amadeo Hollywood Dinner Club."

"Hey, Nurse Devlin," Mel calls out to me. "Congrats from me and the boys." The guys wave a sax, drumsticks, and a trumpet my way before breaking into another fanfare.

Suddenly, all attention swivels to a pair of waiters carrying a huge platter groaning beneath the weight of a massive Baked Amadeo. They settle the confection in front of Cleo and JuJu. Using long matches, Cleo ignites the rum held by eggshells nestled in the peaks of meringue. A waiter carefully ladles more rum into the shells. Blue flames flow down the meringue like lava from a volcano.

Mel and his group open with the first song I ever heard them play, "Five Foot Two, Eyes of Blue." Minnie and DeWitt, Ace and Lily, Patsy and Lynette, even stolid Gerta and Fritz rush to the floor as excited as kids at a prom. As my marathon pals twirl past, memories of that first night back in Houston crowd in on me.

The night I met Zave.

A potent brew of longing and regret threatens to swamp me. Zave, the person who made me believe enough in myself to keep chasing my dream, should be here. I miss him with such a piercing ache that I have to retreat to the shadows to collect myself.

The Melody Makers slide into a gentle waltz that gets the older crowd on their feet. My grandmother and Dub pass by as in sync as if they'd been dancing together for half a century. A hint of contentment warms the icy pillar of despair within me and I start to accept that these two states, contentment and despair, will probably always exist side by side. All I have to do is remember how lucky I am and keep leaning hard toward contentment.

This would have been considerably easier if Mel hadn't summoned Cleo to the stage to provide vocals for "Ten Cents a Dance."

From the first note, I am swept back in time to that moment on the Starlight Pier when we were all waiting for the star to make his appearance.

Before I am ready, Cleo is singing about being rented by fighters and sailors and bowlegged tailors and, though the raw edge of wanting, of hunger for all she could never have, has been smoothed from Cleo's voice, the throbbing poignancy remains. Just as the sheer power of her naked honesty had caused painters to put down their brushes when she sang in the Palace, all motion now ceases.

Again, none of us knows or cares whether Cleo ever danced for a dime with tough guys who tore her gown, but we are convinced down to the hairs that stand up on the backs of our necks that she is a woman who can tell us more than most of us will learn in ten lifetimes about hard times and heartbreak.

I know the lines that are coming and I don't think I can endure hearing them again and remembering when Zave appeared as if she'd summoned him to that sunny pier. I glance at the door and consider leaving, but I hesitate too long and now she is singing about believing she has found her hero.

Biting the inside of my mouth to stop my lower lid from quivering, I applaud Cleo so loudly that she glances in my direction and heads my way.

"Cleo, that was astonishing."

"What?" she answers. "That I stayed in key? Or that I remembered all the words? Come on," she says, plucking her cigarette case from her bag. "I'm dying for a smoke and you look like you could use some air."

Outside, we become two figures in the darkness of a parking lot gathered around the glow of a cigarette.

"You doing okay?" she asks.

"You know," I answer with a shrug. I don't need to say anything more. Not to Cleo. She is the only person who does know. Who will ever truly know.

A car pulls into the parking lot. The ember of Cleo's cigarette tips down as she checks her watch.

"Listen," she confides, "I'm sorry I couldn't tell you sooner, but in spite of you thinking that you're wised up and in the know, you have no poker face at all and I didn't want you spilling the beans."

"What beans?"

"It could have been dangerous. I mean, the Amadeos are happy enough, but other parties still have questions."

"What are you talking about?"

The car's headlights switch off. Doors open. Slam shut.

"Cleo, what's going on?"

Two men approach.

"What's dangerous?" I ask as she steps away.

"Talking to strangers," one of the men answers. "So let me introduce myself."

"Kane?" I ask.

A stream of moonlight pours through a crack in the cloud cover and an entirely different version of the scowling floor judge — one with the beginnings of a full head of silver hair, a broad smile, and a cultured manner — holds his hand out to me. Before I can take it, a familiar pair of broad shoulders steps into the light and both my hands fly up to cover my mouth. "No."

" 'Fraid so," Zave says.

Kane leaves us.

I wobble as my legs threaten to give way beneath me and, as we had from the start, Zave steps forward to steady me. Though I'd strongly suspected and desperately hoped that he was still alive, actually seeing him makes me woozy with astonished relief. I sag against him and it's as if we'd never stopped dancing.

"Zave, I knew you were alive, I just knew it. God, I'm so happy I didn't kill you."

"Imagine how I feel," he laughs, almost breaking the tension.

"Zave," I go on, pushed by the urgency to explain myself before remorse and shame silence me. "I didn't know, I truly, truly didn't know."

I stammer on incoherently until Zave says, "Gravy, don't worry about it."

Gravy.

That breaks the logjam of words. "If I had had even the slightest idea, I never, not in a million years, would have suggested that, that, atrocity."

"Seriously, Evie, don't worry about it. Cleo explained everything. To tell you the truth, I'm glad it *was* an atrocity." Almost joking, he goes on, "I guess it took thinking of having an ice pick shoved in my eye to jolt me out of the lie I was living and realize that I don't actually want to change who I am. Well, it took a shock like that and a guy like this."

Zave holds his arm out and Kane steps into it.

Still stunned by Kane's transformation, I ask, "So you two are — ?"

"Together," Zave fills in. "Unofficially, for years. Officially, just since the fire."

"And you're not . . . ?" I ask Kane.

"A punch-drunk pug?" Kane answers in a cultured voice. "I did do a fair bit of boxing in my younger days when I was trying to prove that I was 'all man.' College mostly. Enough to acquire this." He flicks the cauliflower ear, which isn't nearly as pro-nounced now that it's not sticking off a bald head. Far more disconcerting though than any physical difference is hearing the monosyllabic King Kong speak with such refinement.

"As it turned out," Kane continues, "after the family fortune crashed with the Crash, boxing was considerably more useful in securing employment than my worthless theater degree. The only job I could find was playing the heavy on the marathon circuit. Not the career on the stage that I'd dreamed of, but worlds better than selling apples on a street corner."

"You weren't the person I thought you were at all," I marvel.

"I was the person I had to be to survive," Kane answers.

"We both were," Zave says, taking Kane's hand. "Until he showed me there's a world of difference between surviving and living. And that living is a whole hell of a lot more fun."

Kane lifts Zave's hand to his lips, kisses the knuckles, and tells him, "We showed each other."

They both seem reborn. Light and free and in love. I am radiant with relief. "You're so happy."

"Never would have happened without you," Zave says.

After a quiet moment, I tip my head toward Kane and joke, "I'll bet King Kong isn't even your real name."

"It fit the character, though, didn't it?" he answers.

"The name might not have been real," I say. "But that damn metal yardstick you whacked my ankles with sure was."

With one laugh, the awkwardness almost completely disappears.

"Pops told me to be hard on the home-town heroine."

"Speaking of Pops," I say. "Was he in on the deal from the start?"

The two men exchange a glance. Kane shakes his head and answers, "I don't know what you're talking about."

"Please," I moan. "You two put me through hell. The least you can do now is not treat me like an idiot."

More glances and questioning looks are exchanged. Finally, Kane says, "Evie, take my word, the less you know, the safer you'll be."

Exasperated now, I plead, "Come on, Kane, we've established that you're not a stumblebum palooka. Don't treat me like I'm one. You figured out from the start that the Amadeos planned to torch the place. The tire scraps? The smoke where there was no real fire? You set the scraps on fire to clear everyone out?" When glances and the silence continue, I demand, "Just tell me."

"She deserves to know," Zave says, and tells me, "Well, that was the plan. Which you almost ruined by refusing to leave."

"I'm sorry I had to pop you one," Kane adds.

"And then Zave went back toward what everyone thought was a fire, but was just those smoldering tire scraps? And then, with all that smoke pouring out of the rest area, Zave slipped out through the utility exit. With the money."

"What money?" Kane asks.

"Look," I say, "I *hope* you got the cash. I truly do. You both deserve that, and a lot more. I hope you're living the life of Riley."

"No chance of that," Zave says, pointing a thumb at Kane. "Not with this soft touch here. He sent a big chunk of dough to Suits so he could retire. Paid for Minnie to have her teeth fixed. Gave the pros enough to rest up for a few months."

"Oh, thanks for reminding me," Kane says, pulling an envelope from his inside jacket pocket. "This is yours."

I can feel the thick wad of bills inside. "There's a fortune here," I protest. "You can't give me this."

"We're not giving it to you," Kane explains, pushing the envelope back. "Cleo told us about the speaking you plan to do and we'd like nothing more than to help you illuminate the cruel darkness of ignorance."

I think about all the ways the money will help me get the message out and I crush the envelope to my heart. Ways that might even include me going to medical school with Sofie because I already know how much more weight an MD's word carries than a nurse's. "Will you two have enough?"

"Don't worry about us," Zave says. "I'm dancing in the movies now."

"What? The movies? I thought you were lying low."

"Low as it gets," Zave answers. "I'm working as a foot double in all the big musicals. The audience sees the star's face, then the camera cuts away and the fancy footwork is all mine."

"Foot double?" I echo. "Is that for real?"

"You'd be amazed at how many stars can barely walk up a flight of stairs, much less dance. Business is booming."

"The train," Kane reminds Zave, tapping his watch.

"Right," Zave agrees. "Plus Evie needs to get back to her party."

While we're saying our good-byes, a young man waving a telegram above his head tears past us yelling, "FDR won!! News just came in over the wire. He carried forty-two states. Hoover only got six. It's a landslide."

He doesn't even slow down as he barrels on into the club. I link arms with the two men and decree, "You're not going anywhere until you both come in and toast our new president."

Zave glances over at Kane, who says, "Hell yes. Our guy won, we have to drink to that. We'll thumb it out of here if we have to."

Inside, I grab coupes of bubbly off the first waiter who passes by and we linger in the shadows out of sight, watching the party effervesce with bliss.

Zave whispers, "Denny would be so proud of you."

"God, I wish he were here," I say. "How is it possible to miss someone so much when you barely knew them?"

"You knew him, Evie," Zave says. "He's with you. He'll always be with you. Oh God, look at us. This is a party. We both can't start blubbering. Here" — he plucks my drink from my hand and passes both our glasses to Kane — "Gravy, how about one more dance for old times? For FDR?" I hesitate and he adds, "For Denny?"

"For Denny," I answer, and Zave and I click into dance position like two magnets.

Then I dance with the man who danced with my father. Who brought him back to me. We dance gratitude and farewell. We dance for each other. We don't care and barely notice that the floor around us has cleared.

Instead of a dizzying whirl, Zave and I are the calm center around which all the stars that have lighted my way orbit. Sister Theonella. Uncle Jake. My grandmother. Cleo. Minnie. DeWitt. Ace. Lily. Old friends from St. Mary's. New ones from medical school. And, always and forever the brightest of them all, Sofie.

When Zave twirls me, it reminds me not so much of the cyclone that spun Dorothy into Oz, but of the whirl of air and the rush of wind that whisked her back to Kansas, back to her home.

Before the music stops and all his friends have a chance to crowd in, Zave whispers, "Time for me and Kane to make ourselves scarce. Bye, Gravy, take care of Denny Devlin's daughter for me, will you?"

Before I can respond, Zave is walking away. A path clears that leads straight to Kane. The two men embrace, then kiss. They kiss, as joyously and as freely as any couple mad with love kisses. A shocked silence falls.

I spring forward and, feeling as if I'd suddenly inherited every scrap of Denny Devlin's glamour and charisma, I beam a devastating smile and proclaim, "Hey, everyone! Let's hear it for the man who's gonna get our great country working again!"

I shoot my fist high into the air with each letter as I yell out, "FDR. FDR. FDR."

Like my father, like Zave, I win the crowd over and they join in. Grinning at me, Zave takes Robert's hand in his, lifts it high in the air, and rouses the chanters to such heights that the two men, the purest of lovers, depart to thundering shouts of approval.

Watching them leave, I rub my pin just to make sure it's still there. When I am convinced I haven't dreamed this whole, sublime evening, sheer, unadulterated joy fills me like helium. All that has tethered me for so long falls away and, for the first time, I think I'm finally ready to believe what Marvin the Man of Marvels always used to tell me.

"Evie Grace Devlin, a person can do anything they put their mind to. Why, look at you? Two arms. Kid, the world is your oyster."

AUTHOR'S NOTE

Though I love historical stories that speak to our time, I never expected *Last Dance on the Starlight Pier* to resonate quite as profoundly as it did. Who could have ever imagined that the twenty-first century would bring suffering and despair of the sort that our country has not seen since the darkest days of the Great Depression?

As I was hunkered down, sanitizing my groceries and watching in utter horror as feckless or nonexistent leadership caused hundreds of thousands of needless deaths, compounding the agony of those left behind, who had to say their final good-byes on the phone, I found great comfort in the eerily prescient words of the president who led our country out of the Depression, Franklin Delano Roosevelt.

Though nearly a hundred years have passed, the issues were strikingly familiar. FDR excoriated Hoover's administration for a lack of response to the Depression so complete that our banking system was teetering on the edge of collapse. Roosevelt, on the other hand, had a plan and took immediate account. In his first Fireside Chat after being elected, he explained why all citizens should dig out the savings they'd hidden under mattresses or buried in the backyard and redeposit it in banks.

The next day there were lines of people — kids carrying jars of pennies, parents with their pockets stuffed with cash — around the block.

We saw Americans come together in the same way, when after months of catastrophic indifference and the deaths of half a million citizens, a plan was presented. The benefits of the vaccine were explained clearly and made available. It brought tears to my eyes to see us unite and again line up for blocks — or sit in our cars for hours — to do the thing that would save us. Save our country.

When I passed the bleak encampments that proliferated alarmingly after COVID stole jobs and shut down homeless shelters, I could not help thinking of the tent cities of the 1930s — Hoovervilles — occupied by those who'd lost jobs and been evicted from homes. The culprit that FDR identified was straight out of a story from the day's paper: "For years Washington has alternated between putting its head in the sand and saying there is no large number of destitute people who need food and clothing, and then saying the States should take care of them, if there are."

The parallels continued. FDR spoke of the injustice of one political party that "sees to it that a favored few are helped" while ignoring the worker. He cautioned against spiraling levels of wealth inequality, pointing out that, though unimaginable fortunes were made during the 1920s, "very little of it was taken by taxation by the Government of those years." He warned of the rise of authoritarianism around the globe and how, just as it does now, these strongman regimes threatened the survival of democracy.

I took comfort in knowing that America has been here before. We have faced seemingly insurmountable challenges. And, we have come together and conquered them. We were resilient then and we are resilient now.

That was the lesson I learned from my mother, Colista McCabe, an Indiana farm girl whose father died of a heart attack during the Depression. She also taught by example that the strongest antidote to hard times is laughter. Somehow Collie Mac, as her six children called her, made even the Great Depression sound like fun. As if having little but eggs to survive on during an Indiana winter had been a grand adventure. I heard the echoes of those hard-won laughs in the memories she shared of the time a dance marathon was held at the local Grange Hall.

In her recollection, it had been a jolly community gathering, sort of like a cross between a church supper, with everyone bringing snacks to share, and a slumber party where the "lucky kids" got to stay up all night and watch the amazing sight of competitors who not only slept on their feet "like horses" but kept moving.

That rosy vision was at considerable odds with the version of dance marathons I encountered in the 1969 movie *They Shoot Horses, Don't They?* For decades, the suspicion nagged at me that this film — as superb a piece of cinema as it is — didn't tell quite the whole story of dance marathons.

When I began my research for this novel, I discovered how right I was. Carol Martin's impeccably researched book, *Dance Marathons: Performing American Culture in the 1920s and 1930s,* was a revelation.

CELLOPHANE WEDDING. March 24, 1935

Crescent Studios
Cincinnati, Ohio.

We should all be grateful to Carol Martin for almost single-handedly preserving the extraordinary history of the dance marathons of the 1930s. With grace and precision, she captured the anthropology of this lost world: its fascinating culture, insider lingo, and the remarkable comradery — and competition — between the contestants. It was a world infinitely more complex and nuanced than the one presented in the film.

I was particularly riveted by Martin's account of cellophane weddings and the fact that public weddings of all sorts were so popular at this time because the marriage rate was down by a third since so many couples couldn't afford to start new lives together. It became the perfect metaphor for the relationship between Evie and Zave.

Perhaps the most crucial fact we have lost sight of is how wildly popular these shows were. At their height, dance marathons employed roughly twenty thousand promoters, emcees, judges, trainers, nurses, contestants, and "sloppers," who kept everyone fed. In venues that ranged from, say, a Grange Hall in rural Indiana to a coliseum that could seat five thousand, marathons were held in countless small towns and in nearly every city with a population of fifty thousand.

One such city was Galveston, where the show, pictured below, was held in 1930 by promoter Harold J. Ross. Ross's fifth show in Texas, this one was, as *The Galveston Daily News* reported, a colossal success. "Approximately 2,000 persons" crowded into the City Auditorium "despite the heavy rains."

Galveston in the 1930s is a gift to a novelist. The city was possessed of a dark glamour, created and carefully cultivated by a pair of barber brothers from Sicily, that truly did allow it to remain virtually immune to the depression.

While vacationers and conventioneers drank bonded Canadian whiskey, gambled, and danced to Duke Ellington on this peculiarly enchanted island, the rest of the

country was not so fortunate. For them, a dance marathon offered spectators a bit of distraction, some human companionship, perhaps a warm place to huddle and a roof to shelter beneath for a few hours.

Contestants signed up for lots of reasons: the prize money, regular meals, housing for as long as they could stay in motion. Some sought stardom. And a few even found it: comic Red Skelton, jazz singer Anita O'Day, and actress June Havoc. Havoc was the sister of burlesque star Gypsy Rose Lee and daughter of the queen of all stage mothers, who, in fact, did stick June in pointe shoes as a toddler and market her as the Pint-Size Pavlova.

The intrepid marathoners were emblematic of the resilience, strength, and resourcefulness that we, as a people, have drawn upon time and time again when the dark days seemed darkest and the hard times too hard to overcome.

For them, for us, Roosevelt offered, above all, hope when hope was in dramatically short supply. In a speech he delivered to the Democratic Convention in July 1932 he told us, "Out of every crisis, every tribulation, every disaster, mankind rises with some share of greater knowledge, of higher decency, of purer purpose."

Knowledge. Decency. Purpose.

That is the spirit I tried to embody in my heroine Evie Grace Devlin, who never stopped fighting, always looked for a laugh, and emerged from her struggles having learned the one timeless lesson that history will teach us if we are smart enough to learn it.

We are stronger together.

ACKNOWLEDGMENTS

My first thanks must go to treasured friends Anne Rodgers, Sara Hickman, Tiffany Yates-Martin, Kelly Dennison Harrell, Kathleen Orillion, Diane Campbell, and Carol Dawson and two sublime sisters — Martha and Kay Bird — who, once again, went above and beyond the limits of patience to provide crucial insights, desperately needed encouragement, emergency wine-based psychological interventions, and laughs.

To everyone who joined me on my patio at Club Super Spread — Jason Stanford, Gianna LaMorte, Sam Gwynne, Amy Gentry, Stacey Swann, Mary Helen Specht, Tyler Stoddard, Elizabeth Crook, Steve and Sue Ellen, and Jim and Hester — your company, wise counsel, and generous spirits during a long and lonely time were more heartening than I can ever say. Ben and Sharie Fountain, you both were always there in spirit.

To Kristin Hannah, the most unfailingly generous supporter of other writers, it was a pleasure to walk the same historical path with you.

For the second time now, I am the luckiest author around to have the privilege of working with the paragons of publishing at St. Martin's Press, especially Monique Patterson. A doubt-plagued author could not ask for a more encouraging or insightful editor.

It has been a joy to work with all the A-Teamers at SMP: Jennifer Enderlin, Mara Delgado-Sánchez, Dori Weintraub, Erica Martirano, Brant Janeway, Kejana Ayala, Sylvan Creekmore, Christina MacDonald, Gail Friedman, and Lisa Davis. With an extra dollop of gratitude to Michael Storrings for two glorious covers, and to the charismatically cool Gillian Redfearn, my friend and guide for all these years.

Kristine Dahl, what can I say about my Dahl Baby, my brat sister, except that I bless the day you entered my life. How many years ago now? Since before our children — who are now in their thirties! — were born. Damn, it's been a ride that our aviator fathers would have envied. And one I can't imagine having taken with anyone else.

And, because these are not normal times,

I'd like to offer one slightly abnormal round of huzzahs. With all my heart I thank those who fight every day to, as Franklin Delano Roosevelt said, "resume the country's interrupted march along the path of real progress, of real justice, of real equality for all of our citizens, great and small."

And, finally, firstly, alwaysly, George Jones and Gabriel Bird-Jones. None of it would mean anything without you two, my beloved G-Men.

SUGGESTED READING

The Great Depression

When I began my research, I was overwhelmed by economic analyses of what caused the Great Depression. While it was useful to have that understanding, my favorite overview of the period is the wonderfully illustrated, too-little-known *The Great Depression* by T. H. Watkins.

No one will ever surpass the cheerfully empathetic oral historian Studs Terkel at letting the people who lived America's defining stories tell them, and he was at his finest with *Hard Times: An Oral History of the Great Depression*.

In fiction, a new classic has recently joined *The Grapes of Wrath*. *The Four Winds*, Kristin Hannah's indelible account of surviving the Dust Bowl, brings this period alive in a way that nonfiction can't touch.

Dance Marathons

As I mentioned earlier, Carol Martin's definitive *Dance Marathons: Performing American Culture in the 1920s and 1930s* is the essential book on the topic.

Since there is surprisingly little documentation on such an immense cultural phenomenon, I was grateful for Frank M. Calabria's sociological analysis, *Dance of the Sleepwalkers.*

I might not have been able to write *Last Dance* without actress June Havoc's account of her years "on the circuit." *Early Havoc* brings the hard-scrabble life of a former vaudeville star scrambling to survive to vivid life.

Jazz great Anita O'Day's memoir includes some early chapters on her time performing on the marathon circuit.

The self-published memoir *Marathon Dancer: The Billy Steele Story* by Annette Sevedge contained a wealth of detail that I found useful.

And, of course, I have to cite the novel that led to the film that led to my interest in uncovering the true story of the marathons, *They Shoot Horses, Don't They?* Written by Horace McCoy, a World War I aviator, a sportswriter, and a lettuce picker. It was as a bouncer at a marathon held on the Santa Monica Pier that McCoy found his inspiration for *Horses*. The unrelievedly grim portrait he paints was sparked by his desire to write "the first American existential novel."

Nursing and Queer History

Though I read many accounts and scholarly articles about nursing school in the 1930s, nothing beat the good old Cherry Ames books for capturing a wide-eyed, unjaded perspective on how exciting it was for a young woman with limited options to become a nurse back in those desperate days.

There are numerous superb, often heartbreaking histories of gay citizens in America, but the book that was a godsend for my purposes was Tommy Dickinson's *'Curing Queers': Mental nurses and their patients, 1935–74*. In it, Dickinson examines the plight of gay men who were institutionalized in British mental hospitals and the well-intentioned nurses who administered horrific treatments to "cure" them. I was inspired by the small number of nurses who defied their superiors and attempted to sabotage the barbaric treatments which had a zero success rate.

I found the fiction and memoirs of Gore

Vidal and Edmund White, two of the rare few who wrote openly about being queer in the long, dark years before Stonewall to be very helpful in understanding the mostly bygone mores of that bygone era.

Galveston

Galveston in the 1930s was a spectacularly fascinating topic to research. I read every history of this peculiarly enchanted island I could lay my hands on, but the writer who captured the dangerous allure of this place and time the best was Gary Cartwright. His *Galveston: A History of the Island* is a solid introduction that he expands upon marvelously in the many articles he wrote for *Texas Monthly.*

If you want to dive even deeper into the wondrous empire of vice built by two Sicilian immigrants and frequented by Peggy Lee, Frank Sinatra, Duke Ellington, and a Who's Who of other celebrities, check out *Galveston's Maceo Family Empire: Bootlegging & the Balinese Room* by authors T. Nicole Boatman, Scott Belshaw, and Richard McCaslin.

If you'd like to learn more about dance marathons, the Great Depression, FDR, or queer history in the 1930s, I share reading suggestions and some of the extraordinary images that inspired me on my website: sarahbirdbooks.com.

ABOUT THE AUTHOR

Sarah Bird's previous novel, *Above the East China Sea,* was long-listed for the Dublin International Literary Award. Sarah has been selected for the Meryl Streep Screenwriting Lab, the B&N Discover Great Writers program, NPR's Moth Radio series, the Texas Literary Hall of Fame, and New York Libraries Books to Remember list. She first heard Cathy Williams' story in the late seventies while researching African-American rodeos.